THE
DICTATOR'S
WIFE

Freya Berry studied English Literature at Trinity College, Cambridge, and worked for several years as a financial and political journalist at Reuters and then the *Daily Mail*. Freya splits her time between London and the Welsh coast. *The Dictator's Wife* is her debut novel, inspired by the close observation of the wives of some of the world's most powerful leaders.

THE DICTATOR'S WIFE

FREYA BERRY

REVIEW

First published in 2022 by Headline Review
An imprint of HEADLINE PUBLISHING GROUP

3

Cataloguing in Publication Data is available from the British Library

Hardback ISBN 978 1 4722 7630 8
Trade Paperback ISBN 978 1 4722 7631 5

Typeset in Sabon by
Palimpsest Book Production Ltd, Falkirk, Stirlingshire

Printed and bound in Great Britain by
Clays Ltd, Elcograf S.p.A.

Headline's policy is to use papers that are natural, renewable and recyclable
products and made from wood grown in well-managed forests and other
controlled sources. The logging and manufacturing processes are expected
to conform to the environmental regulations of the country of origin.

HEADLINE PUBLISHING GROUP
An Hachette UK Company
Carmelite House
50 Victoria Embankment
London EC4Y 0DZ

www.headline.co.uk
www.hachette.co.uk

To my parents
For always making time

She is a mother. She is and remains a mother . . .
For at one time she carried the child under her heart.
And it does not go out of her heart ever again.
Leo Frobenius, *Der Kopf als Schicksal*

Perception is real, and the truth is not.
Imelda Marcos, *The Kingmaker*

CHAPTER ONE

2018

The past rarely comes for us politely. She springs out from a half-seen face in the street, assaults us in a once-familiar hall. A sudden visitor, not so much knocking at the door as smashing a fist through the frosted pane.

I raised the teacup to my lips, turned the newspaper page, and there she was, her amber eyes turned to black and somewhere the scent of decaying flowers. Only later, after I had swept up the shattered china, did I realise why I had not spotted the obituary at once. Twenty-five years ago the dictator's wife would have commanded the cover. Now she had been bumped to page three.

I put the paper in the bin, then took it out again, the dark web of ink at odds with the Devon sun. This time I was not imagining it: the whiff of something rotting. The funeral was in three days.

'I'll have to go, you know,' I said to the cat. He glared up at me as if asking why I would do such a thing. I did not reply, though the answer burned nevertheless.

To make sure she is dead.

The plane was small and not busy. I sat in a row on my own, along from some eastern European women visiting home, the glaring yellow of the airline's livery reflecting unfavourably off their tired faces. Long before the dawn clawed at the grubby hotel curtains, I was up and dressed.

I felt the churchyard before I saw it. A hush surrounded it, silencing the gathering crowd. Some observers crossed themselves; others hesitated, hands frozen before their hearts. I stepped through the gate and braced myself: nothing, only the shrieks of the crows in their shabby black. Was I free, at last, of her influence? Perhaps. But I had long since learned that enslavement may be just as imperceptible as freedom.

I found a space among the mourners. They watched with their whole bodies, these people, I remembered now. In this particular corner of eastern Europe, the eyes were larger, darker, with the look of animals calculating whether to run. When I had last come to this country, twenty-five years ago, I had disliked that I was born one of them, a watcher. Here, too, I had learned to be glad of it. It had saved me more than once.

It was surprisingly warm in the sunshine, and as we waited, I began to sweat. In Devon it was winter, but in Yanussia spring had sprung like a trap, though snow lurked still in the shadows of the gravestones. I removed my coat, then my jumper, quickly, uneasy about obscuring my vision. As I did so, the crowd gave a sigh. I wrenched the wool over my head and saw the church doors open.

She who carries the scar remembers; she who gives the scar forgets. An old Yanussian saying, and as I watched that plain wooden box, utterly free of adornment, I remembered. No wonder the government had arranged the First Lady's funeral in such haste. They would all be trying to forget, to purge themselves of the woman whose influence still ran liquid in their veins, who had burrowed into their very marrow. In the trees the crows screamed, but the ensnared faces around me did not look up. I heard someone mutter a single word, and now at last I felt it, that odd mixture of enchantment and dread.

Vrăjitoare. Witch.

Only when the coffin crossed the churchyard boundary, bound for the cemetery, did the mourners exhale, hardly knowing why. I crushed a small heap of snow with my foot. It was over. Marija Popa was gone, her secrets departed with her. Death is a great leveller: it makes everyone uninteresting. The men are always kind and funny, the women beautiful. What happens to the dull, the ugly and the cruel? Perhaps they live forever.

I turned to leave, but as I did so, among the smartly dressed mourning party . . .

'Pavel?'

It was him. Older, stooped, but distinctly him. He turned – not, it seemed, because he wanted to, but because he was compelled. To my amusement, the dyed black hair still clung on grimly, though the underlying colour must long ago have bleached to white.

'Laura Lăzărescu,' he said. 'Those dark eyes. My God. What are you doing here?'

'Same as you.' I indicated the mourning party. 'Only from the outside.'

Cristian Pavel, consummate insider. Of course my old boss had wangled himself an invitation. He blended in perfectly, with his immaculately cut coat and shining shoes, while my hair was mussed and my arms full of clothing. Even as I stood there, my jumper detached itself and fell to the floor. I scrabbled for it, my fingers accidentally making contact with his foot, and rose to find him staring at the point where my skin had met the polished leather. I strangled a smile: he hadn't changed.

But I had. 'Coffee?'

'Actually, I've got a drinks thing . . .'

'Pavel.' My voice was calm, but its undercurrent forced him to meet my eye. I admired the imperceptibility of his hesitation.

'All right. One moment.'

Pavel never was able to resist a challenge. He insinuated himself back into the throng, a crow returning to its murder. Several business cards changed hands. The man retired from the law twenty-five years ago, for heaven's sake. What did his card even say? But there is a certain breed of person who sees a funeral as a networking opportunity, and I felt suddenly grubby, loitering among the gravestones. Her husband wasn't buried here; rather in a far grander cemetery beside statesmen, kings and other notables who had taken the wound of the world and rubbed salt in. Those iron eyes now terrorised only worms; safely interred was that heavy jaw, set against a universe he must have believed had wronged him, or how else could he have done the things he did? I wondered why his widow had not been granted the next-door plot. I would have been the last to suggest Marija Popa deserved more, yet I could not help but feel that this mean little church was cheating her – that if only she had died young and beautiful, they would have laid on the cathedral and throngs of weeping faithful. Like Evita, although Marija would have mocked the comparison. As it was, she had made the mistake of growing old, even unattractive. That surprised me. It was unlike the First Lady not to play a role to the bitter end.

Why had I asked Pavel for coffee? What on earth would we say, could we say, to one another? I sensed the bodies encrusting the earth beneath our feet, their blue-white eyes upturned towards me. Pavel was unaware of my secret, but the dead knew, they all knew, what I had done for the dictator's wife . . .

'Laura? Let's go.' Pavel had returned, tucking his cards away. He didn't offer me one.

We walked onto the Bulevard Unirii, rimed with litter and old snow; the pressure in my head gradually lessened, like the retreating toll of a bell. The city of Poartă had been known, once, as Little Paris, but that was before its alleys were torn open to boulevards, its townhouses mushroomed into monstrous apartment blocks. Yanussia was a tiny country, squashed between Romania, Hungary and Serbia, yet Constantin Popa had decided to build a capital fit only for giants. Before his rule, the country had had modest aspirations, chiefly farming, drinking and spying on neighbouring Romania, which treated it as an irksome younger brother. In the 1848 revolutions, both nations fought for independence from Imperial Russia: Yanussia won where the other regions failed, a fact that apparently surprised them just as much as everyone else.

'Look,' Pavel said suddenly. Above, between us and the sky, spiked the chimneys of the old iron mill. I remembered smoke pouring out at all hours of the day, but now it was empty, its blast furnace stilled, its chimneys greening and silent. An old communist joke, what the Soviets called *anekdoti*, drifted in. Who had told it? Sorin, probably, in a lighter moment.

A factory inspector is conducting his assessment. He asks one worker, 'What do you do here?'

'Nothing,' the worker replies.

The inspector turns to another. 'And what about you?'

'Nothing.'

The inspector frowns. In his report he writes, 'The second worker should be fired for unnecessary duplication.'

No, I probably hadn't laughed even then. Still, it looked like the grand tradition of people pretending to work in return for the authorities pretending to pay them had finally ground to an end. On a wall someone had sprayed furious graffiti. *Turn Up*, it said. A modest ambition. Dreams had shrunk since 1989.

I allowed Pavel to herd me down a side street. He must have been at least eighty, yet his gait was still of someone with places to be. We ducked into a small café, one of those faux-Italian affairs with wipe-down tables, stainless-steel chairs and posters of the usual film stars on the walls. I grated my way into a seat, Sophia Loren pouting down. Her haughty expression reminded me of Marija, and I averted my gaze. It was an unlikely choice for Pavel. I would have expected the bar of some Westernised hotel. I wondered whether his tastes had changed, but then I realised: he did not want to be seen with me.

'You saw last year's Supreme Court ruling,' he said without preamble. 'About the government keeping her jewels.'

'Yes. Couldn't prove she'd acquired them legally.' I sighed. 'What was she, eighty-three? What good were diamonds by then?'

'You expected her to give them up?'

I gazed at the cup before me, the steam making the tabletop waver strangely. 'No. I suppose not.'

'You wouldn't have. If you were her.'

It was such a curious thing to say that I could not think how to respond.

'I haven't forgotten what you were like, you know. Truculent. Always fighting, until the end.' A half-smile. 'As your boss, it could be very annoying.'

A minute passed in silence before he said, evenly, 'First time back?'

'Yes. You?'

He took a careful sip and nodded.

'I would have thought she'd have asked you to visit.' I winced at my own bitterness, but to my surprise he responded by dropping the mask for the first time.

'Why would she? It was all over.' He looked, suddenly, old, the shadows catching up with him like they do on elderly faces, lines webbing across the sockets. So he too had been discarded. Poor Pavel.

Why had he really come? Had that been social climbing at the graveside, or a man burying himself alive in ritual? Had we both in fact returned for the same reason: to verify that those amber eyes had not caused Death to forget his duty? I didn't think Pavel the type to believe in ghosts, yet the Black Widow brushed the earth away from our most secret parts, the parts we hid even and above all from ourselves. Her genius was to make the disinterment feel natural. Even . . . desirable.

The dead were very close now, their long fingers brushing my skin. I knew who they were and what they wanted, what they had always wanted.

Tell him. Tell everyone.

Could I share it, the thing I had carried in my breast for twenty-five years? Few of us have looked the Devil in the eye and turned her away, and Pavel, above all, would understand the nature of the power I had found myself up against. If law taught me anything, it was that people rarely act from natural evil or malice. There are a million little steps to the cliff edge, and even in the leaping moment, the slightest twinge in the muscle or eddy in the wind may change the outcome utterly.

Of course, gravity has only one plan for us. But there are many ways to fall.

CHAPTER TWO

1993

We arrived to an invisible city. The taxi forced its way through autumn fog thick as smoke, the window dirty as if reluctant to let the light in. I knew Poartă was there, felt the capital lurking at the edges of my vision – a spire here, the bone of a bridge there – but every time I turned my head, the thing was gone.

Home. I tested the word on my tongue, probing it for familiarity, for anything that might have lingered in the two decades since I had seen it last, receding from the back of a vegetable truck. Instead I was aware of a deadness pressing down, of things that were broken and had remained so. We passed a man entering a massive apartment block; he stepped inside hastily, yanking the door to, though no one was in pursuit. Forty years they'd had under Marxism, or Bogdan and Popa's translations of it anyway, which were about as true to the original as a badly dubbed bootleg of a Chuck Norris movie. But now the palaces with real gold mosaics were gone, the orchids flown specially from Thailand withered, and all that remained were the stunted figures of the ordinary people, moving warily as if there were nothing good around the corner.

I had returned to work on the trial defence of the very woman whose regime had driven my family away. Marija Popa. The name conjured a glimmering swarm of contradictions. A sumptuous banquet crawling with maggots. Literal blood diamonds. Four years before Jackie O, it was Marija who tore up the First Lady playbook of perma-smile, pearls, and hair set hard enough not to quiver at her husband's more outrageous lies. She had the bone structure of a film star and the mind of a steel trap. There were plans for a Broadway musical in her name. She was glamorous; she was outrageous; she was *fun*. The only fly in the Crème de la Mer was her dead husband and his unfortunate predilection for impoverishing his country and terrorising his people.

There were three of us: senior partner Cristian Pavel, myself, and Jude Greenwood, a lupine-faced senior associate, all of us crammed into the back seat. Pavel hadn't even bothered to ask if I wanted the case, merely dropped the files on my desk, for who would miss what they were already calling the trial of the century? Someone at Harris Stroud Glyn had attached her photograph to the first page, the steel of the paper clip no match for that in her eyes. As if there were anyone in the world who didn't know what she looked like! Her image had hung for years above the ever-frozen radiator in my family's Poartă flat, as if it could provide us with the warmth the metal would not.

Pavel did not ask, and therefore I did not tell him, but in truth I wasn't here for the prestige. It could've been the trial of the millennium, of the Holocene even. Instead the force that filled me, drumming my fingers, clenching my stomach, was not the case itself, but what it represented: a cast-iron excuse for returning to Yanussia, to my past, to the place where my family had broken.

We left when I was seven. Twenty-one years ago now. My father, Ion, was a minor agricultural official; my mother, Gabriela, worked for the famed Iubită empire, a sweet company founded by Marija's adoptive family and run by the First Lady herself. Strangely, our departure was driven neither by political persecution nor poverty; instead, it was as if a light in my parents' minds snapped on and they could no longer bear what they saw, though what that was, they never told me.

It was bizarre, because we had always been faithful to the Party. Marija's smiling face watched us shiver through heating-less winters and boil in un-air-conditioned summers, yet my mother's hugs told me that I was safe, that we were happy, and if Popa in his greed ate up the whole country, well, at least the three of us could live in his stomach together, sloshing around in the dark. We never listened to Radio Free Europe under the bedcovers; we were spotless in our devotion, and whenever a fleck threatened, my parents hastened to sweep it away. When my pet hamster died of cold, they hushed my lamentations, fearful of who might overhear.

Yet still we fled. Some defectors jumped the fence, at the risk of getting shot; others swam the Danube, their papers in plastic bags. The river's waters were fast and treacherous, its borders finely ploughed to show up footprints, because in Yanussia even the earth could be turned against you. The Popa regime hated defectors, presumably concerned that they would spread word of what life was really like, and even now the country maintained a virulent dislike of those who had left, seeing it as a personal betrayal. Our London office had impressed on us the importance of security.

'It can't be as bad as Brooklyn,' I said, half joking. (I'd been in New York on secondment.) In return, I received a glare and the information that only last month the Danube had strewn up the mutilated bodies of a middle-aged couple, claimed by the river they'd evaded fifteen years before.

The real mystery was not why we'd left, but what had happened thereafter. Unlike other refugees, my parents kept no ties with our homeland. In London, they found a house far away from the Yanussian quarter, as if our people carried some invisible plague and they must amputate all corruptive parts completely. They refused to speak Yanussian; even the food my mother cooked was different, mashed potato and Bisto and not a cabbage in sight, though that itself was hardly a tragedy. When a well-meaning neighbour brought around homemade *cozonac*, it went straight in the bin. We became something unfamiliar to ourselves, let alone other people.

Had that been all, I would not have minded. But then it came for me. In the months and years after we arrived, my mother changed towards me utterly. I was no longer her daughter; I was an intruder. Our relationship was reduced to the hot iron of her rages, or the cold fire of her indifference, the livid marks of which I bore on the other side of my skin. Oh, I don't mean there was physical violence – she never laid a finger on me. She stopped, in fact, touching me at all, and there were times when I would have been glad for a beating, if only to feel her hand again.

I did not dare ask why. Sometimes she would reach towards me almost absent-mindedly – but then a shadow would cross her face. She would withdraw, and my heart would crack a little deeper.

It was that remembrance, I was sure, that held the heart of the matter. I tried asking my father, a small, harried man, lines scored around eyes that moved about constantly, as if seeking escape. For a onetime agricultural official, I never saw a man less likely to cause things to grow. In England he'd had to take up as a taxi driver, and I sometimes thought

11

the Christmas tree dangling from his mirror knew him better than I did. Certainly it saw him more frequently. He refused to discuss my mother's change, and when I asked why we'd left, he replied, 'For a better life,' in a tone so flat it was almost funny. At other times he said, 'For you,' and I would replay his tone over and over – was it love, or quiet blame?

I had to find out, but my upbringing had left me stunted, like a plant kept too long out of the sun. Neither parent would hear of me returning to Yanussia, and I had never been strong enough, or found an opportunity impenetrable enough, to defy them. Until now.

I delayed the news as long as possible, although I could have waited for Pavel's dyed hair to turn white and it would not have been long enough. Finally I went down one Sunday: after church, if they'd gone to church, though that too had ended in England, as if their God had been taken away at the border and quarantined indefinitely. My boyfriend Andrei offered to accompany me. I declined, though not before burying my face into his neck, flamingo-like.

The house was immaculate as ever, the short path neatly trimmed, the sofa fat with all the things we could not say to each other. Only the back garden, with its high fences and nobody to look in, was weedy and neglected. Years before, I'd planted a peach stone there and watered it faithfully for months, having been the kind of child who would find a pet item and obsessively focus on it, whiling away the long hours before my father returned to neutralise my mother and me. Even now I could do a Rubik's Cube in thirty seconds flat, a skill that had brought me a surprising celebrity at the kind of university parties I attended.

We had tea. 'I'm going home,' I told the floor. 'I have to take the case or' – I'd practised the lie – 'they'll fire me.'

At first nobody spoke. The room was entirely still, until I glanced at the cup in my mother's hands and saw the liquid reverberating. I'd learned to pay attention to her movements: her words were few these days, and when they came, they were forced through a funnel so narrow that they more resembled a controlled explosion than conversation. Panicking, I began to prattle about how important the case was, how its success would practically assure my promotion – anything to distract from the fact of my return. The tremors in the liquid only widened, reminding me of the film I had recently seen in Manhattan. *Jurassic Park*.

Eventually I shut up, and at last she spoke, each clenched word a knife thumping into its target.

'That – place – is *not* our home.'

'But Popa is long gone, Mamă.'

'*She* is worse! Why – why would you . . .'

She was so angry, the words would not come out. I was born with the umbilical cord round my neck, and in times of stress my hands went to my throat as if it twisted there still. (We never get used to our parents, never.) They flew there now, pressing in until I struggled to breathe.

As usual, it was my father who tried to erect a barricade between us. I had always thought this was for my protection.

'This is a shock, Laura. Can no one else do it?'

'It has to be a Yanussian,' I whispered. 'For the visa.'

The grey wave of his disappointment washed over me at the same time as my mother tried to speak but instead broke into a cough so violent that her tea cascaded onto the carpet. I reached out, but was forced back by the flash in her eyes. Instead my father put his hand on her spasming spine. I hated seeing them like this, a private unit unto themselves.

'Perhaps you'd better go,' he said gently, once the fit had ended. I left, but from the hall I glimpsed her on the sofa, motionless. Waiting. It characterised our relationship, this feeling that I was expected to do something, to know something, to *be* something, and even on the best of our Sunday visits I would catch the serrated edge of her disappointment and know that once more I had failed her.

Her condemnation therefore was not unusual, but on the train home, as I probed the familiar gaps that had reopened along my skin, sores weeping guilt and humiliation, I realised there was something else in her tone.

Not anger, but fear.

If my mother was afraid of me returning, that was exactly what I must do, though I trembled at my own audacity, though it made me feel like a monster. Poartă's train station had been lit by a single light bulb, swinging valiantly against the shadows: I felt like that bulb, seeking to illuminate what had so long been hidden, because the problem with monsters was that the longer you shut your eyes, the larger they grew.

Home. Again I repeated it, and again there was nothing, only a curious rushing in my ears, the sound of something falling. It is an odd thing, to return – it speaks of circularity, of neat revolutions, and it made me uneasy because it seemed so readily true. Yanussia is heavy with fate: it drips from the half-patched ceilings, scurries with the rats in the gutters. Was it irony, to return as a defence lawyer for Marija Popa? Or something crueller, more calculated altogether? The fog gazed at me eyelessly. It didn't have the purposeful industry of London smog; instead, it concealed, with an efficacy that seemed complicit, even deliberate. Thrusting a fist into it, my hand faded, as if becoming less real. I snatched it back and with relief watched it reassemble into flesh.

'Shut that window, Lăzărescu,' Jude snapped. 'Bloody difficult to get a taxi as it is.'

The first three drivers had flatly refused when Pavel spoke to them in Yanussian, the fourth only accepting when I stuffed extra notes into his hand. That had earned me a look, plus a pointed remark about Harris Stroud Glyn's expense account. But after two months living off New York's Murder Avenue, I knew how to persuade reluctant taxi men, though I wasn't sure why they were so wary of taking us to the Hotel Europa. Perhaps they sensed the silken threads that already bound us to Marija. They called her the Black Widow after all, said she'd eaten her husband from the inside out, that it was her fault he had become what he had: a man who put on a different two-thousand-dollar suit each day and burned it each night in case the fabric was poisoned, who kept a listening room behind his office to spy on ministers and ambassadors, and whose only significant political opponent was discovered shot in the head in a hotel room locked from the inside. Constantin Popa had (allegedly) embezzled hundreds of millions of dollars. But he was (undeniably) dead, murdered horribly in the protests of 1989. Instead it was his widow who had turned up at the arraignment, the first step of a trial that would ask how a couple on twenty thousand dollars a year could afford Meissen porcelain, a bed once slept in by Marie Antoinette, a summer palace, a winter palace, a zoo and a personalised train, complete with champagne room and beluga caviar on tap.

She arrived to a packed-out court, half applauding vigorously, the rest howling insults, a comedy and a tragedy all at once. She bestowed her smile upon them equally before listening with sphinx-like calm to the charges being read by a fat official. Even when he came to the serious corruption charges, those that carried the death penalty, she did not flinch. Nineteen eighty-nine had been and gone; Marija Popa should by now have been an irrelevance, yet that slight smile whispered that really she'd been picking her moment all along. Money laundering, fraud, bribery, corruption, obstruction of justice . . . it was an impressive list. Only when the official finished, slightly out of breath, did she raise her hand.

'You have not asked me to state my name.'

The judge rolled his eyes. 'We know who you are.'

'Do you?'

A sigh. 'Go ahead. State your name.'

'Constantin Popa,' she said promptly. The court emitted an odd blend of sound, part gasp, part laughter.

'That is *not* your name,' the fat official exploded.

'Ah. I apologise.' The amber eyes opened wide as mouths; the red lips gave the tiniest smile. 'But you have read out a list of crimes you allege to have been committed by the executive presidency, which was of course held by my dead husband. I thought you might think I was him.'

'We are perfectly aware that you are not your husband,' Judge Ardelean said impatiently.

The eyes widened further. 'I see. In which case, why am I here?'

I had to admire the elegance with which she stooped to plant the seed of doubt. They said that in a marriage it was hard to tell where one person ended and the other began, but how often did that have to be proved in a court of law? Divorce, yes. Money laundering, no. The innocent wife scape-goated for her husband's sins – it was compelling. That day she wore pale blue and covered her head and suddenly the papers were calling her the Virgin Marija. With irony, if not outright loathing, but that was not the point. The words had been gently, slyly put into their mouths like sugar lumps. The mood was febrile, fertile; right now, with the right nutrients, anything could grow.

No doubt she was clever. But clever enough to win? Once again I sensed the tug of plans unseen yet long in the making. Barely six months before her trial she had fired her Yanussian legal team and brought in my firm, Harris Stroud Glyn,

16

setting London's legal circles abuzz. It wasn't clear why she had got rid of local lawyers Manea and Cristescu, but HSG was top brass, so deep-set in the Magic Circle they would've worn pointy hats if they'd had the sense of humour. (They didn't.)

The lack of time made the executive committee nervous – not that they considered declining. Pavel, a natural-born citizen, was brought in, along with Jude, who had an outstanding visa from an abortive coal suit. Last and least was me, a lowly junior associate. The life cycle of an average lawyer, like that of a frog, is in roughly three stages (though with both species there are internal gradations indistinguishable to the untrained observer). Currently I was at the tadpole stage – more than frogspawn, but a lot less than frog – and while Marija's trial might be only a pretext for my return, it was also a major step towards froghood.

Before our departure, I went to the Yanussian embassy, talked my way into the grim little archive and watched hours of old videos of the orphan brat who rose to become queen of Yanussia in all but name. There she was with Ronald Reagan, Paul Newman, Saddam Hussein (and who but she could have been dear friends with all three?). Not that it mattered who they were, these men; they all blurred into the same, even Newman's star wattage fading into the background beside her. It was she who was different every time, laughing, flirting, now in emeralds, now in diamonds. She extracted something from you and appropriated it for herself; I could almost see its trace in the videos, pale tendrils spinning out of those men's torsos. She could have told them two and two made five and they would have nodded along with a giddiness they ascribed to champagne. She was an actress once and it showed, or would have had she been less good at it. Her husband was a keen student of Hitler's charisma, watching and analysing the Führer's old speeches

17

over and over again, but Marija had no need of such lessons. Strange how glamour enchants us, how it makes us forget. A fur coat insists on us ignoring the abattoir.

Up until now we had crawled along the clogged streets like insects expecting to be crushed, but now we turned into a large square and the city decided to reveal itself. I stared.

'Christ. What happened?'

It was a war zone: hundreds of windows smashed, half-burned cars scattered anyhow. The building in front of us was a blackened husk, a Yanussian flag torn and flapping so its leaping hare seemed as though it were fleeing. I fought off the sensation that we should do the same.

'Big government protest two days ago,' the driver said shortly. He nodded at the burned-out block. 'State television building. Fire bomb.'

'Heavy is the head,' was all Pavel said. There was no one around and we drove unevenly across the cobbles, many of which had been torn up and used to redecorate pavements and windows. A solitary cyclist with something red in a basket appeared, heading straight for us. I expected him to move aside, but instead he came on, close, closer, until at the last second the driver swore and swung the wheel, horn blaring as each barely missed the other. I turned round. The cyclist continued on as if nothing had happened.

Jude shook his head. 'Yanussians are crazy.'

No, not crazy. My parents had a chilly, ossified sanity, the kind possessed by those who have tried very, very hard not to go mad. My mother had once been full of grace: I would watch her expansive gestures, arms blooming like the petals of a flower, mouth curving with sudden glee. Now she was immobile, fragile, as if every expression might bring

18

her to shatter, every step cause her bones to break. Sure, the days of forced disappearances were over, the Strajă – the former secret police – disbanded, or rather rebranded, and moved to a glossy headquarters on Bulevard Victoriei. Look, we have a sign outside! Windows! A logo! Yet still the fog pressed in. Yanussia's north was shadowed by Transylvanian forests, greedy and deep; the cities were no better, the streets torn down and rebuilt so chaotically that many houses could not be found on any map.

'This place gives me the creeps,' Jude went on. 'Why couldn't the Popas have dictated in Bali, or Saint-Tropez?'

'Pavel and I were born here, Jude,' I said neutrally. I didn't know much about him, other than that he hated the Beatles on principle. Office legend had it that when a junior had dared sing it to his face, he'd wound up with his tie stapled to his chest.

'Poor you. Are we even meeting Marija today?'

Pavel hushed him, glancing at the driver then upwards, as if afraid of someone else listening. His paranoia was catching. 'What did I say about not discussing the case publicly?'

'Not to discuss the case publicly?'

'Quite.' He lowered his voice further. 'We have an appointment.'

'How the hell did she duck out of prison?'

Pavel smiled. The smile of a shark. 'Our esteemed client's orphanage upbringing has left her with chronic stomach problems. Out of mercy and respect, rather than keeping her imprisoned, the state has seen fit to place her under house arrest.'

I could perfectly imagine what kind of mercy and respect had overcome the government: the kind that could usually be induced by dire legal threats. Half this country hated her, the other half worshipped her. Both were captivated. A

19

newspaper cartoon last week had depicted her as a spider, its web shaped like a map of Yanussia. Now I was here, a fly in that web.

Five more minutes brought us to the cusp of a howling boulevard. The driver stopped.

'No,' Pavel said. 'A little further. Strada Regelui. Across the road.'

Nothing.

'I am telling you, we are not there yet,' Pavel said, impatient.

The driver suddenly hunched his shoulders in a practised gesture, as though expecting a whip. 'No further.'

We had no choice but to get out, disturbing the red leaves that whispered against the high wall. Winter was closing in.

'I don't see the Europa.'

'We're not going there,' Pavel said. 'Change of plan. We're meeting her at her sister's mansion.'

I recoiled, and Jude, getting out of the car, crashed into me. I ignored his swearing. 'What?'

'They tightened the conditions of her house arrest last week,' Pavel said impatiently. 'She's not allowed out at all.'

Oh God.

'So this is . . .'

'Her childhood home. Yes. Is there a problem?'

I clutched at the car door, panic curdling through my veins. This was why the driver had been so reluctant to take us. This was why he was unloading our luggage with his neck twisted as if it had been broken, so that he could not look at what awaited on the road's other side.

Casa Iubită.

CHAPTER THREE

The taxi drove off, the exhaust causing a flutter like that of departing wings. I turned: the wall beside us, directly facing the mansion, was plastered with posters, contorting in the breeze. Each bore a face. Some were old, but most were young; a few were soldiers, stiff in uniform, but the majority were informal, boys in jeans, girls against trees, laughing at something out of shot. They were all different, yet each had the same red word emblazoned across them, a word that turned the knuckles around my suitcase white.

DISPĂRUT, they said, and though my Yanussian was long forgotten, or interred somewhere I could no longer access, I knew, I knew what that meant.

Casa Iubită. A rotten tooth in Poartă's mouth, and my own. It took its name from the family who lived there – the word, with bitter irony, meant 'beloved' or 'sweetheart'. I had never thought I would find myself here. Only last night I'd argued about it with Andrei, he insisting that I find some way to gain access, me refusing. We never argued, never, each preferring to roll hedgehog-like into a ball and nurse our hurts away from view. This was bitter and horrible, ending but not resolving after he pressed his fork so hard

21

into the table that it snapped. Even now I felt used, unable to agree to what he wanted yet weighted down with guilt. For Andrei's family – what was left of them anyway – had also fled Yanussia, and while he understood my personal reasons for taking the case, like my parents he perceived it as a betrayal.

'The Last Supper,' he said drily when we sat down in the restaurant I'd chosen – deliberately fancy, in penance.

'So I'm who?' I smiled. 'Judas?'

He did not refute me, and I flourished the menu to cover the sudden hurt. 'Well, let's spend my thirty pieces of silver.'

I'd braced myself for an uneasy meal, but after we'd laughed at the wine list and ordered beers, he relaxed slightly. He never liked it when I paid, and despite my jest, I didn't want my bribery to be overly blatant. Andrei worked as a consultant, and while he was good at his job, picking out patterns no one else saw, his prickly nature and his evident contempt for the work ensured he was always underpaid. (Only I saw the soft underbelly; everyone else got the spines.) He didn't care, or claimed not to: his real attentions lay elsewhere, for he was also a writer, an unsuccessful one, sitting at the yellowing Formica table he referred to as his desk and stuffing his sentences with anger until they bloated, unpublishable. Last year he'd made a pilgrimage back to Yanussia, looking for evidence of his mother's last traceable days. I had never met Adriana Ciocan, a pharmacist with artistic tendencies, though I'd once found one of her little painted clay pots on his shelf, its colours still bright. It fitted neatly into the palm of my hand. He came in and saw me with it and his face closed.

He had returned from Poartă like a storm, unable to speak, and I didn't dare push him. Until last night we'd never discussed it, though in the meantime his body, always lean, became even more so, as if the trip had compressed him further. I'd come across the sweepings of a smashed glass, or a dent in the wall from where a chair had been thrown, and say nothing, angry at my own helplessness. Last night, less than twelve hours before my departure, he finally told me what he'd found.

The trail had led into – but not out of – a psychiatric hospital, a hospital located in the bowels of the Iubită mansion for several crucial years in the 1970s, until it was abruptly awarded back to Marija's sister, the owner, for services to the Party. It was not a hospital in the true, healing sense. If you rebelled against the state, the logic ran, you must be mad, and could not be pronounced sane unless you recanted. If you did not recant, you were not released. It was even rumoured that a special branch of the Strajă secretly blasted inmates with radiation, so that if they were freed they died of cancer within a few years anyway.

'Some were sent on to proper prisons, or to hard labour. The rest . . .' Andrei gazed into the knots of his spaghetti.

She was not a conformist, Adriana. Not for her the national anthem and queuing for eighteen hours in shifts to buy meat. Rebellion grew within her, a germ that she either nurtured or failed to crush (and in Yanussia, political resistance, like a virus, tended to kill the host). She failed to attend three Party rallies in a row. Her absence was noted. Then she made contact with an underground resistance movement and, ignoring her husband's pleas, started delivering brown packages that bore no address. Her name began to crop up on unseen lists, to be mentioned in long, lightless corridors. It didn't take long for someone to inform on her for 'hostile activities'. A few weeks after that, they came.

Not at midnight, Andrei said. That was too easy. Too *obvious*. They preferred two or three in the morning, once you were in a deep sleep. He still remembered – or could not forget – the fist pounding the door. His father was on a business trip, his brothers and cousins asleep. He went into the hall and his aunt told him to go back to bed. He had never seen her face like that before, and though he was an obedient child, he found he could not move. And then his mother emerged with the officers.

'She was in her thin old nightdress,' he said. 'I remember how frail her legs looked. They were holding her between them, I could see her saggy breasts through the material, and she sagged too; she looked like something broken, even though I'd watched her cook dinner that same evening. I still wonder now whether she knew what was coming. We were a happy family, so I never really noticed my parents. She seemed so . . . so irrelevant beside the agents in their grey uniforms and polished boots. It was as if they'd already taken her away.

'As they left, she asked me to say goodbye, to tell her I loved her. I was the only one of her children awake, the only one. And I'll never forget.' He wasn't crying, although I wished he would. It would have been easier. 'I didn't do anything, Laura. I couldn't move. I just stood there, even when she begged, though she did it quietly as if she didn't want to make me feel bad, right up until they closed the door. And I'll never forget the awful thought I had, that I was *glad* they'd taken her. She was embarrassing, in that thin nightgown with her hair everywhere, looking like the world had been sucked out of her. All that human vulnerability. It was almost obscene.

'You know the strangest thing? The last officer picked up a toy from the floor, a little wooden horse, and came over. My aunt thought he was going to hurt me, but he crouched down, handed me the toy and tousled my hair. Then he said something I'll never forget: "You look like your mother." And he smiled as he left.'

Andrei never saw Adriana Ciocan again. Nobody did. He

went to the National Records Office in Poartă, but her file was missing or destroyed. He spoke to old neighbours, even – especially – the ones he suspected had been informants, and learned of the rumour that she'd been taken to the mansion, but with no papers and no way of accessing the place, the trail had gone cold – until now. I'd already felt like I was venturing into a monster's maw, and his revelation only gave it extra teeth. My anxiety twisted the words in my mouth, and somehow my sympathy morphed into defensiveness, my consolations into excuses. We had made up, barely, before I left, but it was a hastily patched peace and we both knew it was unlikely to hold up through our long separation.

'Laura? Is there a problem?' Pavel was looking at me intently. I could tell him, but what would that achieve? As the most junior, he already saw me as the weak link. I thought of my mother's face that Sunday, how little fat remained in her cheeks and how an unseen force had scooped out the hollows of her eyes, so the raw bones pushed through. I could not jeopardise my presence here.

'No,' I said at last. 'No problem.'

We crossed the howling boulevard, the cars screaming past milliseconds after we reached the other side, as if trying to make a point.

'Why did the lawyers cross the road?' I muttered.

The pavements were carpeted with more leaves, and Jude promptly discovered that beneath this layer was another of dog shit.

'What a charming, functional country,' he said, frantically scraping his shoe.

'Isn't it good luck?' I asked.

25

'That's birds.'

'Lots of stray dogs round here,' Pavel said. 'Popa rolled out the property nationalisation programme and people had three hours to evacuate. Some left their pets behind and they bred.'

'They should shoot the bloody lot.'

We kept on until we reached a beautiful wrought iron gate at the foot of a hill and Jude stopped his complaints.

'Not bad for an orphan who slept and stole her way to the top.' He grinned. 'Not exactly *Annie*, is it?'

Pavel pressed a small bell set into the wall. Two guards huddled in a glass-fronted hut nodded but did not come out.

We waited for what felt like a long time. It began to rain, and somewhere a bird cried, a raucous, grating sound like the squeaking of a gate neither open nor closed. I checked my watch (*I'm late, I'm late*), that faint rushing in my ears again. What would Alice have done had she simply kept on falling?

Finally the speaker on the gatepost crackled: Pavel leapt to it and spoke. After a suspicious pause, the gate buzzed open. The path was cobbled and the guards watched impassively as we struggled with our luggage. Some stones were missing, forcing us to keep our eyes on the ground. Perhaps that was the point. It was quieter here, unnaturally quiet, the boulevard's noise severed by the walls and trees. Even the rain was muzzled.

The mansion, when it appeared, did so all at once, as if it had quickly scuttled into position.

'Oh! How weird.'

It was vast yet squat, two storeys high with a brutish, hulking aspect, and I disliked it at once. The trees crept right up to it, strange trees like long-necked creatures with their arms twisted back. Their fingernails grazed the windows, which were smaller than they should have been, set deep into walls that were either stained or had been deliberately painted an unhealthy yellow-white. The thick columns guarding the doors bulged slightly at the middle, so the viewer felt disturbingly as though they were looking into a fairground mirror. From the roof a glass dome protruded, like a cornea watching the sky.

The peeling black doors opened, disgorging a long, tall figure. A man, dressed in lumpish clothing. Pavel began to speak, but he shook his head and motioned us wordlessly inside.

We stepped over the threshold: heat hit us like the breath of an animal. I had an impression of chandeliers, of things that had been deliberately polished until they sparkled, pinpricks designed to distract from the larger dark. I gasped, the wind knocked out of me, for here was fear – no, *terror*; I sensed it amid the human and inhuman presences, heard it in our footsteps on the shining marble. There was a thing here, a force that breathed and seethed, the bricks and mortar merely an artifice overlaid upon a watching leviathan. I wanted to look yet was horror-struck by what I might see. It was an effect peculiar to that house that I always felt not like a visitor, but a witness.

'In here,' the man said. He gave a sudden smile: his mouth was curiously elastic and I found myself imagining it opening far wider.

'And you are?'

'Ion Apostol.'

Pavel gave the tiniest of starts, undetectable unless one was trained in lawyers' body language, the world's least communicative vernacular. The restraint of the gesture disturbed me more than if he'd jumped three feet in the air. 'Will Mar . . . will the Doamna know we are here?'

'The Doamna always knows.' And he shut us in.

We exchanged worried glances. I thought of what my

mother had said that Sunday, when I had reminded her Popa was dead.

She is worse.

'Lovely,' Jude said. 'Well, I suppose we wait.'

We did, for a long time. My anxiety gradually subsided as the door remained stubbornly, almost elementally shut. I could have believed time had stopped.

We were in a drawing room, large, high-ceilinged and oddly empty for its size. An elegant sofa, three heavy chairs, a solitary pouffe and a coffee table with a laden fruit bowl, its fecundity spilling over into the room. The silk-lined walls were pink, as was the carpet. It was like being inside a body, albeit one gone to seed: empty patches on the wallpaper, pressure circles on the floor. Ghosts of furniture past. The absences, once noticed, began to multiply across my vision, until they were almost more visible than what was actually there. Involuntarily I recalled my mother on the sofa, clutching her teacup so hard I was sure it would break.

Jude picked up a clock from the mantelpiece. Pink and white china bunnies writhed around its face: some sported pantaloons, the rest were naked.

'I believe,' he said, with the air of a connoisseur, 'that this is the most hideous thing I've ever seen. When exactly did the commies arrive?'

'After the war,' Pavel said. 'There were elections after the Second World War. Bogdan's party had people in the voting system, *et voilà.*'

Yes. While the West patched itself up and turned to fridges and washing machines, rock 'n' roll and Toffee Crisps, Superman and Cinerama – while progress, in short, progressed – Yanussia, rather than coming in from the cold, went outside without its coat and shivered. Stanislav Bogdan, dubbed Stalin's bloodhound, made his successor seem almost a bleeding-heart liberal. Almost. The West initially gave Popa a hero's welcome, expecting a reformer, a moderate and potential chink in the Iron Curtain. Instead the Dear Leader cherry-picked the most nonsensical of the Stalinist industrial policies and doubled down. Kleptomania and a spiralling foreign debt brought the nation to the economic brink, while he constantly reshuffled his ministers to prevent them learning anything useful about the departments they ran (not that this set him apart from many Western leaders). When that failed to curb his paranoia, he fell back on a lively series of purges and the expansion of the Strajă.

Jude shook his head. 'Forty years in power, yet this drawing room looks like my Aunt Mildred's.'

We all smiled, reluctantly, but it broke the ice that had crept up on us all. He was right: I had expected a dragon's lair stuffed with treasures, but wherever the money was hiding, it wasn't here. The state might claim Marija's trial was about justice, but I couldn't help think that really it was to shake her like a recalcitrant piggy bank. Most of the Popas' possessions had been seized – Marija's wardrobe proving so large it was hastily stored in the bowels of Yanussia's National Museum – but that was merely the first link in the Tiffany's chain. The rest had yet to be found.

I picked a chair. Pavel sat down on the sofa opposite, one leg slung over the other, his casualness belied only by the crackle in his eyes. I had seen it before, on a case concerning a concrete manufacturer that seemed to prefer round-tripping funds to anything so pedestrian as actually making concrete. When fourteen-hour sessions congealed and everyone else was ready to call it a day, he would insert a knife and twist. He was fifty-five: the black hair he kept dyed to within an inch of its life was beginning to look incongruous. Rumour had it that he was retiring next year, his wife wanting to confirm whether there was a man behind the briefcase hurrying out the door; this might be his last case. Others might have wound down a little, but I knew better. Pavel had a success rate of more than ninety per cent, and he would be ruthless in preserving it, most likely at my and Jude's expense.

I took in the slender pinstripes, the shiny shoes. Yanussian he might have been, but his wealthy merchant parents had sent him to school in England before the borders closed. Harrow then Cambridge had transformed him into the very template of an Anglo-Saxon lawyer, the kind of man who believes all England can be fitted into three boys' schools and two universities. He had the right hobbies, too. Somewhere along the way he'd cultivated an enthusiasm for big-game hunting, and when he invited the juniors round for drinks, I'd shared the bathroom with the drooping lashes of a giraffe.

I thought I understood. There had been a time, not so long ago, when I'd hoped to educate myself as to what to do, which was essentially the same as who to be. Before New York, Carl Mortensen, a partner, had taken me aside at the Friday wine-and-cheese and told me that while my work didn't need any improvement, my people skills did.

'Think about power,' he said, nibbling on his Brie.

'What has that got to do with it?'

'My dear, it has *everything* to do with it. Do you know why I always sit with my back to the window?'

I had assumed it was because he saw the view as a distraction – the HSG office had a staggering vantage across the City, which nobody ever noticed. I often wished there was a code on our timesheets for staring out the window. *11.00– 11.06. Vista appreciation.*

'Because then the other side are looking into the light. It makes it harder for them to see you. Work all you like – in the end, you have to *dazzle* them a little.'

I hadn't yet put this feng shui into practice, but he was

right. I remained the outsider no matter how well I did. On the streets of Moorgate, you could easily tell those who had been born to it, what my mother, with a nose-wrinkle, would once have called fancy men: those whose lives were so much expensive sausagemeat, a refining process that began with the silver spoon and ended with the silver trophy at a Home Counties golf club. Despite himself, Pavel was not like that. Although he would not have seen it so, the establishment had ruined him, leaving him unable to forgive his parents for being both foreigners and shopkeepers. Perhaps hunting was a means of venting his feelings on the subject.

My stomach rumbled loudly in the silence, prompting an eyebrow-raise from the man himself. I reached for an apple, then hesitated, brought up short by the intuition that once I made contact, I could not go back. I checked my watch – a thirteenth-birthday gift from my mother, if you could call it that – and tried to feel lucky to be here. I hadn't lied to my parents: for all my achievements, it was the visa system that had made me a shoo-in. Yanussia might now be capitalist, yet it clung still to its communist bureaucracy, possibly through spite. Foreign visas took months we did not have, so in need of a native-born citizen, Pavel had forgone more senior associates and turned to me. *A convenient set of immigration papers.* That was how he'd described it to the managing partner. I knew it wasn't personal. It wasn't even because I was female; unlike some partners, he didn't deduct ten points from anyone with breasts. It simply offended his rigid sense of rank. Pavel liked order above all things, his fountain pen always at a neat perpendicular to whatever bundle happened to be on his desk, which itself began each morning perfectly clear. I gave no sign I'd heard, but under my desk my fists clenched.

In truth, for the first time, I felt uneasy about my career. I was still performing – in all likelihood I'd be crowned top junior again – but since New York I had found my heart wasn't in it, the black suit I wore every day feeling like someone else's skin. I had always existed at full pelt, chasing something I could not define, running from something I dared not. In law I thought I'd found it: a career that demanded a total absorption I was only too happy to give. I celebrated my job offer by getting blind drunk then marching into John Lewis to buy the exact suit I had seen an associate wearing at interview. From now on, I would fit in. This sharp-lapelled family had agreed to take me on, and I repaid them with slavish devotion. The client didn't matter: an Italian minister accused of spicy activities, the dullest of which was money laundering; oily oil execs under investigation for contract mischief in the Congo; a vengeful ex-wife pursuing her husband over a Ponzi scheme, wringing her pearls as if they were his neck. I didn't care. These weren't nice people, but then nice people couldn't afford our fees. I did the work and I did it well. My mother's anger and silence had stopped my heart, but in my career I believed I had found a way to resuscitate myself.

It worked, or appeared to, the long hours and City culture rendering me outwardly hard and shiny, like a diamond. Yet in New York, working on a Middle Eastern fraud case involving eight clandestine yacht meetings, six prostitutes and a Fabergé egg, I became aware of a lingering flaw, an emptiness no amount of all-nighters could fill. I had wanted to blend in, blurring my edges so closely that you could no longer see the outline; I wanted, at long last, to feel like I fitted. But in America I realised that it wasn't working and never would; that despite everything, still a skinless something quivered.

Andrei had seen it the minute we met, at an alumni event my two closest friends dragged me to, coming over and asking if I was Yanussian. He was extremely good-looking,

32

in a narrow, lean sort of way, but as Sarah and Charlie made themselves scarce with unusual tact, I realised his looks were not the cause of my panic. I had spent so long playing at being English that his question was a shock, as if under his gaze I had turned to glass.

'Lăzărescu,' he said, seeing my confusion.

I looked down at my plastic name badge. 'Oh.'

Only a year later, and eight months after we'd gone official, did he tell me it wasn't the badge at all. 'It was your eyes,' he said, slicing an onion. 'They're like mine.'

I was confused. Mine were deep brown; his, unusually for a Yanussian, were a light hazel.

'Not the colour. The expression.' He paused, the knife hovering. 'Hungry. Your eyes are hungry.'

He was right, and it was my own fault. I had spent the last decade stupidly imagining that if I did well, if I truly succeeded, my mother would love me again. The inhuman hours had always acted as blinkers, shutting off a part of my psyche, making me a little inhuman myself. But that shut-off section had not disappeared; it had merely lain in wait. In coming to Yanussia, I felt myself turning to look for the first time.

I had explained the problem to Andrei, but he was puzzled. He did not need to question his own mother's affection. She was gone, and in a sick and horrible way I envied him. At least he did not have to dance on the wretched high wire of hope, for against hope there are no defences. What did I mean, she did not love me? Could I give examples? But it was not what she had *done*. It was what she had been, and what she had been was absent, not just from the usual school runs, swimming galas, parents' evenings, but from her own self. The real her was locked away deep behind her eyes, inaccessible.

'Why not just ask her what's wrong?' he said, and I

dropped the subject. Our so-called relationship made me feel like nothing, like less than nothing, and I had come to hate the inner badness I must possess for repulsing my own mother, the one person who was supposed to love me no matter what. Asking would tear apart whatever we had left, and my tattered scrap of soul could not bear it.

As for my thirteenth birthday, I never told him. There are some things too excruciating for us even to seek solace.

Suddenly the door moved. We stared. Surely it was not wide enough for anyone to enter . . .

My fists curled, in relief or disappointment I did not know. For the woman who entered was not Marija Popa.

She looked like an overexposed photograph. Yellowed skin like paper, eyes too dark for her face, and thin, painfully thin. I was reminded of those unlucky insects whose chrys-alises are invaded by wasp eggs: the eggs hatch and eat their hosts up from the inside out. The effect was compounded by what she wore: a stiff jacket and boxy skirt, not so much clothing as exoskeleton. I recognised her at once, a crepus-cular presence in the corner of countless photos, the shadow at Marija's side. And while Ecaterina was the elder, there was never any doubt who was in control.

'Doamna Iubită,' Pavel said smoothly, already on his feet. The apparition looked faintly surprised to see him, then recovered and attempted a smile. The dried mouth split, a little seam of red spreading across her bottom lip. She licked it off with a quick flick: the teeth were discoloured, as if she consumed a lot of sugar. Yes. It was the Iubită dynasty who had controlled the famed sweet company, Yanussia's answer to Cadbury's and a national treasure. My mother would often bring home their most famous product, the

34

eponymous *iubită*, and I would hold them in my hand: fat, heart-shaped hard-boiled red candies with soft centres. *Now you are holding my heart*, my mother said. I pushed the memory away.

The business had made the Iubităs rich and powerful, and though the company was nationalised under communism, their future was assured when their adoptive daughter married a young deputy housing minister named Constantin Popa. It added to her allure, for everyone liked candy, didn't they? *Sweet enough already*, the American papers declared when she visited in the late sixties, after Popa had denounced the Warsaw Pact and was still hamming up his role as eastern Europe's maverick progressive, complete with photogenic wife.

Ecaterina did not come any closer. 'You must be Cristian Pavel. A pleasure.'

I hoped we never had to call on her as a witness. She was almost deliberately unconvincing.

'You should not have come,' she went on.

'I am sorry?'

'The Doamna is indisposed. She cannot see you. Perhaps tomorrow.'

'But we have an appointment. I made it myself, a full month ago, with her secretary. A Ms Moraru.'

Marija's adoptive sister gave a small moue of distaste, as if secretaries, like the weather, could not be trusted to get it right on the day. 'Ms Moraru no longer works here. The Doamna trusts me, and only me, with her time.'

'But our appointment?'

'She has taken all this very hard.' Ecaterina examined her nails: I had the horrible impression that the fingertips had been sliced off, but it was only red varnish. 'Yet for you, I will speak with her.' She said this as if imparting a great favour. 'You may return the day after tomorrow.'

'You just said tomorrow.'

'I said perhaps.'

Pavel folded his arms. 'Madam. We are Marija Popa's *defence lawyers*. We must meet her to commence our work. How will she survive in court if she has no one to defend her?'

'The Doamna always survives.'

'The trial is in April. It is October already. Or don't you want your sister released?'

The atmosphere, already chilly, turned to ice. 'You disbelieve my loyalty?'

'I know nothing of your loyalty, madam. I am a lawyer. I care for facts, not beliefs, and the fact is that six months is little enough time to prepare already. The fact is that, as her sister, I would expect you to look after her best interests. It is imperative that we do not delay any longer.'

'It would seem you do not have much faith in your abilities, *maestru*.'

'I have plenty. But I am not so foolish to match that with a lack of faith in the prosecution.'

The black eyes watched him. It was impossible to know what she was thinking.

'So be it,' she said suddenly, and left the room, a bunch of keys at her hip jangling in complaint. Following, we saw her vanish up the grand staircase that swept up both sides of the walls. I hadn't taken the hall in before: it was magnificent, a rose-gold colour that cast a soft blush over even my colleagues' pale faces. (Lawyers come in two shades: ski-tanned or all-nighter pale.) The walls were pink plaster marble of the ruinously expensive variety; under our feet was an enormous Persian rug in pinks and reds, with a curious coiling pattern that made the eye water trying to trace it, while above us chandeliers squatted like great glittering spiders. As with the sitting room, however, it was unnaturally empty. Instead it was dominated by an enormous floor-to-ceiling mirror, completely covering the back wall. The double staircase rose and met it at the landing then divided, the room's bareness forcing the eyes to it.

I found myself walking over.

'Hey,' Jude said. I ignored him and took the first step, then the second. My mirror self appeared, long dark hair brushed straight. I watched her, me, go up the stairs. Andrei always described my body as bird-like, all thin wrists and collarbones. Snappable. The terror had returned, but now it was commingled with something else, something sweeter and harder to refuse. Intoxication. It drew me onwards, upwards: my own flesh tingled, but the stance of the doppel-gänger was easy, thoughtless, unselfconscious in the way animals are. In the background, Pavel paced and Jude inspected his shoes, both of them small and distant, walking up the walls of a different sphere entirely. One of me approached the other, closing in until we were not three feet apart.

I raised my eyes and met those of my double. Concentric circles, white to brown to black. I leaned in, my ears rushing with that sound of falling. I was close now, closer to the depths I had sensed within the house, to the shadow that swirled behind the wallpaper. I could pass through the looking-glass, into it, cover myself in silver . . .

'Come through,' a soft voice said.

CHAPTER FOUR

I glanced up in shock. For in the mirror was a woman, her reflected face as familiar as my mother's.

She was *full*. That is the only way I can describe it. Her mouth, her amber eyes, the soft curve of her neck were so many sensuous lines, each screaming with life. It was as though she had carefully absorbed the world's choicest parts, sucking them up and inserting them beneath her creamy skin for safe-keeping, slathering life over her like butter. She floored me. Outrageous to imagine her hanging from the gallows: I had never met anyone so alive, so *unkillable*, as she. She was fifty-eight, but didn't look it. Beautiful – oh yes, beautiful – yet she knew that she was so much more than that, displaying her looks while also seeming as though anything so obvious was beneath her, demanding to be admired while simultaneously making the transaction uneasy, almost lascivious. I took in the body encased in its red dress like a dagger in its sheath, the black coiled hair, the lips curled at some private joke. There was something mythic about her: a sphinx, a siren, a hydra. Stupid to wonder whether she was guilty of this or that – she *was* a transgression, a living vice, one long sensuous step over the line. She was vivid as blood and she magnetised that hall, so the very air became charged and we found ourselves breathing differently.

'Come through to the drawing room,' Marija Popa went on. 'It is warmer there.'

'Doamna.' Pavel's voice sounded behind me, and with relief I turned to face the real world.

'Cristian. Darling. What a pleasure to see you again.'

Again? But I forgot my surprise in her words, slow and pronounced: the tones of an actress, glittering with promise. We discovered ourselves hanging onto them, pinned there by the awfulness of terror and the deliciousness of intoxication.

Pavel approached the foot of the stairs. With a frisson, I realised he was nervous. I had never seen him so before, not with the most aggressive, wealthy or mad clients, nor even those that were all three.

He stopped and waited. So did the First Lady. I saw that her shoes were white, pure white, gloriously impractical, as if nothing could touch her, much less stain her; as if questions like *Did you do it? Did you know what was going on? Were you active? Complicit?* were gross impertinence.

Pavel broke first and came up towards her, bowing. She laughed and extended a hand, which he kissed. 'After all these years. You are older, Cristian.'

'Whereas you, Doamna, have not aged a day.'

'Ah! Age takes us all. You are married? You have children?'

'Two.'

'I adore children. Delicious.' She turned to me. 'Who is this?'

'Laura, one of my juniors.'

She looked at me, through me. Her eyes were like nothing I had seen, the same colour as the amber pendant I had at home (its little fly trapped within), flecked with shards of darkness. It was entrancing; it was excruciating. I held out my hand, my breath catching in my throat as the smile reappeared at the corners of that mobile red mouth.

Submit, it said, and twenty years fell away. I forgot why I was there, forgot my family, forgot that this trial was a mere pretext, an excuse for the moth to draw close to the flame. Oh, as an adult I knew I hated the Popas, but I had not known it as a child, and the old devotion rose up like gorge. Constantin and his wife had been more than heroes; they had been gods. I grew up in the West, where people didn't believe in anything beyond themselves, but as I looked at Marija, I recalled the primitive magnificence of surrender, the divine glory of self-effacement. *Submit*, the mouth whispered. How I and my classmates had dreamed of such a moment! How we would have cut out our hearts and offered them up, dripping!

Would I yet have done so? I can never be sure, for in that trembling moment, she spoke and it changed everything.

'Laura Lăzărescu,' she said, and she pronounced it the Yanussian way, my mother's way, rolling it around her mouth like a stone. My response was automatic, elemental. A fear that was far older, deeper, overcame this new terror and I shrank into myself, somewhere far beneath the skin. The invisible grip fell away; my own hand fell back to my side. In any case, she had not moved to take it.

The eyes narrowed. She turned away, and I almost sagged, as if her gaze had been holding me up. Not for support, but for inspection.

'And this?'

'This is Jude.'

'Greenwood. Senior associate,' Jude said importantly. He held out his hand: it too was ignored. I felt a certain grim satisfaction, until I realised I was leaning against the mirror as if trying to force myself through it.

'Sister. You wish me to join?' Ecaterina had reappeared.

'It is all right, sister.' Marija smiled, a great indiscriminate sweep. 'We are old friends.'

In the pink drawing room, she chose the sofa, leaving us the three heavy chairs. Pavel and Jude sat immediately, and with belated horror I realised the remaining one faced a wall. I took a step towards it, changed my mind for the pouffe, rejected it as unprofessional, and quite by accident found myself on the sofa beside her.

(*Was* it accident? Even today I do not know.)

I felt the aghast eyes of the others, yet Marija did not look round. I held my position though her presence burned my side, trying not to tremble.

A teapot and a single blue porcelain cup had appeared from nowhere. She did not look like a woman facing death. When she poured, her movements were fluid as the liquid.

'So, Cristian.' She took a slow sip. 'What is it?'

'Well – your defence case, Doamna.'

'Ah! That.' She arched her neck. A tigress? A desert cat, of the kind the Egyptians worshipped? 'I will win.'

'Unfortunately we cannot know that.'

She looked at him as though that were his error, not hers. She was facing execution, yet she seemed to have decided that Death was merely another official to command.

'Over the next few months we have much to discuss.'

'Months? Impossible.'

'Such things take months.'

She purred. 'I am sure this prosecutor will be no match for you, this Dumitru what-is-his-name.'

'Ursu. Dumitru Ursu.'

I thought, she knows exactly what his name is. Her voice was mercurial, its pace shifting, a liquid eddy that caught you off guard. Musicians have a term: *tempo rubato*, stolen time. You borrowed time and you gave it back, accelerated then slowed, that was the agreement. But her speech was not like that – there was no counterbalancing force. She stole time and kept it for herself. A delectable aberration.

'If you like. When you have held power as long as I have, Cristian, you see things differently. Yanussia is having a fit. It will pass. They say they want their money. I say, take it! But I know nothing. How, then, can I help them? Ah, you look at me, at this house, and you think it is impossible I do not know. But see these holes in the walls. See the emptiness of the rooms. They have taken everything, and yet they want more. That is what children do. They take and they take. I should not be surprised. Yet were these same children not suckled on my milk programmes? Were their minds not reared on our literacy initiatives? I was the Little Mother of Yanussia.'

A pang. *My mother belongs to my heart; my heart belongs to my mother.* Her unofficial slogan. We schoolchildren repeated it to her image every morning, hands at our chests, as if ready to remove the organ in question and offer it to her. My own mother, the real one, never took offence at my piety; instead she laughed and chucked me under the chin. 'Thank you, *pisi*. Little cat.'

'Not you! Her!' I squirmed as she picked me up and mocked me gently, claiming the dedication as her own.

'Yes it does, *pisi*. Yes it does.'

'I still am,' Marija went on.

'I beg your pardon?' Pavel said.

'I still am the Little Mother.' Another sip. 'You know, of course, of my Movement for a Million Children. My initiative to create workers gave them their *lives*, and I do not believe they can be so quick to forget.'

The Million Children programme had been one of the biggest hallmarks of the Popa regime, a response to a demographic shortage of workers as the country fixed its sights on Stalinist industrialisation. Four children were expected per family. Abortion was banned; women of childbearing age were inspected monthly by doctors to encourage them to procreate, and to catch any pregnancies before they could be ended. Any pregnant woman who did not give birth was subject to arrest. I myself had been born under the programme. It was disgusting, but it was also hard to hate her for it, because as she said (although the thought made me nauseous), without it would I exist?

'That is all very well, Doamna. But we cannot rely on a change of heart. The First Minister is strong; he will see this case through.'

'Matei Anghelescu?' A ladylike sniff. 'He is a little boy playing politics. Just like his toy president Stoica. They say they want to rebuild the country, yet they go about it by pillaging our past. You do not make a new world by killing the old world's leaders.' She laid a pale hand on her breast. 'They would rape me, Cristian, they would eat me alive, these men who want my flesh. I, who persuaded Nixon to waltz. I, who staked a trade agreement on mah-jong with Chairman Mao and won. Now look at me. This trial is a vivisection, nothing more. If you only knew how I wish I was dead like my husband!' At the perfect moment her breath caught. 'They would not even allow me to attend his funeral.'

As the revolution swept into Poartă, Constantin Popa had barricaded himself into the Communist Party's fortress-like headquarters. There were bars on the windows, themselves of bulletproof glass; the doors were huge iron things, specially smelted in Marovia, as if he'd known what was coming. He was in there for barely a day when, inexplicably, he opened them. The protesters engulfed him like a pack of wolves; they literally tore him to pieces.

Even now, theories abounded as to why he'd done it.

Accident? Suicide? Even four years on, this country did not publicly discuss it. He was buried a month later, after Marija's own arrest. It was true that she hadn't been allowed to attend the funeral. She'd waited outside instead, black dress setting off the pallor of her face and handkerchief clutched to her breast, the image of uxorial grief. God only knew how she had persuaded the guards to let her come. They'd surrounded her, mute and uncomfortable as a crowd watched beyond the hasty barricades, stunned into silence, curiously unable to jeer. Perhaps they were ashamed. When the procession emerged, she forced her way through and flung herself on the coffin, tears streaming down her cheeks, clinging on until two guards dragged her away with expressions very like pity. Had that been grief, or the performance of it? The tears of a distraught widow, or a crocodile?

As if reading my mind, she said, 'Do you believe me?'

Pavel frowned. 'Doamna, I care for f—'

Marija said, quite calmly, 'Cristian, if you tell me that you care for facts, not beliefs, I will have you thrown out of this country and off this case. Facts are nothing, except when used to serve belief. You lawyers believe perception is reality's slave, when in fact it is the other way round. I have always managed to defend myself. No doubt I can do so in court. As if twelve civilians are a match for me!' Another sip of tea. 'But your superiors will not see things the way I do. So give me your answer, Cristian, and as much as it pains your profession, make it a straight one.'

I leaned forward, silently screaming. *Just say it, you idiot.* But Pavel only stammered, 'It is not relevant—'

'It has all the relevance in the world. What use are you if I do not have your loyalty? You think Dinu and I ruled for more than thirty years by letting people *doubt*? One last time. Do you believe me?'

Her teacup was suspended in mid-air. There was no shake

in her hand: she was perfectly still, an animal crouched in the savannah. With mounting distress I saw that Pavel could not speak. This was everything. If he didn't say it, she would fire us or worse, and my search would be lost before it had even begun. I would return to England with nothing – no, worse than nothing, for I would no longer have even the hope of salvation. My parents would never let me come back, and I would never be brave enough again to defy them. This was my only chance. Pavel was paralysed, finger-nails digging into his chair; Jude was gazing at Marija, his mouth half open.

'I do.' The words fell out of my mouth, clumsy, lumpish. Nobody moved. 'I believe you,' I repeated into the silence, black spots edged with gold dancing across my vision. My hands were at my neck; I discovered I was not breathing.

A long moment, then those amber eyes turned to me. I could not read their expression, nor did I know what I expected to see. Surprise? Approval? I had lived a life invis-ible, fearing yet craving to be seen, and her gaze flayed me.

'Very well,' she said, inscrutable. The barometer dropped; the animal sheathed its claws. 'You will remain my lawyers.'

Utter relief. We would stay; I had saved us. But the reprieve was short-lived. She clapped her hands and Ecaterina appeared with a jingle, so quickly I wondered if she had been listening at the door. 'However. I do not like what happens in the corners of my eyes. You will live here, where I can see you.'

I looked urgently at Pavel, trying to catch his attention. It is one thing to venture into the witch's house; quite another for her to put you up, to make your bed, and all that while, at the edge of your vision, the empty oven awaits . . .

But Pavel had eyes only for the First Lady. He agreed. Heedless of our stares, or maybe not so much, she yawned in response, not bothering to cover her mouth. Curled at the top of her neck were hairs too fine to be caught in her coiffure. 'Sister – can we manage?'

'If you wish it, it is done.'

'Angel.' And she was gone, sweeping out without a backward glance. I sat back, the wind knocked out of me.

The angel's smile was immediately replaced by a glare, as if this latest development were our fault. 'There are no rooms ready. Come back at nine.'

Apostol attached himself to us shadow-like, following us as we went back down the cobbled path. My hands shook slightly, reverberating to my words to Marija. *I believe you.* Only words, I told myself, yet I could not shake the feeling that something had been disinterred.

'What's all this?' Jude said. Only then did I notice that the ground near the wall was scattered with detritus: Coke bottles, juice cartons, and here and there, rocks.

Apostol said something quietly.

'What did you say? Dracula?'

I winced. A couple of the more literary, if not geographical, school bullies had called me that, despite my repeated assertion that Transylvania lay over the border.

'*Răscula,*' Apostol said.

'It means to rebel,' Pavel said. 'The Răsculat were the militant arm of the anti-Popa movement. They must have thrown this stuff over. I didn't know they were still in operation.'

Apostol shrugged. 'Just because the sewer has been opened doesn't mean the rats move on.'

I shivered. There was a kind of vibration emanating from him, a low-slung hum agitating the air. I had sensed such a disturbance before in a case involving a kleptocratic African general. It was not the embezzled mining profits that

46

bothered me so much as his eyes: without a doubt they had seen violence, and not as a victim either. Apostol's eyes were the same.

'New faces,' he said, returning my gaze. 'Prettier than last lot.'

'Manea and Cristescu?' Jude said. The lawyers Marija had fired. 'What about them?'

Apostol grinned his elastic grin. 'You do not know? Cristescu is dead. Suicide.'

The wind sighed, red leaves whirling across the path.

Pavel gave him a long look. 'We will return at nine.'

He insisted on hailing a cab three blocks away so no one would know where we'd come from, his paranoia adding another stone to the black weight upon my skull. We flagged one down beside Popa's old ministerial club, whose formal gardens had been exact miniatures of the ones at Versailles. Only when the house had completely disappeared did I sit back, head thrumming, exhausted. I think the others felt the same. And there would be no relenting, not now, living on site. How could I tell Andrei about my new digs? How could I live in that place knowing what had happened?

Pavel turned to me. 'Never do anything like that again.'

'Although it did work,' Jude pointed out. 'A masterstroke, Lăzărescu, pretending like that.'

'Yes.' I looked away. 'Pretending.'

'I'm serious.' Pavel gave me a sharp rap on the knee. 'You heard that man. Cristescu is dead.'

'So? That was—'

'Suicide. Yes. There were a lot of suicides under the Popas. We must be careful.'

I could not help a shiver. I had leapt on the bandwagon of this trial, yet now I was on it, I was discovering the sharpness of its edges, the stench of its cargo, and all the while the driver was picking up speed.

'Jesus, Pavel,' Jude said. 'What exactly have you got us into?'

'I'm saying there are many eyes watching. We don't know their intentions. I want to ensure we don't find out.'

'What about the things we've already found out?' Jude's voice was sharp. 'When were you going to tell us you know her?'

At first I thought Pavel would not answer.

'All right. All right. Yes, I know her. Knew her. We met at Cambridge.'

We gazed at him, stunned.

'Were you friends?' Jude was incredulous.

'No. I only knew her for a summer. Acquaintances really. To be frank, I'd forgotten her. Encounters with the notorious Black Widow – just dinner party fodder.'

'Does HSG know?'

'Yes.' My neck prickled. His tone was offhand, the same I'd heard him use last summer when throwing down terms to the opposite side. He liked to slip in the most important or outrageous demands a few points before the end, when you were least likely to be paying attention.

'But you didn't think to tell *us*?'

'Why should I? You're juniors. And yes, Jude, a senior associate is still a junior. It was thirty-five years ago. I . . . I didn't think she'd remember me.'

'Don't you think that might be why she chose us in the first place?'

'I don't know. Until today, I only communicated with that secretary. Camelia Moraru.'

'Jesus. What was she like back then?'

But Pavel would not answer, only shook his head and made a great show of looking out at the ugly apartment buildings looming into view. We were heading for an early dinner. The fog and rain had dissipated but the sky was dimming, a dull light that flattened everything to shadow.

Distracted, it was not until later that I realised another thing was troubling me: a little whisper as I recalled the languorous way the First Lady had pronounced 'Lăzărescu', rolling it around her mouth like a coin. Only then did I realise.

Though Pavel had introduced me, he hadn't mentioned my last name.

CHAPTER FIVE

We entered the business district. The streets beyond were black, yet here there were street lights, orange wings fluttering on, no doubt to convince foreigners that this was a country worthy of their expenditure. It must have pained this elusive city to offer itself up like a whore to investors and tourists – and lawyers. I'd been rudely reminded of this last time I met my university friends. We tried to meet up monthly, and for once everyone had made it. They sat agog, wine forgotten, as I told them about my trip.

'I forgot you was foreign,' Charlie said in a silly accent, and I blushed. It was the biggest compliment she could have paid me.

'Do you feel bad about going?' Heather – famously, magnificently tact-free – asked curiously, only to be shushed by the other two. The speed of their reactions told me all I needed to know. I'd told myself I was here for my family, but Andrei was right – it *was* a betrayal, and who could tell how that betrayal might deepen? At the mansion I'd almost felt sorry for Marija and her skeleton household. Gone were the fawning visits from Parisian couturiers; no more the Moscow jaunts to see the Bolshoi and drink cognac at the KGB's luxury guest

50

house. But it was out here, in the real world, that the ribs were truly showing. Why are we more shocked by the bankrupt millionaire than the beggar slipping gradually from rung to rung, each layer of degradation indistinguishable to the well-off eye? Why should the height of the fall matter? And yet it does, though it is just as possible to break one's bones falling from the pavement as from a city block.

I had almost felt sorry for her.

I had felt sorry for her.

The realisation was deeply unsettling. If that was how I felt after barely an hour, what would it be like after weeks, months? Tomorrow we began work on what the newspapers were already calling the unwinnable trial. I had to stay focused on my real purpose here, and now I saw that would mean continually reminding myself what she was. Reminding myself of the web.

'Tourists?' the driver suddenly said.

'No. Business.' Pavel looked up with a gleam of interest. 'Tell me – how are things since the revolution?'

For answer, the man spat out the window. 'It is different. Maybe better. I do not have to get razor blades and jeans on the black market any more. I can buy underwear.' He cackled. 'The cold wind always around your *pula*. That I will never forget.'

I almost laughed aloud at the expression on Pavel's face.

'*Pula?*' Jude asked.

Pavel wrinkled his nose. 'You're too young.' Then, in an attempt to elevate the tone: 'What about the political element?'

The little man frowned. 'You are trying to trap me.'

'No, I—'

'Gone, the days where I have to report speaking to a foreigner inside twenty-four hours. But I do not trust you. You are American?'

'English.'

'Ah, the Queen. Very nice.' He visibly relaxed. 'OK, Dinu is gone. He makes us sick.'

'Sick?' For some reason I thought of my mother, coughing and coughing in the living room.

'We are lost. We cannot understand ourselves. Like when you are so cold you almost feel hot, you know? There are so many things missing. Our friends. Thirty per cent of pay if you do not meet quotas. Even the chicken at the market, he only has the feet or wings. Nobody knows what happen to the rest. We joke and say, maybe Yanussian chickens are so efficient they do not need bodies any more.'

'But surely things are better since 1989?' Jude said.

The driver laughed again, not the same cackle, but something more ambiguous. 'Ah, we embrace your Western things. But we do not trust them. We do not know what to do with this freedom. Before, I do not know I am poor, because everyone is the same. I feel it, but I do not know it. Now I know it too. Before, everyone has a job. Now we must fight like dogs for employment. You want to know why it took so long to remove Popa? You think we are scared of him. No! My brother, he worked at the steam mill. Every day they line up and spit on Dinu's picture. He is a peasant with the mind of a fox and the *pula* of a mouse. Everyone knows this. No, we do not rise up because we are lazy.'

'Lazy?'

'We have no expectations. We are taught not to. That is communism. You are born, you get free education, you work, you die. Not like you Westerners, with everything up for the grab. It must be exhausting, no? Here everything is certain. Everybody has a job. So what if nobody is doing anything? Nobody dies of starvation. Many other things kill you, but not that. My sister-in-law is biggest idiot you ever met, but she gets into the Ministry of Automotive Building.' Another cackle. 'No wonder it takes nine years to buy a piece-of-shit Dacia.'

He reminded me of a teacher I'd once had, a slight man with goggling eyes. He never said anything directly seditious, but occasional remarks made us edge away from him, like animals who know one of their number has been marked for slaughter. One day he stopped coming in. We never saw him again, and even though we were young, we were wise enough not to ask.

'What about the Strajă?' I asked quietly. 'Surely that was part of the reason.'

For the first time, the driver fell silent. Jude dug an elbow into my ribs.

'No,' he said at last. 'Of course they are bad. If you try anything real, they hunt you, sure. But Popas are not like Bogdan. They want to appear *progressive*.' He said it as if it were a dirty word. 'Like you.'

He gestured towards us, the car swerving alarmingly. 'So, not so many disappear after that. The torture men, they have to get new jobs. And we find now that little things, little things is OK. I bribe the gas guy, he removes a valve so we get more heat. My neighbour, he writes jokes about Popa's *pula*.' The man was obsessed. 'You want to hear some?'

'Maybe another time.'

'He writes jokes and nobody comes in the night. Maybe they don't care. Or maybe they know that if we say things, it stops us doing things. You only need fear the stonefish if you step on him.'

'What do you think about the First Lady's trial?'

I thought he would spit again, but instead he turned right round to face us, ignoring the screech of a horn. 'My wife loves her. Thinks she is so beautiful you forget your troubles, and you get hope for yourself. Me, I say she should die. But it is a shame. Like crushing the butterfly to the wall.'

※

The restaurant was surprisingly full, silhouettes crowding the window.

'That car,' Pavel said suddenly.

Jude barely looked back, intent on dinner. It was a sleek black Mercedes-Benz, the windows tinted, the driver invisible.

'I saw it when we left Marija's.'

'You're sure it's the same one?' I asked.

A half-smile. 'There aren't many Mercedes in Yanussia.'

'You think it's following us?'

'Yes.'

'Her? Or them?'

'I'm not sure it matters.'

The fog dragged a cold finger down my back. Jude was already inside. I followed Pavel in, trying to shake the feeling of being an insect under a microscope. As the maître d' came over, Jude cast a longing glance at the table beside the window, though the light was half gone already.

'When do you think that might be free?'

Noting his smart suit and English tongue, the man gabbled something and rushed off. Not for the first time, I was ashamed that I could not understand the Yanussian language, a muddled derivation of Romanian that varied so much by region that English had long been the official lingua franca. People did not believe you could forget your own language, but it was perfectly possible. In England my mother banned me from speaking it; instead I spent uncountable hours before the BBC, until the red underlay of my tongue was infested by this new invasive species. English became the structure within which I framed my world, and consequently it felt like a part of me was locked away on the other side of language, inaccessible. Our family forgot our tongue, and somehow that meant we forgot the green plums that grew on the pavement trees, and the way the tarmac smelled in the summer heat; the superstition of putting right foot first when leaving the house, and how to rejoice in an unexpected egg. One by one we forgot it all, and I realised too late that that included who we were to ourselves and to one another. A lightning bolt of need struck me and I reeled. I had to find out what had caused this great silent amnesia. I had to discover what secret had my family by the throat.

'Now you've gone and done it,' Pavel was saying absently.

The host was flapping a tea towel at the party seated by the window: a family of four, clearly Yanussian, eating *mititei* – traditional spicy sausages. A waiter joined him, and there was a commotion, the diners turning to stare. One of the boys, no older than twelve, tried to say something, but the waiter cut him off and began to scold; the brother, who was even younger, piped up in indignation. I watched in horror, wondering at their parents' passivity until I saw a glimmer, and realised the father had tears in his eyes. But the waiter was yelling now, and all at once he grasped the tablecloth and yanked the whole thing away, tumbling the food and glasses together and dragging it off in a crash of china. I ran over, stumbling through the raggle-taggle of chairs.

'Stop! What are you doing?' My voice echoed in the sudden silence, and I felt the other diners' stares on my back. The maître d' looked puzzled.

'English,' he said. 'For you.'

I am not English. I opened my mouth, then shut it again. I was not Yanussian, not any more. This man was a complete stranger, yet even he could see it. It didn't matter that I looked like them. I was in every other way different.

In any case, the damage was done. The family were being hurried out, the waiter maintaining a firm grip on the father's elbow. *There's no need*, I wanted to shout. He wasn't struggling.

'I'm sorry,' I called inadequately as they left. They did not look back, the door swinging cold air behind them. Only the smaller boy stopped on the threshold, half inside, half out. There was no anger on his face; far worse, it bore a weary resignation that did not belong on someone so young.

'We should leave.' I turned, but Pavel and Jude were already seated.

'Sit, Laura. No sense ruining two dinners.'

'Christ,' Jude muttered. 'Didn't expect that.' He was pink about the ears. 'Do they know we're working for Marija Popa?'

'What have I told you about using her name in public? It's not just a name here, Jude, it's an incantation, and you don't know what it'll conjure up. Look at the way Constantin Popa died. You think that's normal, even for a dictator?' Pavel sighed. 'Besides, it's nothing to do with her. They're just used to kowtowing to foreigners and Party members, that's all.'

The nomenklatura had shopped at special stores, eaten at special restaurants, even holidayed in special villas; the most senior got their own cooks and servants, and sod what that meant for the theory of the proletariat. Jude nodded, not listening. I could almost hear him wondering how else he could work his nationality to his advantage and my anger flashed. How dare he? I risked a glance around the room. No one was looking at us, yet I read the deliberate vagueness on their faces. I thought of that unlucky couple, corpses bobbing in the Danube's grey waters. You could search and search for signs of what this place was, hunt for where the people went in the locked boxes of their minds, scrutinise those blank, careful faces until you felt like a fool, and then, the moment you turned away . . .

A sharp pain made me look down. I had dug the tip of my knife into my palm.

I watched the blood well up and thought of something Andrei had asked. *If the Devil went on trial, would you defend her?* It was a tiny violence, the sort we might inflict on one another several times a week. We had been together too long for mere romance to soothe away the pain, but not long enough for mundane toleration to do the job.

'Be careful, Laura,' he said at one point. 'She'll steal your heart and your mind, and you won't even notice until it's too late.'

As I scanned the meagre menu I began to panic. I couldn't lose him, but what on earth would I say, could I say, about our new lodgings? It was bad enough that he wanted us to move in together. New York had allowed me to dodge the question, but when I returned to my rented Bermondsey flat it confronted me again, written in the dust on the window-sill, susurrating across the empty mantelpiece. My friend Charlie often bemoaned the lack of soft furnishings, and I listened patiently and did nothing. The place didn't belong to me – nowhere did. Papering it over with cushions and throws would only have emphasised the facade.

'It always looks like you're preparing to make your escape,' Andrei complained, when I'd been back for weeks and failed to unpack properly. I frowned and he noticed.

'Are you?'

'What?'

'Escaping?' Was it this that had kept him particularly close all evening, trailing me around the flat, sitting watching TV with his hand on my neck?

I laughed. 'No. Where would I go?'

'Who cares? There's the whole world out there, it's all general. But what you have here, it's *specific*. It's yours. It's not about where you go, it's about what you leave behind.'

'You, you mean.'

'Obviously.'

I took in his familiar face, the dimple he was rude about, the little cheek hairs he always missed when shaving. 'I'm not going anywhere.'

'Good. Move in with me.'

I thought – hoped? – I'd misheard, but he was looking at me earnestly, an open door it would be so easy to step through.

'My lease isn't up for six months.'

'So? I can move into yours.'

In the end I told him I'd think about it. We had been together two years; moving in was the logical thing to do, yet I hesitated. He was my first proper boyfriend, and I'd had to learn not just what love meant, but how it worked. Love, like crime, is discussed in terms of commitment, passion. But how did you know if you were loving correctly? There ought to be lessons, schools. How much damage would be averted if only we knew how to love properly? As it was, I carried my love of Andrei as if it were made of glass, terrified it might smash. Often I caught him looking at me with an affection I felt I did not deserve. My friends called him the Stepford boyfriend.

'He's too perfect,' Charlie sighed. 'You don't know what you have.'

She was right: I was too self-occupied to understand another person properly. If he'd put the moving-in question to me before I'd left for the States, I would have said yes, we had grown so entwined. But while I was in New York, I'd found myself uneasily whole, as though he weakened me, or vice versa. In any case, a fortnight later, I received Marija's file. That seemed to enrage him more than either my non-answer or the prospect of a second extended separation, and I wasn't sure whether to be relieved that the topic had not come up again. He had always been angry; never towards me, but it came out in other ways, in rudeness to indifferent waiters, and bruised toes from kicking uncooperative doors. (Sometimes, to my horror, he reminded me of my mother: caged.) Now those futile gestures had died away, replaced by the hot, lifeless atmosphere before a storm.

'Laura?' Pavel was looking at me, and I realised my hands were at my neck. 'Are you all right?'

'I'm fine.' Andrei and I understood each other's past, and that had always been enough to fill our present. It gave us a shared understanding, a secret thread that had drawn us together since that first evening. Only now, with deep fore-boding, did I sense that thread winding tightly around us, threatening to strangle us both.

The wine list arrived and Jude stopped what he was doing, which was inspecting the ashtray to see if it could be used as a bug. The trick, according to Pavel, was to find the pin, which a waitress or prostitute agent would pull to activate. In a country of ten million, there were two hundred thousand secret informants. Popa knew that true control is found not in uniformed bodies, but in uniformed minds.

'They don't actually expect you to order the Yanussian stuff, do they?' Jude flipped through the list. 'I dread to think.'

Pavel ignored him. 'We've got six months of this and more,' he said quietly. 'I hope you're up to it.'

I did not hesitate. I'd already seen off one threat to my presence here. I did not intend for it to be jeopardised again.

'I am.' My voice was calm, my gaze level. Pavel was not the only one who knew Lawyers' Body Language 101. I once watched another partner learn that he had lost a case that had cost him two years, uncountable billable hours, and ultimately his marriage. A momentary clench of the jaw, a slight crack as his fist closed deep in his pocket: that was all. HSG employees were a little like the Spartans, who told of the boy who stole a fox cub, hid it under his jacket, and strenuously denied the theft until he suddenly collapsed and died. Only then did his interrogators realise the fox had eaten away his insides. If HSG suffered from a shortage of infant foxes in Moorgate, well, they compensated in other ways.

The food came. Pavel and Jude had minute steaks, in every sense; I had what claimed to be a vegetable lasagne, though I wouldn't have taken its case. Pavel told us that he'd arranged a meeting the day after next with Marija's defence advocate, Radutu Gabor.

Jude smirked. 'As in Zsa Zsa?'

'Perhaps it would be more professional if you don't enquire,' Pavel said drily. 'He's an eminent court lawyer, perhaps *the* court lawyer in these parts. Jameson's team in London are running a background check for further details.'

'Including his film career, I hope.'

I fidgeted in my seat. The restaurant felt airless, the windows now black and fogged so we could not even see the view for which we had caused so much upset. I had told Pavel I was up to it – I had to hope that was true. I remembered my mother dancing me around the kitchen to our ancient wireless, the green tiles a-whirl in my vision. But the city I found myself in now was colourless, lifeless, held together by little more than bureaucracy and scar tissue.

A prickle at my neck: someone watching. The black car? No, inside – I turned and caught the eye of a youngish man standing up to leave. Not Yanussian: he did not have the sallow features; rather the broad chin and confident, well-fed air of a Westerner. American? He smiled. His mouth was curiously gentle, almost feminine, at odds with his tall frame. I dropped my gaze and poked gingerly at a pasta sheet.

'Pardon me,' a voice said, and I nearly dropped the fork. The stranger was right behind me, coat draped over his arm. A frisson: American indeed. The accent felt so *capitalist*, in this hollowed city.

'I couldn't help but overhear,' he said. His eyes were very blue. 'Are you working for Madam Popa?'

Pavel glared at Jude, who bit his lip.

'You *are*.' He whistled. 'Liked your entrance. Subtle.'

'What's it to you?'

'Oh, excuse me. Patrick Hanagan, First Loyalty Bank.' He thrust out a hand and a card in a practised movement. 'I'm advising the government on all that privatisation work they keep talking about. You?

'Cristian Pavel. Senior partner at Harris Stroud Glyn. The kind of privatisations that saw them sell the Sebeş mine for one dollar?'

Patrick grinned. 'Not much commission on a dollar. Let's say I'm in the market for pricier stuff.' He pulled up a chair beside me.

'So you have Yanussia's best interests at heart,' Pavel said drily.

'I am talking to Marija Popa's defence lawyers, aren't I?' Pavel said nothing. 'If they want to sell off the family silver, they might as well get a good price. You really think you can win? I would have thought this was an open-and-shut deal.'

Pavel smiled. 'We specialise in those that are . . . ajar.'

'HSG. Yeah, I know you guys. The big bad wolves of London.'

Jude positively wriggled at that, taking it as a compliment, and introduced himself. Patrick ordered a coffee, then turned to me. I put out my hand, though there was little space between us: his palm was warm and unexpectedly rough. Not a born city boy, then. My name made him smile that smile again.

'Related to Lazarus?'

'So I'm told.'

The smile widened. 'And do you come back from the dead?'

'It depends on the conversation.'

He only laughed. 'Tell me,' he said to Pavel, 'how do you get your head around her?'

'Around my junior associate?' Pavel was equally flinty. He too got a laugh, the other diners turning to look. He laughed a lot, this American.

'No. Madam Popa. Is she a psychopath or not?'

'That is hardly the question we are here to answer.'

'Oh, sure you are.' Patrick was surprised. 'The Yanussians don't care about whether she *did* it or not. Yes, they want the money, but even Dumitru Ursu knows he's unlikely to recover much more than what they've already found. Trust me, in my profession I've met folk far shadier than mere dictators. There are people out there who can make anything disappear.' He made a *poof* gesture with his hand. 'No, they don't want to know what she did. They want to know what she *is*.'

Pavel looked blank.

'Is she the kind of woman who launders clothes, or the kind who launders money?'

I couldn't help myself. 'What if she's neither?'

He gave me an odd look. 'Did she know what was going on or didn't she? Was she aware of the poverty? Did she help with the embezzlement? Give her blessing to the secret prisons? If she didn't, she's just another loyal, ignorant wife. If she *did* . . .'

His words hung in the air.

'Where I come from, people love a humbug. My driver told me she visited his school, in an outfit like you've never seen, asking them to call her by her Christian name. She was so *clean*, he said. Handed out peaches. Strange, he said, he knew she had eyes only for him, that she had given him the best peach. But each of his classmates, *every single one*, swore the same. There was a huge brawl when she left; the teachers couldn't tear 'em apart.'

Pavel shrugged. 'She's always been good with people.'

'That's what you call it?'

'It was Marija who ensured they weren't left rationing out drugs and schoolbooks like the Romanians. She is aware of their needs.'

'Or their pressure points.' When nobody said anything, Patrick went on, 'How long will the trial take?'

'Impossible to say,' Pavel sniffed, then relented. 'It starts in April. Could last up to a year.'

'Death penalty?'

'Yes. A real *danse macabre*.'

Patrick grinned. 'I'd dance anything with her. It's odd, isn't it? How she forces you to look at her.'

'No,' Jude said. 'She forces you not to look away.'

I opened my mouth to say they were the same thing, then shut it again, remembering those embassy films, her beside Constantin like the sun and the moon. It was true: you could not take your eyes off her. It allowed her husband to get on with what he enjoyed, namely recruiting foreign ministers as spies, stealing US military secrets, and extracting his country's wealth. While she – she was everything and nothing. You could not measure her influence on any known scale, but it was there, like dark matter. Her official positions were token ones – Minister for Language and Culture, Minister for Women – yet it was her charm that lowered the interest rates on their loans and kept the World Bank payments coming as long as they did. The West lapped her up, talked about philanthropy and style when really they meant style and philanthropy. Was that what glamour did (and did the word not mean, originally, *magic* or *spell*) – made you forget about the dark? If so, did it make her complicit, even active in her husband's deeds without lifting a finger? Or were women simply damned if they were beautiful and damned if they weren't?

Patrick said thoughtfully, 'I was watching the fighting in the Balkans. It's a vipers' nest. You know half of these people celebrate Christmas on December twenty-fifth, and the rest on January seventh?'

'Meaning?'

'He means,' I said, 'how on earth can these people get along when their very calendars are different?'

Patrick gave me a quick smile. 'Exactly. You've seen the refugees pouring into Serbia. There are rumours about a Christmas protest against Marija, the fourth anniversary of the revolution. This stuff always spills beyond itself.'

Pavel shook his head. 'Yanussia is the very elbow of the Balkans. It doesn't have the same issues.'

I said, 'Well, it hurts to be hit on the funny bone.'

Pavel frowned, but Patrick laughed again, and I felt my cheeks flush. 'Good point. Well, must go.' He picked up his coat and checked the large watch on his wrist; the waiter, returning too late with coffee, stared at it with a sharp hunger.

'See you around – I hope.' He glanced at me again. As he got into his car, I found myself watching the place where his hairline did not quite meet his collar, exposing the tiniest sliver of tanned skin.

I blinked, and something slammed against the window pane.

'What is *that*?' Jude yelped.

A creature was pressed against the glass, face distorted, mouth gaping horribly, circles of skin compressed into a bloodless white. Its eyes were famished. My vision twisted: not a creature, a person. A desperately hungry person. I could only watch in horror as the waiters hurried to close the curtains; they swung to and the apparition disappeared. Jude and Pavel exchanged looks of uneasy relief, but they and the diners and the waiters and I knew, we all knew, that outside, the man and his hunger battled on.

Hunger. I thought of Marija Popa and her stomach problems, of how, after more than three decades of unimaginable luxury and power, the Little Mother's belly was still corroded by a hollowness that had never left. I felt it now, a childhood craving that went beyond the endless boring bowls of yellow *mămăliga*, my mother pouring in the cornmeal when the gas finally came on at 10 p.m., me standing on the small stool, stirring until it bubbled and popped. Even now, when my parents finished eating, they used a piece of bread to mop up the remnants. A ravenous country, watching, yearning, starving to be fed. The question was – how long would it wait?

CHAPTER SIX

Back to the mansion, where our alternative existence would begin. As we left the restaurant I looked for the black car and disliked that I could not see it.

We crossed the Danube again, the same river Marija and her husband had once cruised down with Saddam Hussein, eating koftas cooked by the dictator himself. *You really think you can win?* The stakes could not have been higher. I had never faced a death penalty charge, and as we arrived, I felt the weight of the soul we carried.

'I'd prefer the east wing.' Jude practically skipped up the drive. 'Do you think we'll get en suites?'

I sighed. 'I doubt we'll bump into Marija brushing her teeth, if that's what you mean.'

Two house staff greeted us, and Pavel and Jude were taken off one way, I another. I tried not to feel like a lamb to the slaughter as I trailed behind Mircea, a grave young man who could not have been much older than me. He seemed human enough, if unsmiling, yet still I sensed the house's darkness gliding out of sight behind the wallpaper, dashing to conceal itself under the floors. The lights had been dimmed and the chandeliers really did look like spiders now, slender limbs trailing; I had to stop myself from ducking as I walked beneath.

We went upstairs (this time I avoided the mirror's gaze) and deep into the east wing. I tried to talk to Mircea but was met with silence, so I looked around instead. Display cabinets empty of knick-knacks, pedestals supporting nothing but air. As if the house had eaten everything up.

We passed a pair of doors larger and grander than the rest.

'Is this Mar . . . the Doamna's?'

He stopped, assessing me, and finally nodded. On the sofa that afternoon I had felt the heat of the First Lady's presence. I felt it now, burning through the wall.

We stopped at a door barely twenty yards away and Mircea produced a toothy silver key. I took a last look down the corridor, noting with a curious satisfaction that the others were nowhere to be seen.

My room contained a bed, a telephone, a chair with clawed feet. A desk with another fruit bowl. The bed was a four-poster, a ponderous carved thing, and I eyed its hangings uneasily. I did not want to be strangled by creeping embroidery. Mircea opened an inner door to reveal a bathroom in flesh-pink marble. A little bubble of laughter: definitely no brushing my teeth with Marija.

The tiles bore a delicate pattern of fossils, ammonites and trilobites.

'I love this design,' I murmured. To my surprise, Mircea replied.

'Not design. Real.'

I looked at him, not understanding.

'They are real,' he repeated. 'From quarry. The workers find, scientists want to examine but tiles must be finished. Deadlines. Quotas. So, chop chop.'

'But that's terrible. Such a waste.' What do we have in the present if the past means nothing?

He shrugged and straightened my suitcase, his motions unexpectedly graceful. I asked myself who he was, this young man with the sad eyes, and how he had found himself here of all places. He seemed to be waiting for something.

'Oh! I should tip you.' I dug in my pockets.

'No, Doamna.' His voice was quiet. 'I do not deserve.'

I had got it wrong; whatever chink had opened between us closed. He bowed and departed, leaving me to stare after him, wondering what I'd missed.

DISPĂRUT. The word on the posters seemed apposite.

It was very quiet. I ought to go to bed but did not want to submit to those pendulous hangings. They had the air of a pitcher plant. Instead I sat on the cold toilet lid and inspected the whorled skeletons on the walls. They reminded me of the crackers that made me gag as a child, manufactured in North Korea from the ground-up shells of shrimp. Bones and leftovers, things with the life drained out of them. Mircea, Ecaterina, the spectre outside the restaurant. My parents. Andrei's parents. Was that what subjugation did, or had some other force sucked the meat of their souls away?

The room seemed dimmer; I shifted on the seat. Family. A neat net of a word. A stranger looks at us and sees what we are in the present moment; our friends will observe a few years deep. Yet our parents see all our past. It puts them outside time, for they knew us before we were ourselves, and so before my mother's infinity I felt everything I knew slipping away. The worst days were my birthdays. They'd been happy once – I still remembered when I had turned six and we took a rare day trip out of Poartă, to where the hay grew long and the pigs, having overdosed on sun-fermented mulberries, lolled drunkenly in the grass. My mother unveiled an unprecedented picnic. They must have hoarded for weeks. Hard-boiled eggs, bananas, real meat sandwiches, and an actual cake, small but resplendent, perfect. She brought it out casually but I saw the pride in her face and perceived even then how she must have begged and borrowed from the neighbours, the favours she would be repaying for months. All for me. I couldn't even finish it for joy and love.

Yes, it was a far cry from the birthdays of later years, of which my thirteenth took the miserable crown. The worst day, the saddest day, the fist-in-my-mouth-so-I-can't-scream day, when I realised we were broken beyond comprehension. There she was, eyes wild, more furious than I had ever seen her, more than I thought it was possible to be. The words tore from her like animals, and I could only cower at their claws.

'You don't know what I sacrificed!'

I still didn't know, and it lacerated me. The maternal forgoing of that sixth birthday had been replaced by something she should never have been forced to give up, not for her daughter, not for anyone. But what it was, she never told me, and after that day I could never have asked. Her secret separated us like a great black wall and all I could discern was its shadow.

I hadn't expected much, that terrible day. As a family we had more or less given up on petty celebrations, last year's consisting of leftovers and *Grange Hill*. Certainly I hadn't expected to wake and discover my sheets stained with red. I was a restless sleeper even then and had thrashed so that it spread, my thighs and calves slick. The awfulness of the gift appalled me – not so much the blood as the sudden realisation that I had a body, with ways and secrets all of its own. It was as if my mind awoke to discover itself atop a loaded gun.

I could not tell my mother. I was just thirteen, raw with adolescence. Thirteen! What a birthday present. It was unacceptable. I must keep it a secret until I was older. Fifteen?

Surely by fifteen I would feel like an adult, more confident, better able to protect myself.

No sooner had I decided this, however, than I realised I had no idea what to do. The tissues bled through within minutes, the carpet tracking my movements in red. My first, shocking test of womanhood and I was failing. I had to show my mother. I had to confess.

I never forgot her reaction. I knew other mothers sat their daughters down and had the Talk, but we would never have dreamed of such a discussion. This was the first and only time we acknowledged it, if you could apply the term to the way she shouted at me, long and loud, as one shouts at a dog that has fouled in the corner. She took it as a personal affront, as if I'd done it on purpose to spite her. *You don't know what I sacrificed.* The words dug things out of me with their nails: shame, humiliation and the knowledge that I'd committed a deep, deep wrong. She made me scrub the sheets and the carpet, standing over me, her face a screwed-up ball. I scrubbed for a long time, cold water and vinegar, the colour staining the water, that bitter, bitter smell. Who would have thought I had so much blood in me? It got under my nails, as if I'd committed a murder. We were studying chromatography at school and I had been enjoying the colours that bled across the filter paper from a single drop of ink. Real blood was not like that: it was sullenly, aggressively itself, red red red, an element all of its own, and already I hated the newly awoken part which was responsible.

I stayed in my room without dinner but did not dare get back into that fresh white bed.

After some hours, the corridor light snapped on, its claws reaching under the door. I crushed myself further into the corner, hands clasped to my throat, trying to keep it all in. If only I could un-birth myself, none of this would have happened.

The door opened and my mother came in, scanning the lightless room with that abrupt motion I knew so well: a slight toss of her head, like a horse doing something it doesn't care to do. She could not see me. Then – oh, so strange – she removed the watch she always wore and placed it gently on the floor. The door closed, the light shutting off as if it had never been.

I crawled to the watch, stared at its silhouette. To give implies a gift, and I did not think this was one. She wore it all the time – I knew my father had presented it to her the week she began work at the factory, but that was all. I wanted to hate it, but it was only an object; you could not blame things for being themselves. Was it an offering? A consolation? No. Some strange part of me thought of it as an amulet, though against what evil I could not imagine.

I picked it up, half expecting it to be red hot. All that night I imagined it winding up my pain, tighter and tighter. When morning came, the watch seemed heavier but I felt slightly better, as if it had siphoned off some of that misery. I wore it from that day on, hiding it beneath my sleeve, though she never mentioned it. Over time I wondered how the thing could withstand it, how it did not spring apart in a coiling mess of cogs and springs, but it never did. The blood came every month, however, and with it the old humiliation and fear.

An external light snapped off: the darkness leapt and I flinched, the watch on my wrist glinting in response. I'd thought Popa's shadow would loom large here, yet it was not *his* presence I felt seeping from the cracks of the walls, toying with the hairs on my neck.

I clenched the cold toilet seat. I had not defied my parents merely to hide in my bedroom. This house held secrets. The Iubită family had employed my mother: perhaps there were private files, or an archive room. And of course there was the hospital.

'You think you want to find things out, but you don't,' Andrei had said. 'My mother, your mother. You never ask the right questions. You sit with your eyes wide open and your hands covering your face.'

My fingers gripped the seat tighter, compressing the fear into ten little balls. I would prove him wrong.

I crept into the bedroom, skirting the four-poster, and silently opened the door. The corridor beyond was black, save for a knife-slice of light twenty yards away. I advanced towards it, the carpet muffling my footsteps: complicit, for now. I came near, as near as I dared – I put my eye to the crack and saw only the faint ghosts of furniture. What was that scent? Something organic, voluptuous, like an orchard after rain. Oddly, it did not feel like there was anyone there. Whereas before I had felt that burning presence, now there was nothing.

I sensed the hall rather than seeing it, an infinitesimal change in the air pressure. A single blade of moonlight lanced down, illuminating the complex coiling of the carpet. It was beautiful, and as I went down the stairs I forgot myself and touched the mirror.

It was so cold that for a moment it felt hot. My hand pulsed as if it had been scalded. I stared at the silverglass: it gazed unblinkingly back. Quickly I moved on, putting distance between myself and it. At the foot of the stairs, I paused. Which way? East. At least I knew the layout. Andrei's neighbour had said the hospital was located beneath the house; it made sense that they would not pollute the luxury above. They would not want screams accumulating mould-like in the wallpaper, blood spoiling the carpets. There would be a door somewhere, I was sure of it, leading down into a deeper dark.

The lower corridor was identical to its partner above, carpeted and lifeless, like a hotel, or an asylum. I had to confirm the fact of the stairs to be sure I had left at all. I passed many doors, but none were right, innocent daytime doors dressed up in cream and gold. You could not have kept prisoners here, or patients, whatever you were calling them. I tried one anyway. An office. The desk bore a name-plate, the stamped lettering reminiscent of a gravestone. *MORARU*. Marija's secretary.

The second room was full of ghosts: chairs and tables and pouffes, rendered phantom-like by dust sheeting, and a horrible one-winged creature that might have been a grand piano. I shut the door quickly, wincing at the squeak.

I was wondering which one to try next when a scent came to my nose and made my heart jump. Chlorine.

A swimming pool? Here? It had been my mother's favourite activity, our favourite activity, in that Time Before. Generally I tried not to recall the sharp blue joy of those afternoons, her laughter shimmering with the water which bejewelled her arms and face. She taught me to swim in Poartă's only public pool, a concrete behemoth in the southern quarter, built while Yanussia was harbouring Olympic dreams. (Popa knocked down a cathedral to do it.) I had no idea how the daughter of landlocked peasants became such an adept, but Gabriela Lăzărescu could move through the water like no one else, utterly at ease, as much sea creature as the person I knew and loved. I swam too, and the further apart we grew, the more time I spent in the pool, two hours a day before school, up and down and back again, over and over: not to commemorate those times, but to defy them. I walked the mile and a half and back by myself, usually in the dark; I won prizes, beginning with club championships and finishing with a national freestyle trophy. My mother did not attend, of course, but I brought the cup home and put it on the mantelpiece, secretly, pathetically hoping for praise.

She came in. It was right in front of her: she could not have missed it. I watched her from the corner of my trembling eye. Then she turned away, and the next morning it had vanished. After that I stopped swimming, much to my coach's dismay.

There was a door at the end of the hall, different to the rest, fronted with frosted glass. I gave it a tentative push.

A tiled floor, two benches: a changing room, and across it another door, again of opaque glass. The chlorine scent grew stronger.

The old spring of defiance welled up. I could do it. I could swim, though I had no costume, no goggles, no idea if the pool was even usable. That first length always captivated me, when the muscles were sleek and fresh and my arms coursed with iron bands of animal strength, slicing through water that itself seemed to urge me on, supporting my weight, rippling my hair. In the pool there is no one else: no conversation, no possibility of connections to be missed or revoked. In the water, and only in the water, I felt I could do anything.

A tug at the edge of my vision. One wall was lined with pegs, all empty – except for one.

A single swimming costume. It hung there like an empty skin.

How different, how very different my life would have been had I returned to my bed and lain there, safe! Some people believe the world splits in two at each decision we make: at these forked moments time stretches thin, and we might see the future if we dared.

I reached out and caressed the costume, half expecting my fingers to pass through it. It was perfectly real. I held it up, and quivered: my size. There were even goggles, twin black eyes, empty. I glanced again at the glass pane, clouded as though someone was breathing upon it.

The hairs on my forearms rose as I removed my shoes, my clothes, my mother's watch. The costume was a perfect fit.

With bare feet and soul I opened the next door. Someone was in the water, doing a slow backstroke.

I already knew who.

CHAPTER SEVEN

She regarded me entirely without surprise. Marija Popa's costume was deep red, her hair encased in a cap of the same colour. I could see her exact outline, and then the light wavered and she looked completely different.

'Come in,' she said. The droplets poured down her face and neck; she *shone*. I watched her kick off again, back arched as if in ecstasy. If I cut my own arm and thrust it into the water, the curl of blood might look like that.

I could refuse. I could turn back, dress myself, pretend I had not seen. But it was too late: when I'd put on the costume, something had stirred into motion, inexorable. The twin shades of terror and intoxication were at my back again, forcing me on.

I donned the goggles; the moonstruck water dulled to grey. Feet on the cold metal ladder, one, two. The chill was a shock, the pool wolfing greedily at my legs as I reached out for the next step, but there was nothing, only the liquid abyss. I sank backwards, and even as the water claimed me, I was plunging into a pool of my own, where the sea-fronds of my mother's black hair snaked around as I snatched at them with chubby infant fingers. Now the water slaked away even memory; I turned my back on the world and swam. Isn't that what humans seek to do, after all – to escape time, which we may only do by escaping ourselves?

I swam one length, two, three, tumble-turning at each end like she'd taught me – but I sliced the recollection away, the goggles turning everything blessedly two-dimensional. I existed only amid the porcelain matrix of the tiles, a blue realm where holding your breath meant you could not sink.

It could not last; it never did. A single point bloomed like algae in my lungs, sucking up the oxygen, an ache I could not outswim. I stopped midway, came up spluttering. She was leaning against the wall, the water lapping at her costumed breasts. We regarded one another.

'It is nice to see a woman swimming properly. None of this ridiculous old-lady stuff. But how do you do the . . . what do you call it? The roly-poly?'

I had expected to detect her taint, seeping like oil across the water, but her childish vocabulary was delicious.

'You mean the tumble turn?'

'Yes.' She watched me expectantly and I found myself wanting to please her. We were in a place slightly outside the usual way: a mirror world, where the rules could be broken. I obeyed and emerged to discover her looking like a cat that has found a new toy.

'Delightful. I must try.' She did not do so. Instead she pulled herself out, the water streaming off her red costume, momentarily taking on its colour. There were strange white marks on her arms, but in that deliquescent light I could not make them out.

'You like to swim?'

I nodded, not trusting myself to speak.

'I love the water. The irony of having a landlocked country. I always teased Dinu that the one thing he could not give me was the ocean. Naturally he took that as a challenge.'

Only then did I realise: on my lips, the taste of salt. She removed her cap, dry black hair cascading from it like a miracle.

'So, here you are. In the monster's lair. Is it so bad after all?' She smiled at my confusion. 'That is the trouble with stories. They are so *easy*. I am the wicked witch, the whore queen. Everybody knows that, and who examines whether what they already know is true?'

'You think they are unfair.'

'No. I think they are not unfair enough. They should have shot me like Nicolae and Elena.' It took me a second to realise she was referring to the Ceaușescus, the conjugal dictators of Romania. 'They would have done, eventually, but they dithered and now the world is watching. They cannot put me against a wall any more, so they are left with a trial. Clearly I must be punished. But for what? That is the question they are careful not to ask.'

'What do you mean, Doamna?'

'I was not the executive president. What power did I have? I was the Minister for Language and Culture, the Minister for Women. Nobody cares about language or culture, let alone women. No, their only reason for this charade is because of who I fucked for thirty years. It makes them uneasy. Communists do not do sex, only reproduction, but it is the only rationale they have.'

The language was lewd, shocking from that blood-flushed mouth. I realised she was performing again, even though I was an audience of one, a junior lawyer, a nobody. Was she simply unable to stop? Did she even believe herself? I looked for traces that might betray the face behind the mask, but she was too clever for that. She was *almost* imperfect. That was the problem.

'They have tried to eliminate sex all these years, and yet here it is at the heart of the matter. As it always is. We women are always blamed for sex. That is the way of the world.'

78

My mouth was open. Surely she could not believe herself? But her expression was deadly serious.

'When Dinu came to power, he was thirty-nine. I was thirteen years younger than him – younger than you are now – when the people's gaze swung its force upon me.' She sighed. 'First Lady. Little Mother. What do these feminine descriptors mean? I was given no power, yet they expected me to hold my own against the most powerful man in the country.'

'You do not have to explain yourself to me, Doamna,' I said eventually. 'I am only your lawyer.'

She smiled, not a cat-like smirk but a full-mouthed grin I had not seen before. It did not quite suit her, and strangely, for the first time, I sensed something normal, something human. Her ugliness touched me in a way that no perfection could.

'Of course. And you believe me, or so you say.' Her tone was delighted. 'I believe you. Or so I will say.'

I could reply nothing to that. I was clutching the pool wall now and my slightest movement was echoed by the water, amplified by it. Body Language 101 suddenly seemed a poor shield.

'What did it feel like?' I asked abruptly. 'Power?'

'Like searing heat.' Her voice was weary; for the first time I felt she had told me the truth. We let the water shimmer between us.

'Do you know what I did?' she said at last. 'I loved them. I loved my people with all my heart, with all my strength. Somebody had to, Laura. God knows they could not do it themselves.'

I was disappointed. She was an actress again, her voice a velvet fist.

'I know you would like to hate me. I will not stop you. History is written by the victors, after all, and these are

79

always men. Labelling someone a monster is so convenient. It means we never have to examine what made them so. But a monster is only something outside its usual context. Communism is monstrous to the capitalists, and vice versa. The Greeks would have abhorred what you label democracy. Only look at the world differently, and suddenly all one sees is monsters.'

'Surely our fear of monsters is that they might eat us up.'

She did not reply, forcing me to continue.

'Surely the problem is that your husband stole hundreds of millions of dollars from this country. And now they want it back.'

I thought she would take offence, but instead she said, 'Of course they do. Yet rather than go after him, they go after his grieving widow.'

'Because he is dead.'

'Is that my fault? You saw what happened to him.' It wasn't a question. 'Perhaps it is guilt that drives them to pursue the woman who devoted herself not to ruling, but to serving. It was I who built hospitals, art galleries, schools. My husband would have come down upon them with a thousand blows, but I put myself in the way. That is what a mother does, is it not? She sacrifices herself?'

A pang at my core. *You don't know what I sacrificed.* What had my own mother given up, and what had I done to force her to it?

'When my husband was exporting our food to pay down the foreign debt, I instigated the milk programmes. When he would have sent every child to the fields as soon as they could walk, I ensured education was free to all.'

I found my voice again. 'I thought you said you had no power.'

'I had no power except that which is granted to all wives and mothers, by a force far greater than my dear dead husband. Every day I rise as a parent. I loved my children. I love them now, even – especially – when they do not love me back. Ah, you are thinking: but she does not have any children.'

I was. Pavel had mentioned her stomach problems, caused by childhood hunger. Had it wrecked her fertility, too?

'That is the truth, and my greatest sorrow. The closest I got was my darling god-daughter. But I am the Little Mother, and motherhood is a role no one can take away.'

I looked away. Perhaps no one could take it from you, but my own mother had done her best to remove it from herself. If she could have scoured her heart with sandpaper, she would.

'When you talk of monsters, Laura, remember this. Half of this so-called new government worked for Dinu. Where are their trials? The Strajă continue as before. Ah, they have a new name now. They have published their files. But everybody knows they are the same beast. These people can barely be bothered to pretend this is a new system, let alone make it so. No. Instead they blame me for their problems. They will execute me, and believe they will feel better. So tell me, who is the real monster? The creature that never pretends to be anything but what it is, or the animal that conceals its true nature even from itself?'

She was lying, she had to be. Yet her conversation reminded me of floating mushroom-like in the pool as a child: with your eyes shut tight it was hard to say which way was up and which was down.

'Marija. Marija Păstrăv,' she said suddenly. 'That was – is – my god-daughter's name. I used to hold her like this.' Her arms formed an empty cradle.

'Where is she now?'

'Still in Poartă, probably. I do not know. Dragos will not let me see her.'

81

She stared down at the water, her amber eyes silver. I had the odd sensation that she might cry. It would have been so easy, so crude, those long fingers reaching out to tug at my heart strings. But she didn't.

I could find her for you. The thought came quite unbidden. By what power had she summoned it?

She glanced up, as if she'd overheard. 'It is probably for the best. I fear little Marija would not benefit from such a connection. I have learned to let go of those I love. Yet you, Laura – you have returned to the land your family once left.' She smiled at my startled reaction.

'You know about my family?'

'No, but I can see you are a Yanussian. Here, where it counts.' She touched her chest. 'Presumably your parents felt we forced their hand. Yet now the prodigal daughter has returned. To help the woman who drove her away? Perhaps. Perhaps not. Forgive me if I have not yet killed the fatted calf. But your name, I think, is apt.' I recalled our introduction earlier, and how the shadows had lengthened with the realisation that she already knew my surname. 'You were dead, and now you are alive. You were lost, and now you are found.'

If I was the prodigal daughter, that made her the parent. Was the insinuation deliberate? *My mother belongs to my heart; my heart belongs to my mother.* Once again I recalled my mother scooping me up to tease me with my own dedication, playfully blurring the two until even I was unsure which woman was meant.

'I am surrounded by people who do not understand me. With you, I think it is different. Ah, you are wary again. Yet you have dared put a hand into the lion's cage. Why do that unless you are something of a lion yourself? I want to keep you close. Cristian, he is too dazzled by me to recognise the person beneath.' She shrugged, as if this were something

82

she could not possibly remedy. 'If I am to win, I need someone who can see deeper.'

'You seemed certain that winning would not be a problem.'

'You seemed certain that you believed me.' She looked at me, through me. I felt her gaze probing my insides, skinning my stomach, my liver, my heart. It made me feel alive.

Did you do it? The question burned. Our eyes met and I knew she detected its smoulder.

'We lie to survive. And survival is more important than anything. Like me, you said what was necessary. I do not care if you meant it – I respect it. I will ask Cristian to give you more responsibility. The boy Jude can do the, how do you say, the oink work?'

I found myself smiling. 'The grunt work?'

'Precisely.'

She was unbelievable, yet I believed her. I had thought that meeting her after years of childhood indoctrination would be like coming face to face with a god. Yet gods are too vast to comprehend, and we cannot care for the incomprehensible. Awe is a sensation, not an emotion. We invest in religion not for care of the immortal, but for care of ourselves, and we are all too mortal. The woman before me was no god: she was, after all, human. I was relieved, and I was overcome.

But even Marija Popa could not quite sweep aside seven years of legal training, a significant portion of which can be summarised as 'there's no such thing as a free lunch'.

'What would you seek in exchange, Doamna?'

Another smile. 'I knew you were no fool. I want to use those sharp eyes and ears. I have not survived this long through luck. I have survived through knowledge. I want you to watch, to listen, and to report back to me.'

'You want me to spy for you.' Didn't they say that spiders, having poor eyesight, relied on sensing vibrations in their web?

'A spy implies two sides. In this house, there is only one.'

I allowed myself to peek over the brink. For the heck of it. For the thrill. She was like that, you see. If I could describe what it was like spending time with her (and God knows in later years I was asked), I would say it was most akin to lingering on a bridge. Perhaps there is a word for that force that compels us to lean over, to dangle something from our fingertips, to feel deep in our stomachs the call of the waiting ground. The kind of thing for which the Germans would have a name.

You mean vertigo, people would say in satisfaction. But I know the word for the fear of falling. I know of none for the attraction to it. How can it be that what terrifies us may also entrance us, despite, *because* of, our fear? I peeked over the edge and saw the rich purple depths. A rabbit hole, bottomless.

But Pavel had warned me. *I* had warned me. Ethics aside, I knew this would only be the start. And for what? For more responsibility? This was already the case of my career. It didn't matter what I was doing – it was enough to be here and not screw up. Lawyers dislike assumptions, but if we won, then my early promotion was practically assured.

And what about the price? Again, I was a lawyer, and despite her charm, I knew a bad deal when I saw it. I would be putting myself under her sway with unknown consequences, and Faust did not sell his soul to the Devil for less time at the photocopier.

'I cannot do that, Doamna,' I said at last. 'I am not a Strajă agent. I am your defence lawyer.'

'So defend me.' Her eyes were black; somewhere a generator clanked into life and the room began to hum. I felt how closely the swimming costume hugged my body. Delicious terror, and awful intoxication, or was it the other way round? I could no longer remember.

'Why do you think I fired your predecessors?' she went on. 'Marku Manea and Aurel Cristescu were First Minster Anghelescu's supporters. They plotted against me. They would have fed back privileged information, misplaced key evidence. They took the case in order to bungle it deliberately.'

I stared. 'How do you know this?'

'Laura, I am not friendless yet.'

If it was true, it was devastating. 'We must move for a retrial.'

'No.'

'No?' I was incredulous. It was an unheard-of violation, a gross corruption of every ethical code.

'What does it matter? They will not drop the charges and I want – I *need* – this done with as soon as possible.' I wondered why this was, what urgency could possibly override such a heinous revelation. 'I have survived this long. My life is all I have left. I *will* win.'

Her tone was so certain, I found myself believing her.

'Those lawyers are gone, but I need your help with the man who will defend me in court. The barrister, I think you call him. Radutu Gabor.'

The lawyers were 'gone'. Her pause had been almost imperceptible. The blithe euphemisms infected (or disinfected) her speech whenever convenient. A sickness entered me somewhere deep, a sunless place even her charm could not penetrate.

'Why not fire Gabor too?'

'He was not part of that firm. Besides, I cannot bring in a foreigner. Only a qualified Yanussian can be my advocate.'

'We can find someone else.'

'No. Radutu is the best. And I . . .' she sighed, 'I am running out of time. But I need to know if I can trust him.'

'Doamna, this is a task for Pavel.'

'Cristian does not even believe I am innocent. Why would

85

he believe me in this?' She leaned in, her voice pure honey. 'One last time. Help me. No one else can.'

The rabbit hole yawed, beckoning. I was tempted. Oh, I was tempted – how could I not have been, despite the offer's paucity? Those of us with overshadowed childhoods crave to feel we matter, and since we lack the resources to create this internally, we seek it externally, usually with disastrous consequences.

I clenched my fist under the water, digging the nails in. I was not here for her, but for myself. I could not afford to risk my mission in any way. To be in thrall to another is to cripple oneself – I knew that better than anyone, toiling endlessly for my own mother's approval, tipping my resources and my strength down that greedy drain. I would not repeat the mistake. I could not afford to.

Slowly I said, 'The London office is already conducting a background check of Mr Gabor. If they find anything, Pavel will let you know.'

Realisation bloomed, a black flower.

'You are refusing me.' For the first time, I had surprised her. The naivety of the very young, or the very powerful.

'Yes.' It thrilled me to push against her. It never occurred to me that whether we leap for the sky or remain on the ground, it is by the grace of the same force. She had almost had me forget who she was. I had *sympathised* with her. She had disguised herself as another person, one whose chest rose and fell like mine, whose eyes revealed pains and disappointments like mine. But she was no woman. She was a spider. Mortensen was right: I did not understand power, which meant I didn't understand people. I braced for her anger and told myself to watch carefully as she revealed her true nature. It would be a lesson I would not forget.

But she only smiled, a light smile, a smile that meant nothing. There was nothing in her face that I could read.

'I am sure you know best.'

She had a unique way of instilling doubt. It dripped from her tongue, trickled its way into the skin, crenulating the fingertips with which I clutched the poolside, hard enough to force myself not to succumb, hard enough that it hurt. She watched me for another moment, two, waiting to see if I would crack.

Then her face changed again, the interest draining away. She yawned, her mouth red, shocking, and rose to leave. Once again I thrilled at her closeness, how I could see her entire shape, her shoulders and her back and her breasts.

Don't go, I almost said.

I thought she would leave without looking back – wasn't that how she lived, after all? – but at the door, she turned.

'One last thing, Laura. I was raised in an orphanage. I know what it is to starve for more. Think about it.'

She was gone. I remained where I was, still clinging to the side, though I had begun to shiver. Along one wall was a viewing gallery and I thought I felt someone watching. I was afraid, because although I had tried to prepare myself for her, to build up my defences, there had been one eventuality so ridiculous I had never considered it.

I had not prepared for the chance that I might like her.

CHAPTER EIGHT

I had turned down Marija Popa. She had flung out her web and I had pushed it aside – for now. Yet the next morning I did not feel triumphant. She would try again, and walking down to breakfast, I trod an invisible line of dread.

I joined Pavel and Jude in a small, unimpressive dining room and we ate in silence but for Jude's complaints about the food: 'I thought it was Russia that had the gulags?'

I said nothing of last night. But the cover-up must have showed, because Jude slyly asked me if I was having women's trouble. If only you knew, I thought drily. As for her revelation about Manea and Cristescu. . . if it was true, well, we were in a deeper pit than I could have imagined. She had said she didn't want to do anything about it, and again I sensed a wider web, hidden threads that I had no hope of perceiving.

Pavel was flicking through the local newspapers. 'Couple of small things about the trial. Letters to the editor. She has some support, you know.'

'Fifty–fifty?' Jude said hopefully.

Pavel laughed. 'More like ninety–ten. But it's there.'

After breakfast, Apostol showed us into the wood-panelled

room off the hall that was to be our office. Marija would join us for an initial meeting, after which we could make a proper start. The walls were a deep red, the windows blessedly large, with views south towards the city. There was a long, heavy table and to my surprise some decent office chairs, while across the hall was a separate, smaller room for Pavel and Mr Gabor to use. Jude immediately christened our room the Lair.

Pavel rolled his eyes. 'The Yanussians love their code names. Popa was called—'

'The Dragon. I know.'

'And Marija?'

'The Dove.'

White. Pure. Peaceful. Of course.

Apostol gave an insincere bow and left us to it.

'Maybe he's the new secretary,' Jude joked. I smiled: it was impossible to imagine this man doing anything remotely mundane; like picturing Dracula at the water cooler.

Pavel said quietly, 'Apostol has always been Marija's dog. He's from Menădie.'

I raised my eyebrows. 'But he works for Marija?'

Menădie was the ugly eastern town where the revolution had begun. It had always been truculent. A small-scale protest broke out the year before and was quickly crushed by miners and thugs bussed in especially, armed with stones and truncheons. People died, and so did the protest. Second time lucky: twelve months later, Natalia Iliescu, a secretary at the state water company, went to buy groceries. Finding neither oil nor flour, she staged a sit-in and was rapidly joined by other women. Someone called the Strajă, but by this time a crowd had gathered. The first agent entered the shop and, in an action that swiftly passed into legend, Iliescu, quick as a fox, flung a tin of tomato soup at his head. The crowd surged in.

The Strajă were unused to trouble. That was the problem. Had they known anything but mute obedience, those shaky fingers might not have pulled that trigger. But they did, and what they hit was not a protester but little Daniel Olteanu, walking home late from helping at school. He was fourteen.

The streets exploded. The order came to suppress at any cost and the police grew desperate, firing hundreds of bullets into the crowds until it became clear that mere lead could not hold back the tide. Despite attempts to lock down communication, the news swept along the roads and the pirate radio waves, protests erupting in its wake. More than a hundred people died in those seven days of revolution, but no one paid a heavier price than Menădie.

'Apostol's loyalty dates from before then,' Pavel said. 'He was with her at the assassination attempt in the seventies. Beat the attacker to death with his own gun.'

A little chill ran down my spine, because that meant one thing. Ion Apostol had been a senior member of the Strajă.

We set about preparing for our meeting with Marija. If the First Lady was convicted, she would be executed, leaving the state to claim Popa's assets. But if she was let off, then it would all revert to her. Prosecutor Ursu had to show either that she had stolen the money herself, or that she knew Popa had. I thought the first outcome unlikely. Even if she had acted directly (and who could say if she had? Just thinking about that pool conversation made me dizzy), I did not believe she would have been clumsy enough to leave evidence behind. Unlike Dinu, who plastered his image across every surface available (a boy in the next-door flat had claimed he stood still too long at a bus stop and had a poster stamped to his head), Marija had used her power to disappear. Not in the conventional sense – she was, after all, one of the highest-profile women in the world – but it was a curious paradox that the more you saw of her, the less you knew. All that hair and lipstick and shopping were merely convenient handholds. You could grasp them in your fist and the rest of her, the real her, would turn to smoke.

The second outcome I therefore thought more probable, though of course the other side still needed evidence. Popa's deviousness had helped us there. He and his principal adviser, Gheorghe Funar, a stocky, powerful-looking man with beetling brows, had known what they were doing. There was not a single checking account in either of the couple's names, and that was the least complex method they'd concocted. Yanussian law meant the prosecution had to prove *mens rea*, or guilty knowledge. Unfortunately, while Popa had helpfully died, Funar was inconveniently both alive and in prison awaiting trial – one of the handful of jailed officials who had lacked the foresight to flee in 1989, or else the brazenness to join Anghelescu's government and declare they'd been with the revolutionaries all along. We expected him to plead guilty, at which point he would become a witness for the prosecution.

Marija was due at ten, but ten o'clock came and went and she did not appear. Pavel drummed his fingers, inspected his tie, then tried to go up to her rooms. The second he set foot on the stairs, Apostol swooped and led him away.

We made coffee, Pavel pushing down on the French press as if he wanted to force it through the table. I had never seen him paralysed like this, limbs trembling with the sheer effort of keeping still. He could not handle the stagnation. And if I knew that about my boss, the woman upstairs would too.

Jude had just opened the window to relieve the stifling atmosphere when we heard a faint sigh, followed by a scream.

91

'Holy shit.' Jude grabbed the windowsill. 'What was that?'

A tree beside the eastern wall was on fire, white flames engulfing it at extraordinary speed. Guards were sprinting up the drive, panicked shouts reaching our ears. One had a bucket of water. A yell – Apostol was running towards them, arms outstretched – but it was too late: the guard had flung the water over the fire, which gave a single, terrifying jelly-fish pulse and exploded.

'Petrol. Must be,' Jude shouted over the din. 'Idiots, they need an extinguisher!'

'We need the fire department. I'll call them,' I yelled back.

'No, you don't speak the language. I will.' Pavel ran to the phone. Jude and I hurried out into the hall and through the front door – even from here, the heat was formidable – but Apostol materialised and forced us back inside.

'But we can help.'

'The only way you can help is by lying down on the flames.' He looked us up and down. 'And I assume you are not volunteering. Might ruin your suits, eh?'

'What's happened?'

'Petrol bomb. I have called the fire department. Do not worry.'

'Don't worry?' I said incredulously. 'About a *petrol bomb*?'

'It is the Răsculat. They have got bored of rocks.' We heard sirens, close and getting closer. 'Stay inside, where it is safe.'

He slammed the door in our faces. Jude and I looked at each other.

'First cans, then rocks, now this,' he said above the sound of the sirens. 'What's next? Machine gun?'

Pavel arrived, slightly out of breath. 'What did I miss?'

Back in the Lair, we watched as the firemen smothered the conflagration, overseen by a small, useless crowd of guards and policemen. It worried me how rapidly our lodgings had become a prison. We'd left England with all sorts of plans and stratagems, yet from the moment Marija had ordered us into the drawing room, our control had been ebbing away.

'It's like we're under siege,' I said.

Pavel shook his head. 'I knew it would be nasty, but I didn't think it'd be *this* nasty. The Răsculat used to stay firmly underground. This seems pretty desperate.' A sudden flare crossed his features. 'They must think we've got a shot.'

I didn't share his confidence – I was too busy worrying about their next move.

A thought occurred. 'You knew that Cristescu had killed himself.' He did not acknowledge my words, but I knew I was right. 'You did. You sent someone to check them out.'

He shot me a dry look. 'All right. I sent a contact before we arrived to arrange a handover. Evidence files, et cetera.'

'And?'

'And nothing. There was nobody at the address. The place had been cleaned out. I've asked London to run checks on them as well as on Radutu Gabor. No trace of Manea so far.'

I didn't want to know, but I asked anyway. 'What do you think's happened to him?'

'If he had any sense, he's run far, far away.' A little trickle of icy water ran through me as he went on, 'They don't play games here, you know. It's all for real.'

Or maybe reality had become the game. It's much easier to treat humans like things if all that matters is winning. I tried to shake off the chill in my limbs, a coldness infused by dread. Cristescu dead and Manea disappeared – and if someone disappeared in Yanussia, they stayed that way. Even if I were inclined to investigate Marija's claims about

93

her lawyers (which, as I had told her, I wasn't) it was a blow.

It ought to have spurred me to keep as far away from her as possible, yet I felt as I had in Cornwall with Andrei the year before. After we'd let the arcade devour our money, he went to buy fish and chips with the remainder. I stayed on the promenade. Huge waves lashed its edges; I stood alone before a force greater than I could comprehend, and as the swells closed in I found I could not move. It was Andrei who came running, chips scattering, and dragged me to safety. 'You could have been swept away!'

He was looking at me oddly, and only then did I realise: I was shivering, soaked to the skin.

We waited for Marija all day, to no avail. The firemen departed but smoke still wisped from the blackened tree. It looked shrivelled and horrible, like a cursed limb. It reminded me of a schoolfriend whose uncle had lost a leg in the war: he told us, bug-eyed, about seeing the stump. A Nazi had bitten it off, his uncle said solemnly. 'With his teeth!' my friend said, demonstrating on the nearest boy as we squealed with joyous horror.

'This is insane,' Pavel said, after a miserable dinner had been and gone. 'Let's recap. What do we know so far?'

Jude shuffled his papers and cleared his throat, then pulled up with an odd, strangled sound. Marija Popa had walked in.

She wore another tight-fitting dress, slashed across the neck so her creamy shoulders were visible. Blood-red again. Did she love the colour or did it remind her of something? If she was a character in a book, she would have been a pop-up: she simply had an extra dimension that flattened everyone else. This was a different woman to the one in the pool. Now she wanted not empathy, but awe. To my surprise – disappointment? – she did not look at me at all.

'Cristian. Were you wanting to see me?' Her tone was innocent. I hid a smile at this mischief, felt her notice. She touched Pavel's arm: he gazed at the spot as if he had been scalded. She was positioned before him, directly in front of the standard lamp, and I remembered Mortensen's theory. Pavel was indeed too dazzled to look at her directly. Was that why she insisted on dazzling him?

'Our interview, Doamna.'

'Oh, yes.' She clasped her hands earnestly, like a schoolgirl at prayer. 'Please, begin.'

Pavel tried not to look flummoxed by this sudden keenness.

'You have registered a plea of not guilty. The good news is that according to Yanussia's criminal regulations, specifically the possessory rights of lands and goods, the principles are in our favour. *Omnia praesumuntur legitime facta donec probetur in contrarium.*'

Normally, clobbering clients with the textbook stunned them into useful submission, but Marija only laughed. 'You will forgive me, Cristian. My Latin is not quite equal to yours.'

'"All things are presumed to have been legitimately done until the contrary is proved." Over the coming weeks we will work through the evidence sent from the prosecution as well as collecting our own. For this I need your cooperation.'

'What can I possibly tell you that the evidence cannot?'

'Well, for example' – he checked his papers – 'the paintings they allege to have been illegally acquired. The Picasso, here.'

'It was a gift.'

'From your husband. I know. But do you have the auction receipt?'

95

The Black Widow sighed. 'You cannot expect me to know the whereabouts of every chit and scrap of the last thirty-two years.'

He bowed his head. 'Of course not. That is why we are here. We are meeting your defence advocate tomorrow. He tells me that he has taken your instruction to pursue the strategy that you were unaware of the business activities of your husband and his associates, and that you believed any funds to have been legitimately acquired.'

I agreed that this was the best plan of attack, but it made me uncomfortable. It was difficult to believe the First Lady was guilty, yet it was equally hard to think she was stupid. Her eyes were sharp as knives.

'No.' The word rang out as if she had struck a glass.

'I beg your pardon?'

'I will not have my husband's good name dragged through the mud.'

'With all due respect, Doamna . . .' I watched with interest as his meaning filled the gap. *Your husband was a liar, a thief, a jailer and an executioner. How much worse can his reputation get?*

Marija let the silence go on just long enough to show she understood. 'His name is my name. I am he, and he is me. That is what marriage is, what love is. Could you name your wife's sins, Cristian, without naming your own?'

'I am not the one on trial,' Pavel said quietly.

'Nor am I. It all comes back to Constantin. But you will not scapegoat my husband. I will not allow it.'

We stared at her, agog. There was no trace of the gallows in her face. Did she think she was immortal? In the pool she had told me survival came before all else, yet even gods may be killed. If she would not allow us to argue that she was ignorant, then either we had to show that Popa's associates had done it without the couple's knowledge (unlikely

96

in the extreme), or somehow, madly, prove that no laws were broken, that all that money was legitimately acquired. From Pavel's inhalation, I knew he had concluded the same. It was ridiculous, like Pablo Escobar claiming he sold face powder. Popa, as executive president, had clearly abused his office, whereas Marija's role and position were usefully ambiguous. In coupling her fate to her husband, her chances looked very remote indeed. And the quicker she lost, the less time I had to seek the cause of my family's grief.

'Doamna, that is a very hard case.'

'Which is why I have brought in very good lawyers. Or so your fees imply.'

Pavel gestured at his files with a certain helplessness. 'Your husband earned twenty thousand dollars a year. Where did the Degas come from? Or the Passe-Partout necklace from Van Cleef & Arpels?' His eye skipped down the page. 'And what about the Iubită factory? They allege that much of its revenue was siphoned off into accounts linked to your husband, and therefore you.'

'Perhaps you should ask Laura.'

I jumped. Pavel too gave a start, as if he had forgotten anyone else was there.

'Why?' I asked, even as my stomach twisted and the answer rose in my throat.

'Gabriela Lăzărescu.'

I stared at her in utter shock.

'Laura's mother? What about her?' Pavel's eyes swivelled back and forth between us.

'She has not told you? Why, Gabriela was one of the workers at the Iubită factory, here in Poartă. All my employees were women.'

I stammered, 'You knew my mother?'

'I remember her well. I knew every one of my employees. She had eyes just like yours.'

97

'But—' I cut myself off just in time, even as her gaze sparkled conspiratorially. She knew what I was about to say: that in the pool she'd said she didn't know my family. She'd lied, of course she had, and I could hardly confront her without revealing our encounter. She had known my mother. Once again I saw her, in her blue overalls, her hair wound up in an old patterned scarf. I'd wait by the door after school just to see her remove it, those black strands spilling out even as she stepped over the threshold, like she was shedding the day's skin and becoming mine again. My mind was afire with all I wanted to know. *What was she like? Why did we flee? Did the change that came over her happen in England, or were the seeds planted here, among your machines?*

'Well,' said Pavel quickly, before I could speak. 'This is a surprise.' He quelled me with a look. 'Let us move on to—'

I ignored the look. 'What did you know of her? What was she like?'

'Laura!' Pavel exclaimed at the same time as Marija said, 'Happy. She was always happy.'

Happy. I sat back, windless. It was the first confirmation I'd ever had of her transformation. The awful degeneration of the woman whose laugh could be heard three flats away, who loved the sun so much she'd sit on the balcony for hours, not caring as her cheeks turned red and the laundry bleached around her. There had been times when I thought I was going mad, clenching the bed sheets into vortices and wondering if I was the one who had changed, who had broken our world in two. But Marija had affirmed it. Gabriela Lăzărescu had once been happy, and that was not a word anyone could apply to the etiolated, angry woman with the pallid skin of one who neither sleeps nor leaves the house.

'Well,' Pavel said at last. 'I doubt an ordinary worker has much knowledge of the higher goings-on.'

'You'd be surprised.' Marija's gaze did not move from my face. 'I had a special relationship with my women. Each of them held my heart in their hands.'

I tried desperately not to react, not to let her grip tighten further. There was a tapping sound: the pen I held was quavering against the desk. I dropped it and it fell with a *thunk*. An illiterate toddler could have read me.

She has me. The thought was clear as a knife.

'Be that as it may.' Pavel moved slightly, putting me out of his line of vision, and hers. 'This is a serious amendment and must be discussed. And there is another matter, Doamna, for which I would be grateful to have your attention. Perhaps we could . . .'

She waited, forcing him to say it.

'Perhaps we could adjourn?'

'Without your juniors?' Her eyes sparkled. 'Very well. Come.' A command, not an invitation, as if it was she who had made the request. She swept out. Pavel grabbed his papers and followed. The room pulsated, once, as though a force had been sucked from it.

Jude waited approximately three seconds, then exploded. 'Junior? *Junior?*'

I sighed. 'Jude. The woman ran an entire country. Do you really think she'll differentiate between junior and senior associate?'

He sniffed. 'Gorbachev did.'

Jude had met Gorbachev at an event two years ago, for about ninety seconds, and hadn't shut up about it since. Everyone at work had at some time been regaled with Gorbachev's opinions on everything from corporate litigation to cocktails.

Marija Popa had known my mother. The thought was electrifying, terrifying. Trick or truth? Certainly we had the same eyes, the same watchfulness, but anyone could have made such a guess. In all likelihood she'd heard the name somewhere and scratched up a staff photograph.

But the truth of it was not the point; she'd been looking for my reaction, and she'd got it. She knew now that I needed something, and a need is the same as a weakness. I trembled. The predator had perceived my wound, and now it was on the hunt.

'I don't mind telling you, Lăzărescu, I don't like it. Why didn't Pavel tell us he knew her? Why didn't *you*?'

Jude's sharp tone jolted me from my reverie.

'It's my mother she knew. So she says.' My voice was lightness itself.

'Be careful. She's like those witches who take a scrap of skin and use it to control you. That'll be why she called Pavel in, whatever he thinks. She knows she's got power over him.'

I suppressed a shudder. He was right. Marija had a hold on me. I half expected to look down and see a pin sticking out of my chest. Despite my defiance of her, despite my promises to myself, in one sentence she had brought me under her spell, and now all I could think about was how well the Little Mother had really known my own mother, and how I could find out more.

'Maybe she thinks power is the only way to survive,' I said distractedly.

'Yeah, and you have to have one fucked-up childhood to live that way. That orphanage has a lot to answer for.'

'Do you think it's true about her stomach problems?'

'Probably. It would explain a lot, that need to fill . . . Ultimately it doesn't matter whether it's hunger or wealth that made a hole where your heart should be. That woman would eat the world if her mouth was big enough.' He paused. 'One thing does make sense now. I didn't tell you before, firstly because it's not my place, and secondly because I didn't think you needed any more Brownie points—'

'Jude,' I said, very calmly. 'What is it?'

'HSG only sealed this case when you came on board.'

I stared at him.

'Hunter, the junior partner, was probably going to get a visa in time. But she didn't want him. Only another Yanussian would do. That secretary, Camelia what's-her-name, was very particular.'

It made no sense. Another Yanussian? It was sheer luck that I was on the relevant team. What if I had been in, say, merger control, or public procurement? Besides, there were other Yanussians to be found elsewhere: Elena at Allen & Overy, Daniela and Ion at Clifford Chance . . .

'So what are you going to do?' Jude was examining his empty whisky glass, his tone deliberately offhand.

Not only had Marija known my mother, it seemed she'd known about *me*. I was alarmed, and flattered. Had she meant that only another Yanussian would do, or that only this one would? The way she had said my surname on our first meeting, its tone implying not just recollection, but recognition . . . I felt like the ant that looks up to discover the magnifying glass, a presence far vaster than itself, watching with the suspended malevolence of a god. Did Marija know what had happened to my mother? Had she somehow *caused* it? And how was this connected with her choosing me, if indeed she had?

Perhaps she merely liked having a hold over me. Or perhaps the reason went deeper.

'Nothing I can do,' I said at last. 'Just wait.' Like the fly in the web, anticipating the attentions of its host.

'Perhaps you're right. Pavel, though . . .'

'Yes.' I was not the only trapped creature around here. I let Jude pour himself another whisky then said, 'What do you think happened at Cambridge?'

'Well, exactly. It's a bloody nuisance he didn't tell us

before. Mind you, you might've said that your mum was her employee. Next thing you know I'll casually disclose she's my aunt.' He sighed. 'You might not know better, but Pavel should. I can't see Compliance being happy, but I don't know what to infer. This place is a shadow-puppet show. This morning I called an old friend in the Cambridge alumni office. Wanted to get hold of a cold, hard fact for a change.'

I knew what he meant, though I was surprised he had detected it. Last night, en route to the mansion, we'd passed a film set, a glamorous melee of trailers, cameras and glaring white lights illuminating a small figure wrapped in furs. A Cold War film, Pavel had said, Poartă standing in for Moscow because it was cheaper and filming licences were easy to get. In the last few years the country had played the Alps, the Mississippi, Spain . . . It could be almost anywhere, and it took a special kind of nowhere to manage that. How could I trust anything I found in a place that so easily shimmered into something else?

'My friend checked the records and couldn't find Marija's name,' Jude said. 'Closest he got was an M. Iubită who attended an English language school at Trinity in the fifties. Probably her, but summer school isn't *exactly* the same thing.'

I frowned. 'Why would she lie?'

'The same reason she wears red all the time. Power.'

Yes. I'd seen at HSG how the Oxbridge name was a magic key, yet that was not the word Marija had used. She had spoken not of power but *survival*. Of what? The Popas had ruled for more than thirty years. Their control had been unbreakable – until, of course, it broke. Until then, what had she needed defending from?

'I suppose you've thought about what it'll be like if we win?' Jude swirled his whisky. 'Bonus season will be fun. Don't shake your head at me, it's not *just* the money. It's the glory too. The Magic Circle are drooling. I heard

Freshfields flew out three partners to get her to change her mind. She wouldn't even meet them.' A direct glance. 'Perhaps she just really liked your mum.'

I didn't take the bait. 'Do you think she—'

He moved suddenly. 'Don't say it.'

Do you think she did it? The question floated like oil, greasy and unpleasant.

'It's not something we should be asking. At least within these four walls.'

I shuddered. 'Our side? Theirs?' I asked, already knowing the answer.

'Who cares? Can you even be sure which is more dangerous? Or who our allies really are? I've watched you at work, bugging the partners with questions. You can't just follow the rules or break them, you have to know *why*. And that's because you make it personal. You shouldn't. It hamstrings you. No one can get along on this damn earth if they're always trying to work out where they fit.'

A hole opened in my stomach. 'I don't do that.'

'Yeah, and my old man's a dustman. Except he's actually ambassador to Ghana, while your mum's a factory worker and your dad is, what, a taxi driver?'

I sought to close the hole. 'I thought you said I was the one making things personal.'

'Sorry.' And he did, temporarily, look sorry. 'How did your parents escape?'

I sighed. 'We left when I was seven. My dad was a minor agricultural official, so he wasn't important enough to get a passport.'

He looked shocked at this admission of mediocrity.

'Jude, if you're going to pull that face whenever you get a whiff of the proletariat, then—'

'Sorry! Sorry.'

'*As* I was saying. The borders were closed. You could take

103

your chances with the armed guards and barbed wire. You could fly over in hot-air balloons. There was even a rock band that hid inside their own Marshall speakers. My father found another way: his ministry was sending a group to an agricultural expo in Belgrade and he talked his way in.'

'I remember those. Showing off the great benefits of communism, blah blah.'

'Exactly. They were exhibiting these prize vegetables supposedly grown by the peasants, though in reality they'd been hothoused for months by Popa's personal gardeners. If they'd sent the real thing, my father said, it would've been an empty stall. He convinced the local officials to let him go along to supervise the unruly peasants. Then he hid my mother and me under some tarpaulins in the lorry, beside the marrows.'

'Goodness. Didn't they search it?'

'They opened the doors at the border, but my father screamed that if they didn't close them quick, the cold might freeze Popa's vegetables, and did they really want to explain that to head office. They shut them.'

Jude laughed, as I'd meant him to. It made it easier. Twenty-one years ago, yet I could still hear the tarpaulin flapping overhead like the wings of Baba Mierlă, the great black bird they said swooped down to gobble up tongues when too many questions were asked. My mother gently reminded me of her, saying we must stay silent as we juddered towards the border, my body melding with the lorry's rhythm until I felt less a human child than a creature of oil and metal.

We came close, closer. The road got smoother, the lorry got slower, and now my mother asked if I remembered how to curl up like a mushroom and hold my breath like in the swimming pool. If you hold your breath, she always said, you cannot sink.

Do it now, she told me, her fear buzzing like black flies. Do it now, and we will be safe.

I folded myself around my knees and tried not to breathe. But it was too difficult, my position too cramped, the road too bumpy. It was only when the lorry stopped and there were angry voices that I began to worry. I should have tried harder. Then we would have been safe. Beside me, my mother had grown stiff as a stone; the tarpaulin was silent, taut, waiting. As the lorry doors were flung open, frozen air and torchlight lancing in, I scrunched my eyes tight and stopped breathing.

It worked. There were more shouts, but the doors shut and we rolled over the border. From there we ascended through Europe until we reached England, our promised land. Somewhere along our journey we became *solicitanţii de azil* – asylum seekers. I knew dimly what an asylum was, and on the ferry, as the freezing Channel winds blew spray into our faces, I asked my mother why anyone would seek one out. She made an odd noise, like a laugh but not, salt water running down her cheeks. That was my first idea of England: a madhouse, and I was disappointed to find its people seemed quite ordinary. I was too busy inspecting every corner of the new house, excited to live in London (though the postman sniffily told us we were actually somewhere called Croydon) and hoping to bump into the Queen, to realise the change: that since the crossing, something had germinated in my mother's breast, a thing that over the years only grew and shook out its ragged black feathers.

If you hold your breath, you cannot sink. That, it turned out, was a lie. We had been falling, all three of us, ever since.

Jude was watching me. 'You work too hard,' he said suddenly.

'Pardon?'

'You work too hard, you're too quiet. And there's the class thing. It's like you're monitoring us to learn how to behave, and that makes us nervous. We wonder what – who – is pulling your strings.'

Again he'd struck a nerve. Was he more perceptive than I'd thought, or were my shortcomings simply out there for all the world to see? I'd worked always to be a chameleon, to do what the others did, which from university onwards mostly consisted of drinking and working and not thinking too hard about anything. 'No one's pulling my strings.'

'Don't bristle at me. I'm only trying to help.' His whisky slopped over his hand and I realised he was quite drunk. 'You're a pretty girl, Lăzărescu. Not, like, obviously pretty . . .'

'Gee, thanks.'

'. . . but there's something about those dark eyes that make a man want to . . .' He closed his hand, then reopened it and placed it against my thigh. It was sticky with alcohol. 'Now,' he went on in a different tone entirely, 'what's your attitude towards the boring black-and-white ban on office dating? Greyer than Pavel's true hair colour?'

I leaned towards him, observing his pupils dilate. 'Listen, Greenwood . . .'

'Yes?' His voice was husky. Wolfish.

'I know you posh types think everyone loves you. But I'm not interested in anyone who thinks intelligence is worn best with a signet ring. Now *get off me.*'

The hand went limp, fell away. 'All right. Jesus, Lăzărescu.' He yawned widely, falsely. 'Tell Pavel I've gone to bed, will you?'

After he'd gone, I leaned back and took a deep breath. We are all puppets to our pasts, and in the past twenty-four hours both Jude and Marija had made it clear that the strings

106

I'd thought cut were yet embedded in my skin. I cringed at who else might have noticed.

We must fit in, my mother had repeated, over and over in a terrified rhythm, as if saying it could make it true. In Yanussia one conformed to survive, but as my schoolmates pressed me up against the crumbling playground wall on my first day, yelling 'Stalin! Stalin!' I realised England was no different. The variation was that here, unlike in Yanussia, we would never be allowed to belong.

That night I dreamed that I looked down and saw a million little hooks pulling under my skin, forming grisly cones of flesh. I turned and followed their strings with my fingers, holding onto them like a blind man, for there was no light. At last I found my parents, clutching the ends. But when I reached for them, they looked at me sadly and turned their backs, and I saw the cords that hung there too, the flesh drooping and bloody, ties that ran down time's lightless corridor until they vanished into the black.

CHAPTER NINE

I awoke at what my mother's watch told me was the same time as yesterday, though the sky was dimmer than before. The days were shortening and the world had changed, the air fresh and crisp enough to snap. It was snowing, autumn's chill replaced by something older, and already a delicate frosting iced the lawn, the noisy red leaves surrendering to the white's calm majesty.

I could not enjoy it. It felt like another step into the shadows. Marija knowing my mother. Marija and Pavel. Last night, as he left with her, I'd glimpsed something in his eyes. The waking leap of a hungry flame.

There was an hour until our meeting with Radutu Gabor, and suddenly I craved fresh air. I took the back stairs, which came out beside the door to the pool. I sniffed gingerly, but the chlorine smell was absent, as if its power did not extend to daylight.

I was about to step outside when I felt it: a soft little stroke down my spine.

I turned. There was another door behind me. Had it been there before? I did not think so, yet here it was, standing quietly, a stranger in a grey coat. It was metal, heavy and narrow. The colour made it hard to see.

Slowly I approached. It was well made, its outline hewing narrowly to the frame, its surface smooth and perfect. Not so much closed as *sealed*, the heavy frame embedded deep into the wall like a splinter.

I thought of stones in front of tombs. Except nobody had rolled this one away.

It's probably nothing, I told myself. Just a . . . a storeroom. But even as I thought it, I saw Andrei again, gazing into his knotted pasta as if its patterns had secrets to impart. Once more I felt Mrs Ciocan's little clay pot in my hand, its colours still hopelessly bright.

Some were sent on to proper prisons, or to hard labour. The rest . . .

I knew I had found it, the source of the dull ache between my ribs ever since I crossed the mansion's threshold. I put out a hand: it shook, but I ignored the tremors and took another step forward, stretching out, trying to hold back the roaring in my ears . . .

Flesh touched metal and I heard the screams. The hinges shrieked into the unnatural morning, but I could not turn back, not now. The gap widened to reveal stairs of damp brick, red and stained, and though my chest gripped like ice, I took them, the first, then the second, pushing through the gathering dark with the effort of a diver descending through the sea. Three, four, five, the air pressure building, my ears still screaming, for here had been horror, I knew beyond a doubt, agony and torment and nails inserted beneath fingernails in awful, precise symmetry. They said that those who passed out from the pain were revived with adrenaline shots to do it all over again, and it was for them that I shut my eyes and kept on down, down, those awful screams rising around me, and suddenly I smelled the breath of someone before me, meaty, fresh, and I opened my mouth to let out a scream of my own, but a huge hand clapped over my nose and lips and I could not breathe, I could not see . . .

I forced my eyes open, back into the real world, and it made a difference after all, thank God, thank God. The hand was removed from my mouth; I choked on undrawn air.

'Hush, Lăzărescu.' Apostol was before me, gazing at his fingers, which glistened with my saliva. He was taller than ever and he blocked the stairs spiralling down. But even though nothing was visible, suddenly I *saw*. A long, long corridor, doorways yawning on either side. Oh, the doors themselves were long gone, safely removed and burned, the floors scrubbed clean, but for that snapping moment I looked through walls, through time, witnessing what I had never seen, remembering what I had never experienced. It took me to a place of numbness, a long, long way beyond tears.

'Naughty mouse. You must not be down here.'

The shadows in his face were all wrong, rising too high up his cheeks. Only now did I see he was holding a torch. It threw the blackness into sharper relief.

'Wh-why are *you* down here? What is this place?'

He wagged a crude finger. The walls were brick too, alive with old stains.

'Naughty mouse,' he repeated. 'Curiosity will kill it.'

He came up towards me, forcing me towards the door. I had found what I was searching for, I was sure of it, but the smile on his face was a dagger and I had no choice but to leave. It was here. Mrs Ciocan had been here and I could not help a small sob at the thought that, in some way, she might be here still. Poor, poor Andrei, that little boy who could not bring himself to say goodbye. I hated it, hated them all, the Straja agent who dared to tell him he looked like his mother, the officials who rubber-stamped her removal, the cosy neighbourhood informants who condemned her: just different heads of the same devouring monster.

I took one leaden step up, then another. On the third, I felt a crashing blow, black and brutal, my whole spine snapping beneath it. There was no time to gasp, no time to save myself. I stumbled, fell, my skull rushing up towards the hard, sharp brick, my arms so much useless jelly. I braced myself for the pain –

Hands grabbed me and set me back on my feet. My body pulsated, heart and head surging with blood as I gazed down at the razor stair-edge.

'Whoops,' the voice came. 'Careful.'

I rounded on him, outrage overcoming my terror. 'You pushed me!'

He held his hands up innocently. 'Me? I am protecting you. Down here it is dangerous. Steps are slippery. Roof might cave in.'

I could not believe his actions – yet also, I could. The rules were different here.

I made sure to hurry up the final stairs, into the light, before saying vehemently, 'You did it on purpose. And curiosity killed the *cat*. Not the mouse.'

He emerged from the black slowly, like a snake from its hole, grinning. His teeth were extremely large.

'My mistake. You are the cat. Of course.'

I was shivering when I entered the pink drawing room, empty but for the rabbit clock's unhealthy tick, its creatures watching with red-rimmed eyes. I could still feel the blow on my spine – there would be a bruise come nightfall – and

111

when I looked in the mirror I saw Mrs Ciocan looking back.

The violence of what had occurred shocked me. It was as if the house had flashed a fin, for the first time revealing its true nature. I had found what I had sought, I was sure of it. Somehow I had sensed the corridor and the rooms – no, *cells*. Who could say what horrors had occurred therein? Survivors of other 'hospitals' had told of torture, of sleep deprivation, of broken fingers and broken minds. Once again I saw that stained brick and shuddered. I had to tell Andrei, though what I would say I could not imagine.

Pavel entered, taking a seat and fussing with his jacket buttons. I gazed at him dazedly. When I'd awoken I'd expected reproach for my questions to Marija – how far off that seemed – but he said nothing.

'How did it go?' I asked eventually, when my pulse had somewhat eased.

'Fine. Fine.' He smoothed his already smooth hair. 'I had only forgotten how . . .' He broke off, apparently finding something of great interest in the armrest. 'She is innocent,' he said finally.

Whatever I had expected, it wasn't that. I gaped at him. Given where I had just been, the notion of innocence was almost funny. I imagined myself breaking into laughter and him doing the same, both of us laughing, laughing until we broke apart entirely.

'You didn't believe her before.'

'I know, but I was wrong. I was wrong.' His face shone with unnatural light, but his words alarmed me more. A good HSG partner would rather swallow his own tongue than admit a mistake. Clearly he was not in his right mind.

'How can you possibly know that?'

'Of course I can't *know* that, Laura,' he snapped, and momentarily he was himself again, the zealotry extinguished.

'I am just saying, when we arrived, well, I did not quite believe her.'

'And now you do?'

'She convinced me. She is innocent, and we have to help her prove it. If we can account for it all with legitimate explanations . . . That is our strategy.' He clenched his fist. 'Her very life depends on it.'

'I see.' I did, and it made me afraid. 'Jude and I think we should be there in these meetings.'

'No! No. I need to see her by myself. Just for now.' His eyes flashed yellow and strange. Then, 'What's this about your mother?'

'Exactly as Marija said. She was an employee at the factory.'

The factory. I considered what I had just experienced with Apostol. That hospital was where Andrei's mother had spent her last traceable days. Andrei thought we were both looking for the same thing, but he was wrong. He was not looking to make sense of a life; he was seeking redress for a crime. I wanted something far more nebulous. I wanted the rest of the story. On that stairwell I had *seen,* however briefly, simply by being there. Before my departure I hadn't been precisely clear on why it felt important to come to Yanussia – it was simply a last resort. But now I understood that it represented a chance to retrace our lives, a chance to gain that stairwell understanding. Our Poartă flat had been bull-dozed years before. No hope there. But the factory – my mother had worked there ten hours a day, six days a week, for decades. I had to visit.

'I don't like it,' Pavel said at last. 'She shouldn't know about your family. And you shouldn't have responded. It gives her a hold on you.'

My mind was still on the factory and I replied absently. 'Like she has on you?'

I regretted my words instantly.

He said nothing for a long moment, forcing me to meet his gaze. 'Perhaps. But unlike you, Laura, I have been in this game a long time. *I* can handle her.'

An image sparked in my vision, that flame I had seen in his eyes, burning. But before I could say anything, Jude bowled in.

'Visitor,' he said, flushing when he saw me, though our altercation last night seemed inconsequential now. 'Zsa Zsa's arrived.'

'Bring him through.'

A man entered, sporting faded black and a mournful expression. I am not good with people. They are a language I can read but not speak, and when I first laid eyes on Radutu Gabor I saw an altogether foreign tongue. Here was someone who had grown up under the regime, with everything that preposition implied. He wasn't short, yet he walked in a sort of crouch as if he wished to appear so, glancing upwards often. I had expected Marija to choose a Rottweiler. This man was more like Chicken Licken, waiting for the sky to fall in.

Pavel greeted him jovially, waving him to the sofa where Marija had sat. Mr Gabor took his place with extreme reluctance, as if he sensed the ghost of her presence, perching on the very edge and clutching his briefcase as though we might snatch it away. Whatever Marija's concerns, he did not look like a man preparing to sabotage his own case. I would have been surprised if he was up to sabotaging his own breakfast. Then again, through our client list I had met dozens of Bad People, most ostensibly the decent sort you would happily invite for tea and bridge with your rich maiden aunt. Always, always we are drawn to appearances.

'Thank you for having us on board,' Pavel said, when Mr Gabor showed no signs of life.

The little man stirred. 'It was not my choice.'

'Ah,' said Pavel wisely, in the tone of lawyerly under-standing that meant he did not understand.

'The Doamna,' Gabor went on. 'She thinks it is too much for me.' A shrug. 'She is right. You have seen the evidence boxes?'

We looked at each other.

'No,' Pavel said at last. 'Nobody told us about any evidence boxes.'

'You did not ask the Doamna?'

I expected Pavel to dismiss this: ensuring proper discovery would surely have been top of his list in last night's tête-à-tête with Marija. But he only dropped his eyes. Jude and I exchanged glances.

'You did not ask,' Mr Gabor said flatly.

'Because we did not know about them,' Jude replied exasperatedly.

Mr Gabor gave a small smile. 'Then you do not know the ways of this country. Here you must ask for what is unknown. You must watch and listen for what you do not see or hear.'

Pavel shifted in his seat. 'I am Yanussian.'

'So I have been told. But it has been, what, twenty-five years?' He cast an unsubtle glance at Pavel's dye job. 'Thirty? You no longer have this country in your bones. If you are to survive here, it needs to be; if you are to win, it must be in your very marrow. I am representing in court, but if the solicitors cannot know what is required—'

'Mr Gabor. You may have every faith in me and my team. I myself am highly qualified, both in this country and in England. I have great confidence in our capabilities for a case like this.'

'Like this?' He let his eyes widen. 'I am the best court lawyer in this country. This is not a boast. And not only do

I know of no other case like it, I think that you will soon join me in my lack of confidence in it.' He glanced upwards again. 'You are a long way from London here. If you make a mistake, the cavalry will not arrive in time.'

'In time for what?' Jude demanded.

Gabor did not answer. 'Our Dear Leader saw this country as something he literally owned. The evidence rooms reflect this. Let us go there immediately.'

Pavel bristled, but we filed out.

'Evidence *rooms*?' Jude muttered.

Mr Gabor had not used the plural unnecessarily. We followed him down the pink-carpeted thread of the west wing, wending through the labyrinth until we came to a door exactly like the rest. He opened it with a flourish. The sight that greeted us would have frightened any minotaur, or certainly one with legal training. Numbered grey boxes were piled from floor almost to ceiling; a narrow arch led to a second room where further containers were visible. We surveyed it with sinking hearts.

'That's a lot of dead trees.'

'Hundreds of thousands of pages,' Mr Gabor said solemnly. 'Delivered last week at my request.'

'From Manea and Cristescu's offices?'

'Again, Mr Pavel, I leave it to you English lawyers, with all your high qualifications, to ask the unknown.' We winced. 'I will leave this, how would you say, *little lot* to you. I suggest you call me when you are ready. Or if you have any questions.'

Pavel snorted. 'Yes. We will call you if we know we need to know something we don't know we don't know.'

'Very good!' He smiled for the first time. 'You will fit right in.' And he was gone, scurrying away like a large black-coated rodent. We stared after him.

'What a strange man,' Jude said.

'Very well thought of in Yanussian legal circles. I suppose that's why she picked him.'

'Talk about a poisoned chalice.'

We began there and then, Pavel dividing the stacks up between us, ignoring Jude's lobbying for calling in paralegals from London.

'No time,' he said shortly. 'Get a grip, Jude.'

I felt a twinge of vicious *Schadenfreude*. Last night might be irrelevant, but it was not forgotten. Yet as I hauled my first cache to the Lair, arms aching, I worried that Jude was right, that we were taking on too much. Six months hardly seemed enough to do the job, let alone find out about my family.

Still, if Mr Gabor *was* planning to sabotage Marija, at least he didn't have much time.

That night I tried to call Andrei, but he didn't pick up. I took off my shirt and caught sight of my back in the mirror: a large bruise bloomed there like a black flower, edged with purple. As I watched, it seemed to spread.

I slept with the light on, because when I turned it off, all I could see was red brick, stained.

CHAPTER TEN

I finally got through to Andrei the next morning. The light was clear and crisp; there were no shadows, and by the time he picked up, yesterday's horrors had retreated, hiding themselves somewhere I could not reach.

'I'm here,' I told him quietly. 'In the Iubită mansion.'

At first he did not believe me. Only after I'd given a precise record of the events leading us here (once again I was uncomfortably cognisant of our loss of control) did he finally say, 'You have to get out of there,' followed swiftly by 'What have you found?'

I told him. Of the grey door, and the stairwell with its old stains, descending into the dark. Of my impression of a corridor lined with lightless rooms. Of Apostol, and how he had prevented me from going any further (I left out the push: I didn't want to scare him). But the daylight leached the power from my words and the account I gave was puny, free of the teeth of the actual events. I'd opened a door. I'd been interrupted. And what had I actually seen? Nothing.

'You have to try again.'

'I thought you wanted me to leave.'

'Yes, but you can't, can you? You're trapped.'

Hearing it from another's mouth brought the full weight crashing down. For a moment I could not speak.

'Try again,' he repeated. 'I need more. Something concrete.'

'There won't *be* anything concrete.' As I said it, I knew it was true, and it made the prospects for my own search infinitely more bleak. 'Things slip away around here. Or they're erased. You don't know what it's like.'

'Of course I don't. You're the one working on her case.' His tone was bitter.

'Andrei, it's because of this case that I had the chance to do what I did.'

He snorted. 'Just because we're able to jump off the cliff doesn't mean we should celebrate the steps that brought us there.'

He guilt-tripped me into promising to try again, and it was with resentment that I replaced the receiver. He was wrong about so many things, not least that I could not leave. I would go out into the streets, I decided, and in doing so I would re-gain some control. It was still early. I'd do it right now.

I was halfway down the drive when the first guard appeared. He said nothing, only watched with black eyes, head rotating on its stem as I ducked past. The air was cold, the sky white. Old leaves crunched under my feet, their corpses spiking up above the snow. I kept on: another guard materialised. Again he said nothing, but this time when I tried to pass, he stepped smartly in front of me, blocking the way. The gate was barely twenty yards distant; I could see it, and the empty street beyond. I tried moving in the other direction: the guard mirrored my movements. Now I saw the guard hut door open and disgorge several more, their expressions as smooth and empty as granite. I halted. The man before me remained where he was, silent and implacable. There was nothing in his eyes to take hold of and the blankness was frightening; he was not even looking at me. It was almost as if I wasn't there.

'So it's like that,' I muttered, trying to appear offhand. With feigned casualness I turned and went back up the hill.

If I was ever going to get out of the grounds, if I was ever going to explore the factory, I would have to find another way.

But the way was not forthcoming, not least because when our work began in earnest, we had barely enough time to eat, let alone conduct covert investigations. Each morning Jude and I rubbed the tiredness away and sat down with a box each. Many files had been looted from the Popa palaces, including a hidden vault harbouring thirty locked Louis Vuitton suitcases. The documents spanned everything from interview transcripts and company accounts to bank cheques and private letters. I got used to seeing Popa's signature, an ugly squarish scrawl. The money was splurged on Manhattan real estate, Asprey serving dishes, Tiffany's pendants, Persian carpets, gold taps. I saw shopping not for pleasure but for mania, consumption for someone with a lot to spend but even more to hide.

Then there was the art. Jude somehow laid his hands on poster images of paintings from the couple's vast collection, all but one of which had been traced by the authorities. He tacked them to the walls, lending the Lair the feel of a kleptocrat's student bedroom. Bonnard. Rothko. Matisse. More than one Monet. Dozens of priceless pieces had ended up in the Popas' assorted palaces and penthouses, excepting a Goya, a Rembrandt and a Klimt, which had been sequestered in Swiss bank vaults. Jude pointed to an image pasted in pride of place above the mantelpiece: a woman, abstracted by the exuberant arches of cubism.

'Do you know what this is?'

I took a guess. 'Picasso?'

'Not just *any* Picasso. *The Woman in Red.*'

Even in abstract she was beautiful, her lovely curves filling the frame, seated loosely with one hand in her hair. The image should have been static, yet with those sensuous, swooping lines it was like staring into a flame.

'This is the one Pavel asked Marija about. Is it of her?'

'No, but it could be, couldn't it? Last seen in the Champs-Élysées apartment of one of Popa's fixers. When French police raided it a couple of years back, they were met with nothing but a cleaned-out interior and a smile. Someone tipped them off.'

'They even dress the same.' Pavel was beside me, looking up. 'Red. The same colour as the Yanussian flag.'

I blinked. Was that really the link? 'Have they found the original?'

'Not yet. But it's the last and best piece, so I imagine they bloody want to. They say he bought it for eight million.' Jude grinned. 'You could probably buy Poartă for that.'

Pavel sighed. 'If the authorities find it anywhere remotely connected to the Popas . . . well.'

We returned to work. I reviewed the charge sheet while Pavel and Jude waded through the evidence trove.

Money laundering, contrary to the 1937 Organised Crime Act. On 21 January 1974, the defendants CONSTANTIN R. and MARIJA L. POPA, with the aid and assistance of aforementioned associates, caused approximately $32,000,000 to be diverted from the Yanussian Oil Company to nominee accounts in Switzerland and elsewhere, in order that these dollars could be fraudulently exchanged for Yanussian piesta and used to purchase certain personal property, and for investment for the benefit of CONSTANTIN R. and MARIJA L. POPA.

From in or about September 1982 up to on or about October 1983, the defendants CONSTANTIN R. and MARIJA L. POPA, with the aid and assistance and through the efforts of their associate GHEORGHE M. FUNAR and others, unlawfully, wilfully and knowingly did transport approximately 150,04,682 YPR ($50,234,893) in cash and works of art in foreign commerce, which funds and works of art the defendants knew to have been stolen, converted and taken by fraud, in violation of Title 12, Yanussian Code, Section 49.

On and on it went, for dozens of pages. I worked away, taking notes and consulting the shelves of heavy statute books while the others talked strategy and witnesses.

The oink work. The words danced mockingly in my head.

It helped a little that Marija was an older woman, and that her adoptive family had long been rich. If our position was that no wrongdoing had occurred, we would try and show that much of her wealth had been made over many years through prudent investments. The remainder, we would argue, she had no reason to believe was suspicious.

Mapping out the money trail meant we could track what the prosecution could spring on us – when they might be able to claim that Marija had reason to know, or worse, prove that she had known. Hunting money. This was what I loved, what I excelled at: the odour of a backdated document, the telltale whiff of someone being too clever. Over this stinking midden we would pour the delightful fragrance of legitimacy. But the task's sheer size made our job as hard, if not harder, than the prosecution's. Easier to attack than defend. It would have been far better to argue that our client didn't know anything, but as she didn't want that, we were stuck.

Such was the time pressure that we hardly broke for lunch. Instead, Mircea, the staff member I met on the first night, brought sandwiches, which we ate ravenously, dripping grease over the Xeroxed pages. I could always tell which piles were Jude's: they were almost see-through from the fat of various animals.

'It's like she *wants* us to fail,' he said for the umpteenth time, through a mouthful of brisket. Privately, uneasily, I agreed, though what her motives were I could not guess.

I'd wondered what had happened to Marku Manea, Marija's previous lawyer, with his case reallocated and his partner dead. Yanussia was not the kind of country you fled easily. Two days later I found out.

'They've found him. Marku Manea.' Pavel was reading a small article. His tone was flat.

'Where? How can they be sure?'

'In a forest. Took them some time to make a formal ID. He'd been there a while and there are – bears, and so on . . .' His voice faded, then revived itself. 'But yes. Dental records. They're sure.'

Jude and I exchanged worried looks. 'Do you think—'

Pavel shook his head virulently. *Don't say it.*

We spent so much time now stopping up our mouths that it was a miracle there was anything left to say. I'd told them already about the guards, and Pavel had nodded, apparently unsurprised that we could not leave. Jude, while professing himself 'creeped out', was also unconcerned. 'What's there to see in this dump?' Mr Gabor was able to come and go as he pleased, so it was only I who chafed at our incarceration.

And what of the Yanussian? He took the news of Manea in the manner of quicksand, the information sinking in without trace. He carried something about him, but I did not think it was subterfuge – rather, a deep, heavy sensation of loss. It reminded me uncomfortably of my mother. It shimmered in his glances up to the heavens, in the sudden jerks he gave for no apparent reason, making those around

123

him lean away unconsciously, as if it might be catching.

He said nothing about Marku Manea, but a few days later I found myself alone with him and could not help myself. The fear had become an iron file, grating every movement. The only way to alleviate it was to learn more.

As soon as I asked, he was on his guard. 'What do you wish to know?'

Those two deaths, and our new habit of silence, made me timid. 'Were they any good?'

'The best.'

'Did you . . .' *Did you see them betraying their own client?* 'Did you like them?'

'Yes. I was at law school with Marku.' I was surprised: I had expected him to deny any connection.

'What do you think happened?'

He looked me full in the face and I leaned back involuntarily. 'I think they made a mistake.'

I was afraid, now, but I regathered myself. 'You know why she fired them, don't you?'

He shook his head. I looked at him hard. In the short time I had known him, he had never hesitated to refute our ideas. Now he was silent, and though his face betrayed nothing, I tasted something in the air.

Guilt. The tang was unmistakable, my palate honed by my profession. But why? Because he was betraying Marija also, and unlike his co-conspirators he had escaped punishment? Or something else? Either way, it was clear he knew more than he was letting on.

Eventually I said quietly: 'Are you afraid?'

'That the same thing might happen? No, my dear. I am very, very careful. If you are worried for yourself, don't be. Mr Pavel is very careful too.'

I didn't know whether to be relieved. I wasn't sure my faith equalled his.

Noticing this, he sighed. 'Here we have a saying: to have a curly mind. It means to have unusual ideas. I prefer to think of it as seeing things differently. In England, these happenings would be greeted with horror. In Yanussia, we have the curly mind, and so we shrug. Manea and Cristescu made a mistake. But we endure. Life goes on.'

He went out and I sat back, gazing into the abyss between us. The curly mind, indeed.

Curly, or twisted beyond recognition?

CHAPTER ELEVEN

I called my parents. Partly to ask about my mother's connection with Marija, and partly because I was scared.

My father picked up. I thought of him standing in the bare little hall, of the curtailed grass outside, the sticky neon 'Fish n Chip's' sign opposite. Our world. All happy families sound alike; every unhappy family has its own distinctive timbre, and as we crouched at dinner listening to the shouting from next door, our little room filled up with the almost-said. I existed at the tip of my tongue, somewhere behind my gritted teeth.

In truth, my parents were the reason I had become a lawyer. I spoke out because their presence strangled me, argued cases because I could not argue against my family, defended other people because I could not defend myself. They might hate that I was here, but when Marija Popa's files had dropped on my desk, like manna from heaven, I'd caught a glimmer of something I had not seen in a long time.

Hope.

I began gently. He was and was not like my mother: kind and considerate but also shut up, made inaccessible by some private grief. It was too much to expect him to help me with his wife – we rarely if ever went beyond small talk, and I did not like to push him. He possessed a frailty I could not bear to break.

'Are you safe?' he said bluntly, cutting across my description of our daily activities. I was surprised and pleased: his words eased the grey presence hanging over me. I reassured him without giving details, then felt encouraged enough to ask: 'Tată, do we have any friends or relatives here? I thought I might look them up.'

Silence. Then: 'Why on earth would you do that?'

'Just if there were any old connections. Anyone you wanted to make contact with.'

'There is no one.' His tone was cold. In the background I heard my mother coughing, a long, hacking sound, as if someone had taken a pickaxe to her throat.

'Surely there must be *someone*. Old neighbours. Cousins I don't know about. Or maybe' – I braced myself – 'maybe I could ask Marija.'

'Laura, stop this. Stop this now.'

'She remembers her, Tată. She remembers Mamă. I could ask her—'

'*Stop!*' His anger snapped my neck back. He sounded like my mother.

'What about Ecaterina? She controls the factory. It would be nice to visit, see where Mamă worked.'

'Laura.'

My mother's voice grabbed at my heart. Where a stranger would have heard only her urgency, I heard everything, all the little scrap of life we had shared.

'You mustn't talk to that woman. You must not go to that place.'

'The factory? Why? What happened?'

'Do not ask about what you do not understand.'

'Then *help* me understand, Mamă. Don't keep me in the dark.'

She had to force the words out. 'Laura. *Pisi*. Please.'

Pisi. Little cat. She hadn't called me that in years. Tears pricked my eyes.

'You have to tell me why,' I repeated. Her breathing was butterfly quick, rasping down the line, but the unerring fear of recent days pushed me on, my desperation for relief making me braver than I had ever been. 'What happened with her? And the factory? Why did we leave?' I drew myself tighter. 'Is it to do with . . . with what you sacrificed?'

There was a cry and a bang, simultaneous: I looked wildly around for its source before realising it came from the phone. She had dropped the receiver.

'Mamă?' Nobody replied, but I heard another cry and my father's panicked voice. 'Gabriela? Gabriela?'

'Tată?' I said, horribly afraid. 'What's happening?'

No response, only my father repeating my mother's name in tenderness and desperation as I listened helplessly, berating myself for pushing her. The line went dead. I had asked too many questions, and the great black bird Baba Mierlă had swooped down and stolen my mother's tongue after all.

It turned out she'd had something resembling a panic attack. My father told me the next day that he had taken her to hospital. I was shocked.

'But she hates hospitals.'

'I know.' His tone was grim. 'I had no choice.'

'But she's home now?' His silence was frightening. 'She's still there? Why?'

'Just some routine checks.'

'Was it . . . was it my fault?'

There was a long silence, and eventually he said, 'Look after yourself,' and hung up. It took some time to prise the hands from my neck. I'd heard nothing since: when I called, nobody answered, and I was growing desperate. Our parents dictate our vulnerabilities; I'd finally plucked up the courage to ask about our history and I'd come away with worse than nothing.

No, not nothing. I had known my parents feared Marija and her husband, but it seemed they were afraid of the factory as well.

I had found one once. A single *iubită* candy, still in its bright red wrapper. I stared at it for a long minute, nestled at the bottom of a drawer in their bedroom. My mother didn't want me to visit the factory, yet she'd brought a piece of it to England. She must have loved it once.

I didn't dare open it, instead taking it in my palm and tracing its shape with my thumb. *Now you are holding my heart.*

Why didn't they want me visiting? What had happened there? And was that thing the reason why we had cut ourselves off so utterly? I had to find out before it was too late.

In the meantime I had a job to do, not that it was giving me any cause for hope. By the time of our next meeting with Marija, we had appraised the legal situation more fully, and what we appraised was bad.

'There's too much,' Jude said.

I agreed. 'Maybe we should tell her so. Discuss a change of strategy.'

Pavel and Mr Gabor snorted at me in unison. 'As we say here, you are getting drunk with cold water,' the Yanussian said.

Pavel agreed. 'It's useless. Even without the risk of

professional misconduct, what do you think the chances are of her listening?'

'This is bad, Pavel, and you know it.'

'We're only a week in. There's still time for us to—'

'What? Find out that the money's been in a sock under her mattress all along?'

'She's right,' Jude put in. 'Marija could *die*. This strategy makes no sense, we all know it. The only question is why she's so keen on it.'

I thought our boss would explode, but he only sighed. 'Get back to work.'

I expected Pavel to try and keep her to himself at the meeting, but Mr Gabor insisted on sitting in, so we juniors were allowed to stay. Last night the Yanussian had cleared up to go home as usual. He was on the cusp of putting some files in his briefcase when he saw me watching and smoothly put them back.

Marija swept into the Lair, coiling herself up like Grendel's mother. I hadn't seen her since she revealed she knew my own mother, and I wanted to see – what? Some acknowledgement, while also fearing exactly that. She might have looked at me, but the glance was gone too swiftly to be sure.

'Have you read file three in this series, Doamna?' Pavel jumped straight in. 'The one about the yacht?'

She sighed. 'Which yacht?'

Popa had of course had his own yacht, finagled out of a Middle Eastern ruler whom he was equipping with oil rigs, and kept at a secret naval base on the Black Sea.

'The *Osiris*.'

The *Osiris* belonged to a Yemeni arms dealer. According to the charges, the dealer, on Popa's orders, had arranged to supply a safe port in exchange for a succulent commission. In the cargo hold, snuggled like sleeping babes, were fourteen bars of pure gold.

She picked up the file, no animation in her face. I was surprised. She'd said she'd do anything to ensure survival, yet we might have been asking her to read the cricket scores for all the interest she showed. I wondered what she was waiting for, where her thoughts roamed beyond this wood-panelled room and the four of us staring at her with varying mixtures of anticipation, anxiety and, yes, desire; beyond this mansion with its ticking clock and grey door, slicing off old screams; beyond this city, constricted by hills, the very landscape contriving to limit her horizon.

'If we turn to page nineteen.' Pavel had gained some confidence in the last couple of days; for the first time he seemed in control. 'The *Osiris* docked on the twentieth of June 1977. Three weeks previously, your private secretary sent a fax to Steven Wright, chief executive of the Bahamas Overseas Bank, requesting a meeting in Berlin.' He flourished the sheet. 'Do you recognise the fax?'

She inclined her head.

Mr Gabor picked up the thread. 'The prosecution has a photograph of Wright, here, on the thirteenth of June, on the balcony of the Hotel Adlon Kempinski in West Berlin. Do you know this individual?'

'Really, are all these questions necessary?' She smirked, and this time there was no mistake: her eyes went directly to me. 'What are you, my mother?'

Oh God. I had hoped, wildly, that she would not use the hold she now knew she had. But I should have remembered that apex predators do not summit the food chain through brute strength alone – they do it by exploiting weakness. The old. The sick. Or in my case, the fucked-up.

Mr Gabor wisely did not respond.

'Radutu, he is only on the third floor. Is it likely I will know someone who stays on the third floor?'

He nodded, unfazed. I realised he had been expecting this

131

answer and felt her realise it too. Her eyes narrowed almost imperceptibly. She would not like being predictable.

'Page twenty, Doamna. This time he is on the penthouse balcony.' His expression was perilously close to smugness. 'The next photo is from that same day. Your husband is on that balcony with him.' Popa was wearing one of his trademark black coats, specially lined with the skin of bears he had killed. 'Later, you, on that same balcony, alone.'

Yes, alone, elbow resting lightly on the rail, cigarette loose in her fingers, staring towards the Wall and the Brandenburg Gate. What had she thought about the Wall, scarred and graffitied, more than a decade away from being torn down? And what about the moment it had finally fallen? I'd watched it myself, one of the secretaries wheeling in a TV, the whole office stopping to watch in silence as that stone domino toppled, its shock waves rippling through the plains of Bulgaria, the forests of Czechoslovakia and the ragged streets of Bucharest, culminating at this woman's doorstep. Her regime was gone, her husband murdered, and now she faced this trial. Did she envy Dinu? She spoke of survival, but was that what she wanted, really? Was it not far worse to linger on when your shape in the world has lost its meaning, the earth spun on its axis leaving you behind, so that only your dusty imprint was left, cartoon-like, to drift on air?

Another image. 'This man is Isaiah Burns. Vice president of Overseas Bank. Purpletons, the asset tracers employed by Anghelescu's government, discovered fourteen gold bars in an OB account. The account is traceable to your husband. What do you say to that?'

No response.

'I ask you this, Doamna, because it is what the prosecution will ask you. What will you answer?'

He waited. Nothing. Her poker face was excellent, yet why did I feel that her mind was on another table altogether?

Pavel leaned forward, his frustration visible. 'If we are to make this strategy work, Doamna, these discussions are imperative. This is but the first of many. I really must recommend—'

'I am done for today,' she announced. She was not even looking at them.

'Doamna. Marija . . .'

She gave him such a look that his voice died. Then she was gone, leaving the four of us sitting there like fools.

My head spun. With the crack about my mother she had declared her hold on me. The cards were on the table. The game had begun.

Jude twirled his pencil. 'How are we going to prove she's innocent if *she's* not interested in proving she's innocent?'

Mr Gabor looked worried. 'Indeed. I am not confident in this strategy. She is, how would you say, not in her heart?'

'Her heart is not in it?'

He nodded.

'Well,' said Pavel through tight lips. 'Where the bloody hell is it, then?'

CHAPTER TWELVE

We found out a fortnight later. In the interim, the prosecutor, Dumitru Ursu, announced a press conference. Jude, frustrated and fretful, perked up.

'It'll be packed.'

'Irrelevant. We have a job to do.'

But it was not irrelevant, and Pavel knew it. As the trial loomed, interest was spiking among the international press; the trickle of interviews he was busily declining had become a flood. Our client was a hypnotic blend of Joan of Arc and Imelda Marcos; both goddess and she-devil, princess and tyrant, martyr and uber-bitch. The trial and its verdict would say something about this newly democratised nation that was still working out what it was, and by extension, what it was not.

Meanwhile we toiled with increasing futility, burying ourselves in paper piles as high as snowdrifts and just as unforgiving. The disputed purchase of a northern hunting ground. The alleged theft of IMF loan money, diverted to the purchase of antique rifles, a stuffed crocodile and other essentials. I wondered what had happened to the crocodile. I pictured taking it home and setting it up in my narrow hall, jaws open, always smiling for visitors.

'You know,' Jude said privately to me, 'arguing that neither she nor Popa have done anything wrong . . . it's not so much closing the door after the horses have bolted, but after the stable has burned down.'

'And the debris cleared.'

'And the ground sown with salt.'

We grinned at one another despite it all.

'We'll keep at it,' I said. 'We're making progress. What else can happen?'

In the universe's infinite game of whack-a-mole, Fate heard our levity and made its move.

'Shit.' Pavel entered. 'Shit, shit, shit.'

'What?'

He threw a thick glossy magazine onto the table. Jude and I fought a brief, silent battle for it. I won and he was forced to slink around and peer over my shoulder.

It was a copy of *Vogue*. There, gazing dreamily from the cover, was none other than Marija Popa.

FIRST LADY TELLS ALL. Marija Popa of Yanussia talks love, labels and litigation – plus her latest bold political move

'Uh-oh,' Jude breathed.

I riffled through to the relevant page. *Tea with the Black Widow: Eva Williams meets the woman who made communism sexy*, the headline squealed. I recognised the journalist. Last year she'd written a profile calling Osama bin Laden 'darkly handsome'. She must have brought a photographer, for here was the First Lady, in every image dressed in black.

'Jesus, what's the theme? Sexy funerals?'

Jude had a point. Here was Marija gazing soulfully out the window, dressed in silk trousers and a blouse just sheer enough. Here she leaned elegantly against a table smothered in flowers. Was that a tear in her eye? I saw someone who could be whatever she wanted, who could mould and remould herself like so much clay. You could turn and see the very opposite of what you expected, move to strike and find your weapon long gone from your hand, and only then realise that you yourself had thrown it away. 'Are you afraid of her?' Jude had asked me earlier. She was a caged creature, all parted lips and glittering eyes, yet those eyes spoke of a freedom that went beyond bars, a liberty that came from knowing yourself absolutely and understanding other people. She was uncaged in a way I could never be, possessed of a limitlessness I had not even known existed before we met, and now that I did know, nothing could be the same.

I was not afraid of her. I envied her.

On a cold winter's day, the gardens of the mansion on the hill are frozen. The deep snowdrifts and frosted window panes create an aura of mystery, as if in this palace a princess might sleep. We are in Yanussia, named by the Romans for their two-faced god Janus, its position balanced between East and West. The god's eyes seem closed today; the streets are quiet. Inside, perched on a Louis XVI chaise longue, I wonder: does anything bloom in this country?

The answer is given when the iroko doors open and out steps Marija Popa, style maven, philanthropist and former First Lady of Yanussia, looking far younger than her fifty-eight years . . .

I skipped a few paragraphs detailing her expensive outfit and dewy complexion.

How do you solve a problem like Marija Popa? A conundrum dressed in diamonds, a mystery wrapped in furs. Four long years have passed since revolutionaries upended her country and murdered her husband. Marija herself (she immediately asks that I use her first name) lives under house arrest. This mansion is no more than a gilded prison, where, a bird in a cage, she awaits trial.

'It is just the latest trial for me. It has been hard, unimaginably hard, even before this case,' she says. 'All I wanted was to love my people. Yet the things they are saying about me! I think I was naive.'

A sad smile lights up those beautiful amber eyes, sharp in a way that implies contacts, though she wears none, and said to have ensnared the likes of eastern European strongmen Josip Broz Tito and Nicolae Ceaușescu. Even Ronald Reagan, a fervent anti-communist, is said to have described her as 'bewitching, dammit'.

Of course Ms Popa is not just referring to literal trials, but rather the long, difficult years navigating the troubled waters of the Cold War; the strains of statehood; and her marriage to Constantin Popa, the man she rebranded and introduced to the world as Dinu, maverick spirit of the Eastern Bloc. Does she miss him?

'Every day,' she replies, touching a ring on her slender finger that she wears always, a constant reminder of the man she lost.

I squinted at the ring. I could not recall ever seeing it before.

'Life in power is hard. Marriage is harder,' and she smiles again. That is her special elixir, the common touch that made her a gift to ordinary people and a lightning rod for a jealous elite. While the latter focused on internal power struggles and international posturing, Marija built hospitals and schools, rolling out a

137

universal milk programme and raising the literacy rate to 98 per cent. Her office is bedecked with humanitarian awards.

'I am only a woman. I did what I could with what I had,' she shrugs when I point this out, making light of her achievements before adding that she could 'sort' the ongoing Balkans war 'in five minutes, if only they would let me'. As someone whose little black book comprises everyone from Marlon Brando to Adnan Khashoggi, it is difficult not to believe her.

Still, she is not, of course, 'only' the wife of Constantin Popa. As the adoptive daughter of Yanussia's powerful Iubită family, she is a business tycoon in her own right. The Iubită Companie – think an eastern European Hershey's – manufactures the famed sweets of the same name (the word means 'sweetheart': they are given as gifts by men to their wives or girlfriends). In a very modern twist, Marija is not just a First Lady but a businesswoman as well. Long before 'girl power' became a rallying cry, she introduced an all-female staff to the Iubită factory and built on the brand's popularity to the point that the sweets were included among the country's weekly rations, along with other staples such as cooking oil and bread.

'It is important to have joy in life,' she says. 'A woman should be able to enjoy a candy when she wants.'

She herself has famously found joy in her very feminine love of fashion. Over the decades her extravagance has captured the public's imagination: personal sessions with Valentino in New York, private tours of De Beers in London. On one trip to Givenchy's Paris couturier, she racked up a bill of three million dollars. I express envy at her black Dior outfit today and she waves me away with a smile. Red is her signature colour; it reminds her, she says, of the poinsettia her adoptive father planted.

BOMBSHELL

The question on everyone's lips, of course, is what will Yanussia's Little Mother do next?

'Once the case is out of the way? Why, it is obvious,' she smiles. 'I shall run for office.'

I cannot help a little gasp – of shock? Relief? She looks at me as if she knows what I am thinking, even if I do not.

'My people need me. They are suffering. All the promises of 1989 have been broken. The so-called revolution was nothing but a coup. Why accept an imperfect version of what was before? [Current president] Petre Stoica is like the chocolate teapot. The same with Matei [First Minister Matei Anghelescu]. I shall run for the presidency on my own terms.'

She takes a sip of tea. 'Already my associates are seeing such support for me. The people tell them time and again, "No more of this limbo. Bring us on to paradise." My husband may be dead, but I have not given up my country's cause.'

Yanussia's presidential elections are in eighteen months' time. A survey this year found that less than a quarter of Yanussians believe that life has improved since the overthrow of the former regime . . .

I sat back. This was why she had shown no interest in our interviews: all along she had been planning to announce her presidential bid. It was why she wanted us to argue that she was innocent, for how else could she return to power? It also explained her reluctance to seek a retrial: it would delay matters further, and anyone under investigation could not run for office. She needed the case wrapped up in order to launch her campaign.

Jude rubbed his eyes. 'She can't.'

'She can.'

'She won't.'

'Oh, she would.' Pavel was kneading his temples with his fingers, as if trying to shape his thoughts like dough.

'It's just a stupid women's magazine. Nobody will care.'

'No, it's dangerous,' I said slowly. 'The threat of a presidential run backs them into a corner before we've even begun. They'll fight like wolves – not to mention the jury haven't been chosen yet.' Jury information was public in Yanussia. How many jurors would vote her innocent knowing a presidential run would follow? How many would risk essentially going on record as not just supporters, but enablers?

Pavel nodded. 'We have to stop her. Make her retract.'

But how? I ran my fingertip down the glossy page, down that glossy face, so smooth it seemed a sacrilege to hunt for cracks. I wondered if Ursu had seen it and what his reaction would be. As for running for the presidency . . . She would do it, I knew, and what was more she would probably win, not despite what she was to this country, but because of it. Half of them might hate her, but the other half? All those posters and miniature shrines, all those little girls and boys who had grown up with her image of womanhood branded in their skulls – I doubted everything had been destroyed since 1989. She had carved her name too deeply for them to simply erase her, and as for those who despised her, well, the opposite of love is not hate. The very fervour of their loathing spoke to the pull they felt. She had made herself not a politician but an addiction, and now she had dared to point to their withdrawal symptoms and say, here, let me help with that.

A voice breathed beside me. '*I can't* . . .'

I glanced up. Pavel was staring at the magazine as if trying to bore a hole in the paper.

'What?'

He gave a guilty start. Jude and I exchanged looks.

'We can't let her drive herself to her death,' he said in a different tone, wrapping his fist around the magazine. 'I'm going to speak with her about a plea bargain.'

He went out.

'She'll never go for it,' I said. 'Even if they drop the death penalty, she'll still get life.'

'It's madness. Doesn't she *want* to survive?'

'She'd see prison as a living death. She'd rather be truly dead. With her it's all or nothing.'

'At this rate, it's going to be nothing. What a fuck-up.'

I sighed. 'Got a cigarette?'

Jude rummaged in his pocket. 'Didn't know you smoked, Lăzărescu.'

I didn't. But I needed a shot of something, and in the absence of tequila I took it and his lighter and went out into the cold white air. The snow was a constant presence now: every morning we awoke to find the drifts a little deeper, as though we were sinking into a wintry grave. I remembered waking up as a child to find school shut for the day (just as well – we had run out of paper the previous week) and making a snowman with my mother instead. The soft red cold of my blood-flushed hands. Fitting both of my shoes into one of her footprints. She lifted me before her, put my feet on hers and we walked like that, laughing at our slow, bumbling tread, her hands on mine.

I lit the cigarette. I could not see any guards, but I had no doubt that if I set off down the drive they would appear like so many ghouls. Somewhere in the gardens a bird screamed, the same bird I had heard on the first day and several times since. I could not work out if the cries were sympathetic or mocking our imprisonment. It sounded like a door half opened, a promise unkept.

There was a path leading down to a side gate – I didn't bother to try it; there was a guard there, watching me narrowly – but I turned round and walked up the slope. The house was in the hill's eye, which made it difficult to see from the road, though when I looked back I saw Poartă clearly enough. It seemed a doll city, cars dawdling up and down the boulevards that sliced through it like a knife through a cake. Harmless but for the white monolith of the Parliament at its centre, an albatross around its neck. Popa and Ceauşescu competing to come up with the biggest pile of bricks. Dinu had eaten out half a mountain's worth of marble and had the army bulldoze a fifth of Poartă's once-beautiful old city to do it, and it wasn't even finished. In what struck me as a very communist state of affairs, it would now be more expensive to tear it down than finish it off. I imagined the same applied to his Moon Institute and all the other uselessly exorbitant dreams. Why is it that the richer and more powerful you are, the giddier and more irrelevant your fancies? Must kings and billionaires reach for the stars rather than the starving? The truly rich are irritable with it: like a parasite, money burrows under the skin and creates an itch. The clients we served had reached a certain level only to become conscious of a higher one still, and the higher they climbed the more they became aware that there was another, final plane, one they could never touch, not for any price.

I turned my attention to the large hills hemming in the city. The closest, to the west, was the smallest. From it rose a huge statue, unfinished and partly shrouded by scaffolding: the figure of a woman holding one arm out before her, grasping at nothing. Her face looked odd, and it was several moments before I worked out why.

She had no eyes, only empty sockets. It was no mistake – someone had carved her that way. The face was turned towards me, gazing blankly at the mansion, at Marija.

North. Always her expression would be in the shadows.

I inhaled deeply, then broke out coughing as the smoke burned my throat and my breath-frost mingled with it, grey polluting the white. It reminded me of my mother on the phone, the sound of someone with blades in their throat.

The cloud speckled out. In its place walked a ghost.

I stared, wondering whether to call for help. (But who ya gonna call, Laura?) It was horrible, with baggy white limbs and a void where its face should have been. Its hands and feet were . . . yellow?

My vision shifted. Gloves, boots and a mesh visor. Less ghost than ghostbuster. It rounded the west wing and vanished.

I followed, crunching through the snow, then winced at my own footprints. I should not leave traces. What if the house was watching, keeping record? How was it that mere bricks could live and seethe? It reminded me of Apostol, as if the house was his familiar, or more unsettlingly, the other way round. I'd kept well away from him since that hideous encounter on the basement stairs, but he had a habit of appearing silently, suddenly. Yesterday, I had been pouring coffee when I felt eyes on my back, the exact spot where I still bore his bruise: I turned to see him there, and an ugly pain in my hand alerted me to the fact I was now pouring coffee on myself. I had the horrible feeling that he had *meant* it to happen. He had unusually wide nostrils, and I pictured him scenting my cigarette smoke and setting off on the trail as if stalking deer. In the frosted silence my body was too noisy, too obtrusive; not just the snowy footprints but the blood pulsing in my ears, the rush of my hat against my hair, my bones and joints grinding along in a mass of vulnerable flesh.

Was that how Marija wanted us to feel? Hunted?

I rounded the house and there was the figure, bowed over a wooden box about three feet high, one of six in a neat row. The snow here had been carefully swept away.

At my approach the figure straightened and flapped its yellow hands. I stopped and it returned to its box. It appeared to be listening. Then it took a bag from a pocket and withdrew a white lump, like rock but too deliberately shaped to be natural. With immense care it raised the lid of the box, then, bracing itself, in one swift movement placed the brick gently inside and replaced the lid. The whole process took less than three seconds; I thought I detected a hum in the frosted air. Then the figure reached up and took hold of its hood. With a tug the mystery collapsed. It was Ecaterina.

'Hello,' I said. 'What were you doing?'

'Beekeeping. Put that out.'

I looked down: the cigarette had burned down almost to my fingers. I bent and inserted it into the snow with a faint hiss.

'You keep bees?'

'Evidently.'

This was unexpected. I had not imagined this dried-up, bloodless creature nurturing anything, yet in her eyes was a light which very much resembled passion.

'What was the rock?'

'Not rock, cane sugar. They burn through a lot of honey. The sugar is a substitute so they have enough for winter.'

'Why not give them more honey?'

'If you give honey from another hive then disease can spread. So I make this candy instead.'

The Iubiță candy queen, feeding sugar lumps to her bees. I smiled. 'You must really like them.'

'Not so much liking, as needing.' She paused, assessing me. 'Do you know what happens to bees in winter? No? Well, I suppose you know about the queen. The worker bees, they surround her with their bodies. They flutter and shiver. It keeps the hive warm and the queen alive. But they must not stop, not even for a moment. The queen is the most important thing.'

I grinned. 'I think I know how they feel.'

Her eyes gave a pale shimmer of amusement. It encouraged me. We spend our conversations constructing ourselves for others to look at. Yet even as we do so, we long to glimpse a chink in our counterpart, who is busily doing the same, and for their weakness to knock a hole through our own so that we may peek through the ramparts and see one another for the first time.

'Don't bees die after they sting?'

'Only honey bees, and only if the victim's skin is suffi-ciently thick. That includes us. The stinger is barbed so they cannot withdraw it. So yes, my bees would die if they stung you, though it is only the females that sting.'

'What about the males?'

'The males are drones. They feed, they mate, they die.' Another shimmer.

'I suppose the sting is a last resort.'

'Yes. If I knew I had to surrender my nerves, my abdomen and my digestive tract, I would think twice.'

'Does it hurt?'

'Of course it hurts.'

I gazed at the humming boxes. 'Do they know?' I said at last. 'Do they know what will happen?'

Ecaterina turned her face to the sky; for a moment she reminded me of Mr Gabor. 'I pray that they do not.'

I shuddered. The hive was an entity whose survival depended upon thousands of creatures enslaved by a single mind, a mind that could and would have its own foot soldiers disembowel themselves for protection. What breed of power could exert such control? And was it a tragedy or a mercy that its army could not comprehend their own sacrifice?

In the trees, the gate-bird cried its grating cry. I scanned the black limbs but saw nothing. 'What is that?'

'I don't hear anything.'

'I . . . Never mind.'

We walked around to the front door.

'You have settled in?'

'I was born in Yanussia.'

'But you grew up in the West. In the elbow society, we call it. This is a land of eyes and ears. The difference is greater than you think.'

'My mother worked in your factory. For the Iubită Companie.'

Ecaterina gazed at me, a cloud of breath half obscuring her face. 'Did she now?' Her voice was careful – but not, I realised later, surprised.

'Did you know her? A Mrs Lăzărescu?'

She shook her head, a little too quickly. I thought of my mother, how she'd told me not to visit the factory. There was something there, I was sure, and my parents did not want me finding it. She was out of hospital now, my father had told me, but still weak. I envisaged her in bed, drinking cup after cup of the hibiscus tea she swore by, its scent a reminder of times when I had been ill and she sat beside me for long hours, reading, humming, living. It made me sick to defy her further – but nor could I tolerate being kept in the dark. I had lived there too long.

I could not leave the grounds by myself, the guards had made that much obvious. But an authorised visit? I took a

146

deep breath and said, 'If you would allow it, I'd like to visit the factory sometime. To see where she worked.'

'I am afraid it is closed.'

I smiled my best smile. 'Surely you have a key?'

She frowned. 'You should go to lunch.'

I quashed my disappointment – I would try again – and asked if she was coming. I had never seen her eat; I wasn't sure that she did. Then again, Marija never joined us at mealtimes either. Perhaps they lived as chameleons were once reputed to do, feeding on air.

'No. I must visit the local prison. I go every week to bring food, and company.'

'Is that safe?'

'Is anything? Some are officials from the regime, some are people imprisoned by those same officials. It is a terrible thing to be forgotten. But we forget what we should remember, and remember what we should forget.'

'Surely we owe it to ourselves to remember everything we can.'

'You are young. Someday you will learn that forgetting can be best.'

I tried to imagine what she must have seen over the years, what luxuries, what horrors. Purges and banquets, blood and flowers, and that red stairwell slashed through her childhood home. She must know about the hospital and the crimes that had occurred within. How had she felt when the Strajă came knocking?

I swallowed and said instead, 'You think they will forget themselves enough to hand her the presidency?'

She laughed, a dry little sound. 'My sister is unique. The rules do not apply.'

'Tell me about her.'

'No. We have been bound together as long as you have been alive, and years before that. Besides, you have your files.'

I shook my head. 'It is hard to understand someone from paper alone. In any case, what our files contain is always less interesting than what they do not.'

'You think to understand her?'

'I am her lawyer.'

'You are an associate, and a junior one at that.'

We gazed at one another. I thought of her in all those photographs of Marija and Dinu, standing off to one side or behind, so she appeared in fragments. Unnoticed yet omnipresent, as if she could not exist outside the frame. Why did she remain here? *She* was not under house arrest.

At last I said, 'I believe you know how that feels.'

The eyes narrowed; I held my breath. But at last she spoke.

'Marija and I have a special bond. It began when we were young.'

'Because you became sisters?'

'Because she once did me a favour. For a price.'

'What did she do?'

No answer.

'The price?'

Her mouth split. 'What do you think? You call me a junior associate. You are more right than you know.'

'Was that wise? To create such a bond?'

'A worker does not choose its queen. But it does not mean they do not love her.' She sighed. 'You know, I suppose, that Marija's parents died when she was seven. She grew up in an orphanage in the north. I do not have to tell you what that meant. They were never as bad as Romania, but even so. The tales she told . . . "Playgrounds" that were nothing but bare concrete squares. Dormitories with rows of silent children staring from tiny beds, so deprived of stimulation as to be virtually language-less.

'Yet she waited two years before someone adopted her. I

do not say it took two years for someone to come along. I mean, she actually turned people down.'

I gaped at her. 'How? Why?'

'She was waiting. Waiting for my parents. Not them specifically, but someone like them. Wealthy. This was before communism, when people could afford a good life and a conscience. When Marija saw my mother's camel coat, she knew she had found her family. Her will is more than iron. She is the strongest person I have ever met.'

I said slowly, 'If the orphanages were so awful, her Million Children movement must have made them even worse. All those unwanted children.'

'You do not know. Of course. Marija undertook the biggest renovation of the orphanages this country has ever seen. Under her, they became respected institutions, with proper care and education. She vowed her experience would never be repeated.'

I frowned. 'I've never heard that.'

'No. Unusually, she did it without telling anybody. Constantin would have forbidden her. As it was, she was three quarters of the way through before he found out. Rather than stopping her, he decided to take the credit.'

Could I believe her?

'If that's true, she should tell people. They should know what she did.'

Ecaterina examined her red nails. 'Tell me. When something very, very bad happens to you, and you run away, when do you feel safe enough to look back? When, even, do you stop running? Marija made sure the reforms went through, but she wanted nothing to do with those institutions otherwise. Childhood is full of monsters, Laura. The great lie of adulthood is that we have defeated them.

'She told me once about a fight that broke out. The orphanage staff had grown tired of beating them, so they arranged something more . . . inventive. They lined them up opposite one another and told each child to punch their opponent. Then the other person would hit them back. Marija was a troublemaker, so they deliberately put her across from her best friend.

'Can you imagine, Laura? Can you picture what it is like to have a home that is no home at all?'

I did not answer. But I could.

'I was fifteen when she arrived and thrilled to have a younger sister. I loved her immediately. And when she grew up – well, it is hard to be a woman in this country, when "mother" and "wife" are just different words for "slave". She found a path and took me with her. She put me in charge of the Iubită Companie when my parents would have given it to my cousin because he was male. She gave me back this house. She has always been able to do what others cannot, with everything that implies.' The pale eyes bored into mine. 'I know that this country looks at her and sees a monster. But I see the woman who saved me.'

I looked away. Had Marija told Ecaterina to talk to me? Was it all even true? If so, how had she not only escaped those horrors but been brave enough to do something about them? The Little Mother had the curious double-sidedness of a Rubin vase. You could perceive one image, or another, but trying to see both at the same time made your head spin. I wanted Marija to be innocent; I wanted her to be the wicked witch, stuffing children into the oven. I could not decide what she was, and that was the torment. Ambiguity is the enemy of peace of mind, and I understood enough by now to know that she used this to her advantage, dancing on the shards of my doubt, of Yanussia's. For what could you do when you strode up the path to the gingerbread cottage, flaming torch in hand, only to find that the witch was charming and her oven contained only cakes? (And yet

150

just as you leave, embarrassed and relieved, the whiff of roasted meat . . .)

Ecaterina was staring at something a long way away. 'About the factory.'

My head snapped up. I hardly dared breathe.

'If you wish, I will arrange a tour.'

I began to thank her profusely, but she cut me off and went inside. A moment later she reappeared. 'One thing, Laura.'

'Yes?'

'I say this as a warning. Not everything in our history can withstand revisiting.'

She went inside, keys jangling faintly at her waist. I remained where I was, humming with my own success even as I wondered what I had got myself into.

Think of the Devil, for it was then that I saw her.

Marija Popa was gazing down at me from the second floor. She ought to have been dulled by the glass, but a beam of sunlight had lanced upon her, transfiguring her into something more than coloured flesh. As I watched, she leaned forward and breathed upon the pane. I felt the warmth of it as surely as if I were the glass. The cloud it formed obscured her face; the pale moon of a fingertip appeared. She was writing something.

Come.

CHAPTER THIRTEEN

The scent hit me first. Delicious, intoxicating, accompanied by a deep warmth. Outside it was winter, but in the Black Widow's chambers it was always spring and everywhere there were flowers, unseasonal, beautiful flowers, piled high in elaborate displays of white and pink and green. I was unable to think, enveloped in this glossy perfection. Lilies, amaryllis, orchids, lost in their own gorgeous eruptions. The nearest petal was so vivid it looked fake, yet when my fingertips made contact (a faint shock), it possessed the unmistakable suppleness of a living thing.

She was still at the window, her back to me. The room was pink: the wallpaper, the lighting, the thick carpet, which muffled all sound. The atmosphere coiled itself around my shoulders like a fur stole and settled there. Without the flowers it would have been stultifying; with them it was stupefying. I understood that this was a place apart from the usual way of things. Like a seed vault or a nuclear bunker, it reached beyond time, pointing to a different way of seeing. I could just make out her message on the window pane. She had not written it mirror-style, so I could read it, but the normal way round. The effort, she was saying, would have to come from me.

But in this she had made a mistake – again. First in the swimming pool, and now here. The mistake was that I was good at puzzles. The First Lady was a case file to be cracked, and the more time I spent with her, the more I was beginning to understand her, every moment in her company another click of the Rubik's cube.

'Are you very angry with me?'

I ignored the glitter in her eyes, the glamour she sought to throw over me. In law it is vital to control the narrative. I had so far failed to wrest back control. The stakes had never been higher than now.

'The presidency,' I said.

'I meant it.'

'Why now?'

'Why not?'

'It makes things difficult.'

'For me, or for you?'

'Both.' I took a deep breath, balancing on the filament. We watched each other. 'A retraction?'

'Impossible.'

I let my eyebrows rise. 'I did not think you believed in such a thing.'

'In the presidency?'

'In impossibility.'

Now it was her turn to pause. 'Pavel was here. He proposed a *plea bargain*.' She said this as if it were a dreadful swear word. 'I need my people to know I am coming for them. I will not back down. I cannot.'

'So you refused.'

'Of course.'

'Then why am I here?'

For the first time, she was silent. My heart was racing; I thought she would detect it pulsing in my chest.

'You want someone to talk you down from the ledge,' I said, 'but you will not grant Pavel the satisfaction.'

'You think I will grant it to you?'

Maybe not. But you don't deny it.

'Judge Ardelean, the jury – whatever they think of your case, they will certainly be swayed by the prospect of your return to power. Why not wait until after the verdict to launch a campaign? If you are exculpated, you can do what you want. But if you do not retract, they will push for the death penalty no matter what happens.'

'No. Without power, I am nothing. The cards have been dealt. It is your job to play them.'

'We cannot play poker if you are playing chess.' I took a deep breath, thought of Carl Mortensen's words. *Dazzle them a little.* 'A retraction is not what you think. We can turn what looks like weakness into hidden strength. Wait until they demand the retraction, then capitulate. They will think they have you running scared.'

'And won't they?'

I smiled. 'Doamna, do not tell me that you are unfamiliar with the practice of saying one thing and doing another. Of course it is your decision, but you may wish to portray yourself as an old woman' – her eyes flashed at that – 'being bullied by the new, young, male government. You may say that this regime claims to be about choice, yet it cannot trust the people to elect its own leaders. That you, who have already dedicated more than three decades to public service and wish to devote more, are not only barred from running for the presidency, but may also be executed for the crimes of your dead husband.'

There was a small jewelled box on her desk, nestled among the scattered humanitarian awards. She picked it up and weighed it in her palm.

'What if I do not fear death?'

I considered her. 'I do not think you are afraid of dying. But you are afraid.'

The gleam in her eye would have felled nations. 'Oh?'

'You do not fear death,' I repeated with more certainty, gathering my courage and everything I had observed since our first meeting. 'You fear . . . restriction.' As I said it, I knew it was true. 'You cannot bear limits being placed upon you. I don't mean walls or prisons,' for she had gestured around her as if to say, look, here I am under house arrest, and I am not afraid. 'You have long learned to operate beyond them, even to relish their transgression. You love breaking rules, yet you cannot abide the rules themselves. You don't want form placed upon you if you can't supersede it; you don't want a role if you can't surpass it. You want to be everything and nothing. You place survival above all, but survival is just another word for possibility.' I nodded at the paper knife on her desk. 'You would have no hesitation in plunging that into your heart if you thought it the only way to elude their power. But death at their hands, on their terms, is the ultimate circumscription. It is this that makes you afraid.'

Silence. A grand piano crouched in one corner, black wings furled. Did she play or did she merely like the idea of music, with its beauty and its control, its rules made only to be broken? I waited, ignoring the sweat on my palms, not daring to blink. I knew I was right. She had chosen her creeds carefully over the years, inlaying them one upon the other like the finest filigree. She did not believe anything until it became useful to her, and then she took it to the point where it hurt: herself, or other people, or a nation.

Eventually she said, 'I can make this retraction. Or I can tell you about Gabriela. Choose.'

I stared at her. 'You would sacrifice your case just to talk with me?'

'No, Laura. *You* would sacrifice *your* case to talk with *me*.'

The opportunity uncoiled, a reptile in its cage. It would be so easy to release it, to allow myself to find precisely what I had come to seek. It was everything I wanted. Of course her case would be damaged, but it was already damaged. Perhaps we could still win regardless. If not, well, I would not be promoted. She – she would be executed. Was this truly what she was offering, what she was willing to sacrifice? Was it a test? Or did she believe she would win no matter what? It was exactly what I wanted, what I craved. I was tempted . . .

A slight breeze blew through, setting the plants a-whisper. It shook me to my senses. It didn't matter what she believed. It mattered what *I* believed. Finding out about my family was important: it mattered beyond everything; everything but my own integrity. I had lost so much along the way, I could hardly bear myself. The realisation was a blow to the head: it was for *this* that I had come to Yanussia. In tracking my mother's secret, I was in truth hunting a way to live with myself. My client had just put her life in my hands. Nothing is as important as not hurting people. I could not risk it. Not even for this.

'Make the retraction,' I said, though the sacrifice was great enough for the very syllables to hurt.

'Why?'

'The past is not as important as the present.'

'Wrong.'

'You would prefer I had chosen differently?'

Her eyes were locked doors. 'I did not say that. And yet . . .' She opened up the box she held: inside was a tiny ballerina, leg and back arched in arabesque. As I watched, the figure started to rotate on its axis and a tune began to play, a fragile thing too eerie for a lullaby. I stared, hypnotised. 'And yet you will not help me look into Radutu. The past is everything we are and will be. I have placed my fate in Radutu's hands, exactly as I just placed it in yours. How can I trust him without knowing who he is?'

I saw then how she had trapped me. The whole conversation had been leading to this point, and my own decision had cornered me. The dancer's tune sharpened; the air acquired a tang that had nothing to do with flowers. Salty, meaty. Like blood. I had thought I could regain control, yet once more she had so easily plucked it from my fingers.

'If you make this retraction,' I said heavily, 'I will look into Mr Gabor.'

Constantin Popa's widow smiled, wide and slow. 'Start in the National Records Office. Where they keep family archives.'

'We have an agreement, then.' I was careful not to phrase it as a question.

'I will tell Cristian to make the retraction.'

'Without—'

'I shall not mention you.'

'I cannot leave the grounds unescorted. Your guards have made that clear.'

'I will help you. Watch for my sign.'

'Doamna,' I said, hand on the door. 'The choice you offered me. Was that a test?'

'No, Laura.' Another smile. 'But this will be.'

The box snapped shut: the music stopped and the ballerina was gone, collapsed into her own secret workings. I had vowed not to be drawn into shadows, yet when I looked now, I saw nothing but.

I took my cue and left, the reverberations ringing in my ears, drowning out the silence.

CHAPTER FOURTEEN

All day the phone rang constantly: Jude and I fielded no fewer than seventeen press calls requesting comment on Marija's presidential bid. The queen had put the other side in check and everyone was awaiting the next move.

There was no point any more in pretending I wasn't in the game. I too was a pawn – had been since I stepped off the plane, or even since her files had hit my desk. Struggling was worse than useless; as every fly knows, it only entangles you further. I tried to escape to call the London office, but Pavel would not let me leave. It was as if the Lair had truly become its namesake, guarded by a jealous dragon. And there was another concern, fresh and horrible: with every move I made for Marija, my search for my family seemed to retreat a little further.

The callers were from every paper I'd heard of and many I hadn't: the national newspapers, of which the *Popor* was the biggest, but also the *New York Times*, *The Times* of London, *Le Monde*, the *Corriere della Sera*, all of them thirsting for more. Despite himself, Jude got into a conversation with one.

'That was a historian,' he said when he finally hung up.

'A historian?'

'Yes. She's doing an op-ed for the *Popor*. She says she was invited to stay with Marija for a week in 1988. She's writing a book about their time together.'

I felt a small stab of – what? Jealousy? How curious. With some effort I set it aside.

'"A charming taboo", she called her.'

'Will it be a hatchet job?'

'Maybe. Maybe not. Most of the papers want to tear her down, but I think some can't quite bring themselves to. She's too wrapped up in their psyche. It's like self-harm.'

Between the calls and trying to escape Pavel, I had a job to do. We were working through the most serious charges, those that carried the death penalty. I hoped that Marija's retraction would lessen the pressure, but it didn't mean that she would change strategy, and as I gazed at the uncompromising pages, black and white with no room for the grey she excelled at, I felt the noose tightening.

Later, we received yet more ill tidings. Gheorghe Funar, Popa's key adviser, had pleaded guilty, which meant he could now give evidence for the prosecution. It would be doubly hard to argue the Popas' innocence if the other side had the testimony of the mastermind of the operation.

'This isn't working very well, is it?' Jude said to no one in particular. I prayed that Marija would make her retraction soon, and that my impending search of Mr Gabor's files would prove successful.

The National Records Office. Where they keep family archives. I gripped my pen as her meaning finally assailed me. What if the place housed not just Mr Gabor's file, but my parents' as well?

What if it housed mine?

Again I saw the web stretching before me, threads glistening. I'd thought that helping her and helping myself were at odds with one another. But what if I was wrong? She knew already that I wanted to find out about my mother – I had stupidly made that much obvious. I knew by now she was never *not* calculating; she must have realised she could help me. The question was, why? Kindness? Entrapment? Or both?

I had no hope of telling the difference, but I seized the opportunity. The next morning, the dragon mercifully went out for a bit and I fled my tower to call the London office. Jameson picked up and I asked for their report on Marija's previous lawyers, Marku Manea and Aurel Cristescu. If I was to investigate Mr Gabor for treachery, it made sense to start with the unlucky original traitors.

'It's not ready yet. Did Pavel tell you to pester us?' he grumbled.

I barely hesitated. 'Yes.'

'Nasty business. Be careful out there.'

My eyebrows shot up. Jameson only cared about his filing systems, crooning over his neat rows of cabinets with a tenderness matched by a dislike of the messiness of people. It was the most human thing I'd ever heard him say, and deeply disconcerting.

He read out what they had so far. It wasn't much. I replaced the phone, picked it up to call Andrei, then put it down again. I'd tried calling several times of late, and every time he didn't answer, I was shamefully relieved. Love, romantic love, is all we need, or so we are told. But if that was so, why was I here, digging away? Why was he angry enough to ignore me? We had always said that no matter what, we had each other – the kind of thing you say earnestly to one another after a crappy day. But I was slowly realising it wasn't true, that the other person wasn't enough, for either of us.

The phone rang, making me jump. 'Jameson?'

It was my father. I sat heavily down on the bed. 'How is she?'

'Fine.'

'What about the tests?'

Did I imagine the slight hesitation?

'Nothing. Everything's fine.'

I wanted to grab the pair of us and shake until something fell out. Instead he asked me whether I'd remembered her words about the factory, and now it was my turn to conceal my hesitation.

'Yes.'

'Good.'

It wasn't a lie exactly. I did remember, but I never said I would comply. In a court of law, it'd likely have been fine. But the court of family is a different matter: the judge is partial, the jury unbalanced, and the sentence is life, made all the harsher because you serve it in your head. I had to get to those archives, and the factory, before it was too late – for me, for all of us.

The sky turned red and dim and I was relieved from my brooding by a flurry of excitement among the staff. Jude and I collared Mircea in the hall and learned that we were to attend a dinner that evening in honour of an artist friend of Marija's. Apparently a big deal in Yanussia, he went only by the name of Sorin.

'Like Madonna,' I said to Jude.

'Ooh, I hope so.'

The manservant shrugged. It was this artist, he went on, who was building the statue of the woman on the hill.

'That bloody great thing?' Jude said. 'Gives me the willies. What's it supposed to be?'

Mircea simply shook his head. At that moment, someone hammered at the front door: the noise was startlingly loud, reverberating round the hall, and the handle began to twist and turn with great violence.

'Think that one's for you, mate,' Jude said.

161

Mircea advanced cautiously, the handle writhing like a living thing. We watched as he took hold of the lock, braced himself – and was almost knocked over by the creature that flung itself upon him in a mess of hair and torn clothing.

'Jesus!' It was a woman, wild-eyed, thrashing like a demon. We retreated in shock. Other staff were flooding in, but as they glimpsed the intruder, they gasped and halted even as she attacked Mircea, clawing at his face. Jude ran forward and got hold of one of her wrists, but her strength was phenomenal, made monstrous by desperation. Amid the din, the shouts and the running feet, I was struck by her silence, unnatural, horrible, as if she was no longer a person but a force, pared away into inhumanity.

'A little help!' Jude yelled, and the rest of us shook ourselves and ran over. Several men took hold of her, and it was then that she began to scream. It took a second to recognise the words, or rather one word, repeated over and over.

Marija! Marija!

The cry ripped from her throat and I could not help it – I froze. Neither before nor since have I heard a voice under so much strain. I wouldn't have been surprised if it had torn her vocal cords in two. She kept screaming, on and on, awful and ear-splitting, rattling the chandeliers, threatening to crack the great mirror from side to side. *The curse is come upon me.*

It took four members of staff, plus Jude and Mircea, to wrestle her out of the door and into the arms of the apologetic guards.

'No idea how she got in . . . Must have climbed . . .'
They carried her away.
'Who was *that*?' Jude asked the general assembly. Mircea

162

was clutching his cheek, blood dripping through his fingers. They shook their heads, mute, but in their averted eyes I saw: they knew exactly who the stranger was, and why she was so desperate to see the First Lady.

CHAPTER FIFTEEN

It was too much. The bruise on my back had awoken again, as if my body had lost the ability to heal itself. I found myself desperately needing Andrei. A port in a storm. I called him and he picked up immediately.

'I've missed you.'

'I miss you too.' His tone was guarded.

'I haven't managed to find out anything else,' I burst out. 'I'm sorry.'

'It's OK.' It was not OK. My heart clenched. Could he not give me a break? Did he have to be so unforgiving? Andrei divided the world into the neat boulevards of 'must' and 'must not', with no room for the messy alleyways and cul-de-sacs of 'could' and 'could not'. It made him a bad writer, and it divided us now. Or was I merely making excuses for myself?

'Some madwoman tried to break into Marija's house,' I said instead. 'She seemed obsessed with her.'

'What did she want?'

'To see her, I guess.'

'To eat her, you mean. Or be eaten.'

I could not think how to reply, but that salty, meaty tang

was fresh in my nose and mouth. I asked how he was, and he began telling me about his latest writing project, a one-man play about the injustices of a ruler referred to only as 'X'. I pictured him cross-legged on the ironic granny-print sofa he'd 'rescued' from a skip, his slim fingers expertly making a roll-up. The image's familiarity brought a rush of warmth, as his tone – and yes, the content – lulled me into a state too comforting to be called boredom. Perhaps that was why I said what I did.

'Andrei. Let's do it.'

He stopped mid-sentence. 'Do what?'

'Let's move in together. When I'm back.' A sudden puppyish optimism swept me. I would solve the problem of my family. I would win the case, and return to him, triumphant. I could picture us now in a shared apartment, him cooking, me playing sous chef, laying the table with the plates we would find at some niche market. Why not? Other people managed to be happy. It could not be so hard.

But the silence stretched, and the optimism wobbled. 'What do you think?'

'I think . . .' The pause was deadly. 'I think we should wait until you're back.'

'But I've just decided. And you have already. Haven't you?' My voice wavered.

'Yes! Yes.' But he didn't sound too sure. 'Don't worry about me, Laura. Worry about you.'

'Meaning?'

'I haven't changed my mind. But you – *you* might change. I don't think you understand that this is going to affect you in ways you can't imagine. The person I move in with might not be the person who left. Even this conversation . . . you're keeping something from me, I can tell. You've never done that before. Oh, you've always been locked away – God knows I've devoted the last two years to hammering at the door. It's only now, though, that I'm afraid of what lies on the other side.'

There was nothing I could say to persuade him. I found myself practically begging him, his hesitation creating a certitude in me that I could never have managed on my own. But he was immovable. To my shame, in the end I told him to shove it, then hung up and cried self-righteously until it was time for dinner.

At the appointed time, I went down to the usual small dining room with Jude, who took in my red eyes but said nothing. The place was empty, until Apostol popped up from nowhere and gestured for us to follow.

'Speaking of the willies,' Jude muttered as the bodyguard led us further down the passage, the same one that would eventually come to the grey door. It was different with the lights ablaze, or maybe not so much.

Andrei was wrong. He had to be.

With a spade-like hand, Apostol showed us into another, far grander dining room. Jude went in first, me following behind, and as I did so, I felt a hand against my lower back, the exact place of my bruise. I turned in shock. Apostol met my eyes, held my gaze. Then he was gone.

It was a struggle to focus on the dining room. The long mahogany table could have seated thirty but was laid for only seven, with a fruit centrepiece resembling a controlled explosion. Rows of cutlery flanked shining plates, each with several crystal glasses set above them like moons; over the last, closest to the door, Mr Gabor was positioned like a dark star.

'I thought you were with Pavel?'

'I was. Mr Pavel said he had private matters to discuss with our client.'

166

Jude and I frowned, just as Marija padded in, a tiger burning bright, trailed by our boss and a stranger I took to be the artist. Everyone in the room turned helplessly towards her. I saw her then as she must have been, wooing foreign dignitaries, joking with arms dealers, that raw animal magnetism made further alluring by its semi-concealment beneath tailored clothing and perfect make-up. Cats carry a parasite that makes mice forget to be afraid – here, you never forgot your fear, but the helpless, trapped attraction was the same. Once more I heard that desperate woman screaming her name.

'Enough,' she said. A fox fur was wrapped around her throat: its sly glass eyes watched me. 'Enough of being hidden away.' She clapped her hands, two gunshots, and everyone started. 'You sit there. You, there. Where is my sister?'

'Speak of the Devil,' Jude murmured as we heard the faint jingle of keys. Ecaterina entered, followed – no, *propelled* – by Apostol.

'Sister! We have found you at *last*.' The lightest of emphases.

Not for the first time, I was struck by the difference between them, one so flush with life, the other so drawn and desiccated. I wondered how Ecaterina had borne it for so long, all those eyes drawing the same conclusion. She seemed even paler than usual, her bloodless mouth pinched.

'Doamna, I am not hungry today.'

'Sister.' That word again; the ties that bind. 'The hunger torments your belly as much as it does mine.'

Whatever colour was left in that hollow face drained away. Only yesterday Ecaterina had talked of their bond, but just then it seemed more of a stranglehold.

We took our places. Marija sat at the head; I was beside Jude, at the far end, which annoyed me. Ecaterina sat opposite, next to Pavel, her head bowed like a dead flower. Mr

Gabor was hardly more lively. I watched him throughout dinner and he did not look at Marija once, or rather, not directly. I could not work out if his evasiveness was suspicious or normal, if that was a word I could use any more.

The artist, Sorin, broke the silence, speaking in Yanussian. He looked to be in his early thirties, slim, with quick eyes and prominent cheekbones, dressed in coarse clothing of navy and tan. Peasant clothing, yet clearly he wore it because he was a painter, not because he was poor. When had I learned to tell the difference between poverty real and assumed?

'English, please,' Marija said. 'For our guests.'

He switched over, barely missing a beat. His English was no less smooth, his manner familiar. He must have been one of the regime's favoured artists, perhaps *the* favoured artist, given that vast statue. I wondered what he thought it was, and what she thought it was, and whether or not they were the same thing.

'I am saying, today my union had a speaker from France. He explained the international art market to my illustrious peers. They could not understand it. They are horrified to learn that now people will only buy paintings for what they are worth.'

Marija was amused. 'They must miss those nice payments from the state.'

'Precisely, Doamna. Ah, they liked to pretend it hurt their art, to work for the government. Yet they are fat as hens. Now the capitalist fox is in the pen . . .' He smiled.

'Sorin, you are too gruesome.' The food arrived, hands sliding salmon steaks before us. The skins had been removed, the ribbed pink flesh visible. Ecaterina looked as if she was going to be sick.

Ah. She was anorexic. Of course. One did not get so thin

this side of the grave otherwise. It struck me as a horrible irony, for the heir to a sweet empire to be unable to eat. That must be the cause of this rupture: she did not want to eat, and Marija had insisted on her presence so she could ensure she did.

Not a stranglehold – an embrace.

The First Lady turned to us. 'The West criticises us for our policies, yet what is capitalism but a blood hunt? Whereas my friend knows what it is to be nurtured at the breast of the state.'

Sorin smiled back, and I was rather repelled by this puppetry. He explained that he was a son of the Movement.

'What movement?' Jude asked.

'The Movement for a Million Children, of course.'

'You were all my children,' Marija said, and my stomach gave a little flip.

'I was the ten thousandth child,' Sorin said. 'That's how we met.' He turned to Marija. 'Without you, I would not exist.'

Marija laid an affectionate hand upon his cheek, and for a moment they really did look like mother and son. That is, until I glimpsed something behind his eyes, pinned, wriggling. It disturbed me, but the next moment it was gone, leaving me unsure if it had been there at all.

Without you, I would not exist. Was that blessing, or blame? Not all mothers are good, after all, and within his brightness, a brittleness lurked. It reminded me of a university friend whose father had walked out. Her cheeriness was relentless, her bedroom plastered with inspirational quotes, the mirror with smiley faces.

'I held him at a week old,' Marija said. 'Sorin was the first major milestone of the Movement's success. He was a sensation.'

'The Doamna was kind enough to take an interest in my

169

education. It was she who encouraged me to go to art school.'

'And I was right, was I not?'

'Doamna, you have never been wrong.'

She laughed. 'Sorin likes to tease me. He does this with everyone. When he was young, I took him to Buckingham Palace. He was the same even then. There was another time with Kissinger – Henry insisted on personally escorting me around the White House garden, he wanted my tips on orchids—'

'You met the Queen? I didn't know that,' Pavel interrupted. His hair was unusually dishevelled, as if fingers had repeatedly run through it. What had happened in their meeting?

Marija gave him a scornful look. 'Pavel, you are, as they say, like the bird with the head in the sand.'

'The ostrich,' I said quickly as the plates were removed and dessert, tea and coffee brought in. Pavel flushed, but I hardly had time to feel guilty, because finally, finally she looked at me, a glance like the sweet lash of a whip, landing and withdrawing as soon as it came.

'Precisely. Your Elizabeth and I got along famously. She invited me onto the royal yacht.' Her eyes sparkled. 'I was her favourite, you know. Beyond even Tito.'

'All that man cared about was clothes. You know he used to want to be a waiter, just so he could wear the suit?'

'Come, Sorin. There is nothing wrong with fashion.' She caressed the fur stole at her throat. The glassy eyes seemed to sparkle. 'These prosecutors are rummaging in my closets, hoping to find skeletons. But all they will find are my beautiful clothes.'

Pavel, who had raised the lid of the sugar bowl and was staring minutely at its contents, laughed suddenly. The laugh was shut off as soon as it began, but not quickly enough to miss its trace of hysteria.

If the artist was surprised by this, or by Marija's extraordinary statement, he showed no sign of it. 'Doamna, you have always walked in beauty.'

'Ah, I insist upon it. My clothes, my jewellery, they are my amulets. My protection.'

Protection. Survival. She spoke the language of the hunted, yet who was her hunter? It was as hard to believe in her fear as in a tiger's. Yet when I looked again at the dead animal at her throat, I did see a strange kind of armour.

'I demand beauty for my people also. Perhaps my friends should see. What do you think, Sorin? A trip to the gallery?' They locked eyes and something passed between them. 'That was one of mine, you know,' she said to the room in general. 'Just beside the National Records Office. Tomorrow?'

Her gaze fell meaningfully on me: I hesitated, then gave the slightest of nods towards Mr Gabor, who was mournfully watching his saucer and did not notice. This was it. Tomorrow I would investigate. Tomorrow I would look up the files of my family.

'Perfect,' Sorin said. 'I hear you are all working much too hard.'

'No such thing,' Pavel grunted. He replaced the sugar-bowl lid at last – a faint *chink* – but his eyes did not leave it.

'Come, Cristian, it will do you good.' Marija lifted her chin so the chandelier illuminated her features, chasing the shadows away. 'You were not a child of the Movement . . .'

'No, Doamna. I am far too old.' And he looked it. He and Marija were virtually the same age, yet while the years had only heightened her beauty, sculpting the fat around the cheekbones and eye sockets, bringing her into sharper definition, he was sagging around the neck and jowls, blurring round the edges. He had aged in the last few weeks; the hand on the table trembled slightly.

'Age brings wisdom,' she said.

'No. Age brings pain. We are not what we used to be. We cannot do the same things and expect the same results. Sooner or later, something breaks.'

An expression flitted across her face, the same expression as when an owner goes to pat a long-faithful dog and is suddenly unsure it will not bite.

'Well,' Sorin said lightly. 'Let us hope it is not this delightful tea service.' He picked up his cup. 'Wedgwood?'

But she was not listening. She was watching Pavel minutely.

'I have made a decision,' she said. At her tone, my breath caught.

'I shall retract the statement I made to *Vogue*.'

Pavel looked up sharply. 'Retract?'

'Yes, Cristian. Rescind. Reverse. Or' – she waved a careless hand – 'you may say I was misquoted. Taken out of context. Whatever it is people say when they bow to pressure.'

I watched my boss. I heard his thought – *What pressure?* – as clearly as if it had been my own, but then his features were washed with relief. Her gaze fluttered towards me, pregnant with meaning. It lasted barely a second, but it was enough. I held the glowing coal of our shared secret. Many years later, I still recall the warmth of it.

'And the trial,' she went on, as if nothing had happened.

'Y-yes?'

'We need a different strategy. I no longer wish you to focus on proving legitimacy. I want you to make me not innocent, but ignorant.'

We gazed at her in disbelief. I had thought retraction the greatest possible victory. I hadn't dared dream that she would rethink her strategy in consequence.

'I heard about Gheorghe Funar's plea. We need to win. It does not matter how. If this strategy is not working, we need another. I knew nothing of my husband's business matters, and I wish you to prove that to the prosecution.'

'Hot damn,' Jude murmured, while I fidgeted beside him in quiet exultation. After weeks of toiling at a plan we knew was unlikely to come off, we finally had an opening. By shackling herself to Popa, she had weighed herself down with his sins. But this – this meant we could uncouple her from that load, and with some gravity-defying legal tricks we just might have a chance of setting her free.

The rest of dinner was spent amid Pavel and Mr Gabor's polite murmurings, both trying to hide their elation. Afterwards I walked out to the hall alone, where the chandeliers glimmered darkly.

I unlocked the front door, stepped out into the cold. There were no stars, only a thick orange smear where the sky should be; the bird I had heard yesterday with the strange creaking cry was silent.

I gazed up at the door's exterior. Despite the intruder's rough treatment, the handle was miraculously intact. The wood, however, looked different. I squinted in the gloom, and at what I saw, all triumph fled.

It was gouged with long scratches, carved deep into the paint, the wood beneath exposed like organs.

To eat. Or be eaten.

The air carried the after-reek of inhuman desperation, and something smooth and pale was lodged in the varnish. I extracted it, held it up, then dropped it in horror.

It was a woman's fingernail. A perfect oval, whole and neat, but for the bloodstains around its rim.

I went leadenly to bed, the carpet sucking greedily at my feet. Every time I thought I'd found something good here, evidence was sprung upon me to the contrary. I felt like Gretel, faithfully following the breadcrumbs, unaware that she'd never find her way home.

As I passed Marija's door, I heard something. Pavel's voice.

I had seen people press their ears to doors in films; never had I imagined doing so in real life. It felt foolishly over-blown, lending the scene an air of unreality. At first I thought I was mistaken, for the voice was wholly different to my boss's precise tones. The hysteria I'd heard at dinner had returned, along with something I'd never heard before: a Yanussian accent, low, slanting.

'Surely you must see,' he was saying.

'I don't *see* anything,' Marija said coldly. 'I see nothing. I owe you nothing.'

'That wasn't what you told me before I came.' He was almost whining now. 'Before I came, you said—'

'I know what I said.'

'This is not enough.'

'No. With men it never is. Cristian, darling, we mustn't have these upsets. It will bore me.'

'Marija . . . Doamna . . .'

'Release me.' Her tone was hard as bone.

'Forgive me. It has been so many years . . . Do you remember the day we went punting? You wanted to see a friend, so I took you all the way to Grantchester. Two miles. You wore a blue dress. A flower in your hair.'

'Ah! In the autumn? We ate apples from the trees?'

'No, Doamna. It was spring. There were daffodils.'

'In which case, I am thinking of your friend Sidney. I remember he took me once. Such fun! But spring? Daffodils?' A pause, as if for thought. 'No, I do not recall.'

Finally Pavel spoke again. 'I said I would try my hardest for you, Doamna, and I will. But you have me on a string and you have to give me something. A sign. Anything at all.' And then, barely audible: 'I cannot relive that summer. It is torture.'

'Torture? Oh darling. What on earth would you know about that?'

'I mean it, Marija. It won't be long before something breaks. Either the string, or me.'

A silence, then her reply came in a hiss. 'You would threaten me?'

'I . . . No, I . . . I didn't mean . . .'

She laughed, clear as ice. 'Get out.'

Pavel stumbled up; hearing him, I fled.

CHAPTER SIXTEEN

Pavel and Marija. Marija and Pavel. I turned it over and over in my head, tormenting myself. Did he love her? Did she love him? I could not believe the latter, and if the former were true, I feared for us all.

The London office of Harris Stroud Glyn technically closed at ten, but there was always someone working late. I knew because it was usually me. I put in a call to Risk & Compliance, and Jameson picked up on the third ring.

'Laura, if your team bug me about Marku bloody Manea one more time, I'm calling pest control.'

I made my voice as light as possible. 'It's not about Manea.'

'Or Cristescu?'

'Jameson, you wound me. Pavel just asked me for a copy of the details for the Popa case. Should be on the system.'

'I'll fax it to you.'

'Thanks. I need it asap.'

The phone clicked off. Eight minutes later, time that I spent pacing my small room, the pages arrived. I scanned them hastily, heart thumping: reputational issues, money laundering risks from fees, any possible conflicts of interest. It was the protocol for every case. Pavel had said he'd informed HSG about his connection with Marija. If so, it would be here.

I read the filing. I read it again, praying I was wrong.

'Jameson? Are you sure this is everything?'

'Of course it's everything.'

I gripped the phone. 'There's nothing missing? No extra page?'

'Lăzărescu, there isn't a Post-it in this building that I don't know about. If you're missing something, it's because it doesn't exist.'

'Right. Sorry. I just . . . Never mind.'

'I won't.' The line went dead. I sat on the bed and took several deep breaths. The argument with Andrei, the stranger's fingernail, it all seemed a mote in the eye of this latest development. Jameson was more basset hound than man, and he was right: if a document wasn't there, it didn't exist. If it didn't exist, then Pavel had lied. And if he had lied – my stomach flipped – it was a major transgression. No matter that it had been three decades since he'd known Marija. No matter that he hadn't seen her since. The Office for the Supervision of Solicitors hated anything that could affect a lawyer's advice. They banged on and on about the importance of being fair and open, at the threat of being struck off.

Once more I replayed the desperation in Pavel's voice, the Yanussian accent he must constantly strive to conceal. My throat constricted. Exactly how fair and open could he be while harbouring a decades-long infatuation? And that was aside from the internal problems created. No matter how dirty the client, when it came to processes, HSG prided itself on being cleaner than God. To be otherwise exposed it to significant risk, and most partners would rather risk their own children than the firm. That Pavel had not disclosed this was a serious matter, the disciplinary consequences

177

significant. In sum, it just wasn't worth the risk. Why, then, had he thought it was?

'New day, new strategy.' The man himself dumped some folders on the table. His suit was immaculate, his hair groomed and sleek. I tried to square this impeccable lawyer with last night's crawling creature. He did not look like a man who had risked everything, but I remembered that fingernail, pale and desperate in the moonlight. She could drive you to the extreme edge.

'So rather than proving Marija is innocent, now we have to prove she's stupid,' Jude drawled. 'Great.'

'Yes. It *is* great. This just got a thousand times easier and you know it.' Pavel caressed the folders. 'Given our school trip this afternoon, let's start with the art. What's wrong, Laura?'

I realised I was staring. I had almost forgotten our new instruction. It is one thing to prove someone is innocent. Ignorance is a whole different ball game. Pavel was right: it did make our work easier. But it also sent us back a few paces when we already had precious little time to spare. So far there had been many snakes and very few ladders.

'I was just wondering – is this the only strategy? Not that I don't think it's a good one,' I added hastily, seeing him begin to mantle like a ruffled goose, 'but I feel like there's more we could do. Something we're missing.'

'Such as?'

I was forced to concede I had nothing.

'We don't have time to waste on fancies. Let's get to it.'

'I'll take the Picasso,' Jude said quickly.

'I hoped you'd say that. I need you to track down the

178

auction receipt. There's a tranche in the evidence rooms from Christie's. Off you go.'

Jude's face fell as he realised his mistake.

'Before you do, listen, both of you. We have to win. We *have* to.' The tension in his voice was a steel rod. 'If we don't, she dies. It's as simple as that.'

Jude went out, banging the door unnecessarily behind him.

'Laura, I need you on diary duty.' He waved to a stack of Xeroxed papers. 'I want you to go through every single one of the committee minutes. Check if Marija is among the attendees – let's pray she isn't – and cross-check them with her official schedules. Wherever there's a hint of them discussing finances, I want to be able to place her a hundred miles away.'

I worked away, trying to distract myself from last night. As I did, I took some heart. She was not named as director of any companies, nor was she noted as present at many key meetings. Indeed, she was often far away, skiing in the Carpathians with the Minister of the Interior, or visiting Yves Saint Laurent at his villa in Marrakesh.

Jude reappeared. To my amusement, he was rumpled and dusty, with a large ink blot on his cheek. He hadn't found the Picasso receipt, but he had discovered that many of the other disputed paintings – including the Matisse, the Rothko, the Bonnard, and the three Monets – had been 'borrowed' from the Yanussian National Gallery by the Popas. Forty paintings in all, weighing in at over two hundred million dollars. Naturally, none were ever returned.

'We can check the gallery records today,' he said excitedly. 'Speak to the curator about the loan terms.'

Pavel frowned. 'Have you found the Picasso receipt?'

'Well, no, but—'

'In which case there is no "we". Laura and I will go.'

It looked like someone wasn't going to the ball. Cinders shot me a furious look. 'Pavel, *I'm* the art expert here. My aunt is an international curator. I've been to the Tate more times than Laura's had hot dinners. I interned at Sotheby's, for Pete's sake.'

'Thank you for your curriculum vitae, Jude,' Pavel said drily. 'Now unless you wish to find yourself disseminating it further, please return to the evidence rooms.'

Jude flounced off, just as a name in a diary entry caught my eye. *SLS*. I'd seen it somewhere before.

I grubbed up the charge sheet. There it was. I'd admired the acronym's symmetry before. An allegedly illicit payment of $200,000 had been made from the central bank to a company account of that name. Three days later, the money was withdrawn in full, from a local bank. The prosecutors said this was just another example of siphoning off state funds, but it struck me as unusually straightforward. Other transactions were far more complex, and the withdrawals generally made in more exotic locations than Sibia, a ratty little town in the east. I brought it to Pavel's attention.

'Sounds like another dodgy tax foundation.'

'I don't think so. Its headquarters are in Sibia. She travelled there on the same day the money was withdrawn.'

'Oh dear. So they can prove the link.'

'Yes, but isn't that a little atypical, to be so obvious? We have to ask her what SLS is. Maybe it's not what we think.'

Something glimmered in his eyes. Embarrassment? Fear? He must be thinking of last night's encounter. Little did he know that I was too.

'I could go,' I said airily. It was cruel, but it jolted him into action.

'No. No. I'll do it.'

He went off clutching the files like a supplicant, and returned less than ten minutes later.

'SLS stands for Wood-Carving Society in Yanussian.'

I frowned. 'And it's an actual wood-carving society? Not a front?'

'Apparently so. It's a local community initiative giving employment to women and children. Spoons. Sculptures. The workshop is in a sort of preserved village for Western tourists.'

'Sounds too good to be true.'

'She says that they were running low on funds, so she organised a grant. Then she paid a personal visit and gave them the money in cash.'

'All at once? Why?'

'Says they got a discount on their raw materials if they bought in bulk, and she wanted the money to go as far as possible.'

We looked at one another, each hunting for credulity in the other.

'Well,' I said at last. 'This is very good news.' If the prosecution were wrong about this, it could shed useful doubt on the rest.

Pavel summoned Mr Gabor and explained the situation. The little man's eyes gleamed. We could argue that not only was Marija not using the money for personal gain, she was also busy doing good. Even more damningly, it showed the prosecution had not done its research.

Shortly before eleven, we were interrupted by Sorin. The artist shepherded us away from our desks, ignoring Pavel's half-hearted protests. A staff member was sweeping the stairs, so I was forced to go round the back way to fetch my coat. I'd carefully avoided the route since that time with Apostol. Now I approached the corridor's end with mounting apprehension, hearing every step, feeling the house's eyes on my back. The grey door was still there, quiet, innocuous, doing nothing at all.

I should try again, I knew I should. I had promised Andrei. I hesitated, my breath coming quick and shallow, suddenly cold all over. The metal shone so brightly I could see a figure in it, vague and smeared.

I could hear Jude and Pavel's voices, faintly, a long way off. If I didn't rejoin them soon, they would come looking. I would do it now, quickly, before I could talk myself out of it.

I grasped the handle and gasped: it was freezing, far colder than the surrounding room, as cold as the mirror on my first night. I pushed it down, pulled – and nothing. It was locked.

I moved off immediately, fetching my coat and immediately putting it on, seeking to warm myself up. I had tried. And that was that.

'Look at you – three little vampires.' Sorin mocked us gently as we stepped blinking over the threshold. 'Let's get you out in the sun.'

He grinned, and despite the chill still hugging my torso, I could not help but respond to his lightness. He was a pond skater, dashing across the surface, weightless, never looking down, never stopping lest he sink. Some people travel lighter through this life than others, and I was blind enough to think he was one.

It was now a month since we'd moved in, and I hadn't once left the grounds. I had, in fact, barely left the house. Oh, at the beginning I had chafed against my perceived incarceration, but over time the trapped sensation had dwindled. What was there outside for me anyway? I had no desire for another encounter with the guards, or Apostol. The mansion was Marija's entire world – why not mine? At dinner I had glimpsed the soles of her shoes: pure, unstained white. Was she even allowed outside? I didn't know.

We were no longer allowed to meet the car at the gates, so we waited outside the house. As the trial neared, security had been stepped up, and while it had not stopped last night's intruder, it was an uncomfortable reminder of the tightness of our time frame. It was November already: we had barely five months left and so very much to do. Guards now permanently patrolled the street and garden, eyes flicking from left to right, cigarette butts littering the paths. Their blankness had swelled with their numbers: they looked like the sort who would shoot a man for something to do.

'At last,' Pavel muttered as a smart Mercedes pulled up. He went to open the door at the same time I did. A leather bag was slung over his shoulder, and as we leaned together, I heard a faint *chink*: he leapt away as if he had been scalded. The sound reminded me of something, but I could not identify what.

'Not ours,' Sorin chided. 'Safety first, Mr Pavel. You cannot simply get into any car you please.'

The door opened of its own accord. A familiar face looked up and an American accent drawled, 'Well, would you credit it?'

Patrick Hanagan, the banker we'd met on our first evening. He got out. 'Mr Pavel. How are you? And Laura.' His blue eyes, like extracts of sky, met mine. To my discomfort I felt my face grow hot.

'This is Radutu Gabor. And this is Sorin, a noted artist,' I said to deflect his attention, though not before I sensed his amusement.

'What are you doing here?' Pavel asked.

'I have a meeting.'

My boss bristled. Professional caution, or jealousy? 'With whom?'

'I'm not here for your client. Keep your panties on.' I clamped my mouth shut at his turn of phrase. 'I'm here for her sister, Ecaterina.'

To my surprise, he pronounced her name with a passable Yanussian accent. She still had not arranged the factory tour. I would have to remind her.

'What business do you have with her?'

Patrick gave an airy wave. 'She's a long-time First Loyalty client. I said I'd look in. What are *you* doing here?'

Jude had materialised. 'We live here.'

Once again his gaze turned to me. 'Do you indeed?'

He went inside as our own car arrived, crackling over the cobbles.

'Close your mouth, Jude,' Pavel said irritably. 'Why aren't you in the evidence rooms?'

Jude sighed. 'I just had to come out and see. There is something about rich Americans. *Isn't* there, Laura?' he said slyly.

'Don't you have a receipt to snuffle out?' I snapped back.

I settled myself in the back beside Pavel, who placed his bag on his lap with extreme care.

'What's that for?'

'For any documents we find.' His tone was curt.

'We're going to need a bigger bag,' I joked to alleviate the sudden tension. Silence.

As we passed down the drive and out the gates – I felt a thrill crossing the threshold – I looked back. Patrick was gone but yet another car had drawn up. A small woman stepped out, spoke into the intercom and was immediately buzzed inside.

'Who was that?' I asked Sorin, who did not bother turning around.

'The hairdresser.'

'She's allowed to visit?'

184

He tossed his head. 'The Doamna made it a condition of her house arrest. She'd rather be seen dead than without a blow-dry.'

I thought of that coiffed hair, the just-so make-up, the creamy skin that must need God knew how many expensive oils to maintain. She talked of living in beauty, in an encasement of it, like a larva. Rather than a reproof against inner turmoil, were these perfections in fact symptomatic of it? Inserting hairpins with a barely suppressed violence, not so much keeping up appearances as shoring them up at any cost? She literally made herself up daily, and I wondered when, if ever, the cracks would begin to show. Had she ever considered escape? I doubted it. It was not her style; a spider does not leave its web. Instead we were being sent out, little emissaries questing on her behalf. I had my orders. She had provided the set-up. Now I had to execute.

The Yanussian National Gallery proved to be an enormous faux-classical confection, amidst a square crammed with cars parked anyhow and thousands of dirty pigeons with oil-slick necks. One pecked at my boot and I jumped away. The rest of the square was girded by dull official buildings and ramparts of filthy snow, guarding something scarcely worth keeping. A pinched-looking woman walked by, a live goose in her arms. It was squawking and thrashing, white feathers drifting to the ground to mingle with the grey. At the square's centre was an empty plinth, defaced with graffiti.

'That's the Ministry of Agriculture and Fisheries. The Ministry of Justice. Over there, the Central Bank.' Sorin pointed to each. 'And that short one is the National Records Office.' I dug my nails in at its nearness. 'The Strajă's files are there – what they didn't manage to burn, anyway. You go in and show ID for yourself or whoever you're looking up. National identity card is fine.' His eyes flicked to me.

An ID card. Shit. Yanussians always carried them. The question was, where was Mr Gabor's, and more importantly, could I steal it? Marija had not forewarned me, and I realised this was deliberate. As she had said, this was a test.

'There you can find out who was spying on you. Your horrible children, or your horrible husband. A fun day out for all the family.'

'Have you been?'

'I don't have any children, or any family. Lucky me.'

'And the plinth?'

'Used to hold a statue of Popa. Naturally it was torn down.'

There must be many similar plinths across the city, now supporting nothing but air. The old joke had been that his statues were Yanussia's most prolific crop.

But Pavel was not listening, instead staring over my shoulder. Even before I turned, my dread uncurling, I knew what it was.

'Ah. The old communist headquarters.'

Counter-intuitively, it had been built in firm fascist style, all perfect limestone rectangles and thin, flat columns. Most striking were the doors: twin iron behemoths, recognisable from a thousand news segments. Now they were closed, but in the TV reel spooling through all our minds, they yawned horribly wide.

'This was where Dinu hid on that last day.'

He had died, right there, between those immutable doors. I shuddered and for the millionth time asked myself why he'd opened them. He must have heard the baying on the other side. He could not have believed they would show mercy, so why – *why* – had he done it?

'Funny to see it,' Pavel said.

'Oh yes. Funny.' Sorin took a gulp from a hip flask and

I caught the faint whiff of plums. Țuică: Yanussian brandy. 'They're putting up a plaque.'

The gallery interior was large and marbled, and seeing Sorin the ticket woman waved us through with an anxious smile. At first glance it looked like any London gallery: only on closer inspection did the verisimilitude rupture. A tatty broom propped against one wall; in the corners, exposed wires tangling like snakes.

The cloakroom attendant was so thin I worried the weight of our belongings would snap her in two. The hangers she guarded were empty. I wasn't sure whether the people of Poartă had better things to do, or if the place had been cleared out for our visit. Marija had been accustomed to private sessions at the famous department stores, once spending two million dollars in a single Harrods blowout. They had given her a discount. The press, of course, had loved it. Perhaps she wanted the same for us. Or perhaps she wanted to keep us away from any real people.

My mind turned to theft. Undoubtedly this was the best place to do it, and I was a good finger-smith. Why? Let me say only that in my first year at HSG I worked on the case of a little old lady with a fondness for Chanel twinsets, pince-nez, and kleptomania. Since much of my work was really babysitting her to guard against mischief, we spent a lot of time together, and I learned a thing or two.

Therefore, as Mr Gabor handed over his coat and briefcase, I turned and accidentally walked into him.

'Sorry.'

Nothing in his trouser pockets, and his jacket was pocket-free. I was in luck.

Pavel insisted on keeping his own bag at his side, 'for

the documents'. Sorin summoned the director, a nervous-looking woman with greying hair who wrung her hands at his request.

'Only two at a time to see the records,' Sorin said at last. 'She insists.'

'Radutu and I will do it,' Pavel said. His eyes flicked to the clock, as if he had somewhere else to be. 'Laura, just amuse yourself. Meet back here in an hour.'

I wandered off, but it wasn't until halfway down the first gallery that I noticed the pictures. It happens often: thoughts and memories crowd my eyes, and when the world comes back into focus, I have no idea what I was doing in the interim. I check for anyone looking at me askance, but there never is, and I don't know whether to be relieved or concerned that I am such an effective automaton.

I paused in front of a still life: a dead hare, draped for some reason across some lemons. Their waxy skin had a dull gleam mirrored uncomfortably by the creature's eye, reminiscent of Marija's fox. In the next painting flowers huddled in a vase; beside them, another lemon. Both images were rendered with a faithfulness that was exceedingly uninteresting. The cards bore no names, just dates and the medium. I tried to think of any famous Yanussian painters but drew a blank.

The next room was more modern. An oil painting showed round-faced peasants cavorting by a gingerbread-esque house, done in vibrant and unrealistic blues, purples and pinks. I recognised its style and that of its successors. Naive art, everything bright, bouncy and above all harmless. I wanted to scratch at it to see what lay beneath.

The final piece was different. The stodgy houses were still there, but now they were blanketed with blue-edged snow, the viewer almost feeling the chill. The sky was as near black as it was possible to be; the hills crouched in on themselves, concave with shadow. For some reason I thought of my mother, and Mr Gabor.

Naive. I had heard the word in another context – the term for an animal that does not recognise its predators. I looked at the date: 1989. I remembered those huge iron doors and shivered.

'Hideous, aren't they?' Sorin was leaning against the entrance, watching me. 'Marija's pets. She would insist on keeping them.'

A sudden panic gripped me. 'Has Pavel finished already?'

'No. Still rummaging through old loans. As if who owns what matters in a place like this.' He picked something invisible off his lapel. 'There is a difference between what you own and what you have. Exploit that, and you'll always be rich.'

I frowned, trying to square the loyal puppet and the pinned, wriggling thing. So much of my time here was spent trying to see two or more things at once, like those Magic Eye pictures where a pattern masks another quite different image. Look through the orderly squares and see the crocodile, jaws open, weeping with laughter.

'None of yours, then.'

'No, thank goodness. I'm a sculptor. Three dimensions. Makes for better lies.'

'That's what you think these are?'

'What else? The government owned the publishing houses and the galleries. If you bought a typewriter you had to register it with the police. Truth to lies, lies to truth. Every good dictator's playbook.' I looked back at the painting, at its heavy, hungry night, as he said, 'Power. The oldest story of all.'

'What was it like? What was *he* like?'

'What does it matter? He's gone.'

I gestured at the paintings. 'Is he?'

189

His smile didn't reach his eyes. 'You're smart, I see. Be careful.' A sigh. 'He wasn't anything, Dinu. He wasn't polite. He wasn't nice. He wasn't educated, or bright, or charming. But he knew what he wanted, and he would do anything – *anything* – to get it. That was his only talent. I wonder if there is any other worth having. He liked getting one over on people. He liked to win, but he loved to see others lose. He didn't like religion – God was the one person he couldn't get a hold on. That's why he made informants of the priests.'

He came closer, looking not at me but at the deep blue night.

'I saw it when I accompanied them both on a deer hunt with Ceauşescu. Dinu was annoyed, kept complaining how Nicolae hadn't invited them for a bear hunt. He liked nothing more than standing by a lake at sundown, watching half a dead horse being placed where the creatures went for water. But Nicolae said he was saving them for Tito.

'We rode out, the four of us and their aides. That fat peasant Elena stayed at home. Dinu bagged three or four animals, Nicolae six. That Romanian idiot wanted to outdo Dinu. As a guest, it's good manners only to kill a few and leave the rest for the host and breeding. Dinu hated losing at anything and Nicolae was taunting him.

'We set out for home, but Dinu told us to wait. He had a good voice – you did what it said automatically. We all turned to look. The sky was red, I remember, and beneath us a herd of wild deer had come to the lake. Twenty or more.

'Dinu's gun rang out: a single deer fell. I watched Nicolae the whole time – I remember he gave a polite smile of approval. The gun fired again, and his smile wavered. Then again, and again, and again. Nicolae stepped forward to stop Dinu but thought better of it, instead gazing like a slack-jawed fool as the shots went on for minutes.' He took a gulp from his flask. 'When the smoke cleared, the entire herd lay slaughtered, the blood running from their bodies and mingling with the red of the lake. Nicolae ended his shooting season there and then.'

I studied his face. The lightness had gone, replaced by emptiness. Or were they two sides of the same, tarnished coin?

'What did Marija do?'

A queer expression. 'Nothing. She just watched.'

Strange. I could imagine the scene, the blood-red sky, the massacre. But the First Lady, stood to one side like a spare limb – I could not picture that at all.

'What were they like together?'

'Oh, she could control him. But it is like having a mad dog on a leash. Yank it back and it might turn on you.'

'Did they love each other?'

'Could they have built all this if they didn't? We assume that love contains an essential goodness, but look at these men who crush the world. Hitler and Eva. Mussolini and Claretta.'

Silence, dust motes drifting in the dull winter light.

'That huge statue of the woman. It's yours, isn't it?'

'The Gallows Hill monstrosity. Yes, it's mine.'

'That's what it's called?'

'Ah, no. That was the name of the hill. The nineteenth century was an innocent sort of time. They liked to kill people in front of everyone. Marija would have been hanged up there.' I was surprised by the strength of my reaction, and tried not to show it. His eyes flitted to me. 'But the regime brought all that stuff underground, renamed it Justice Hill. Such is progress.'

'Surely people see through it.'

'These days people see what they are told to see. You have your friend Marija to thank for that.'

'I think you mean *your* friend Marija.'

He gave me a look I could not decipher. 'Of course.'

'You know why I'm here today, don't you?'

His eyes widened in alarm, but he said nothing, only pressed his finger to his lips so hard they turned white. 'Haven't you worked out what my statue is yet?' he said quickly, changing the subject. 'It's blind old Lady Justice. The regime commissioned it.'

'So how come—'

'How come it's still going ahead?' He laughed. 'I thought you were smart. Marija always gets what she wants. Her method is simple yet ingenious: she makes you want it too.' He yawned; the lightness flitted back, like a shutter reopened. 'It is all very boring. Very *serious*. Aren't you tired of being serious? Even under the Popas we had jokes. What is the difference between painters of the naturalist, impressionist and socialist realist schools?' He paused. 'The naturalists paint as they see, the impressionists as they feel, the socialist realists as they are told.'

'Ha.'

A wry smile. 'No, it is not funny, but that was not the point. The opportunity for laughter. That was the point.'

'Was there so little to laugh at?'

The smile faded. 'Oh, there's always plenty to laugh at. It just depends on your point of view.'

His tone was chilling. He went to leave, then turned back and said, 'Make sure you see the next room. Camelia loved it.'

'Camelia?'

'Ecaterina's secretary.'

'I thought she worked for Marija.'

An odd smile. 'Like I say, it all depends on your point of view.'

After he left, I checked my watch. Ten minutes before

Pavel and Mr Gabor returned. Quickly I moved on to the final chamber, where hung a single huge painting of a foppish young couple in a wood. Nineteenth century. The man was pushing his companion on a swing and the painter had shown her at the apex, feet kicking inelegantly from her full red skirt, a secret that should not have been shared, her pink mouth open. At first it appeared she was laughing, but then I saw the man's expression and realised she was screaming.

Out in the lobby, I looked around. No one there. I hurried across to the cloakroom, went to lift the little latch on the door – and jumped back as the stick-thin attendant appeared.

'The director wants to see you,' I said.

'I cannot leave these.'

'It's fine, I can look after our things. No problem.' I gave her my best smile.

She considered me, then shrugged. I could see her thoughts. Who cares? Life: just people telling you what to do, then you die.

She went off and I clenched my fist in victory. Seven minutes, assuming they weren't early. Plenty of time. Quickly I let myself into the cloakroom to where our coats hung neatly, Mr Gabor's in the middle. I checked the pockets. Nothing.

Somewhere above, a door opened and I heard Pavel's voice. They were early! I frisked the coat again. Nothing beyond fluff and a mint humbug. In the briefcase? But that was not practical if he was stopped . . . What about *inside* the coat? I tore it open. There! Two pockets, tightly zipped. Now I heard footsteps descending the stairs. The first pocket yielded nothing. The second contained a wallet. I flipped it open, rummaging through the small wad of currency. There it was: the ID card, and also a photograph of a woman looking over her shoulder, smiling. I stuffed the photo back, restored the wallet and shoved the card into my pocket just as the company rounded the corner.

'Laura. Let's go.' Pavel's eyes flicked towards the clock again before he spotted me in the cloakroom and frowned. 'New career?'

'The attendant went off, so I was getting our things.'

He and Mr Gabor seemed to accept this, but the museum director was frowning, wondering where her staff member had gone. Quickly I whisked the coats off their hangers. Pavel was watching the clock again.

We got in the car without incident, but I did not relax. As we bounced across the cobbles, I noticed how Sorin's seat did not indent around him, as if he weighed nothing at all.

After five minutes, heart in my throat, I said, 'Wait.' My voice reverberated oddly: Pavel had spoken at the exact same time.

'I've left my scarf,' I said.

'I have to stop in on a friend.'

We looked at one another.

'Why did you not say before?' Sorin was irritable. 'I told Marija we would be back.'

'You go ahead. I can find my own way.'

'Same.' I tried not to speak too quickly.

He gave us both a long look. 'Do not take a taxi to the mansion by yourselves. It is not safe. Here, ask for this place. You will fetch up close to it.' He scribbled an address on a piece of paper.

I thanked him and said, 'Pavel, why not leave your bag with Sorin?'

Pavel stared down at the item in question. I noticed how tightly he was gripping it.

'Take these,' he said at last, and withdrew a bunch of papers, practically shoving them into the sculptor's hands. Once again I heard that faint, mysterious *chink*.

The car pulled away; we regarded one another. I couldn't help it: I looked away first, the distraction momentarily lifting from his features.

'Hope you find your scarf.' And then, disconcertingly: 'Be careful, Laura.'

I could not make him out any more. These days he walked with his head in the clouds, but at other times there seemed nothing but clear sky and he saw for miles.

He strolled off with a fresh casualness, heading north while I retraced my way south, back towards the National Records Office and through a food market. It was busy, crammed with arguing women with scarved heads and bagged eyes, black-haired traders with stalls and black-haired traders with no stalls, only blankets on the ground, wares nestling amid rotting vegetable matter and half-melted snow. I pushed through, trying to be quick while avoiding the pallid apples, limp carrots, skinny courgettes. To my Westernised gaze, they seemed pitifully underfed. My father was always unable to comprehend the sheer mass of available food in England, where every vegetable seemed pumped full of rainbows. We eastern Europeans had thought ourselves at the vanguard of industrialisation, measuring our progress by the smoke clouds belching from our factories, by the breathless reports of exceeded quotas. Yet it transpired the real revolution had been happening elsewhere. In the drizzling quiet of English fields there were no quotas. They simply had enough. Communism obsesses over quantity; capitalism does not need to.

I passed a shop, a proper one. In its filthy windows, cans of preserved fruit and milk canisters had been arranged at persuasive intervals, daring the viewer to point out the shelves were virtually empty. The old Yanussian joke: 'If only I had a little more to eat, it would be like wartime.' Here I understood why Sorin sought out laughter, why my parents' fridge was always crammed with food.

It was slow progress and I keenly felt the need for haste. I would arouse suspicion if gone too long, and questions were the last thing I wanted. I tried to hurry through, but the street narrowed and the air developed a meaty tang, the wares shifting colour to flesh-pink and gristle-white. Shelves of tear-shaped ears, trays of trotters, and a whole pig's head straight out of a Golding nightmare, its eyes a nacreous blue. I could not bring myself to come any closer to push by. At least the cold was keeping it all refrigerated.

I was passing a trio of dangling hams when to my shock, through the fleshy hangings, I saw Pavel.

He must have doubled back after we parted, and his initial ambling walk had changed. No longer did he look like he was heading for a social visit; now he hurried along, head sunk into his collar, bag cradled in his arms like a child. Or maybe a delivery boy.

My palms tingled. It was only because the market had impeded me that I had seen him at all. Automatically I followed, tracking him through the stalls, shutters of meat opening and closing between us. Where was he going? This was the very centre of town and the buildings were all offices or government departments, plus the occasional ancient church that had escaped Popa's clearances. Not a house call, then. Nor were there any business meetings scheduled for this afternoon. Had Marija given him a secret task also? The notion pricked me, until I recalled the conversation I had overheard, the desperation in his voice. They were not the tones of a man inside the castle of her confidence. Rather he was scratching at the door, begging to be let in.

Sooner or later, something will break. Something, or someone? Either way, I could no longer rely on his judgement.

We crossed the river, the murky water slow and black. It moved like it had a grudge, like everything round here, as if daily life was only passing time before vengeance could be taken. I realised we were heading back towards the square, and began to panic that we had the same destination. I felt horribly exposed, even though he looked neither left nor right, walking with a knife-blade of purpose at his back.

The street suddenly yawned around us, the skyline cut apart. I was right: we were back in the square. If he saw me now, I could always say I was fetching the scarf. Despite this, I tried even harder not to be seen, though not via the ridiculous ducking and weaving that you see in movies. The way to be invisible, of course, is to do nothing of interest at all. I walked on, glancing through my lashes. Perfect – at least until I ran into someone. Incredibly it was the goose woman from that morning, or perhaps the same woman and a different goose, or the same goose but a different woman. Either way, I was immediately embroiled in a furious one-sided argument, goose and woman hissing with equal vigour. I stepped back, apologising, all the while desperately looking for Pavel. The woman, or perhaps the goose – I was starting to have trouble telling them apart – regarded me with anserine cunning and thrust out a hand, I suppose for money, but I had been existing in the cashless, world-less society of the Iubită mansion for so long that I only stared at the hand stupidly until, with a huff of feathers, the two of them flounced by.

Where was Pavel? I cursed, scanning the square. I couldn't lose him now. The gallery? But we had just come from there, and he had not flinched when I said I was returning. The massive doors of the former communist headquarters were closed and the Central Bank seemed unlikely, the Ministry of Agriculture and Fisheries more so.

My eye fell on the fourth and final side. *Gotcha.* A whisk of Jermyn Street tailoring. Of course, it was madness to follow him in. I could go no further.

But he had just walked into the Justice building. And that meant I had a pretty good idea of who this 'friend' might be.

The question was, what was Pavel doing – or more worryingly, delivering?

No time to fret now. I withdrew the scarf from my pocket, turned on my heel and headed towards the long, blank brow of the National Records Office.

CHAPTER SEVENTEEN

The NRO interior had the size and feel of an aircraft hangar, the ragged carpet rapidly petering out, surrendering to bare concrete. Behind the front desk, huge metal shelves receded into shadows the thin strip-lights could not penetrate, dwarfing the clerks scurrying around their base. I shivered: it felt like nothing good could spring from here, that even if I found something on my past, it would be poisonous, corruptive. Here were a million files, stretching to some ten miles, a snaking labyrinth of paranoia and dread. The Roman Empire had never really consolidated its grip on this country, yet the Strajă had achieved a stranglehold with nothing more than some cunningly vague laws and the useful belief that everyone was guilty of *something*. Here were illicit copies of house keys, recordings from microphones hidden in kitchen cabinets, lists of borrowed library books. They'd domesticated human rights abuse, and these everyday viola-tions were somehow just as invasive as far worse crimes. Unlike the protesters who'd killed Popa, the Strajă hadn't bothered battering down the front door: they'd sneaked in the side entrance, crept through the living room window, insinuated themselves under the doormat.

Now I was here, on behalf of the woman whose husband had controlled it all. How much had she known? How tainted was she, and therefore how tainted was I by association?

No time to think about it now. (Nor did I want to.) A passing clerk had just shot me a suspicious glance and I could not afford to look out of place. I had Mr Gabor's stolen ID in my pocket and a job to do.

With deep trepidation, I approached the desk. A poster informed me that illicit requests were subject to prosecution. Great. If I was caught misappropriating public records, our defence could fall apart, not to mention that I would be fired, or worse. I'd been so fixated on finding out about my parents that only now did I appreciate the sheer appalling risk of the operation.

'ID,' the unsmiling official said. I handed my passport over. He photocopied it with an unnecessary amount of ceremony and my heart sank further. A box-ticker. The last thing I needed.

I filled in the form, trying to make my handwriting usefully illegible. He inspected it, sniffed, jabbed a finger.

'Occupation?'

'Lawyer.' There was no point lying. He glared as if I had chosen my profession to spite him, though I think if I'd put 'marine biologist' or 'Morris dancer' it would have been the same. He wrote my name on a card (I knew already that his handwriting would be neat as type, and just as featureless), and slipped it into a plastic square on a string.

'Wear this at all times. Files are to be read in the reading room. You are not allowed to take anything out of the building. The removal of items is a prosecutable offence.'

I did not doubt that. A small woman at the exit barriers was being searched so thoroughly that a filched Post-it would have struggled to make it through. I took the lanyard; then, keeping my face impassive, withdrew Mr Gabor's identity card. This was it: the moment I would succeed or fail.

He looked at me as if I had deposited a turd on his desk. Not encouraging.

'What is this?'

'My employer. I'm not here for myself, I'm here for him.'

'You are only allowed to see your own file.'

'He wants some details and is too busy to come down.'

He was already shaking his head mournfully, but I saw the sadistic little gleam in his eyes. The kind of man who, if you saved him from falling off a cliff, would sue you for treading on his toe.

'No.'

'But—'

'*No.*'

'I'd like to speak to the manager.'

He drew himself up to his full, insignificant height and I realised my mistake. 'Domnişoară, I *am* the manager.' He jabbed a finger at the warning on the poster. 'Your file and immediate family members only. That is the rule. Find your reference card and give it to the clerk. *L* is that way. Good day.'

The blow was crushing. I had entered into a bargain with Marija: I had to see it through, or I would be out of the country, off the case, or worse. Manea and Cristescu had failed her, and look what had happened to them.

In a daze I came to the file index, no more than a series of flimsy handwritten Rolodex cards in alphabetical order, giving a location number by surname and forename. I shook myself into sensibility. I would address my own family first – that, I reminded myself, was my main purpose. Marija's mission was secondary.

Why did I not feel that way?

I began flicking through. The answer I had so long sought

could be under this very roof, the thing that had changed my mother so utterly. Perhaps she had been arrested, even tortured. It would account for her alteration, if not for her attitude towards me. Hope, dread, anxiety, guilt, each flicked through me in time with the Rolodex's pages, the latter most of all. I hadn't minded attempting to claim someone else's file, but my own family's? When something has been so long denied, it is hard to feel you have any right to it.

There they were. Gabriela Lăzărescu, and, a few cards on, Ion Lăzărescu. I picked them up gently, as if they might tear apart at my touch. Maybe here at last was a portal to the past, to the real reason my family had broken.

Something tugged at my attention. I looked back at the Rolodex, moved aside the card of Lăzărescu, Kristof . . .

Lăzărescu, Laura.

CHAPTER EIGHTEEN

I don't know how long I stood there, knees slightly buckled against the wooden cabinet. It was here. *I* was here. I had never dreamed that someone would create a file on my seven-year-old self. Who had believed a child still in need of a bedtime story was a threat? Had they planned to recruit me, waiting until I reached the ripe old age of eight or nine? Or had we already fled, and they were compiling this information so that one day they might have their revenge? I saw that ballerina turning on its screw and asked myself: had Marija known?

A sharp voice unfroze me. The manager was happily berating an old man on an obscure subsection of rules and regulations. I was not here for myself, I remembered. With the manager distracted, I seized my opportunity, scurrying through the ranks of Rolodexes until I found *G*.

Members of the public were not allowed into the stacks. Instead you took your form and index card to the gloomy reading room, where scattered shadows bent over the long tables. A severe-looking woman checked my form, then another clerk, a man with an unusually pink complexion, took my three *L* cards and dived with them into the shelves. I sat down to wait, keeping my thieved index card hidden.

How was I going to get at Mr Gabor's file? Marija had not given me an easy ride: on the walls were more signs warning of prosecution. I suppose they did it to ensure that neighbour did not spy on neighbour. They must have had enough of that already.

The clerk was gone so long, I began to worry he'd got lost, swept away by the currents of those eddying secrets. The Strajă claimed that 96 per cent of informers had been recruited willingly, but the longer I sat there, the more I felt the assertion's grim hilarity.

But none of it mattered, because soon I would have my mother's file, and my father's, and I would know what had become of us. A fever came over me as I picked away at the chair's tatty leather, to the chagrin of the elderly woman four seats along. I thought with a pang of Andrei's visit here the year before, and was disgusted at myself for having been jealous of him. I would not let the grey door divide us. I would fix us, just as I would fix my mother and me, for unlike Mrs Ciocan, she was still alive. I was not too late. Whatever happened, I was not too late.

The clerk reappeared and went to the reading room woman, who consulted the card and the form again. Both were frowning deeply. I stood up, but he shot me a warning glance and I sat back down, itching to know what was going on.

Eventually he came over and I saw he carried just one file. But which one?

'Laura Lăzărescu?'

I nodded, not trusting myself to speak.

He placed the file before me. It was a skinny brown snake of a thing, disappointingly thin.

I turned it over. It bore my name.

I licked my lips. 'The . . . the others?'

The colour in his cheeks intensified. 'They are not there.'

'How can they not be there?'

He shook his head miserably. 'I do not know, Domnişoară. I checked with our records. No one has come to *L* in the last week. That is my section, but I have seen nothing.'

'Someone has taken them away?'

He shifted, uneasy. 'It is not allowed.'

'I don't care what is not allowed!' The old woman glared and I lowered my voice. 'I *have* to see those files. How long have they been gone?'

'Again, Domnişoară, it is impossible to say. I am sorry.'

I kneaded my eyes, wanting to bury my head in my hands and cry. I had been so close, but this was just another dead end. I had nothing.

No. Not quite nothing.

My hands shook slightly as I picked up the file, observed closely by the clerk, who was too curious now to mind propriety. The cover sheet bore my name, my place and date of birth, my old address, parents' names, nationality, citizenship, education level, foreign languages, occupation (none) and known political affiliations (ditto). It was, indubitably, me.

What was in my parents' files that meant they had been removed? What was in my file that meant it had not? And had mine simply not been taken, or had it rather been *left* for me to find?

A piece of string around a button held the thing shut. I unwound it, slowly, the ballerina turning with me.

Inside was a single piece of paper, face down. I had expected – what? An erupting jungle of accusations, shrilling with secrets? Certainly not this quiet, civilised little rectangle, smaller than an A4 page. I brushed it on the blank side. It was unexpectedly smooth. Glossy. The kind of paper used for photographs.

I turned it over and stared.

CHAPTER NINETEEN

The photograph was in colour, but faded, glued along its top to thick card. It showed a group of some forty people, all women. They were in a factory, recognisable from the vast space and gleaming machines, their light catching the women in a halo. There was a large sign on the back wall.

IUBITĂ, it said.

The women – employees in their overalls – sat in neat rows. Most held a baby or toddler. They *looked* like mothers: they bent over the offspring on their laps, their responsibility no longer to present themselves foremost to the viewer. It was a formal pose, but the photographer had apparently caught them by surprise, because no one was looking at the camera. They were ignoring their infants in favour of another woman, expensively dressed, sitting front and centre with magnetic poise. She was mid-conversation, yet the lipsticked mouth was open to precisely the right degree to exaggerate her beauty. It was spontaneous, yet so perfect it could have been rehearsed. What person could lure a mother to forget her child?

Marija Popa. She was talking to the person on her left, a woman with hair worn shorter than the rest. This one was clearly unaccustomed to being photographed, caught between speaking and posing so her face was smeared with movement, the dark eyes as obscure as her companion's were clear, so dark it seemed someone had bored two holes in the paper. She, too, held a baby on her lap.

I did not need the smile in her eyes, nor the gleam of the watch on her wrist, nor the list of names inked carefully along the bottom, to know her identity and that of the child. A child with those same eyes, gazing up at me through the years.

It was my mother. The baby on her lap was me.

I felt now the warmth of her body, the weight of her arms around my chest. The old ghost of her love against my cheek, and the sweetness that gathered in her hair. Watching her stuff pickles into jars, vinegar stinging my tongue; the smiley faces we drew on the fogged window panes, and the crack as she took down the half-frozen laundry, when even your eyes felt cold in your head. I remembered all of our love, its whole universe: her, and myself, and what we had been to one another.

'It is you?' The clerk jerked me back to attention. I wondered madly if he'd recognised my infant self, before realising my fingers were compulsively brushing my mother's face.

'Yes,' I said at last. 'A long time ago.'

I had been right. The factory was at the heart of everything.

A sob choked me. *Mamă*, I thought, reaching out in my mind, though neither the photograph nor its flesh counterpart could hear. *Surely, seeing this – seeing us, as we once were – you can one day forgive me?*

But the clerk was now pointing at the woman beside her. I felt a stab of rage at the interruption.

'And she?'

The question thrummed in the air.

'Yes.'

'Ah.' There it was: a softening in his expression, a dazedness that I had lately begun to recognise. A switch flipped. I was back on the hunt, the film in my eyes gone.

I hesitated, then whispered, 'My mother belongs to my heart.'

I had to strain to hear his reply, his voice soft for such a big man.

'My heart belongs to my mother.'

And I knew what to do.

The reading room clerk frowned when my new friend lumbered over and asked if she wanted a coffee break. A whispered conversation ensued, but at last she went off, holding up both hands and then one again, in a gesture that unmistakably meant 'fifteen minutes'. As soon as she was gone, I hurried over.

'She says no one in or out until she comes back, or she raises alarm.' I winced. 'She is punctual, that one. Second stack down, tenth shelf on the left, then on the right halfway along.'

The clerk had completed Marija's motto. He was one of her supporters, a shadow population that I was beginning to suspect was far larger than I knew. I had told him who I was, and after his excitement died down we were able to agree on a plan. It was risky to trust him, but Marija, as usual, was right. She still had friends.

'I hope it will work. It is quiet today. If you see anyone, do not look at them. Just keep going.'

'Thank you,' I said. 'From me – and from her.'

His eyes gleamed. 'Go!'

I plunged off among the stacks, ears roaring with the

silence. I could just make out that I was in a narrow alley running all the way across the building, between one series of shelves and the next. The shelves towered above, many times my height; my mother's watch, counting off the seconds, was near invisible in the gloom. The clerks used flashlights, but my ally and I had agreed it was too risky. I kept moving, counting off the shelves under my breath. Four, five, six . . . I tried to be quiet, but my feet pattered along the bare concrete floor regardless, dust and mould filling my nostrils. Piles upon piles of pages, some stowed neatly in files, most simply tied with raggedy string. Some stacks were over a foot high, and I wondered to whom they belonged, and why they'd had the dubious honour of such close documentation. I hoped that whoever they were, they had come out all right in the end.

Nine . . . or was that ten? I stopped and cursed. How could I have lost count? There was precious little time before the clerk returned and discovered I was missing. I could not afford to waste it at the wrong shelf.

I clenched my fists, thinking. Then I took a chance, hurried along one more shelf, and dived in.

Fulga, Furdui, Fusu . . . I muttered the names under my breath, straining to see the spidery handwritten labels. Halfway down on the right, I stopped. G. Yes. I scanned the shelves, praying it was not too high up.

Someone walked past along the narrow alley I had just left and I flattened myself into the shelves, trying to ignore the crawling on my skin, secrets swarming over me like poisonous beetles.

They passed and I exhaled, dust tracing the cloud of my breath.

Gabert, Gabin . . . Gabor. There it was. Radutu Alexandru Gabor. The file was fatter than mine – a lot fatter. I gulped, rechecked my watch. Ten minutes. No time to waste. I took it down and began flicking through, thankful that my profession had given me plenty of practice with speed-reading. It seemed he'd only been under surveillance for a year. Nine minutes. There were transcripts of family phone conversations, notes of his daily errands, the route number of the bus he took to work, how much coffee he'd bought at a local store. Six minutes, and still nothing out of the ordinary, or at least not this strange, sick ordinary that they had built . . .

A word caught my eye. A name. I reached out blindly to steady myself; at the same moment, a noise made me look up and I saw, through the gap where the file had been, my sadistic little acquaintance from the front desk.

He was replacing a folder, chin lifted in concentration. He hadn't seen me – yet. Soundlessly I shifted to one side. What now? I already knew that if I tried to walk away the concrete would betray me. All I could do was stay absolutely quiet and wait for him to leave.

Yet the seconds ticked down and still he lingered, straightening the files with little grunts of satisfaction. One minute gone. Then two. My fists clenched. The clerk would return to the reading room in less than three.

Desperate, I took a step, then another.

A single, treacherous sheet of paper escaped the pile and fluttered to the ground, the noise carrying clearly along the silent shelves.

'Valeriu?'

I was frozen. He repeated himself, then I heard him moving. He was coming. No more time – what I had seen would have to be enough. I could not keep going down the shelves; this series of stacks was the last, leading only to the wall. The poster advertising prosecution flared in my mind; I could not be caught here. So I did the only thing possible: I scooped up the page and fled, back the way I had come, running down the shelves, outstripping him as I reached the aisle and wheeled to the right, back towards the reading room. I kept expecting to hear his shout, the sounds of pursuit, but there was nothing, and I did not dare look back.

I didn't stop until I was nearly at the reading room, and then at last I slowed, trying not to attract attention, praying the female clerk had not yet returned.

She hadn't. I was safe. I bolted past the desk and seated myself as before. The old woman was now fast asleep, snoring gently; my friend was nowhere to be seen. I hoped there was a non-threatening explanation.

The photograph was still on the desk. I could have lost myself once more in my mother's eyes, in the fat, happy baby on her lap. My fingers tingled. I couldn't leave it here. I couldn't relinquish my past again.

The female clerk reappeared, a mug in her hand. I had been there perhaps thirty seconds. She looked surprised then infuriated by the other clerk's absence. I scooped up my bag, informed her that her colleague had been summoned by the manager, and asked if I could leave.

A brusque nod. 'Leave your files in your place.'

A hole opened in my stomach. I didn't look back, but I knew what I had done. It was not just my file I'd left at my seat. I'd also left Mr Gabor's. I'd been so flustered by the manager's appearance among the shelves, then distracted by the photograph, that I had forgotten to dump it.

I could do nothing but smile politely and leave, praying she would not notice its mysterious materialisation, that my ally would find it and tidy it away. Quickly I walked away, certain that I would hear her shout, or the sound of the alarm, but the front desk was close now, and I kept on, and I was at the exit, hand extending to push the door open, so nearly free—

'Lăzărescu.'

211

I almost cried out. The manager had appeared from nowhere, as if pedantry gave you superpowers. He was blocking the exit, deep displeasure on his face.

'Y-yes?'

He shook a slow finger. My heart dropped like a stone. What would they do to me? Arrest? Interrogation?

'Bag check,' he said.

I tried not to smile in relief, until I remembered what was in said bag. He patted me down and grunted.

'Open up.'

I held my breath as he checked the bag thoroughly, running his fingers through the side pockets, fishing out chewing gum and keys, even opening my wallet.

'What is this?' He held up a little box.

'Tampons.' I had recovered myself; my voice was perfectly level.

He gave another grunt, this time of distaste, rummaged around some more for the heck of it, and eventually nodded. 'Go.'

I took one step through the exit, then another. Nobody was behind me. Nobody chased me down.

'One more thing.' His voice rang out, catching me by the throat. Slowly I turned.

'Tell your boss he is the one who must come. For each person must face his past for himself.'

CHAPTER TWENTY

I entered the mansion aflame with adrenaline and grim triumph. The hall seemed brighter than usual, the chandelier blazing fire, lending the person in the mirror a golden, artificial gleam. In there I was not plain old Laura Lăzărescu; I was a creature of sinew and dreams. On this side Alice, on the other, the Jabberwock.

My bag was on my arm: inside it was a tampon box, and inside that was the photograph I had stolen, rolled up neatly among its cotton companions.

I opened the door to my room and there she was, sitting on the bed.

'Well?' she said, and my cheeks flamed.

'Radutu Gabor.' I took a deep breath. 'He was born in Menădie. He has – had – family there.'

'Menădie?' She was very still.

'Yes. There was a sister.' I paused, remembering the photo I'd found in his wallet of a kind face, a face well-lived. 'She had a son. You remember the protests there – not 1989, but the year before. The miners were brought in to crush them.'

The miners tended to be loyalists and had frequently come

in useful to the regime. The ones in Menădie were particularly vicious.

'Well, there was a clash, and people died. One of them was Mr Gabor's nephew. There were lots of phone transcripts between them.' My voice wobbled. 'He was only in his twenties.'

'Who did it?' Her tone was calm.

'Does it *matter*?' A young man had been killed. I was disgusted with her, and with myself for being her accessory. I bit it back and said, 'It was a scrum. No one was charged. Six months later, his sister killed herself. They say from grief.'

I didn't say the obvious: that ultimately it was her fault. Everything was her fault. The deaths of that young man and his mother were on her hands, as was Mrs Ciocan's and so many nameless others. It made me sick.

'You should probably get rid of him,' I said heavily. She gave me a sharp glance, as if she had detected my feelings. 'Mr Gabor, I mean. I cannot see how he could be unbiased after something like this.'

Marija tilted her head to one side, then said, 'Elena Gabor was married to a grocer in Menădie. His son, Oscar, did not like the profession. He left school aged sixteen and became a miner.'

I stared at her, running through the implications.

'He was twenty-three when he died. He had found time to beat up a couple of girlfriends before then. Not a nice boy, I think, though of course his mother loved him. Radutu was close to his sister, and one of the few who could get through to her son. But evidently it was not enough.

'When the chance came for more violence, he took it. He came in on that bus with a cudgel to beat up protesters. This was his home town, remember. Menădie is not large.

'Someone threw a stone, and it rebounded off a building and killed him. It wasn't thrown by the protesters, nor by

214

the police. One of his fellow miners did it. And yes, within a year, Elena killed herself. But her son's death was an accident. A stupid, pointless accident.'

My mouth was open. 'You knew all along.'

'Yes.'

I sank into the clawed chair, overwhelmed by how much I had risked. And for what?

'You *knew* it had no bearing on Mr Gabor's loyalty.'

She smoothed the coverlet. 'How do you think I found out about Manea and Cristescu's treachery? Radutu told me. He discovered what they were doing and came to me. He told me everything. He swore that he knew nothing of their actions and that he would never do the same.'

'Why would you trust him?'

'Because he is a good man, doing a good job. No more or less than that.'

'You didn't trust *me*,' I said, suddenly furious. 'That's why you sent me along. I risked this case for you. I risked prosecution. I could have lost my job, everything. I thought at least it was for something useful. A test of my capabilities, not my loyalty.'

'It *was* useful. Is one not as important as the other? I have met many clever men, but only the loyal ones were of any use. Intelligence without integrity is destructive, dangerous. But nor do I have need of a faithful idiot. Radutu is one of this country's leading lawyers. He has proved his worth, and when he came to me he proved his loyalty. But you, Laura? You are a junior lawyer, the daughter of a pair of defectors. Untried in every sense.' She smiled. 'But today you performed a service. I am grateful. And who knows? You might have discovered something else in those files.'

I tried to brush her gratitude aside. 'That young man died.'

'It was an accident.'

'No, it wasn't. Not really.'

'Laura, you are not here to hold my husband's regime to account. Or my husband. Or me. You are here to do your job.'

She was right, but it didn't help. 'There isn't a traitor at all, is there?'

'Oh, there is. Or rather, there will be.'

'I don't understand.'

'Because you do not understand this country. You are correct, I do not think it is Radutu. But Yanussians do not make one plan. We make many. Even if a little old lady is going to see her grandson, she has five different ways to travel depending on the weather, the public transport, the neighbours. Manea and Cristescu were working against me, but they will not have been alone. The other side will have planted many seeds, and soon we will see which have grown.'

'But nothing's happened.'

'Not yet.' Her face was grim. 'But it will. That is why I had to test your loyalty. In the times to come, I will need you.'

I will need you. The words sank in, displacing my anger. Despite the risks, I *had* proven myself. And of course, I had the photograph. Our eyes met and then she stood, brushing past me to leave. Did I imagine it, or had she come a fraction closer than necessary?

'Pavel,' I said slowly. 'I followed him. He went into the Ministry of Justice.'

She stopped. '*Did* he now. Do you know why?'

'No. But I can imagine who he met.'

'Prosecutor Ursu. What on earth could Cristian want with him?' She bit her lip, white sinking into pillowy red. 'You think he is working against me too?'

'There's nothing to suggest that.'

'Why then does he go in secret?'

216

I shook my head, then remembered something. The *chink* emanating from Pavel's bag. It was the same sound I had heard at our dinner: the sound of a sugar-bowl lid being replaced.

Following a hunch, I said, 'Doamna. Do you remember Catherine the Great's tea set?'

The Bleu Celeste service created for the empress was a masterpiece, a hundred and sixty pieces of gilded china, exquisitely wrought. The factory at Sèvres had become the *manufacture royale* through the influence of Madame de Pompadour, Louis XV's mistress, whose Versailles collection rivalled only the king's. After her death, Catherine the Great, another powerful woman with a taste for luxury, ordered a service of her own. A single 'ordinary' Bleu Celeste teacup and saucer might fetch thousands, but the Catherine the Great pieces, not being for sale, were priceless. The set resided as one of the most perfect treasures in St Petersburg's Hermitage Museum, until the Kremlin donated several pieces to the Yanussia National Gallery in thanks for Popa's about-face on the Warsaw Pact. The items, including a sugar bowl, an ice pail and a teacup, were soon 'borrowed', never to be seen again. Asset tracers reported that they were smashed during a particularly boisterous Party banquet in the mid-eighties. Or were they?

'The sugar bowl at dinner yesterday,' I said. 'That was it, wasn't it?'

Her expression was impassive, but I would have been willing to bet the entirety of Catherine's crockery cupboard that if I examined that bowl, I would see what Pavel must have seen: the telltale *EII* – Ekaterina II. The imperial cypher. Perhaps Marija had hidden it from the asset tracers in sentiment for her sister of the same name. As for the missing teacup, I remembered the one she had sipped from on our very first encounter, a delicate thing of bright blue . . .

I didn't ask. Instead I said, 'If that is so, and Pavel realised this, he had no choice but to turn it over to the prosecution.'

She let out a soft hiss. 'But I have client privilege.'

'Not if your lawyer somehow obtains physical evidence. You know how this works, Doamna, or at least you ought to. He realised what it was, and that meant he could not suppress it. Unlike in English law, your system says he has an ethical obligation to hand it over. Don't worry, he won't reveal its source, and he'll have arranged the handover so as not to implicate you.' No wonder Pavel wouldn't check his bag into the cloakroom.

'How certain are you?'

'Reasonably.' But even as I reassured her, I felt an under-current of unease: why hadn't he told Jude or me? Perhaps he was trying to protect us – or perhaps something else was going on.

Marija shook her head mutinously. 'I liked that sugar bowl.'

I couldn't help it: I had to smile, and after a moment she smiled back.

'I could ask him about it.'

She sighed. 'Not yet. Let us wait. See whether a seed grows.' She placed a hand on the door and paused, a ring sparkling on her finger. 'I am glad you found what you did at the archives. I thought you might be someone who is constrained by rules, but you were not afraid to overstep them when the time came. Tell me – was there anything else?'

I thought of the photograph in my bag. I felt its burning presence, could almost trace its outline from the corners of my eyes.

I gazed at her levelly. 'No. Nothing.'

After she left, I leaned back, winded, gazing at where she'd sat. The coverlet bore the neat imprint of her bottom, the twin stars of her hands. I wondered how long she had been there, waiting – waiting for me. Her perfume hung in the air.

Slowly I withdrew the photograph from its small box.

Some years ago, walking alone on the South Downs, I had found a bird trap. Inside it hopped a solitary magpie. One for sorrow. I recalled my father's words: magpies are vicious. Even he found them hard to like. They forage for ticks in the backs of domestic animals, picking at their flesh with sharp beaks, causing infection. They are more than gleeful treasure-seekers: their probing makes them cruel. This one carried the blue of its wing like a handbag, into which a greedy old dame might secrete stolen treasures.

I examined the cage. There was a door on top by which the creature had presumably entered. It would have hopped onto the small treadle and its weight would have closed the door: trapped by itself, by its greed for the waiting dish. The food was gone but the cage remained. I gazed at the bird through the mesh.

'Bait, not food,' I said sadly. An important difference. The magpie watched me with glossy black eyes, a pinprick of alien intelligence. It made no sound. Out of fear?

I inspected the mechanism and found it simple. No padlocks. I could open it by myself, if I chose.

If I chose.

Inside the National Records Office, hunting my past through those endless shelves, I had felt like that magpie, picking, picking away. I had been greedy for secrets and now I was locked in. Knowledge is supposed to open up the world, but it can also narrow it to almost nothing. The new government had made the Strajă archives publicly available early on, billing it as a step towards transparency. The international community praised them for it, yet long after the world had moved on, these people were still reeling from the revelations therein. You might discover that the woman with whom you queued for soup bones had been an informer. Or your ten-year-old son. Or your best friend. Knowledge is a plague: Andrei's experiences had shown me as much, but I hadn't paid attention. Visitors to those archives should have been met with hazard barriers warning of infection.

I thought about my lie to Marija. I thought of Pavel, and the grip she had on him because of their shared history. My past was her choicest weapon: to overcome it I had to come at her from a position of strength. Concealing the photograph from her was the first step to regaining that strength, because for the first time, I knew something she did not.

This was my reasoning, yet as I picked up the photograph again, I could not help thinking of that magpie. I'd wondered whether it had been there long and when the farmer would drive by, tractor wheels chewing up the grass. I imagined him opening up the cage, seizing the bird and wringing its neck.

Only later did I discover that sometimes the first bird is left inside and kept fed and watered. Its presence draws other birds in. Like their companion, they too become trapped; unlike him, however, these birds are slaughtered, while the first bird, the call bird, hops and trips and sings, knowing that every snared fellow is another lease of life for himself. Soon the fields are empty of that raucous song.

The fingers that held the photograph began to tremble. My parents' files had been taken. Mine had not. I had been in Yanussia long enough now to know such omissions were not accidental. I had lied to her, but I should have realised by now that she was always three steps ahead. A piece of my past had been parcelled up and left out for me, tempting and juicy. I was being *allowed* to see this. And with my eyes shut tight, the after-image glowing in my mind like my mother's watch snared in the camera's flash, I could think of one word, and one word alone.

Bait.

CHAPTER TWENTY-ONE

Eight days later. Dumitru Ursu's press conference was in three hours and I resented the distraction. I'd hidden the photograph at the back of my wardrobe, but it didn't stay there: instead I found myself taking it out repeatedly, first thing in the morning, last thing at night, even making excuses in between to sneak upstairs and gaze at what I had lost.

Marija's retraction had been published four days previously. *First Lady Bows to Pressure* was the line in the broadsheets, while the tabloids ran with items like *Black Widow Scurries Back to Her Web*. Though the headlines were largely hostile, the articles themselves bore traces of inner conflict, criticising an undemocratic heavy-handedness in First Minister Anghelescu's government uneasily reminiscent of the prior regime. Marija's statement about wishing to 'devote yet more of my life to public service' was widely quoted, and I hid my pride at my words being used almost verbatim. Yanussia's biggest private TV channel was planning a live debate on the matter, and a petition backed by Popa loyalists calling for her immediate release had garnered close to ten thousand signatures. Meanwhile the Răsculat, the anti-Popa extremists, had threatened to march on Parliament unless Anghelescu publicly ruled out a plea bargain, which he did twelve hours later. It didn't affect us – Marija after all was dead against such a thing – but the wasps' nest had been well and truly prodded. The previous night, I had fallen asleep to the sound of a few dozen protesters chanting her name – whether in support or condemnation, I could not tell. We expected Ursu to make reference to the reversal today.

Ursu. The sugar bowl. Was that the only business my boss had with him? I was watching Pavel, but we were so busy it was hard to do so too closely. Jameson had finally sent over the report on Manea and Cristescu, but its findings were bland, useless. Any explanation of their deaths had been efficiently rubbed out.

I also still felt that we were missing something in our defence strategy. It was all very well arguing that Marija was ignorant, but we needed a rabbit in the hat to dazzle the prosecution. Something still nagged at my subconscious, and when I wasn't poring over my mother's photograph, I was poring over the files, seeking to identify it. Jude had started calling me Fido, 'because you're like a dog with a bone'. I felt the pressure we were under as an almost physical force, crushing down from all directions.

Andrei saw Marija's retraction and called. I'd tried him several times before, half-heartedly, still annoyed by the moving-in question and guilty over the now-locked door. But I only succeeded in getting his flatmate Craig, a bore who did family law and was convinced we had a lot in common.

Apparently my boyfriend was in an odd mood, however, because barely had we exchanged pleasantries when he said, 'I see the bitch is on her way out.'

'Andrei!' I was shocked by his venom.

'What? You hate her too.' I did not reply. 'I said, you hate her too.'

'Of course.'

'Of course,' he mimicked, and suddenly it was him I hated, his know-it-all tone and his inability to see people beyond their gross outlines. 'Did you try again?'

I didn't need to ask what he meant.

'Yes. Andrei – it was locked. I'm sorry.'

'Are you.' His voice was flat.

'Yes!'

'There's something up with you.'

'Nothing's up.'

'There is. I can smell it.'

I shifted uneasily. 'I'm a thousand miles away.'

'Exactly. You have a fall coming, Laura. I want to save you, but you have to want to save yourself. You're too far from home, and you're losing perspective.'

Whatever I lost in that moment, it was not perspective. 'What if I'm not?' I said loudly, the pressure of the last few days bursting forth. 'What if I see things correctly, and you're the one warping everything?'

His voice was very quiet. 'Is that how you see me? Warped?'

I sensed the ledge and the dizzy drop beyond. 'No. No, of course not.'

He sighed. 'I need you, Laura.'

'I need you too.'

'Come home, then.'

His request incapacitated me. Andrei hated asking for help. He wouldn't even ask for directions. I knew how much it must have cost him, and I knew too how narrow our little ledge of happiness currently was.

'What about the door? Your mother?'

'It's done. It's over. You say you tried. I'm sure you did all you could.'

The guilt was immense, the pull of his words extreme. He needed me.

But so did someone else.

The question was simple. Who mattered more?

'Laura?' His voice was quiet, yet I heard its challenge. 'Please?'

My reply was little more than a whisper. 'I can't.'

A long silence. Then he hung up. After all, what was there left to say?

A restive quiet hung over the Lair that morning as anxiety about the press conference set in. I worked doubly hard, seeking to dispel the ache in my chest.

Sorin peeked round the door. 'Can I join you for the conference? World is watching, et cetera.'

Pavel frowned, but could hardly say no. He did not like anyone to be in the Lair but ourselves and Marija. I understood the security concerns, but unless I was imagining things, he had become even more paranoid since his clandestine visit to Ursu. I hadn't asked Pavel what he'd been doing that day, partly because Marija had told me not to, partly for fear he might ask me the same question. But I wondered. Pavel was by nature protective, not secretive. Why hide a sugar bowl from his own juniors? We could have helped him. I could have dropped the thing off myself. Why had he felt the need to play delivery boy?

A phone rang in the little office across the hall, and he hurried out. 'That's for me.'

I made a coffee – I'd never liked the stuff, but I'd wanted to fit in, and that meant drinking what everybody else drank – and returned to work, now involving the dubious acquisition of a Cartier collection that would've made Liz Taylor blush. A tiara, three diamond necklaces, a sapphire bracelet, etc., etc., the whole bundle estimated at £6.3 million.

As if who owns what matters in a place like this. Sorin's words came back. I looked over at Jude and the small pile of National Gallery papers. (The auction receipt for the Picasso had never turned up.) In the beginning, Marija had wanted us to argue for her innocence. That meant proving, somehow, that no laws were broken. I had thought it crazy. But – I gripped the edge of my chair – what if it wasn't?

As if who owns what matters in a place like this. Sorin was right, but what if he was more right than he knew? I hurried over to the shelf of statute books and twenty minutes later I had it.

'Stop hopping around,' Jude said irritably.

'Jude.' I pointed excitedly to the sheaf of loan certificates. 'What if these paintings weren't stolen?'

'Excuse me?'

'Look at this.' I put the open book down before him. 'Specifically, the articles on the transmission of goods between central state institutions. The transmissions are made by the order of the head of the institution that owns the goods.'

'So?'

'*So*, Constantin Popa, as the ultimate head of a communist state, also has the ultimate say-so on any state assets. As the general secretary and head of the Party, he and his central committee are the body of the state.' I stabbed at the relevant point. 'They allocate bailment.'

'Bailment.' Jude sat up suddenly, a gleam in his eye. 'In other words, you transfer the physical possession of an item while maintaining ownership.'

'Exactly.' I paced back and forth. 'All the paintings except the Picasso have now been reclaimed by the government. The other side will make the argument of conversion in bad faith – that Popa took control of those paintings and didn't intend to give them back. But his regime was interrupted in 1989, so how can they know?' I thrilled with realisation. This was it, the magician's rabbit I had been trying to identify. 'He never actually sold those paintings, just stashed them away. We can argue that he was always intending to return them – he was just murdered before he could. Also, since he was top dog, they'd have to find him guilty of violating his own bailment. And you can't steal from yourself.'

'By Jove. You're right.'

I knew it was good, and what was more, we could apply it to almost every painting, the exception being the Picasso: since it had been purchased by Popa personally, the problem was not bailment, but the source of funds. I half expected Jude to go to Pavel himself, but to his credit, he told me to go.

Pavel was sequestered across the hall, in the small private office he and Mr Gabor shared. The murmur within told me he was still on the phone. I hopped back and forth. He had been in there ages. An electric thought: what if he was speaking to Ursu? I leaned in. I was getting quite a taste for eavesdropping.

He was speaking in Yanussian. I cursed my ignorance, until an English word snagged my attention.

Rupert, he had said, quite distinctly. Was that the person on the line? I was disappointed. I knew no one of that name.

'Lăzărescu.'

I turned, every organ suddenly tight. Apostol was behind me.

'Listening?' he said, with a knowing look.

'Just waiting for my boss.'

'Ah. Like the old days. I also spent much time . . . waiting.' His irises were just too small for the eyes; there was too much white around them. 'You know, Lăzărescu, what I do before I come here?'

I understood. He must have seen comprehension burst in my eyes like a blood vessel, because he smirked.

'Yes. The Strajă. Not many people know, but we are friends. So I tell you.'

'Friends?' I could not hide my incredulity, the bruise on my back a gruesome reminder. 'After what you did?'

His grin widened. 'Of course. Because if we are enemies, you would not be here.' He moved closer. 'There is only order and aberration, Lăzărescu. That is why we have the watchers and the watched. To stop the chaos.' A massive hand coiled over my own. 'That is where I took a bullet for the Doamna. I will watch her, always.' He leaned in: his breath was hot meat. 'And for her, I will watch *you*.'

I wrenched my hand away. His answering grin reminded me of a rat-catcher's: not clever, exactly, but cunning enough to know which way his prey will run.

When he'd gone I rubbed my hand furiously against my skirt and turned back to the door, cursing the interruption, for not only had the conversation within switched to English, it had also become an argument.

'Why would Anghelescu . . . I see,' Pavel was saying hopelessly. The First Minister. What on earth had Pavel got himself into?

'Rupert, listen. Listen to me. I meant no offence. This should not mean that you . . .'

So Rupert was the person he was speaking to. I knew the Yanussian government pretty well from my legal research, as well as the justice department and courts. Of all the king's horses and all the king's men, there was no one with such a name.

'Rupert, please. There is no need to do this.'

His words and tone reeked of a hopelessness that made me very, very worried. It sounded like he had tried to do something and it had backfired, and now there was no one to put Humpty together again. Marija had said a traitor would emerge. Was that what was happening, here, now?

I leaned further forward, and as I did so the door sprang open. Pavel stepped into the hall and I almost fell headlong into his chest.

I regained myself and leapt away, holding up my documents like a shield.

'What are you doing here?' His voice was choked. 'Were you *listening?*'

'No! Just, um, waiting.' Apostol had poisoned the excuse and I hated him all the more for it. 'I think I've found something.'

'Later. I'm busy.'

'But . . .'

He walked off, his back stiff and perfectly straight. I watched him go. We were a long way away from the Moorgate office now. There, everything was shining glass: the walls, the tables, the voices of the posh secretaries telling clients to call back. But the mansion was dense wood and brick, and it seemed that whichever way I turned, I found walls that had not been there before.

CHAPTER TWENTY-TWO

I returned to the Lair, hands shaking slightly. Just what had I overheard?

'Laura?' Mr Gabor was there. 'Jude said you had a plan?'

I tried to shut out my thoughts, and told him.

'This is good,' he said slowly.

'I thought so,' Jude put in. 'Fucked up, but good.'

'Let me think.' The Yanussian closed his eyes. The lids were so thin as to be almost translucent.

'This is what we do,' he said at last. 'We take this and, as you say, run with it. Conversion – essentially, theft – is an intentional exercise. It can be committed by buying, selling or altering the goods, or most critically by refusing to surrender the goods to the owner. But the National Gallery never asked for its paintings back.'

'They wouldn't have dared.'

'No, of course. But that does not affect the facts.'

'What about the duration of ownership?' Jude said. 'The earliest "loan" dates back to 1978.'

Mr Gabor smiled, and for the first time I saw not Chicken Licken, but a shark. 'The 1977 robbery.'

'The what?'

'In 1977, the gallery was robbed. A very famous incident. They vaulted the fences and drilled through the wall. A Matisse was taken.'

'So?'

'So we argue this was the inciting incident. It became clear that the country's national treasures were not secure. Therefore the Popas took them into custody for safe keeping. And where is safer than the palace of a dictator, or a Swiss bank vault?'

We gazed at one another.

'It's audacious,' Jude said.

'So is she.'

I knew then, thrillingly, that we were on the right track. There was no point Marija facing the gallows with a toy gun. She needed a blunderbuss. The court must be blindsided by her brazenness, intoxicated by her spirit. Her effrontery – our effrontery – must take their breath away, such that they found themselves unable to speak against her, or even speak at all.

We hammered it out as the time to the press conference ticked down. Sorin arrived two minutes before the hour, followed by Pavel, who avoided my gaze. It was too late to bring him up to speed before the conference, and I even wondered whether it was a good idea to do so. It implied we were on the same team, and right then I was not quite sure if that were true.

We crowded round the television, tuned to the state channel. It showed a podium bristling with microphones, at the base of the steps leading up to the now-familiar hulk of the Ministry of Justice. I looked sidelong at Pavel to see if I could detect, well, anything – the rendezvous, the phone call, the deceit. He did look pale, but it seemed these days he always did.

'Those poor sons of bitches,' Jude said. 'Why are they doing it outside?'

'Maybe they want to discourage an audience.'

He snorted. 'Do this lot look discouraged to you?'

Jostling before the podium was a small army of cold but determined reporters and cameramen. Confined by metal barriers, they stamped their feet and fiddled with their equipment, their breath coming in clouds. Behind them thronged an even larger mass of regular people; before them all, guarding the podium, was a ring of policemen. And with good reason. The crowd was restless, the individual faces I could pick out tense. I wondered if any of them belonged to the Răsculat. Pulling out, the camera showed eddies and swirls, people moving to and fro with a half-controlled energy that spilled out of the screen in invisible pixels and infected the room. I found myself drumming my fingers; Jude fidgeted with his pen, Sorin with his glass. Pavel, by contrast, was abnormally still, except for snapping at Jude when he inevitably dropped the pen. Mr Gabor was folded into himself, briefcase perched neatly across his knees. I thought of that overfed NRO file and could not work out if I felt bad for rifling through his life.

No, that wasn't true. I did not feel bad, it was as simple as that. Through Marija's test, I'd learned not only about the strength of his loyalty, but of my own. I could not lie to myself any more: I was involved, whether I liked it or not. The rushing sound in my ears had returned over the last few days. More than that: it was growing, rising to a roar.

'There's something you have to understand,' Sorin said to me. He was draped casually over his chair, though the hand that gripped the whisky glass was white. 'The reason why the Yanussians are bothering with this trial. They want to put Menădie and Popa's death behind them. The UN still bash them over the heads with it any chance they get. They want to show they can play at justice with the big league.'

232

'And are they playing fair?'

His lip curled. 'I said they were playing. I never said anything about fair.'

Eleven o'clock came and went. I checked my mother's watch repeatedly, the restlessness of the crowd multiplying like so many bacteria. There were shouts of discontent. Perhaps they were yelling political slogans, or perhaps they were just cold.

Dumitru Ursu finally emerged at quarter past, trudging down the steps to the podium. I'd not seen him before and I watched now with interest. He was just shy of fat, with a round face and sharp eyes. I pictured him pawing over the sugar bowl and found the image distasteful. Behind him were four more policemen, lumpish with black body armour, like scarab beetles. Unlike their peers, they carried guns.

'Ursu. He's lost weight,' Sorin said. I looked at Pavel, but his face betrayed nothing of the meeting I guessed had occurred between him and the prosecutor. 'I know it doesn't look like it. He's under a lot of pressure. The Strajă trials were more or less a joke. He needs to put *someone* on the gallows or the things will rust away.'

'So, harmless?' Jude said.

'Is a wounded animal harmless?' Sorin said softly. 'No. He needs this conviction more than ever.'

Ursu began speaking quickly in Yanussian. Sorin translated.

'He is saying this will be a fair trial. Despite the insulting doubts of the UN regarding the capabilities of Yanussia's courts, the country has sworn to take this burden onto its own shoulders. He and the government want above all to see justice served . . .'

His voice faded as he concentrated, but as the prosecutor rattled on, it was evident that his message was not going down well. The crowd brandished their signs, their shouts

233

growing louder. The policemen behind him shifted uneasily but Ursu gave no sign of noticing: he kept his eyes fixed on the pages, only raising his voice slightly. Then he paused, licked his lips, looked dead at the camera and said something else. The crowd moaned. Sorin gasped.

'What?' Jude and I were craning forward in our seats, as if that would help.

'I thought this might happen.' We turned as one: Ecaterina stood in the doorway, her voice low. How long she'd been there, I had no idea – I hadn't even heard the telltale rattling of keys. She looked even more bloodless than usual. I could not imagine her state of mind, seeing the threat her beloved sister faced.

'He is bringing forward the trial date,' Sorin said.

'*What?*' Jude was on his feet.

'It is no longer in April. Judge Ardelean has seen fit to move it.'

'To when?'

I glanced at Pavel, but he was staring blankly, silent and rooted in his chair. 'Pavel?' I said quietly, but again it was Sorin who answered.

'January the third.' A shadow crossed his face. 'The same day my statue is to be unveiled.'

Jude's jaw dropped. 'But it's nearly December. That's barely a month away! How the fuck do they expect us to be prepared?' When nobody said anything, he went on, 'We'll apply for adjournment. Or breach of fair trial.'

Sorin's voice was distant. 'It won't work.'

'They can't do this!'

'I assure you they can.'

Jude gazed at him hopelessly. 'But she could *die*.'

He was right. If we could not find a way to push back the date, our time was now lethally short. It would be virtually impossible to have a viable case ready in four weeks. It was a ridiculous move: it would completely wreck Yanussia's claims to an impartial justice system. How could Ardelean have done this? But no – he was known for being fair, if stern. This move must have come from the very top. Had the President and First Minister felt threatened enough by the spectre of her presidential bid that they had pressured the judiciary? More importantly, had Marija seen this trade-off coming, and if so, was it confidence or madness that made her think she could win regardless? Or had this development been spurred by something else entirely?

'Pavel?' Jude asked hopefully. I was struck by our boss's expression. There was shock, certainly, yet also something that on anyone else would have looked like guilt. Before I could wonder whether there might be more to my sugar-bowl theory than met the eye, we were distracted by a particularly loud chant. It grew and grew, swelling into a tsunami that bore down on Ursu, who visibly flinched, and all at once his words began flowing faster. The change of pace was a mistake. His fear became audible, and that which is primal in us all pricked up its ears. It sent the crowd wild. As a single organism they charged on the podium, the reporters screeching as their pen collapsed, the policemen shouting and brandishing their batons.

Pandemonium. But now another faction was pushing back – the organism split in two, breeding – Marija's supporters, waving banners bearing her face and yelling for Ursu to continue. Sorin's face was so close to the screen his nose was practically touching it, all pretence at casualness gone. At the very crest of the wave, Ursu finished speaking and turned to make his escape. The mob burst into hysteria. A questing tentacle overwhelmed the other faction, scything through the remaining journalists and into the black ring of police. Carnage, shaking the crowd until it became divisible. A baton smashed into a red-haired woman, who fell even as more people flowed around her, men in old overcoats, students in faded Levi's, irrepressible despite the violence. I sensed long-pent-up rage seeking release on both sides, the police using their batons with far more force than necessary, the protesters so furious they hardly seemed to care.

Yet the black-uniformed ring was winning, driving the crowd back. Ursu was being bundled away, up the steps of the ministry, towards safety. Three more seconds and he would be gone.

Then a lone figure smashed through the line and ran, faster than I thought possible, straight at him. Five yards, four, three, and a tiny flash, perhaps of silver, the image too imprecise to see, only the exploding fury of the crowd and the armed policemen twisting like deadly eels. Two loud bangs and the figure – no, the *woman* – collapsed on the ground and was still.

CHAPTER TWENTY-THREE

Nobody moved. All was chaos, until an enterprising camera-man found an angle. The picture jumped and the prone woman's face slammed up against the screen.

Jude and I jerked forward simultaneously.

'That's—'

'I know. The madwoman. The one who was trying to get in.'

I stared at the body, dressed in red, and at the rosebud mouth agape in surprise. She was about my age and blood had spilled around her like milk, mingling with the dirt of the street.

'Lăzărescu,' Jude said. 'She looks a bit like you.'

His words sent a shiver down my back. I wanted to turn and look at the others but was afraid of what I might see.

'That's no madwoman,' Sorin whispered. 'That's Camelia. Marija fired her the month before you came.'

Camelia Moraru. Marija's former secretary – or Ecaterina's. The latter had moved right up to the screen, a skinny hand over her mouth.

'What the hell?' said Jude.

'Why would she—'

There was a confused babble, everyone talking over one another except for Ecaterina and Pavel, who remained silent. Ursu was completely invisible, buried under a pile of gleaming black uniforms. It looked as if he had been overrun by beetles.

'Is he OK?' No one could answer. The seconds passed, soundtracked by the panicked shrieks of the scattering crowd. Madly I thought I heard the rabbit clock ticking.

At last a space yawned at the centre of the officers. Ursu lay there unmoving. We held our breath.

At last a shaky hand reached up. The prosecutor was pulled to his feet. The crowd sighed – in relief? – as he shook himself, patting his torso as though checking it was still intact. He took one step, two, then they swept him up the steps and inside the Ministry of Justice. The massive doors closed and he was gone.

Several people clustered into view. Civilians, not police officers. One man took Camelia's pulse, while another placed an ear close to her mouth. Unusually for this part of the world, he was blond. The two of them looked at one another and shook their heads, even as an ambulance siren began to wail. Someone produced a sheet; together they covered the body. Only a few shallow bumps in the cloth suggested there was anything beneath it at all.

'What on earth possessed her?' I said aloud, half expecting Ecaterina to answer. Instead she was staring at the screen, eyes wide, one hand compulsively playing with the keys at her hip. I hadn't thought she could get any paler, yet any remaining blood had drained from her face. She looked as though she had seen a ghost. I looked again at the television, but the scene had not changed. There was only the covered body and the two men bent over it.

'What are we going to do?' Jude asked. Any popular support for Marija would have just evaporated. It didn't matter whether she was really behind it. It was only a matter of time before Camelia was publicly identified and people drew the inference for themselves. Not to mention the changed trial date. Just when I thought we'd found firmer ground on our strategy, our case had been dealt a double body blow. It was hard to ignore the shadow of the gallows.

'The only thing we can.' Pavel's jaw had tightened, the guilty confusion brutally shoved aside. 'We get back to work. Jude, come with me.'

Jude opened his mouth to protest, then thought better of it. Still Ecaterina had not moved: only when the picture changed to a news broadcast did she blink and come to life. Pavel and Jude went out, and she followed a moment later, casting glances back at the screen as if in disbelief.

I sat at the table, the words before me blurring, meaningless. I thought of Camelia clawing at the door, screaming her former employer's name. Why had she tried to kill Ursu? Did she believe she was saving Marija, or condemning her? Either way I could not comprehend the scale of the sacrifice. What had possessed her? Or rather, who?

'She did it on purpose,' Sorin said flatly. I started: I'd forgotten him. He was standing by the mantelpiece, staring intently at its marbled surface.

'What?'

'She knew that would happen. What we just saw was suicide.'

'It reminds me of . . .'

'Of how Popa died? No. Camelia was sacrificing herself. That was not what Dinu did at all.'

'How do you know?' I demanded.

'I was there.'

I stared.

'I was there,' he repeated. 'I saw it with my own eyes. He knew it was over. The sharks had smelled blood. But those walls are three feet thick, and the doors, well, you've seen them. They're enormous. They can only be opened by remote control. He could have stayed there forever, or at least long enough to organise an escape. Yet after seven hours, he opened them – or rather, they opened.'

I frowned at the twist of meaning, but he was still staring at the mantelpiece, as if what he had seen could bore a hole through it.

'I watched the crowd pour in. It was . . .' He stopped. Found the words. 'They tore him to pieces. They were ordinary people, but when they saw him, they became something else. I watched people stumbling away, dazed, their hands stained red. One man had a bloody mouth.'

'Why did he do it?' I whispered.

'That's my point – he wouldn't. He would never, *never* have opened those doors. Constantin was a survivor; they both are. It is their greatest gift. Possibly their only gift.'

'Maybe he just gave up.'

The sculptor's tone hardened. 'No. It would never have occurred to him. Survival was the only thing that mattered. Yet those doors opened, and by the time they were done, there was hardly anything left to bury.'

Voices were coming down the corridor, angry voices, headed for the Lair. Sorin's whisper, in contrast, was barely audible.

'Someone made a sacrifice that day. But it wasn't him.'

CHAPTER TWENTY-FOUR

'It is quite simple, Doamna.' Pavel's face was white. He and Marija were toe to toe, and for once, she was not doing her languid, disinterested act: she was furious, cheeks scarlet, a strand of hair coming loose, and in her eyes – worry? 'Did you have anything to do with what just happened? Or are you going to tell me it was the Răsculat?'

'How dare you.' Her voice was a hiss. 'How *dare* you.'

I quailed, but Pavel was past that. He drew himself up. 'This gravely damages our case – your case. I must insist you answer.'

'You think I put that silly girl up to that?'

Lăzărescu. She looks a bit like you.

Camelia Moraru. Just another silly girl, manipulated and eventually overtaken by forces she did not understand. I closed my eyes.

'Why not? Someone must have.'

'I know my employees. Always Camelia was impulsive. And if she had managed it, what would that have achieved? These prosecutors are like cockroaches. Kill one and another comes in its place.'

'You'll forgive me, Doamna, if that does not sound particularly reassuring.'

'I do not need to reassure you! You are working for *me*, not the other way around.' She brushed the loose strand aside angrily, then yanked out her hairpin so the whole lot came tumbling forth in a dark river. 'You should be worrying about the new trial date, and the disaster it spells. You have hardly any time left to do your job.' She jabbed the hairpin in his direction like a knife and he reared back. '*If that is what you have been doing.*'

Pavel went very still. 'What are you implying?'

'You should get to know your country better, Cristian,' she said quietly. 'In Yanussia, there is always someone watching.'

Jude and Mr Gabor looked utterly confused, but my stomach lurched. Once again I saw Pavel entering the Ministry of Justice. I gripped the armchair's back. Could *he* have arranged the date change? Could he have betrayed her, because she had rejected him, or because he was jealous? If it was true, we would be off the case and out of the country – if indeed we were allowed to leave. Once again I thought of Manea's fate.

I shook myself. This was Pavel. *Pavel*, for heaven's sake. The man who had sat me down on our first case together and talked about his love of doing what was right, speaking with a passion that I didn't see in many partners. He wasn't just in it to win. He really cared about his clients – perhaps too much.

His voice was quiet. 'Marija, I have always acted, and continue to act, in your best interests. If you do not believe that, then fire me.'

'You think I will settle for firing you?'

Pavel gazed at her. Then he spread his arms wide, as if facing a firing squad. 'You want to do more? Then do it.'

I couldn't move. Nobody could. This was it, the moment when my future and hers could be wrenched apart, shattering my past in its wake. My heart was going *thump thump thump* in my chest, bees swarming under my skin.

'Lăzărescu?' Apostol popped up in the doorway like an ugly mole. Everyone turned, outraged at the interruption.

'Yes?' Foreboding filled me like blood; my voice came out small and cracked.

'Phone for you. Urgent.'

CHAPTER TWENTY-FIVE

The plane's stale roar filled my nose, my ears. The sign in front informed me brightly that my oxygen mask was above me, my lifejacket under my seat. Why bother? If we crashed, what would a little plastic cup achieve, even if I did put on my own before attending to anyone else's? *If you hold your breath, you cannot sink.* Wrong. We would fall, we would hit, we would die. I almost craved the cleanness of it. Anything was better than the spreading stain of living.

My mother was dying. Anaplastic thyroid cancer, my father said down the phone. I might have expected him to stammer over the unfamiliar word; the fact that he did not told me far more than I wanted to know. She had days left. Perhaps hours.

Four days' compassionate leave, Pavel said, Jude stuffing my passport into my coat as I stumbled out the door, limbs refusing to move as they ought. I'd dug around in the wardrobe for the photograph, but it wasn't there, though I'd cleared it out in a desperate hunt, leaving the clothes where they fell. Without its proof, I was naked, unprotected, but even that did not matter, for she was dying and she had not told me. I remembered those hospital tests. She must have found out then, and that was weeks ago.

The driver went the long way round, despite my pains-taking instructions, remaining mute as I shouted at him with barely controlled hysteria.

'Bitch,' he yelled, magically finding his voice as I scrambled out without tipping and ran up the drive, my suitcase banging against my legs. I was freezing cold; I'd left my coat in the car, and thought stupidly about running back to retrieve it. But the notion vanished at the sight of the front door. My front door. Home.

My father's taxicab was parked on the drive, silently offering to take me away again. Instead I went to knock, but my hand froze. Yellow light slanted through the pane, as if in warning. I tried again, with the same result, as if the door wore a protective barrier. For whom? Me, or them?

My mother's watch glinted on my wrist. It said that we had run out of time.

Then my father opened the door and blinked at me in the light, surprise written across his face, as if he had expected a different, more shadowy visitor. I embraced his inadequate frame; he turned with hideous, mechanical formality and led me up the yellow-carpeted stairs. One of the pictures on the wall was out of position, the discrepancy capering madly in my vision. The steps were blurred and seemed far too few, my foot meeting the top with a sickening thud.

The bedroom door was closed. My breathing came short and shallow. This was our moment of redemption, our chance to save ourselves. There was so much to say. Here at the last my mother and I would talk, and all the years and hurts would trickle away.

I reached towards the handle, but my father seized my wrist.

'Listen to me. She is very, very vulnerable at the moment.'

245

'I know, Tată.'

'Please don't upset her. Since you went to Yanussia, she has not been herself.'

'She missed me?'

He shook his head impatiently, as if this was an irrelevance. 'Your going back made her . . .' He stopped, choosing his words. 'It has given her great pain.'

I exhaled, my voice shaky. 'So this is my fault.'

'No, *pisi*, that is not what I meant.' In his eyes there was pity and . . . what? Blame?

'Why did you both hate me going? What's wrong?'

His cheeks were pinched, sucked in by whatever secret they shared. 'Nothing. There is nothing wrong.'

'If that's true, then why shouldn't I go home?'

He moved suddenly towards me, anger in his face, his voice low and furious. 'Home? You did not go *home*. You went into the lion's den! Into the house of the woman who did this to us!'

'Did *what* to us?'

He would not answer, his narrow chest rising and falling in the hall's blackness.

'She is just Popa's wife,' I said, my anger rising. 'She didn't *do* anything to us.'

His face was bleak. 'Laura. Do not talk about things you do not understand.'

'Then tell me what I'm missing!'

'I cannot.'

'As ever. You two have always shut me out. I'm not a child any more, Tată. I haven't been for a long time. Mamă saw to that.'

'She loves you, Laura.'

'Does she?' My voice rang out shrilly, and he winced, whether because of the volume or the words I could not say.

'Of course she does. Stop seeing shadows where there are none. It is that – *that woman* who is making you like this.'

'No. It was this woman who made me like this.' I indicated the door. 'You have given me nothing but shadows all these years.'

'We are not talking about the past.'

'No. We never do.' I was furious now. We were here at the edge of the world, looking over the brink, and still he denied that anything was wrong, as if the water was not pouring away beneath our feet and the way ahead not an abyss. 'I'm sick of your stupid secret. I've lived under it for too long. Don't try and claim this has anything to do with me going back. This has gone on for *decades*. Do you understand, Tată? This has been my *whole life*.'

'Why, Laura?' he asked, not listening. 'Why did it have to be *this* case? Of all the ones in the world . . .'

'Because I was asked to do it! Because it's my job. My responsibility. Remember that – responsibility?' I smiled savagely. 'You know what, Tată, I don't think you're angry at me. I think you're jealous.'

'What?'

'Yes. Because I have a successful career, while you've struggled ever since we left. I'm sorry, but that's not my fault. You were the ones who decided to leave – God knows why, since you refuse to tell me. I've made something of myself here, despite you.' The rage rose to fill my whole being, and I spat, 'It's not my fault taxi driver was the best you could do.'

Immediately I wished I could take the words back, but it was too late.

'That's what you think we are? Jealous?' I'd never seen such an expression on his face. I could have reached out; I should have, oh, I should have, but my small, stunted soul was incapable.

247

'I don't know. And right now, I don't care. What I do know is that you and Mamă have shut me out for too long, and I'm going to put things right.' And though he reached out to stop me, I wrenched the handle and went inside.

Did I believe my own words? Did I truly believe that this time I could fix us? Despite everything, I think I did. Hope – sweet, treacherous hope, one hand gesturing to the light, the other twirling a knife – blinds us all.

CHAPTER TWENTY-SIX

The bedroom was half lit, the curtains drawn, though the unhealthy orange of the street lamp greased the surfaces of everything. A figure lay on the bed, face turned towards the window.

My mother.

It was not my parents' bed in which she lay, and it was this unfamiliarity more than anything that shook me. A hospital bed, strange and new, the head forced upwards as if it, like its occupant, had been broken in two. The air was pungent, earthy and vegetal. Aside from these aberrations, everything was normal, the chair with clothes draped over it, the glow of the street light, somewhere the meow of a cat. Everything as usual but the bed, and the person who lay in it. My anger fell away.

'Mamă,' I said, and my voice wavered, mangling the word into a question. No reply. I moved closer, a child again: there was no chair, so I knelt. The bed was higher than I'd thought, leaving my head barely level with her lap. I stared stupidly at the yellow blanket until it gave a faint twitch. Only then did I raise my head and dare look at her.

It was her, and it was not her. She gazed back, her

expression unreadable. It was the same look she always gave me, a wall I could not scale, only this time there was a – a thing squatting on her throat. I understood nothing about that fatal gland that sits at our throats in the shape of spreading angel wings, but I had pictured it small and neat, like an Adam's apple. No. Her whole neck was swollen, black and monstrous. My hands flew to my own throat in sympathy and fear. I wanted to run.

She made an awful rasping sound: it took a second to realise it was her breathing. Alarmed, I forgot our rule about never touching and put out a hand, then stopped.

'I love you, Mamă.'

Nothing. My father shifted behind me, but I did not turn. I tried again, said her name, told her that if I'd ever hurt her, I was sorry. She tilted her head a little so the light fell rancidly upon her face. The wall in her eyes remained; in vain I hunted for cracks. The photograph should have spoken for me, but here, now, there was no one to speak for me but myself.

'Will you tell me what I did? Tell me what I did wrong, Mamă. Please.' My voice was a whisper.

Her dried lips, ridged with black, parted. She began to speak, or at least made a sound, but was immediately overwhelmed by a coughing fit so prolonged and brutal I almost wished she were dead, anything to end those vicious spasms tearing chunks from her throat. All those times I had clutched my own neck had been a ghastly foreshadowing of this moment. I turned my head so I could not see.

At last it ended, though it was a while before I dared speak.

'Mamă? What did you want to say?'

She did not move. She was no longer looking at me at all, instead gazing up at the ceiling at the scythe of a passing car. The curtains had fallen open: the 'Fish n Chip's' sign flashed through. The aberrant apostrophe had stopped working and I was briefly glad until I remembered where I was and how ridiculous it was to be relieved.

You don't know what I sacrificed. That had been the constant refrain, the weight I carried, on and on, staggering, falling, but always somehow getting up, until now. I could bear it no longer. I had to know what she had done for me, and what I had done to drive her to it, for since we had fallen apart, I had not lived, only endured.

'I know you don't love me. It's OK. I know. But please, Mother. Mamă. Please. What happened to us? What did I do?' It all came tumbling out, not just words, but chunks of my heart. 'I've tried so hard. I love you. I'm sorry that wasn't enough.'

Silence. Her mouth did not move, but her eyes were agitated now, darting across my face.

'She can't talk, Laura,' my father said.

'Yes she can. Yes, she can,' I said fiercely. I managed to put my hand on hers. It was thin and dry, the veins as delicate as the skeleton of a leaf. How long had it been since we'd last touched?

'No more secrets. No more silence. Please, Mamă. For me.' That was it; I had no more.

It took a long, long time to forgive myself for this scene. I believed then that knowledge could fix a thing. But only wisdom can do that, via the kind of truth that lies far beyond what has been said and done.

The tiniest movement. She looked towards me again, and all at once she was *there*, my mamă, not this exhausted husk but completely herself, right there behind the eyes, the woman who had danced and laughed and taken me swimming and whirled me around in the living room as I choked with giddy excitement, the woman with whom I had shared condensed milk, eating it straight from the tin and licking the spoon, who had dried laundry and washed rice and counted sheep, who had buried her nose in my hair and stroked my cheeks for no reason: all the thousand thousand simple huge little things that make up a family, that make up a life.

Her blackened mouth parted; my soul lifted. I strained every nerve to listen.

But the words never came. Her eyes, searching mine, closed, though the lids remained open. She turned away. I knew it was for the last time.

For a few seconds I remained precisely where I was, as the neighbour's car gasped and the street lights flickered and that last small, infant hope died in my arms. I clamped my mouth shut, digging my fingers into my eyes so nothing could come out or in. Then I stood up and left.

'Where are you going?' my father hissed, following me onto the landing. I put a finger on the wonky picture frame, correcting its position. It was that or punch through the wall.

'I'm leaving.' Oh Mamă. I knew nothing then. Forgive me.

'How can you?'

'Tată.' I looked him full in the face and saw, with what could hardly have been called satisfaction, a faint patina of embarrassment. I was not crazy. I had to remember that.

But he reassembled himself quickly. That was our family all over, smoothing over the cracks, pretending not to notice that we were falling to pieces.

'Your mother is dying.'

'She doesn't want me here. She didn't even tell me she was sick. You did.'

'Because I knew she wanted you here.'

'Really? How? Did she ask?'

252

He didn't answer that. 'Just because she can't talk—'

'She can. She just doesn't want to. She doesn't want . . .' Even after everything, I still choked on the words. 'She doesn't want *me*.'

'Laura. You're being ridiculous. How can you abandon her?'

I was near the bottom of the stairs now, looking up at his face, half cast in shadow. Only a fool does the same thing over and over again in the hope of a different result, and I had been that fool. Even in my blackest hours, I had always told myself that things would get better. It had taken me this long to realise that this was no more than a story to hold back the grief. I was too old for stories now.

'I'm not the one doing the abandoning.'

I went down another step, but my father came down one too, as if there were an invisible cord between us, and now I saw the rest of his face, its hurt, its despair, and a part of me unclenched. My mother was one thing, but my father was another. He was different. He *had* to be different. It was true I had no idea what he thought about, all those hours in his taxi with only the radio for company; no idea what kind of a man chose to spend his days encased in a metal shell, only allowing paying strangers in. Even I was not permitted inside, though as a child I'd often begged him. Yet equally, he had always been supportive, congratulating me on my career, showing interest in how I was doing. Of course he had never been able to heal the splits my mother left in my skin, but could anyone?

At once I was ashamed. We were, after all, family. Our wounds ought to bind us together, even if we received them from each other. I would not run away. I would stay. Until the end.

I stepped towards him, put out a hand, and—

He flinched. His body convulsed, slightly but utterly,

entirely visible to my unnaturally heightened senses. It took over his whole frame, his limbs, his face, an alien snap in his eyes. Then whatever it was departed and my tată was in its place, reaching towards me.

I backed slowly down the remaining steps, my breath fluttering madly in my throat. I saw that he knew exactly what had happened, and that he would never, ever acknowledge it. At long last, I realised.

It was not just my mother. It was my father, too.

The splits tore wide, wider, down to the very bone. Clumsily, holding myself together only through will, I picked up my small suitcase, opened the front door and stepped out into the cold night, the tears freezing as I went, walking as fast as I could and at all costs keeping my face turned away from the house and the people I had so long, and so wrongly, called home.

CHAPTER TWENTY-SEVEN

The worst thing you can do is destroy someone's hope. How else to explain the grief of betrayal? The cradle falls away and we fall with it.

I went straight to Andrei's flat. I didn't know if I had a place there any more, but I had sub-let my own apartment and it was too late now for a flight back to Poartă. Without my coat, New Cross station was freezing, and I thanked God that the light in his block was on. My back and shoulders ached and my heart felt huge, distended, as if trying to burst out of my chest. I was past caring, I told myself. It was not until much later that I realised 'past caring' really means 'caring so much it has consumed all else'.

Someone came out of the building and I slipped in past them. I did not want to press the buzzer and hear his surprise, thrown into spiky relief by the crackle of the machine. I did not want to detect a slight pause, replete with our last conversation, before he said, 'Come up.' I wanted to fling myself at him, into him – to eliminate our differences by insulating myself within his body, burrowing into the crevices of his ribs, secreting myself in the chambers of his heart.

I knocked at the door. He opened it wearing pyjamas,

and clacked his tongue in surprise. I tried not to feel like a fly in his food.

'What—'

I told him what had happened, the words pouring out even as he tried to manoeuvre me onto the sofa. I talked at him as he finished his dinner – Craig poking his head in then thinking better of it – waving away a proffered forkful and talking on and on as he washed the plates and his hands because he could never sit still with greasy fingers. I saw the hurt in his eyes after our last conversation, and how he was trying to forget it in order to console me, and my heart broke a little more when he nodded and occasionally said, 'Well done. Well done.'

'I haven't done anything well,' I said, when the words had stopped.

He finished washing up, watching the last suds vanish down the drain.

'You came back.'

That hadn't occurred to me. Suddenly he opened his arms and I went to him, pressed myself in. I had expected to feel safe, but instead I experienced a sudden jolt of hunger. I leaned in closer, my face against his chest and neck. I entwined my fingers through his hair.

'Are you sure?' he whispered, and for answer I led him into his bedroom. I needed to obliviate myself, and I did.

He must have known he was being used.

The next day I awoke early, exhausted, to discover he had slept on the sofa, though I could not recall asking him to do so. I buzzed with a preternatural energy, my limbs restless; it was all I could do not to run.

Andrei's phone rang. It was my father.

'How did you know I was here?'

His voice was weary. 'You're my daughter. I know you. Just as I know you want to come back.'

'I can't. Not after yesterday.'

'Don't be silly. You can always come home.'

'Can I? You don't want me there, Tată. Nor does Mamă.'

'Of course we do.'

'No you don't. Not really. I *saw* you. You wouldn't let me touch you. Why? Why did we leave? Why does she treat me like she does? What in Christ's name have I done wrong?'

A rumble, a controlled explosion. '*I can't tell you.*'

I gripped the phone. 'If you don't tell me now, when she's dying, then when?'

He sucked in his breath. I waited on tenterhooks. For the first time, I really thought it would work. I sensed that at long last I had got through, that he would unbrick the wall of secrets between us and we would see each other for the very first time.

And then I heard it. My mother's voice in the background, distorted yet recognisable. A single word.

'Don't.'

I put the phone down. It did not ring again.

We would never reconcile. I repeated the fact of it to myself, thinking that it would toughen me up, as if a hard heart were something to be desired, as if to go through the world without hurt is the route of a strong person and not a sociopath. She didn't care. She had discarded our last chance forever.

I knew I would never see her again, although looking back, I could not have known it, not really, not where it counted. There are so many planes on which one can exist,

257

and the small, shallow one at the surface is the easiest of all. Many of us never venture beyond it, believing ourselves content with our television and our gossip and our dinner. But to push oneself down into the giant, silent deeps, into the true essence of things – that requires a gentle compassion, a wholeness of consciousness and spirit. I wouldn't do it, and I told myself it was because I didn't want to. Instead, each time my thoughts turned that way, which they did every second, I trained my concentration furiously on Marija, scything through the water; on the photograph I had found at the NRO, from which I still reverberated in disbelief. The photograph might have been bait, but had it not fed me, in a way my mother never had? I'd watched that magpie in its cage, wondering whether to release it; in the end, I'd passed on, not looking back, as it screamed its fury behind me. But at least you knew where you were in a cage. At least there was no dread hope of freedom.

'I have to go back to her,' I said, seating myself at the kitchen counter as Andrei made hard-boiled eggs. 'She needs me.'

He nodded again, peeling an egg, not looking at me. I watched the white skull emerge.

'Good plan.' The rest of the shell came away. He tore off the soft filmy membrane and held the egg out to me.

'I'll have to check the flights.'

He froze, the egg still in his fingers. 'What?'

'The flights,' I repeated. 'I think there are only two a day.' I had no idea if Marija had fired us, or what I was going back to, if anything – the new trial date might have made it hopeless. But the case was all I had. My mother was dying, but Marija Popa was very much alive. I would sacrifice everything to make sure I kept it that way.

He stared at me. 'You're going back to Marija.' He set the egg down and I stared at it stupidly as he rubbed his jaw, trying to remember the last time we had said 'I love you'. Even in my head the words felt worn thin as that membrane, too easily torn to pieces.

'I thought . . .'

'What?'

He shook his head. I picked up the egg and bit into it. He hadn't boiled it for long enough, and the yolk burst, yellow gunge splattering my chin and my fingers. We might have laughed. Neither of us did, and that, I think, was the death knell.

'Andrei . . .' The air between us was thick, impassable with all we were not saying. It obscured our view of one another.

The moment passed. I packed my few things as quickly as I could, and when he closed the door behind me, I knew I would not be back.

The taste of egg lingered all the way through the flight and the ensuing train journey into the city centre. When we went through a tunnel, my reflection slammed against the glass and I pictured the yolk bursting across my face, its deep yellow merging with the orange street light on my mother's swollen cheek. It made me want to throw up, and when we arrived into Poartă station, I did, vomiting into a discarded plastic bag as my throat burned acid and I almost choked, a sound horribly reminiscent of my mother's coughing. Dizzily I wiped my mouth; looking up, I saw a solitary light bulb, swinging in a manner that brought me to the bag a second time. Slowly I slid down the wall, luggage and caged chickens skating past, my hands pressed to my burning throat. Everyone else was busy. Everyone else had a groove into which they fitted. Everyone except me.

I had wanted to belong. That was all. That was why I was obsessed with what had happened to my mother: because from the moment she changed, there was nowhere I fitted.

I made it somehow into a taxi, and although Sorin had said not to give people the exact address, right then I did not care. The driver mumbled the usual reservations, but I must have looked such a sight that he relented. The streets were almost deserted; it was not until we were almost there that I saw any signs of life.

Protesters, more than a hundred of them. They were not chanting, nor waving banners. Rather, they were waiting. The taxi attracted excitement, and they crowded round, forcing our pace to a crawl. A raven-haired woman threw herself against the window, and with a shock I saw that she was brandishing a noose.

Evidently I was not the one they sought, however, for they allowed us through. The guards, who looked as if they were regretting the boredom they had suffered hitherto, opened the gates so we could drive through the frozen grounds all the way up to the front door.

I stepped out. It was quiet, windless, the trees unmoving, the protesters unheard. Even the gate-bird had fallen silent. Someone had already opened the door, a welcoming slice of light spilling across the snow and a warm breath on my cheeks. I looked up towards the east wing and saw a figure silhouetted there, waiting for me.

I was back – I barely hesitated at the word – home.

CHAPTER TWENTY-EIGHT

We had not been fired. Jude met me and gave me a hug: 'Our clogs aren't popped yet.' Later, he outlined what had happened. It seemed the news of my mother's illness had jolted everyone to their senses.

'Marija in particular became very forgiving. We agreed to put it behind us. I'm sorry about your mum, Lăzărescu, but really her timing couldn't have been better.'

I didn't take the remark as callous – I knew he meant well – and besides, I was too relieved for it to matter.

'Are you going to be OK? There's no time to waste with this new trial date. Pavel and Mr Gabor applied for adjournment and tried to argue breach of fair trial provisions, but Judge Ardelean is sticking to his guns. Radutu reckons he's being pressured from the top. The press have been going berserk, even the pro-Marija commentators. Looks like the love affair is over.'

'Love affair?'

'Between her and the media. Sorry, pal, but we need you.'

Neither he nor Pavel commented on the brevity of my visit. The latter unlocked the small office and hustled me inside, muttering gruffly that if I needed anything, if I needed more time . . .

I stared at the nearest thing on his desk, an inventory with an alphabetised list of assets traced by the authorities. A Rembrandt, a Renoir, a roll-call of Rolexes. Then on to S, beginning with 'Saab 9000 (3)' and moving on to 'Sèvres Bleu Celeste, ice bucket, sugar bowl, teacup.'

The sugar bowl. The clandestine meeting with Ursu. The trial date, and whether Pavel had anything to do with it. Camelia. It all felt so impassable.

'Laura?' Pavel's voice was gentle. 'Do you need more time?'

S culminated with 'stuffed crocodile'. I wondered what the crocodile had made of his end of the deal, whether he too felt as if his insides had been ripped out and his eyes replaced with glass. No, I did not need more time.

'Good. Good.' There was relief in his voice, and who could blame him? Our time was running out. I *had* run out, might have believed the clocks were all broken had my mother's watch not continued to tick defiantly on my wrist. I wondered vaguely if I should remove it, the only relic I had.

Enough. It was over. There was no longer any hope of restoring what was broken. All I could do was find out why it had.

But as I gazed at the inventory, I was aware of a spreading warmth in my belly. Here I had a second chance at redemption. My family had made it clear there was no place for me, but here, in Yanussia, I would carve one for myself.

'Pavel,' I said at last. 'Can we still win?'

At any other time, with any other case, the answer would have been a brash affirmative. I knew we were in trouble when he regarded me for some time and at last said, 'I don't know, Laura. But we can try.'

I restarted work. I felt nothing but pure determination to battle against the odds, against myself. Every morning I picked up the phone with shaking hands to call. Every morning I put it down again, unable to find the courage.

Slowly but surely we made progress, and though every second was now against us, I could see our team were doing well with what he had. We put together the defence statement, the jury and defence bundles. Mr Gabor and Pavel attended the pre-trial review. They seemed to have decided that grief had made me fragile: one wrong word and I might shatter. Perhaps they were right. In those ensuing days I vibrated at such a frequency that I worried I might myself do the breaking. I constantly surged with that curious energy, my every action and reaction in overdrive, throwing myself into work as the files danced across my vision in increasingly exotic tessellations. The photograph was nowhere to be found, and I knew now that I would not find it. I drummed my fingers uncontrollably. I choked on nothing, Jude bringing me glass after glass of water I could not drink.

On the seventh day I found myself in my bedroom, in my hands the telegram I had known was coming. The envelope's seal was already broken.

The funeral was in a week, my father's words said.

It was as if he'd pricked me with a pin. All that unnatural energy hissed out of my pores and I could not move. The paper slipped through my fingers, snapping at me in the way paper sometimes does. I stared at where it lay on the floor, broken-backed.

She was dead. My mother was dead.

You'll never know why, a small voice said.

I didn't cry. I couldn't. *Funeral*. Such a crumpled little word. What was it for, anyway? To remember the person, to pay respects. But what if their memory scarred, and the price you'd paid far too high? We have all the procedures in place for sincere emotion. There is always space beside the grave for the weeping widower, the distraught daughter. But what if our true feelings are less whole-hearted? The wedding you would rather not attend; the funeral for the person you did not really have, and so could not really lose. I had tried to grasp my mother but she had slipped through my fingers, and now she was gone.

My first thought was to call Andrei, but we were gone too, dead in all but name. The holes in my skin stretched wider, mouths yammering for pain. I *wanted* to feel pain. There is a second self which knows all our secrets, and I wanted confirmation that I was human, that I was somebody's daughter, not a cut-off nobody. I needed to weep because I was *supposed* to be weeping. I wanted to watch myself act out Grief, to feel ennobled by my own distress, but the stage remained empty. Nothing.

I don't know how long I was there before somebody knocked. I came back to myself and realised I was in my bedroom, huddled on the chair with the clawed feet. The feet seemed to be trying to gain purchase on the ground.

The knock came again. Apostol opened the door.

'She wants to see you.'

Of course she did. The telegram's seal had been broken, and it angered me. Whatever Andrei thought, I had returned to Poartă because I had a job to do. Yet that opened envelope had revealed the cords still threaded through my skin, and I was sick of being a puppet.

We went down the back stairs (why not the ones in the hall? I realised dully that he did not want to be seen). The grey door emerged like an unwelcome guest, its metal glinting in the half-light.

I had had enough of shadows. I was done with secrets which promised so much and gave so little. This whole house needed to be wrenched into the light, its entrails exposed for the world to see. As we reached the foot of the stairs, I surged suddenly forward, away from him, towards the door. Apostol let out a strange noise, half yell, half snarl, and grabbed for me, but I arched like the cat curiosity had not yet killed and eluded him, body snapping back then forward again. I had only a millisecond before Apostol would be on me, and I knew this time he would not settle for a mere push; this time he would beat my head into the door until the metal did his work for him. I wrenched the handle but it would not turn, and I shook it with an awful death rattle, praying it was no longer locked, then all at once it was opening, wide, wider, and a hand grasped my wrist and pinned it to the bone, but the door was open and I could see . . .

The stained red stairs were no longer there. There was only a breeze-block wall.

It was as if a plastic bag had been placed over my head. All the air was sucked out, the only sound the howling in my ears. Though Apostol's grip was painful beyond belief, I reached out and placed my other hand against the wall. It was real. Hard, yet with that strange, slightly porous crumble to it. The pieces looked old, limned with white cement.

'It can't be . . .'

Before I could do anything else, I was whipped around, my head slamming back into the stone so I felt the shape of my own skull, outlined in flashing pain. Apostol had me by the throat, this man who had spied for the Strajă and beaten another to death with his own gun.

'Where is it?' I hissed. 'The basement.' The grip was forcing the blood to my ears, tracing the ribbing of my windpipe. Was this what being born had been like, with the cord around my neck? Imagine those first few minutes, when all I knew was pain.

'What basement?'

'You know . . . what I mean.' I forced the words out. 'Where are the stairs?'

'No stairs. Bricked up years ago.'

'You're lying.'

'Am I?' He smiled, wide and slow. 'You don't know what truth is any more.' His free hand traced lovingly down my waist, and my breath froze. 'Pity Marija has taken you for herself.'

Something dark in me thrilled, even as the grip around my neck loosened: he shoved me viciously so I stumbled away from the wall, my throat engorged, alien. Just like my mother's.

After that, I went quietly. I had nothing left. We walked back along the lower floor of the east wing, all the way to the hall. At the main stairs Apostol turned on his heel and went *behind* them. There, partly hidden, was a short corridor I had not seen before. The staircase rose above it: I could have reached up and touched its serrated edge. We were neither in the east wing nor the west, but somewhere in between.

We stopped and he turned to me, twirling a key in his fingers.

'You don't know what truth is,' he repeated. 'But I am your friend. I will help you.' Another twirl of the key. 'You remember what I told you before? That there is only order and aberration?'

I refused to speak, but that only made him smile again.

'Truth can be either, Lăzărescu. That is what makes it so dangerous.'

Before I could say anything, he opened the door and pushed me inside.

CHAPTER TWENTY-NINE

My first impression was of unexpected light. Not the yellow-amber of the house's interior, trapping us like flies, but the pure, elevating white of daylight. I felt as though I had just woken up. Was I outside? I had lost my bearings completely. Yet it was warm, and gradually I noticed that while the walls and floor were brick, the roof was glass, or must be, arching somewhere high above and letting the light stream in. I cannot tell you the relief it brought.

I was in a beautiful garden, resplendent with fruit trees and flowers. It was less a real place than a fable; I wondered what the lesson was to be. A conspiracy of green, leaves curling gently around themselves as if preserving secrets, rills of tinted shadows running in and among them in delighted congregation. I felt like one of a crowd. The trees seemed to have been placed precisely so as to bring maximum delight, their fruits evenly spaced so as to be pleasing to the eye. I saw oranges, lemons, cherries, all in unreal jewelled hues. Strawberry plants and melons loitered at my feet, scenting the fresh green air. Each was picture-perfect: someone had made them so, carefully drawing out the faultlessness in every plant, every fruit, every leaf, extracting form from nature's very formlessness. You could have painted it from any angle and been handed a perfect composition. This was not gardening. This was playing God.

'The Winter Garden.'

The voice made me start. Marija Popa had appeared on a small path tailing into the foliage. She wore a complex dress also of green, fastened with buttons all the way down the side. If I half closed my eyes, her body merged with the plants. I had seen her coiled like a spring, yet here she was softer, more essential, her waist two arcing stems, her finger-nails the dappling beneath the leaves. She was smiling like the sun.

'You call this winter?'

'It is a misnomer, I admit. Here it is always spring. Or summer. Whatever I choose it to be.'

I realised then where I was: beneath the glass dome, at the heart of the mansion. At the heart of *her*. The shadows in the greenery acquired a deeper tincture and the edges of the leaves seemed to sharpen. A Venus flytrap.

Don't lose your head, I told myself. Don't lose your head.

'Do you like it?' she asked, a light in her eyes as if she could read my thoughts. I put up my guard.

'You shut things in and expect them to thrive.'

'No, Laura. I take them in and nurture them until they do.' She rolled my name around her mouth, and for a second it was my mother standing there, her eyes no longer black but green as the plants around us. 'This was my favourite place as a child.' Her voice became soothing, channelling itself along a path as well marked as the brick beneath her feet. 'I spent hours here with the plants. I suppose it was my father who gave me the passion. I used to follow him around with a watering can, tending his roses, his poinsettia . . .'

She was doing it again, weaving a narrative around me

like a spider. I recoiled. She must have seen my expression, because the performance came to a halt. I risked glancing up: the sky was eyeball-white.

When she spoke again, it came from a different script, or even – could it be? – no script at all.

'After the orphanage, my new parents showed me this.' Her voice was quiet. 'And . . . well. I could not believe it. I had never known a world capable of beauty. It was the first place I truly felt at home. When Dinu and I built our first palace, I wanted something similar. No, not similar. Identical. I created another garden, built to exactly the same specifications as this. He did not care for it. For him, beauty without function was not beauty at all, whereas I knew beauty could keep me safe. I had my way – at a price.' Her voice lowered. 'Always at a price.'

I waited for her to elaborate, but she only said, 'The plants would not grow. We questioned the gardeners. I flew in experts from your Kew Gardens. They could not say what was wrong, only that they were sick. I was so sad. I felt it was my fault, as though I had lost something inside me. We began importing them. Dinu's ambassadors smuggled specimens in their diplomatic cars. Many died.' She sighed. 'We made it work, but it was not the place I wanted. It was sad and disappointing. I should have known. You cannot force something to grow, or rather, if you do, it will not live very long.'

I said, 'You opened my telegram.'

'What did you expect?' Her tone was simple, direct. 'You think I have survived this long by respecting others' privacy? It has been decades since I had any privacy of my own.'

'Because you were powerful!' I burst out. 'Because you and your husband *chose* this. Because you fought tooth and nail to get to the top and stay there!' The unnatural energy was coursing again, the words spitting in my mouth like fireworks. 'It doesn't matter whether you did what they allege. You could have done anything you wanted. You could have made life *better* for people, but you didn't.'

I broke off, breathing hard. Marija was motionless, her eyes burning black fire, the leaf shadows mottling her skin. After the telegram I had forgotten how to be afraid. Now I remembered in full.

She removed a brown envelope from a pocket and held it out to me. 'Look at this and tell me what you see.'

I took it, and as I withdrew its contents, a great weariness burst over me. It was the photograph.

'You stole this.'

'No, *you* stole this. You say I have helped no one. I will help you now. I remember Gabriela Lăzărescu. She had shorter hair than most. It failed to cover her face. I recall that, because she looked like she wanted it to.

'The watch on your wrist. It is hers, no?' She was looking at it and I thought I detected a magpie flash in her eye. 'I recognised it the first time we met. You wear it to keep her close.'

I said flatly, 'Why did you not tell me from the first that you knew her?'

'I did not know whether I could trust you.'

I said angrily, 'I have proved myself. I investigated Mr Gabor for you. I have done enough.'

'And yet Dumitru has moved the trial date forward by three months,' she snapped. 'That man is slow. This is not his style. Someone has pushed him to it, him and Ardelean. The seed has begun to sprout, exactly as I said it would. There is a traitor, Laura' – my mother's pronunciation again; it flayed me and I could not tell if she knew it or not – 'and if it is not Radutu, it is someone else. You told me Pavel was delivering a sugar bowl. What if you are wrong?'

'You told me not to ask him about it. You have him on a string, Doamna. If *you* want to ask him, be my guest.'

Her eyes narrowed dangerously. 'On a string?'

Too late I remembered where I had heard the phrase. They were the exact words Pavel had used the evening he had pleaded with her.

'You spied on me.'

'You opened my telegram. We're even. No – not even. I proved myself to you with Radutu's file. You said you could trust me, but you have given me no reason to trust you.'

A tiny vein pulsed in her temple: I felt that for once I was looking at her, the real her. It gave me no satisfaction. Whatever game she thought we were playing, we were at stalemate.

Suddenly she turned and said, 'Come.'

I followed. Why not? My mother was dead, after all. There were no paths left but this. We walked along the coiling brick, hemmed in by green, drawn into the garden's leafy heart. I was Eve, trailing the serpent.

Don't lose your head.

The path twisted and turned upon itself, a narrow tendril, almost organic in its own right. There were more fruits on the bushes, red fruits I could not identify, clustering in as if offering themselves up to be eaten. I was careful not to touch them. Eventually the hedges opened: we were in a small clearing directly under the dome's eye. Beneath it was a circular space lined with stacks of square cages, each cage holding a single fluttering occupant. At the centre of them, in the garden's very heart, a fire danced in a raised pit.

'For my husband,' Marija said. 'It is kept burning, always.'

'And . . . and the birds?' They had fallen silent at our appearance; as ever, I could not decide whether to be horrified or enchanted. I was beginning to think they might be the same thing.

In answer, she put a hand against the nearest cage. A small thing of intense yellow – a canary? – began to cheep urgently within, peeping out with that peculiar sideways avian gaze. I sensed its fellows rather than seeing them, an ongoing spasm of minute movements, green and blue and red flashing amid the wires. I caught the scent of blood, and flowers.

'My birds.' She smiled. 'They make it hard for me to die. Who else would love them so well?'

'You call this love?'

'Why not? That was.' She pointed at the fire, moving towards the bench beside it.

'What do you mean?'

And she explained. Explained how love was a monster of many heads; explained how her marriage, far from being a bond of equal power, had in fact been one of enslavement and terror.

'It was not always that way. Before we married, I was smitten. I was an actress, a rising star; he was the housing minister, newly minted. At an after-show party he came up and told me how extraordinary I had been. We were eating smoked salmon canapés with lemon, and as he talked, he squeezed the lemon piece in his fingers until there was no juice left. I watched those fingers and knew then that they would take me, or crush me in the trying.' Her voice was clear, with no trace of self-pity. 'We married after barely six weeks, still strangers. He liked me, liked my beauty. He showed me off to his comrades and noticed early on how I opened up his conversation. I made him appear charming rather than surly, gregarious rather than mute.

'It did not take long to realise that he saw me less as a person than an aperture. Through me he could pass into the world and transform it. At his bidding I insinuated myself with old Bogdan, whispering in the ear of the Dear Leader and the other nomenklatura, watching those hairy little orifices open like flowers. Why did I do it? I suppose because

I was good at it, and because even then he had a way of making you do what he wanted.' She was staring at the flames, deep into the fire's heart.

'I was effective – too effective. When Bogdan faded, he anointed my husband as his successor. By the time of the election, Dinu's appointment to the presidency was little more than a formality. And I – I became his First Lady. I was twenty-six. I was so young, Laura, so unbelievably young, young enough to stand beside him as they cheered and allow myself to fantasise that now he had what he wanted, it would be enough.

'But then I found I was infertile. The doctor told me that my womb had been wrecked by childhood hunger, that there was nothing they could do. Everything changed from that moment. You see, Dinu had pictured a dynasty. His rule would not end with his own death: it would march on, for generations. "We could be the new kings," he would whisper at night. My diagnosis drove him half mad.

'He sent the doctor to one of the new secret prisons, but the whispers got out anyway. My husband, the Father of Yanussia, could not even fuck his wife properly. They said I was cursed, that I was barren as a desert, my vagina full of dust and snakes.' I might have expected a catch in her voice, a crack; for her to hunch over in self-protection. But her tone was smooth, her back unbowed.

'The first beating came shortly after. It was the longest, and the worst, but it was not the last. He beat me until it scared him, until he wept, and the more afraid he was, the more he had to continue. And I realised that his only way of overcoming fear was by inflicting his power; that he would force himself to keep going until he vomited and long past that.'

I stared at her. Whatever I had expected, it was not this. It was impossible to subjugate her, or so I had always thought.

She was a creature entirely of her own, entirely free in every sense that mattered. Yet I felt her truth.

'Afterwards he was sorry. He brought me a goldfinch in a cage, filled a ballroom in our summer palace with red roses and fucked me among them, heedless of the thorns. When I stood up again, my back was a lake of blood.

'Alone in my apartments, I laughed at the bird. I assumed it was a sick joke, but after a while, I realised he was too stupid for metaphors. I offered him other women, hoping they would satisfy him. But the strange thing about Dinu was that he couldn't bear to be unfaithful. Power was his way of fucking the world, of violating it with himself, and if he could not fuck me, he would find other breeds of violation. We were bound together for life. The kind of love that is a death sentence. He could not sate himself any other way, so there were many more beatings, and many more flowers, but never any more birds. So I bought them for myself.' Her eyes were twin hollows. 'Each time it happened, I took a bird home.'

I regarded the cages, and at their sheer number something fell away in my heart. Popa must have thought he knew everything about everyone. Discovering he did not even know his own wife's body must have driven him wild.

'I replaced them when they died, so I would never forget what they cost me.' A hundred living, fluttering scars. I clenched my fists at the scale of it, at the horror.

'One day I will set them free.'

I found some words. 'You could set them free now.'

Only then did her voice waver. 'No. Not until after the trial. That is the only thing that can liberate us from his influence.'

I told her she needed to tell someone, that we could argue coercion. She laughed.

'They would not believe me, and if they did, they would

not care. All men want to make the world quiver. Dinu beat me because he could not bruise my country to his satisfaction. First Minister Anghelescu is no different. Nor is Ursu. Why else do you think they call him the Bear?'

We were on the bench, sitting beside one other. I wondered why she kept the fire burning; whether he had told her to do it, and even after death she did not dare disobey. The flames cast a red light on our faces, on the photograph I still held. She looked at the image and smiled.

'You look just like my god-daughter.'

'Marija Păstrăv.'

'Yes. She had eyes like yours.'

'Why was this in my file?'

'You were a Iubită child, Laura. The Iubită children were of vital importance.'

Something in me flared and died. 'Importance?'

She said, quickly – only later did I realise too quickly – 'My employees became the pilot for my Million Children Movement. I had insisted on an all-female workforce. It was perfect. They were faithful to me, those women, every one. They knew their duty. They and their children – my children – showed that my Movement could work, and it did. It was my greatest triumph.' Her eyes glittered. 'It kept me alive. I used it to convince Dinu that my barrenness was a blessing, not a curse, that I could pull strength from my weakness like a rabbit from a hat. I told him that I would use public sympathy for my own infertility to start a national programme that would flood his fields with workers. His Little Mother would birth not two or three children, but a million.'

I could not help but think of all those other women, the ones who had lived in terror, going to war against their own bodies and the possibility of pregnancy. The ones who ran a desperate gamut of old wives' tales, poisoning themselves with photochemicals, scalding themselves in hot baths, lifting weights until their muscles tore.

'I know what you are thinking. But in Yanussia, a wife is little better than a slave. The one thing men cannot take from us is our gift of life. The Movement worked. It made us more than just lesser versions of men: it made our bodies more than theirs, made them sacred. A space in which we could exist.'

A space to exist. Wasn't that all I wanted, all anyone wanted? I looked at her, gleaming in the light, and saw what she had done. The Little Mother had transformed herself into a symbol. She had weaponised her own infertility, and in doing so made herself untouchable. Hadn't she?

'We don't have much time,' I said at last.

'No.'

'We might not win.'

'Yes.'

'Are you ready for it?'

A faint smile. 'Do I strike you as someone who will lose?'

There was something else, then. More tricks up her sleeve, more bullets in her gun. I said only, 'Let me visit the factory. I need to know.'

She said nothing for some time, staring into the flames.

'Very well.'

A warm, honeyed relief spread in my belly, but before I could thank her, she spoke again.

'Your namesake. Lazarus of Bethany. Jesus brought him back to life, did he not? Do not look surprised. I was born a Christian.'

Until an hour ago, I could not have imagined her believing in anyone but herself.

'It is a good story. It gives people hope.' The fire leapt in her eyes, the heat grazing her cheeks as if seeking to burn off her skin. 'I once heard a story about Lazarus. About how Jesus went to the cave where he lay, and how the disciples watched in amazement as their dead friend emerged alive. But there was something the disciples did not see, and Lazarus himself never told a soul. Only his sister, Mary, heard him weeping in the night and got it out of him.

'What Jesus never told anyone is that the process of resurrection is one of immense pain. It is a pain that does not belong to this world, so much pain we cannot imagine. What Lazarus told his sister, deep in the night-time, was that it hurt so much that he wished he were dead.'

The fire seemed to have had its way, for her skin was raw and her eyes full as she said, 'Sometimes, Laura, the thing we believe has saved us – well, it may in fact have wounded us beyond repair.'

CHAPTER THIRTY

Late that night I sat in the bath, long enough for my finger-tips to corrugate and the water to feel neither hot nor cold but merely an extension of myself. I didn't want to go to bed, because as long as I stayed awake, I was still in the same day that my mother had been alive.

Thus I lingered, water tracing down my cheeks so it looked like I had cried myself a bathful of tears. Pushing the tap with my toe, I wondered if I had ever truly been awake, if I had ever let the world in properly. My mother on her deathbed. Marija and those caged birds. I needed another way to experience the world, to cram myself with it, to dine, feast, gorge upon life so I could confirm to myself that I had lived, and there was a difference between this side and that other.

I believe I already knew then where that portal resided. It shimmered, susurrating the tips of my consciousness. My mother had not given me the answers I sought, but another woman could.

I closed my eyes and pushed myself down, down into the water.

Morning came. The barrier of night was between us

forever; every successive night would be another splicing. I'd found a bottle of sleeping pills on the pillow, though the door had been locked all day. I didn't question it. There were enough questions already. The little capsule overpowered me with ease, and as I dressed that morning, fumbling with my clothes, I thought I saw another Laura in the mirror, watching me with an unreadable expression. I flung a jacket over it and she vanished.

At breakfast, I was surprised to see Ecaterina. Naturally she was not eating, only watching in mild disgust as Jude sprayed crumbs across the tablecloth. I remembered now that I had seen her after the press conference, as I left for the airport. She had virtually run into me outside, hair and eyes wild. I remembered her aghast expression as Camelia's body was covered. I had attributed it to grief for her secretary, yet the more I thought about it, the more I realised it was not poor Camelia who had produced that expression. Marija's sister had been staring not at the body, but at the blond-haired man beside it.

She had not responded to my distracted apology but instead continued straight on, as if there were a hidden path from which she could not deviate, though her coat was thin and her feet drenched in snow. I had thought she looked like the White Queen, weeping for a wound not yet inflicted.

This morning, she looked different again. Not wild, nor aghast, only a cold composure.

'The tour,' she said without preamble. I noted the red around her pale eyes. 'We are to go this afternoon.'

I blinked at her stupidly.

'The Iubită factory tour,' she said impatiently. She glanced at Jude, who was engrossed in his toast, and in an undertone added, 'My sister thinks it is an excellent idea.'

Marija's reward. I sat back in my chair, once more sensing the tug of the web. I had not expected her to act so soon, and the implications sprang out. My mother had not wanted me to go – it was practically the last thing she had said to me. It would be a final betrayal.

But I felt the pull of the photograph. No matter that she was gone, that I could never fix us. I had to find out what lay beyond that shining Iubită logo, to prise it off the wall and see what crawled behind.

Pavel entered. He seemed mostly back to normal, but I had not exactly attended him closely of late.

'Pavel.' Jude ran a finger through the leftover jam on his plate. 'Apparently we have another school trip. The Iubită factory.'

A frown. 'Impossible. We have no time.'

'The Doamna has requested it especially,' Ecaterina said smoothly. 'Two hours only. You can work late instead.'

'Late?' Jude muttered. 'Later, more like.'

'She told me to inform you she believes it . . . important for your understanding.' Another glance at me. 'The Doamna will brook no arguments. We leave at two.' Then she was gone, a faint musky scent lingering, like paper or beeswax. She was growing more insect-like, thinner than ever, skin stretched tight over her jaw.

'More distractions. Just what we need,' Pavel said heavily.

Jude shook open a newspaper and swore. 'They've found her.'

'Who?'

'*The Woman in Red.*'

We stared at the headline. The Picasso had been located in a Swiss bank vault by a hotshot new team of asset tracers. If they had proof it was purchased illegally, as was rumoured, we were in real trouble. *Little Mother – or Big Liar?* ran an editorial denouncing the discovery, as well as the *Vogue* story and Ursu's attempted assassination. To my horror, and Jude's excitement, our photos were on the inside pages, a special feature on the Black Widow's defence team. The images had been pulled off the HSG website and made me feel hideously exposed. Huffing in exasperation, Pavel went out to make yet more phone calls.

'This is awful,' I said. What must it be like for famous people? When Marija looked in the mirror, did she see her head or a headline?

'I know,' Jude replied, holding the paper up so close his nose was almost touching it. 'Your picture is *terrible*.'

'Jude.' My voice sounded small to my ears.

'Don't worry, I'm looking out for you. When this is over, I'm going to sort you a photo shoot.' He glanced over. 'You're looking pale. Have you checked under your bed for vampires?'

'That's Romania.'

'I wouldn't be so sure. I feel pretty undead these days. Plus I've always imagined Pavel as sleeping upside down, like a bat.'

I managed a smile. 'Thought about it a lot, have you?'

'Seriously, this place is draining my life force. Don't you feel it?'

Surprised by this admission of weakness, I said nothing.

'Come on, Lăzărescu. Trench spirit and all that.'

'I don't feel like that. I feel . . .' I stopped.

'Like what? Come on. You can tell Uncle Jude.' He did, bizarrely, look avuncular then. The wolf had been tucked away.

At last I said, 'I feel like I'm falling.' Faster and faster, and I could not stop no matter what.

I spent the rest of the morning navigating a maze of kick-backs illicitly received for everything from Second World

War reparations to road-building contracts. Pavel gave us the not-unexpected news that with the altered trial date there would be no festive break: after Jude put up an almighty fuss, citing the 1926 Slavery Convention, he finally granted us Christmas afternoon off. I wondered how his wife had taken it. An HSG partner's dedication was measured in absences rather than coffee spoons, and I wondered if it ever haunted Pavel, all those regretful should-have-been-theres, the myriad lonely if-onlys. What would he do when he retired? He would don his Church's shoes, tie his careful tie, then remember, and stop, and – what?

Was I any better? I had always wanted to become a lawyer, or at least had always told myself that I wanted to become a lawyer, and they had seemed the same thing until now.

But I was incapable of broader speculation. This case had become my whole world, and it was easy to believe that if I set foot outside Poartă's boundaries, I might melt. Perhaps it was the pill I had swallowed, for I took that morning's news of the outside world with mild disbelief. Funar had complained about his treatment in prison. Clinton was celebrating the North American Free Trade Agreement. The Croatians were seeking to purge their language of Serbian influences (*okolotrbusnji pantalodrzac*, or 'around-the-waist pants-holder', would now replace their four-letter word for 'belt'). I knew these things were true, but I did not believe them.

Had I been wholly honest with myself, I would have said that even Poartă was blurring at the edges. The mansion, and the magnetic presence within, had become my only reality.

At 1.55, Pavel dropped in to remind us of the factory trip. As if I could have forgotten. I was brimming with dreadful anticipation.

'Be ready for two o'clock sharp. We can't afford to waste

any more time.' He was already dressed for the outdoors, but he turned to the mirror on the wall of the Lair, tugged on his lapel in dissatisfaction, and said he was going to change.

'I don't know why he's bothering,' Jude said once he was out of sight. 'That scarf makes him look like Rupert Bear.'

I started. 'What did you say?'

'That stupid yellow scarf he insists on wearing.'

Why else do you think they call Ursu the Bear?

Jude whistled a little tune, stopped, peered at me. 'You all right, Lăzărescu? You look like you're about to throw up. Please don't. I'm a sympathy vomiter, and after that I tend to faint.'

'It's nothing.' My thoughts were wires, sawing back and forth.

'Where is Cristian?' Ecaterina appeared, looking displeased.

'Here.' Pavel returned in a coat that looked exactly the same as the previous number, the yellow scarf coiled around his neck like a snake.

Rupert Bear. Dumitru Ursu. The Bear.

There is a traitor, Marija had said. *Or rather, there will be.*

Could Ursu have been Pavel's mystery caller? I had dismissed the possibility after hearing Pavel address him as Rupert, but now I remembered my boss's words on our first full day here. 'Yanussians love their code names,' he'd said.

I tried to recall the details of that phone conversation. *There is no need to do this,* he'd said – no, pleaded. Then at the press conference that same day, Ursu had moved the trial date. Coincidence? I didn't think so. But had Pavel really sabotaged our case? If he had, he faced massive negligence exposure. He could be sued. Our team would, of course, be fired, and who knew what Marija would do. (Once more I thought of Manea and Cristescu.) The case would likely go to a retrial; I would have said the entire case could collapse, but I doubted that would be allowed to happen. They would force her to trial one way or another, and meanwhile the prosecution could feed off our turmoil and grow fat. I needed to speak to Marija immediately, but when I tried to excuse myself, Ecaterina snapped, 'No. We go *now*.'

Her tone was so febrile I could not but obey. We shuffled meekly out.

Outside, the day was still as ice. My brain was fevered, whether from Pavel or the pill: every thought felt heavy, a dragging pressure behind the eyes, and the cold was a relief. It had snowed heavily overnight; the trees held out frostbitten limbs. All was layered in a thick silence, broken only by our crunching feet and Ecaterina muttering about lateness.

'I do apologise,' Pavel said with unusual contrition.

Ecaterina sighed. 'No, it is for me to apologise. In truth, I am upset about my bees.'

'What bees?' Pavel and Jude asked at the same time as I said, 'What happened?'

'A hive's lid fell off last night,' Ecaterina said, ignoring their question. 'They died of the cold.'

A shiver went through me that had nothing to do with the freezing air. 'An accident?'

'Yes,' Ecaterina said tonelessly. 'An accident.'

'Can't you just get another?' Jude's face was waxy from cold.

'If your child died, could you just get another?'

'Ah.'

'Yes. Each hive has its own character. They are individual. Irreplaceable.' She went on, softly, so I had to lean in to catch the words like snowflakes: 'Like people, if people made sense and were beautiful.'

We got into the warm waiting car, Ecaterina in front, the

284

three of us behind, me squashed in the middle. Mr Gabor was in witness interviews all day, speaking with people who might help explain away some allegedly corrupt payments from foreign car manufacturers. A huddle of protesters met us at the gates but there were fewer than previously, presumably deterred by the cold.

'Wonder if that Christmas Day demonstration will happen,' Jude remarked. 'It's freezing.'

We drove onto the long stretch of Bulevard Noiembrie 22, which sucked us down towards the Parliament building and spat us out the other side, over the grey Danube and down the Bulevard Unirii. My thoughts should have been on my mother and the factory. Instead they were all on Pavel. Before, there had been nothing to tie him to the moving of the trial date – more than a week had elapsed between his visit and the press conference. But if he had in fact spoken to Ursu the very morning of the conference, that all changed. Had he deliberately conspired to change the trial date? Perhaps that was what jealousy did: took you and the world and wrenched the pair of you out of any comprehension.

I didn't know what to do, and my thoughts chased one another around as we passed the giant Parliament and the ugly communist apartment blocks. Buildings left by giants – or rather, men pretending to be. Through the windows, a woman adjusting a clothes line; the exposed backs of photo frames.

To my relief, we turned off the boulevard and the road narrowed immediately, the buildings lessening in stature and morphing into sagging traditional houses, roofs embedded with almond-shaped windows, like eyes. It was the first time we had seen anything older than this century, thanks to Popa's clearances. Marija had described his hands squeezing the life from that unlucky lemon. She had told me about

285

the physical scars he'd left, but what about those she and this city carried within, on the other side of the skin?

The landscape became industrial, or a fossilised version thereof, scattered with the bones of abandoned factories, backs turned on one another in the snowy landscape. Some bore scorch marks; most windows were broken. The spaces between buildings were littered with toffee-chunks of concrete, spare tyres and the occasional dog.

'We're here.'

'Here' was a large, square white building, its address showing us to be at 159 Strada Iulie 6. I noticed immediately that its windows were unbroken, though here and there were red brick scars where the paint had fallen away. An enormous billboard loomed: *IUBITĂ COMPANIE*, it said in swirly font, beside a faded image of a beautiful woman being kissed by her beautiful husband. With a pang I recognised the logo beside them: a fat red cartoon heart, bursting with light. The *iubită*. The sweethearts. How many times had I seen my father shyly present one to my mother?

But darling, she would say, I already work in the factory. They give me extra for free. And he would answer, I know, but how could I give my heart to anyone else?

I rubbed my eyes: the ghosts disappeared. Our car was met by security guards, but when they saw Ecaterina they nodded and waved us through. The tiled lobby was clean and empty.

'Where is everyone?' Jude asked.

'It's Saturday,' Pavel reminded him.

'Yes, it is Saturday, but also there are no workers,' Ecaterina said. 'At its height this factory had a staff of eight hundred women. They were known as the lucky eight hundred. Everyone wanted a job here. Now . . .' She lit a cigarette, a point of red flaring against the white of her skin, and pressed a

286

switch. For an odd moment it seemed as though she had buzzed like an insect, but it was only the strip-lights turning on to reveal a huge factory floor, yellow beams arcing off silver steel. With an intake of breath, I beheld the room from the photograph. There was the metal sign; there the machines; there that curious silver halo around the heads of my companions. But the benches and the women with their babies were gone. I was gone. I grasped the nearest pillar for support.

'The factory,' Ecaterina said, the pride shining so strongly through her voice that I half expected to see my mother's afterglow drifting down the aisles. Her soul had been forged here. And, perhaps, broken.

We walked on through, past a series of enormous vats. Pipes of incomprehensible purpose ran across the ceiling and hurled themselves in. I tried to focus, to detect what it was that had upset my mother so much. This was my only opportunity. It was my suggestion of this visit that had caused her panic attack, which in turn had led to the hospital, which had led to the diagnosis, and her keeping it from me until the last, when I had knelt before her and nothing had happened. In my guilty mind the chain of events had clotted, coagulated, so it seemed to me in some strange way that it was the factory, and my eagerness to visit it, that had killed her.

'The gummy bears,' Ecaterina said. 'The mixture is stirred and sent to the pouring machine. Then it goes into the starch moulds. I keep one as a reminder.'

We clustered round. It was a large tray covered in some white floury substance, several inches thick. It had been stamped or moulded into dozens of bear-shaped hollows. In the solemn atmosphere they were somehow – ridiculously – totemic, like Iron Age corpses in a peat bog. I didn't like these creatures: they reminded me of Ursu. Jude put out a finger, apparently to poke a hole in the powder, but

Ecaterina shot him such a look that he gave a small cough and delicately used the digit to tuck a lock of hair behind his ear.

'Now, the gummy snakes.'

What was I looking for – or rather, what was I being allowed to see? I rubbed my eyes again, a hot prickle. Why did I feel like the hungry magpie, gazing through the wires at the temptations within? Strange beyond strange, to think I had been here once before. I wondered why that photo-op had been set up in the first place. I itched to look at its offspring, but I had left it in my room, hidden safely away again inside a jumper in my closet.

No, not safely. I knew well enough by now that if Marija wanted something, there was no stopping her.

Pavel threw an unsubtle glance at his watch. 'Perhaps we can skip the snakes and see the *iubită*?'

Ecaterina smiled for the first time, ignoring his impatience. 'These are our pride and joy. Famous through all Yanussia.'

'Famous sweets?' Jude was sceptical.

'You forget, there wasn't much of anything, and what there was tasted like nothing. The *iubită* were different. They are, how do you say, a national treasure. Like your Cadbury's but more so, a tradition going back more than a hundred years. Sweethearts, you would call them in English.'

'You were supposed to give them to your wife or girlfriend,' Pavel said. 'To prove your love.'

'Yes. They were so popular they were rationed. Three a week. They had separate queues in the grocery shops. Everyone envied the women who worked here because they got a certain amount for free – like your mother would have done.' This last was to me.

'So Marija ran this?' Jude said eventually, as the silence stretched like a gummy snake.

'At a government level it was run by the Minister for Industry. Alexandru Ungur.'

Jude frowned. 'Isn't he still in that position?'

'I believe so. I no longer pay attention to politics.' Her shrug was as artificial as her sweets, and I wondered why. 'I was the general manager. Marija was more of a . . . figurehead. As Minister for Women she liked using the factory for public relations. The all-female workforce, for example.'

I recalled Marija talking about her Movement and the factory's role therein. *It kept me alive*, she'd said. They did not sound like the words of a figurehead.

Her sister's eyes flickered upwards, just once, and I followed their direction. Above us was a tiny mezzanine room, little more than a box. The windows were of tinted glass: whoever was within could look out, but nobody could look in. I caught Ecaterina watching me, and with a frisson I knew exactly who that had been, who had curled up in there, gazing down upon her kingdom.

'The factory has been closed since the revolution,' she went on. 'There is no money.'

'When will you reopen?'

'When there is money,' she said, opaque, and walked on ahead before any of us could ask when exactly that might be. We went upstairs, past the liquorice machines on the second floor – 'I have never much liked the stuff' – and up to the third.

'Not exactly Willy Wonka, is she?' Jude murmured in my ear, and I nodded. Any golden ticket would have withered to ash. The childish magic that ought to have whisked about was absent, leaving only the taste of sweet times turned bitter, of cavities without the chocolate.

Ecaterina opened her skinny arms wide. 'This is where we made the *iubită*.'

To my disappointment it looked precisely like the floor

we had left behind. Even the vat to my left seemed to bear the same scuff mark. Perhaps we were trapped in an infinite loop, and in many, many years they would find our dusty outlines lined up neatly beside the bears' hollow corpses.

'When the winds blew towards the city, one could smell the hot sugar in the air.'

'What do they taste like?'

'They are like, what would you say? Gobstoppers. But not too large, and with a soft centre. You have heard maybe that they call Yanussia's female workers the hamsters. Because they work, work away with one of these in their cheeks. Each batch takes two days to make. The *iubită* do not allow for haste or imprecision. They demand patience and care. Like love.' Again I caught a dusty something in those dried eyes, like furniture covered in sheeting. A mutter, a memory. A time when things might have been different.

Angry voices from below interrupted us and a second later a guard came running up.

'An intruder, Doamna, trying to get in—'

'I tell you, I'm not an intruder. I am a *friend* of Ms Iubită.' The voice coming up the stairwell was laconic, American. Even as I turned, I knew who it was.

'We know him,' I said, as the guard gabbled on. 'It's all right. We know him.'

Patrick came over, shooting me a quick look of thanks. His hair was untidy from the wind, his cheeks cold-pinked, and the odd shock of that soft, feminine mouth.

'Patrick Hanagan,' he said to Ecaterina, making a small bow. 'I'm real glad to meet you at last.'

Pavel shifted. 'I thought you met the other day.'

'Sadly we missed each other. My fault. Got my dates wrong.'

'That is hardly a rationale for breaking in—'

290

'Who are you?' Ecaterina interrupted. 'How did you get in?'

'Forgive me, ma'am. I work for First Loyalty Bank.' He gave her a card. She was about to put it straight into her handbag when he added, 'I *am* a friend of your Minister for Industry, Alexandru Ungur.'

That man again. Ecaterina looked from Patrick to the card and back, and there passed between them something I could not decipher.

'This place is great,' he said. 'Reminds me of Hershey's in Pennsylvania.'

'You had better stay with us,' Ecaterina said. 'We will finish the tour.'

The frown lines in Pavel's forehead carved deeper as she showed us the spinning machines that whirled the *iubită* around with dye, using five tonnes of force to compress them into solid candy. Before, these mechanisms had blurred with movement; now they were utterly still, caryatids marbled to museum-like immobility. I had recently learned that Greek statues had not always been that solemn white of antiquity; originally, they had been painted in gaudy colours. It was unsettling because the association I had with them was not what their makers had intended, and therefore not their true nature. I had the same sensation now. Whatever I sought was here but hidden, lurking in the greased spaces between the metal, flitting into the strip-lights with a faint moth-like sizzle. Perhaps there had been some kind of industrial scandal, years before Chernobyl. But Iubită didn't deal with nuclear waste or oil spills. It was just a sweet company. And everyone liked sweets, didn't they?

'Thank you,' Patrick whispered into my ear, so close that I felt the soft warmth of his breath. My neck tingled.

'The process stops them getting brittle.' Ecaterina saved me from replying. 'They are in fact the same machines as the drug companies use to make pills.'

The comparison made me uneasy. Wasn't this what the place was, after all? A drug factory, churning out products to sate the masses, distracting them from the bitterness of life with a sweetie?

'What's up there?' Jude pointed to the back corner where the stairs rose again. Unlike the black iron of the ones below, these were of whitewashed concrete and had a clinical look.

'Research and development,' Ecaterina said. 'No, you may not go up. It is forbidden.'

'Why?'

'Marija had it installed. She wished to bring out new products.'

'Seems kind of a serious outfit.'

'Marija's projects were not my business.' Her voice was cold. She beckoned to Patrick, and the two of them moved off, speaking in an undertone.

I glanced back at the stairs. Jude was right: they did look serious. I was both deflated and unnerved by our visit. Nothing was here, yet everything was. Perhaps I could wait until the others were distracted and run up. . .

But Pavel interrupted, insisting we needed to get back, while Ecaterina insisted just as firmly that she needed to give Patrick a proper tour before bringing him back to the mansion.

'You're staying with us?'

I feared for Pavel's frown: any deeper and it would be engraving itself into his skull. Patrick only grinned.

'Just for a few days. For convenience's sake.'

'In that case, let's go back separately,' Pavel said. 'There won't be enough room in the car with him as well.'

'He can find his own way,' Patrick offered, lighting a Winston. For the first time I noticed the thin gold band around the fourth finger of his left hand. A hot, unreasonable coal of irritation landed deep in my stomach.

Pavel ignored him. 'If we may, we will get a taxi,' he said to Ecaterina. 'We have much to do.'

Outside, the clouds had broken into a blizzard, hurling pieces of themselves down upon us. Fat snowflakes rushed into my eyes, furring up my lashes so I could hardly see. A strange dizziness overcame me and I grasped hold of a railing for support, my glove coming away rimed with ice, a frozen lump of disappointment sinking through my centre. The pill again? I didn't know. What was clear was that I'd met another dead end. I still had nothing.

We made it to the main road and searched in vain for a taxi.

'*Fuck* this,' Jude snarled, stuffing his gloveless hands under his armpits as he peered into the storm.

'Let's go back inside,' I shouted. But the guards had pulled down the gate and disappeared. The cold was a punch in the head, the wind tearing through our clothing and the snowflakes howling sideways, drawn away from the factory as if by some unseen force. The dizziness worsened as I followed their path: they seemed to coalesce at a spot across the road, blurring into a long white shadow. Blearily I watched as the shadow gradually condensed into form, a form that twisted and reshaped itself uncountable times every second, coiling in and out of itself as flakes rushed into my eyes and mouth, melting on my hot tongue, until finally I made out its shape.

My mother. She beckoned to me with frosted fingers.

Tears sprang to my eyes, mingling with the dissolving snow. I had found her after all. I had done something right for once, and she had responded, she had come for me. I would rid myself of my unnatural heat and the two of us could spiral away into the air together, two snowflakes, unique, yet identical.

Overcome with yearning, I lurched towards her. *I'm*

coming, I called voicelessly, but even as I did so, I remembered my mother was dead, and the face was twisting and it was no longer her but Marija, lips bared to reveal teeth whiter than snow, and I heard the alarmed shout of a man – no, men – and a huge shape exploded through the storm with unnatural speed and charged irrevocably towards me.

CHAPTER THIRTY-ONE

A whiplash of consciousness and I was back in myself. I was lying on the freezing street, the cold soaking through as if I were sprouting icy wings. Two blobs loomed in my vision: as I gazed up, they wobbled and became Patrick and Pavel. The former looked concerned, the latter furious.

'What the *hell* do you think you were doing?' Pavel was shouting. 'Running into the road like that. You could have been killed.'

The taxi bumper was barely a foot away. Jude was talking to the driver. Everything felt unreal. I might have been floating several inches from the ground, as if those wings had taken flight. The blizzard had eased, the sky reassembling into wholeness. What about . . .?

I twisted my head – *God*, that hurt – and saw, across the road, a small snow-covered tree. It was the very approximate size and shape of a person.

I had to start seeing what was really there or I would get myself killed. This seemed, suddenly, very funny indeed.

'Well?' Pavel demanded.

'Just getting us a cab,' I said, and began to laugh hysterically. Patrick at least found this amusing.

'Are you all right?' he asked, as Pavel carried on about the idiocy of juniors. 'The taxi stopped just in time, but you slipped on the ice. I saw you from the factory. Let me check for blood and bumps.'

Before I could speak, he ran a gentle hand through my hair. A single snowflake fell between us and settled on my cheek.

'Laura Lăzărescu,' he said thoughtfully. 'Looks like you do come back from the dead after all.'

He helped me up, and the heat of the car's interior restored whatever life was still missing. The memory of those two figures, shifting together within the same body, melted away.

Curious, the thing we call reality. It is a misnomer. The world is filtered first through our senses and then our minds. Add in our attention and inattention, our memories, our hurts, our hopes, and we are left with a window that is cracked and warped, not to mention papered over in places. We tell so few people who we really are, even ourselves. How could I know what Pavel was up to? Or how my mother had really felt? Or what had happened at the factory? I'd taken another pill and now I was lying on the bed, stroking the arm of the clawed chair. The real world is not out there, but in here. So it was that while I knew that snowy mother/Marija had not existed, I also knew, in the sense that mattered most, that she had.

The heaviness of the morning had gone: now I felt nothing but a strange lightness. I would not have been surprised to reach up and discover myself scalped.

'Curiouser and curiouser,' I told the claws.

Footsteps outside, lurching and slow. I opened the door. Mircea. I was surprised – it was after eleven. The manservant heard me and turned, jerkily. The web over my eyes slipped down enough to realise he was drunk.

'Where are you going?'

He pointed dramatically down the corridor at the cream door twenty yards away, even as I heard someone else moving heavily up the back stairs. The lightness vanished, replaced by alarm: I pounced on him and dragged him inside. He moved easily for a tall man, and not for the first time I was struck by his grace, even in this inebriated state, and asked myself whether it had been intended for another use.

'Sit,' I whispered, and he plopped like a child onto the bed. The slashes on his cheek that Camelia had inflicted had healed; in their place were three thin brown scars.

I pressed my ear to the door: the footsteps slowed, stopped. Apostol, it must be, prowling the corridors. I clenched my fists, desperately hoping Mircea would remain silent.

'Hey! Come in!'

I watched aghast as the door handle slowly began to turn . . .

Not Apostol. Sorin. I sighed in relief. 'What are you doing here?'

'Looking after him. He's upset.' He nodded at Mircea, who was rummaging through my bedside drawer.

'Stop that!' But he had already retreated across the bed with his prize. Chewing gum. He unwrapped the silver paper and slipped the little white strip into his mouth, which looked red and raw. He was a mess, collar askew, shirt stained, reeking of alcohol. The difference between this Mircea and the one I saw sealed up each day was shocking.

'Wrigley's,' he said blissfully. 'Used to collect.'

'You collected gum?'

He laughed. 'In my dreams. We have no such fancy things. As a child I find only skins.'

It took a moment to work out he meant the wrappers.

'People throw them out of train windows. You can still smell the . . . the . . .' His eyes lost focus.

'The mint?

'The mint. Gum skins. Orange skins. Banana skins.'

I tried to imagine what it must have been like, this childhood spent among detritus. To know only the cast-offs, the outline of the world.

'We are peasants,' he went on. 'What do we have? Nothing. We have money, but we can only buy chicken bones. Even the heating. When we walk down the street in winter, we say, shut the windows! You are letting the cold out.'

A hiccup. I wondered whether he lived in the present tense on purpose, and whether it might not be better to follow suit.

'But all different now! Everything different after the revolution. Oh yes. We spend a year feeling pleased with ourselves. Another year, we are still pleased. We wait for change. Change will come soon, we say. You will see. And another year comes, and another, but the underneath does not change. Yes, the queues are less. Yes, we can drink Coca-Cola. Bread and oil everywhere. And fancy things. Only now we cannot afford them. This the revolution, oh yes.' He broke into a croaking, hysterical laugh, but I was distracted by his hands. One lay open, slack on the bed, but the other was clenched tightly around something. He moved and there was a flash. No, a glint. Something metal.

'What's he holding?' I asked Sorin.

'It is human to change,' Mircea interrupted forcefully. 'If it is good, if it is bad – that is not the point. It is real. It is life. To be always the same is what animals do. That is what they want. They turn us into beasts.'

I leaned towards Sorin. 'Why is he upset?'

'Haven't you been listening?' He paused and went on,

flatly, 'He asked to come out with me. Should have known he couldn't handle it.'

I had once thought the sculptor a creature of lightness, yet his face was now heavy, his complexion dull. I remembered the looming opening ceremony for his statue, up on its lonely hill. Like it, he seemed under construction, unfinished. Some people are stand-alone buildings; others go through life scaffolded, as it were. The scaffolding ought to be temporary, intended to be dismantled, leaving the building whole and complete. Yet somehow the day never arrives, and as a result the removal of a crucial pole or joint at any time can see the whole collapse.

'How are preparations? For the unveiling?'

'It's the social event of the year, if you can say that in January. They'll put the scales into the hands of Lady Justice. Anghelescu himself will do it – or rather there'll be a plaque saying as much.'

'That's great.' When he said nothing, I gestured towards Mircea. 'I'm just trying to understand.'

'Are you.' His voice was flat. 'Will that help us, do you think?'

'Surely it's better to try?'

'Such a conscientious little Westerner.' His tone was ice.

'What's the matter?'

'You think we give a shit about your understanding? You think you can just turn up here and we will open ourselves up to you like whores?'

I was stung. 'There's no need to play the victim, Sorin. You were as much a part of the regime as anyone.'

'I had no choice!'

'Everybody has a choice.'

He laughed. 'Spoken like somebody who's never truly had to make one. Two options are not the same as a choice.'

'Who are you trying to justify yourself to? Me or you?'

'Justice, nothing. Survival. *That* is what matters.' I stared at him. He sounded like Marija. 'If you knew anything about us, you would know that. It is always better to survive than to wake up one day and find yourself disappeared.'

'Isn't that what happens anyway? Without our principles, we disappear?'

He made no answer, instead digging into the wall with a fingernail, sketching patterns I could not discern. It was a writing I was so close to being able to read, hieroglyphs that would shake the world if I could only understand.

'Tell her about yourself, Mircea,' he said at last, not looking at me. 'Tell her about your dancing.'

Mircea fell still. Gum half hanging out of his mouth, he began to speak in a dull, practised monotone, as if he had long since grown sick of the tale.

'I am a talented child. Too talented. They see me dance at a competition in my village and they take me from my family to Poartă. I live with other children who are . . . useful. They want us for state parades and shows. There is burning rubbish along the roads. The food queues are so long. Still, we dance, or sing, or say poems they tell us to write. But the dances are not our dances. The songs are not our songs. We are just puppets.' His face hardened. 'We all begin to hate our talents. And so we hate ourselves.

'One day I hurt myself. My leg. It breaks one day when I am practising. The Doamna hates what is ugly, what is useless. I think I do not care, because I hate dancing now. But I do care.' His voice cracked. 'I do.'

I saw that easy, ruined grace, saw with a chill what it meant.

Sorin grabbed my arm. 'Do you see, Laura? Don't let them keep you in the past. Seize control of your life. Never let someone else do it for you.' His eyes burned into mine. 'I told you about what happened to Popa in that square.

300

Do you understand? Do you understand what the Popas made us? What *she* made us?'

I shook my head, dizzy, and he cursed. 'If only I could make you *see*. Do you remember that story I told you about the hunt, about Popa slaughtering all those deer? Well, I lied. It wasn't him who had the gun.'

I stared at him.

'It was her. *She* did it, *she* killed those creatures rather than let Ceauşescu humiliate her and Dinu. She will never, ever bow to anything, and she'll repay in blood anyone who tries.'

My head was light as air; I walked among clouds. 'I don't understand.'

'That's because you're not listening. Listen now. It might save your life.

'I told you about Dinu's death, about how it's never been clear where she was when he died. But I know that they were having a private meeting when it kicked off, so unusually they were alone.

'I know the layout of those buildings, Laura. She couldn't have left the complex. When he died, she must have been somewhere close by. The official version is that Popa opened those doors himself, but they omit one crucial thing.'

'What thing?'

'*They never found the remote control.*'

A lump in my throat then, a single word flashing in letters of blood-red. *Survival.*

'I . . .' I tried to speak, but the scent of flowers was in my nose, the sparkle of stars in my vision, clogging my senses. I could not believe him. I didn't want to. Already my mind was making excuses for her: that the proof was flimsy, that any disgruntled official could have done it, that it was impossible to know if he was telling the truth . . .

It was a long time before he spoke again, his voice low and hopeless. 'I'm too late, aren't I?'

'What is this?' Mircea cut in. I turned, the sculptor's words crawling all over me. He was holding the photograph.

'*Iubită*. I never like them anyway.' He peered at it closely. 'My sister works there. She is sick.'

I felt nauseous. 'Give me that, please, Mircea.'

'I will show this to her. Maybe it makes her happy.' He went as if to put the photograph in his pocket, and I couldn't help myself: I lunged for it, grabbing hold of the little piece of card to which it was attached. We both froze. I met his eyes, and in that moment the power balance shifted. Even, or especially, in his inebriated state he sensed it, and I will never forget the expression that slithered across his face: an awful sapient gleam, a predator's acknowledgement of prey. The scars on his cheek seemed suddenly more livid. He stood, never letting go of the photo, and only now did I realise how tall he was, how his limbs moved with an athlete's strength. I took an involuntary step back. Sorin was motionless, watching. He would be no help at all.

Mircea leaned towards me. I stepped away again, and now the wall was at my back. He came closer, close enough to feel the wine heat of his breath, to see the unnatural drunken shine of his eyes. The forefinger of the hand that held the metallic thing traced slowly down my cheek.

'You think she wants you,' he whispered. 'But she has no wants. Only uses.'

He reached for me and I did the only thing I could – I wrenched my hand down. The photograph ripped away loudly from the backing: the sound, shocking in the silence, broke us apart. Mircea crumpled into himself, dropping the paper and retreating across the bed, one hand over his face, the other still clenched around the mystery object. The lights around us hummed.

'What is that you're holding?' I was careful not to look away, nor to move for the photograph again. He did not look up. 'Show me,' I commanded, feigning control. This time he opened his fist.

It was a corkscrew. Not the domestic variety, safely encased in plastic, but the kind used in restaurants, little more than a handle atop a long, twisting dagger. He had been holding it so tightly that its shape spiralled down his palm in blue and purple.

The outline of the world.

'I'll take that,' I said brightly, holding back the shaking. The lingering menace in his eyes fled; child-like again, he handed it over. I put it in a drawer and closed it firmly. Then I turned to Sorin.

'What the hell—'

'They take it, you know.'

'Take what?'

'Who and what you love.' He was not looking at me but at something far away. 'They take it, and make you hate it. This is their power.'

I stared at him, at the sickly pallor of his face, the slight tremor in his sculptor's hands, then back at Mircea and his wasted fluency. In that moment they looked identical.

After I had released them both, watching as they walked unsteadily back down the corridor, in the opposite direction to Marija's rooms, I picked up the photograph. I had ripped it from its backing, but miraculously the image itself remained intact. I went to put it back in the wardrobe, but something made me stop. I held it up to the light – and gasped.

Crosses. Dozens of crosses in black ink. I turned the photograph over. Someone had taken a biro and, with the same care as the names had been written, drawn dozens of neat X's on the back. With the card blocking the light, they had been invisible. Now I held it up and saw how they had been positioned. Nearly three quarters of the women bore a mark, slashed exactingly across their smiling faces like plague victims. None of the children were touched, but their mothers' desecration was shocking.

A sudden, frantic thought. I looked, knowing before I saw it.

My mother had been marked too. I turned the card again, gazed at the corresponding X. Unlike the others, it was not faded. It was meatily fresh.

I heard a sound, an animal hiccup. It came from me. Where simple grief ought to have been was something altogether more raw and complex: the terrible, terrible strain of *not knowing*. At last I understood Andrei, cramming his sentences with desperation until the words vomited and died. I could no longer ignore the hole at the centre of things; I could no longer continue being myself, or the hollow creature that had come to pass as such. Andrei and I had fallen apart because he wanted nothing but to look, and I – I could not bear to. He was right. I went about with my hands over my eyes, telling myself I was searching for answers.

I lay down, still fully dressed. Something had been done to my mother: the crosses proved it. Just like Adriana Ciocan, she had been a victim. But of what?

At some point the pill must have kicked in, for I could not have slept on my own. I dreamed I was in a spinning machine, tossed around and around until I was a heart-shaped lump, solid all the way through.

CHAPTER THIRTY-TWO

'Hello. You've sprung a leak.' Patrick was sitting cheerily at our breakfast table, a glass of orange juice before him. Behind me the toaster snapped to. It was such an ordinary domestic scene that I was swept with a wild urge to laugh.

The dreams had pursued me through the night, and even now, in the daylight, I had to blink hard to remove those crosses from my dizzy eyes. Or perhaps it was the sleeping pill. Either way, when I reopened them Patrick was still there.

Jude was helping himself to toast. 'How did you find your first night?'

'Fine, except for my bed. Some monstrous four-poster thing. Thought it was going to swallow me up.' He gave a mock shudder.

I rubbed my eyes. 'Why are you here again?'

'I told you, Ecaterina and I have some business. Easier to do *in situ*.' He pronounced it *in si-chew*, which for some reason I found charming. 'Anyway, don't you want to hear about your leak?'

'I beg your pardon?'

Patrick waved the newspaper. It was the *Popor*, Yanussia's biggest daily. Marija's face was plastered over the front. Since she had hardly been seen in public these last few years, the press had to make do with their archives, and this image was particularly popular. She was stepping out of a car, and either the sun had been setting or the cameraman had caught an unfortunate angle, because despite her usual Hollywood smile, her face was all wrong. She looked mean, low, cunning. Like an animal.

I took a gulp of coffee, trying to rid myself of an odd metallic taste on my tongue, as Patrick read aloud.

'Someone gave an inventory to the press of all the Popa treasures found so far.'

'You speak Yanussian?' I said in surprise.

'Well, I'm sure as hell not perfect, but I don't need it to translate half this stuff.' He squinted. 'A Renoir. Rolexes. Hermès . . . hmm, handbags, I think. Sèvres porcelain, whatever that is. Oh, and a stuffed crocodile. Classy.'

'Where?'

'The world's piggy bank. Switzerland, of course.'

My heart sank. Jude snatched the paper and groaned.

'Indeed.' Pavel entered, looking pale, followed by Mr Gabor. 'It's old news, of course, to us and the prosecution. What are you doing here?' This last was to Patrick.

'Oh my God. Do you guys never stop?' Patrick was still smiling, but there was irritation in his eyes.

'He and Ecaterina have some business,' Jude inserted helpfully.

Pavel frowned. 'Of what kind?'

'That's not really anything to do with you. I'm not asking about your case, am I?'

'Good point. Perhaps you could leave while we discuss it.'

Patrick toasted him with his orange juice. 'Once I've finished this, I'll be out of your hair.'

Pavel seemed happy to wait in silence until this came to

pass, but Gabor said quietly, 'They tracked these items down two years ago. Ordered a freeze on everything. Naturally the precise items were never made public – until now.'

'It's the worst timing,' Jude said. 'With the trial so close.'

He was right. Nothing titillated the public like good old-fashioned loot. A similar leak had hit my colleagues last year, working to defend South American officials accused of siphoning off hundreds of millions of dollars from the state oil company. Some journalist had tracked down their ill-gotten gains (cars, paintings, jewellery, prostitutes – apparently the one thing money can't buy is originality). In the ensuing public outcry, HSG lost the case.

'The question is,' Mr Gabor said, 'where did this come from?'

Pavel eyed Patrick evilly. '*He* could have leaked it.'

Patrick held up his hands. 'I arrived yesterday night. When did I have time to nip over to the *Popor* offices?'

'Well I don't know who else it could be,' Pavel snapped. *There will be a traitor.*

A cold knife-blade of memory sprang out of the day I had returned to Poartă; of Pavel asking if I needed more time as I stared and stared at nothing.

No, not nothing. Rolexes, Sèvres porcelain and a stuffed crocodile.

'But you do know,' I said, my tongue thick, not daring to look up from my glass of juice. 'That list was on your desk.'

The room tipped into a hot, thick silence.

'What?' Pavel's voice was very quiet. 'What did you say?'

'Laura? Are you sure, old girl?' Jude said with forced jollity. 'Can't rely on feminine intuition.'

'I saw it after my m . . . when I came back from England. It was on your desk.'

'I don't recall it,' Jude said.

'That's because it wasn't in the Lair. It was in the small study.'

'What are you suggesting?'

I forced myself to look up. Pavel was very still, watching me. I thought of that hurried visit to the Ministry of Justice, of the sugar bowl, of how he looked whiter and more strained by the day. I thought of his conversation with 'Rupert', and how Ursu had announced the trial date amendment so soon after. I had not confronted him, deferring to Marija, but had that been a mistake?

'All I'm saying is I saw it on your desk, and now it's in the national press.'

'Strange indeed,' Gabor said. 'Mr Pavel?'

Pavel's face was a mask. It seemed detached from the person beneath, utterly different to the man I knew. In that gap lay everything that mattered.

'What is going on?' Ecaterina had entered, dressed in a padded black jacket that suited her not at all. Pavel attempted a smile: the effect, with his uncooperative features, was ghastly.

'It is nothing more than a blip, Doamna. Just some bad PR.'

Mr Gabor laughed bitterly. 'This case is nothing *but* PR. You know that as well as I do. Is this woman a charming, how would you say, shopaholic? Or is she a malicious thief, as bad as her husband ever was? The court has chosen its jurors, but I would not count on my country's inclination to shield them from this news.'

'Isn't that what you want?' Pavel said hotly. 'To see her in prison? Don't think I haven't noticed your looks, your little comments. You don't even like her.'

'What has like got to do with it?' Mr Gabor spat. 'This is not about like, Cristian. Nor is it about love, whatever you might think!'

Love. The word had been said at last, and though I had suspected it, hearing it aloud was shocking. Love that had lured Pavel here. Love that had forced his hand, strangled his judgement. I had wondered why Marija would want to manipulate her own defence lawyer into breaking. But what if, rather than leading him on, she had in fact refused him, and it was this that had made him snap? I dug my nails into my palms. He could not love her, not really. He did not understand her, and love without understanding is infatuation at best, obsession at worst, a giddy balloon left to dart higher and higher until reality grounds it or causes it to burst.

Pavel did not respond. 'What about you?' he said to Mr Gabor in a voice of deceptive calm. 'You're from Menădie. Oh yes. I know about that.'

The air went out of the room. It was a low blow, even from Pavel. He had found out what I already knew when the results of London's background check came back the other week.

'I'll leave you guys to it,' Patrick said awkwardly, making us all jump. He stood and knocked his half-finished juice glass over: the sticky opaque liquid, bits floating in it like flies, cascaded over the offending newspaper and drenched Marija's smiling face, distorting her features beyond recognition.

Mr Gabor was absolutely still. 'You think I destroy my own case?'

'I think you have motive. Your home town was shot to pieces.'

'You believe that all Yanussians are like Popa. That we will pursue our own agenda over doing what is right.' His posture had unbent from its usual crouch and he looked taller than he ever had before, as though he had concealed his true height from us all along. 'Did you ever think that

309

I might instead do what is right – not *despite* the Popas, but *because* of them?'

Pavel jerked his head. 'All I know is there are two people who work in that office. Two people who have the key. I don't know what you lost in Menădie—'

'No! You don't know what I lost, or who.' His eyes were fire. 'You think I took this case for fear of Marija? No.' Again, softly: 'No. It was not fear of her, but memory of another. I try for justice because it is my job, because once in a while someone must do what is right. So that we do not fail. So that the darkness does not claim us.'

A great weight settled in the air. I remembered the photograph I had found in his wallet the day I stole his identity card. Once upon a time I had thought of him as Chicken Licken, waiting for the sky to fall in. But he was not waiting. The sky had already crashed down. The force that bent his tall back was not expectation, but grief.

Nobody spoke. I think we all felt ashamed. Oh, we lawyers tell ourselves we do what we do because it is right, that we defend the indefensible because someone has to. But how many of us truly hold ourselves to account, day to day, in any profession? It is easy to gesture grandly at the scales of Lady Justice. How much harder to grasp them yourself, tight enough for the hand to bleed?

'Let us go to the study and see if the list is there,' Ecaterina said at last.

It was only a short walk across the hall, but it seemed much longer. Mr Gabor and Pavel went first, while I followed beside Ecaterina. Her cheeks were pink with the unhealthy aura of fever.

We crowded into the tiny study and searched, circling the room, bumping hands and feet. The press of bodies was surreal, each of us breathing the others' air. Another sweep of nausea. Was this how we would end, stalked by suspicion and counter-suspicion, until the whole collapsed? A-tishoo, a-tishoo, we all fall down.

'Nothing,' Pavel said, at precisely the same time as Mr Gabor. We stared at one another.

'You have heard what I have to say,' Mr Gabor said quietly. 'I suggest you now have a word with your juniors.'

CHAPTER THIRTY-THREE

Mr Gabor and Ecaterina went out. Pavel turned awkwardly to us. I almost felt sorry for him. He was a far cry from the man I had seen in action only last summer, those concrete executives watching in horrified fascination as he ate the other side up. Then again, I wasn't exactly in great shape myself. I felt as though I might never sleep again.

He asked us whether we had leaked the inventory to the press. I had expected outraged bravado from Jude, but he reacted like a hurt child, folding up and muttering about the Spanish Inquisition. If he was guilty, he ought to have ditched law for the acting profession. At last Pavel turned helplessly to me.

'Did you . . .?' He was unable to finish. I would have respected him if he had interrogated me properly, like the lawyer he was, or rather had been. My mouth burned with a bloody metallic tang, his clandestine visit and phone call festering on the tip of my tongue. Should I confront him, even though what I knew I did not believe, and what I believed I had no way of knowing?

I glanced at Jude, hoping for help, but he looked the picture of misery, shoulders hunched and eyes gazing at the floor. Pavel stood there with his hands open, empty. Had he been aware of his feelings towards Marija when he took the case – a simple university crush left to suppurate over decades and now grown monstrous? Or had he been caught unawares and laboured on in the mistaken belief he could cope? Either way, I was unable to answer the only question that mattered.

Did loving her make him more or less likely to betray her?

The prosecutor had moved the trial date. An inventory had been leaked. These were significant obstacles, but not existential ones. My mind churned. Pavel had been in this game a long, long time. He was a superb lawyer. If he'd wanted to destroy the case, he wouldn't even have had to get off the plane.

No. These events were damaging, but the real threat came from the divisions they were causing within our team. We had mere weeks before the trial began; tearing ourselves apart this late in the day would be catastrophic. My fingers tingled: I knew whoever had done this had reasoned the same.

But if the traitor wasn't Pavel, then who was it?

'I think,' I began slowly, observing him tense, 'I think we should all get back to work.'

We did, though it offered no solace. Our rhythm had been disrupted and now we twitched to a more malign beat, each of us conscious that someone, somewhere, was working against us.

There was a rap on the window and our assumed casualness was immediately belied by the start we all gave.

It was a bike messenger. Pavel ripped open the package, watched all the while by the rest of us. Is there anything that saps the strength so much as distrust?

'Alexandru Ungur's pre-trial interview,' he said, pulling

out a video cassette. 'And the same for Dragoş Păstrăv, the old Minister for Fisheries.'

The name pricked my ears. Păstrăv. The father of Marija's godchild.

'Let's watch. They should be asking about those suspicious central bank loans to the Yanussian Oil Company.'

Jude fetched Mr Gabor and we clustered round the TV like the world's most depressing movie night, each of us reluctant to meet the others' eyes. Alexandru Ungur proved to be a large man, sweating from two fleshy pouches on his chest that were clearly visible through his too-tight shirt. The sheen on his brow glimmered in tiny white pixels.

'He looks like a fat Kelsey Grammer,' Jude said.

'Ungur was and is the Minister for Industry,' Radutu said. I wondered if he had got Jude's reference. It did not seem likely. 'He set the output quotas. He has the Stalinist mind. More, always more. Quantity not quality. He is not popular, but he is powerful. He was close with Anghelescu even before 1989. I am surprised they have managed to get him. You have heard of the Grand Canal?'

'Venice?' Jude said eagerly.

'No. Marovia, in the west. It was his idea, to take coal from the Danube down into Yugoslavia. The workers were political prisoners. They were forced to dig fourteen hours a day.'

'I've never heard of it.'

'No. It became too expensive. All that work, all those lives. Wasted.'

We waited in silence for the interview to begin. The interrogator arrived, invisible off camera, his presence marked only by an increase in Ungur's sweat patches, the marks seeping across his paunch so it looked like he had been shot in the chest. They did discuss the bank loans to the Yanussian Oil Company, but the interviewer moved rapidly on to the

Iubită empire, in which he seemed to have a particular interest.

'I don't understand. Why are they talking about this? The Iubită Companie is way smaller than the YOC,' Pavel said.

'But it is important. Up here.' Mr Gabor tapped his head.

I wasn't necessarily surprised that they were interested in the business. Perhaps they thought it had been used for laundering. But then the questions ought to have centred on the usual areas of revenue reporting and group structure. Instead the interviewer was asking detailed questions about the factory's operations – nothing to do with the accounts at all.

Ungur's interview ended inconclusively and ran straight on to Păstrăv's. If the Minister for Industry had been nervous, Păstrăv was far worse. Rarely had I seen a man look so afraid.

'What's his problem?' Jude asked.

'He orchestrated the 1987 coup,' Mr Gabor said. 'He spent the rest of the regime in prison. I am surprised he is still alive.'

'There was a coup?'

'No. Not in the end. Popa crushed it before it could come to anything. We are not sure how.'

Marija had never mentioned this. Was that why she no longer saw her god-daughter? It must have been quite the betrayal.

Onscreen, Păstrăv had begun to speak – no, to gabble. He could not have been more dissimilar to the reserved Mr Gabor, yet I was reminded of the lawyer. They shared the same invisible aura of loss.

The interviewer asked a question and Păstrăv leapt agitatedly in his chair like a trapped salmon. The interviewer asked the question again and now he began to scream.

'Laura.' Pavel stopped the tape. 'I need you to go through

the Iubită accounts. See if there's anything we need to worry about.'

'Now?'

'Right now.' He ignored Jude, who was making outraged faces at this usurpation, and nodded encouragingly. I was being fed a bone, a chance to prove myself. Why did the prospect no longer excite me?

As I left, I took one last look at the screen. Guards, headless due to the camera's frame, had rushed in to restrain Păstrăv, whose features were contorted with anguish. But what struck me most were his hands. They were held before him, twisted into claws, as if seeking to strangle something invisibly in his grasp.

I worked as hard as I could, my days dizzily frantic, my nights spent in a sleep the pills made too unnaturally deep to be refreshing. But I couldn't not take them, for then I only lay awake, the bed hangings twisting into monstrous forms.

It was worsened by the fact that the Iubită accounts were not cooperating. Usually I liked numbers. They had rules, and I found this comforting. But this time I could not make them add up. I wondered madly if this were simply the way of the new universe in which I found myself, where numbers went their own secret ways and I might brush the sky with my fingers, picking out strawberry pips of stars.

It turned out that Constantin Popa had effectively used the Iubită Companie as his very own piggy bank.

'In 1982, the business made one point eight billion YPR in revenue.' Pavel and Mr Gabor nodded. 'Six hundred million dollars, or thereabouts, with the *iubită* themselves accounting for most of that. But their actual profits were just twenty million – a margin way off for their category. I had a look, and after the usual SG&A, they had a massive brand licensing fee of more than a hundred million. No points for guessing who the licenser was.'

'Proof?'

'Well, the money went to a shell company. After that it's pretty much untraceable. But I found a GZ Suisse statement from 1983 belonging to an account we linked to one of Popa's associates. That year it received three payments totalling just over one hundred million dollars.'

'Any evidence that she . . .' Pavel waved his hand.

'Nothing with her name on it, as always. But this was her family business. Her sister was general manager. Even though it was nationalised, is it really possible she didn't know? And there's another thing.' I explained the other curiosity about the accounts: that, bluntly, they made no sense. Their research and development spending was off the charts.

'So?' said Pavel impatiently.

'This is a sweet company with about twelve different products. Where's all that money going?'

But Pavel was not interested. 'No time to waste hypothesising. I need you on other things.'

I had to drop it, but still I wondered. The extra money must have been going on something. But what? The question refused to disappear, drifting down rows of silent, shining vats.

For the next couple of weeks we worked like slaves. Jude and I found ourselves compulsively glancing up at the clock, every second allowing its hands to tighten their grip. London tried to send in backup but was unable to get visas. Every night we stumbled to bed, eyes like sandpaper, only to wake up the next day and do the whole thing again. I was accustomed to all-nighters, we all were, but this was both a marathon *and* a sprint. Bribes from foreign companies in return for approving import licences. Funds diverted from domestic financial institutions. The mysterious disappearance of gold bars from the Yanussian Central Bank. It seemed like everything was against us, and by Christmas afternoon it was difficult to feel festive. Pavel had threatened to cancel our pitiful half-holiday altogether, but eventually he bowed to Jude's protests, seeing the sense in them. We had been working around the clock and we were exhausted. He satisfied himself with merely keeping us until mid-afternoon.

The moment he let us off, Jude announced an outing to the International Hotel's English bar. Pavel went to meet friends. I considered following him again but decided against it. He was not the person betraying our case, and besides, I was growing sick of shadows. This country seemed to absorb anything tangible. Sorin had remarked on this the other day.

'It's funny watching you all snaffle through your precious files. As if Marija would leave any trace. What are you expecting, an X marking the spot?'

I smiled, but he didn't. He was thinner than ever; the hip flask seemed always in his hand.

'I heard the statue's done. Ready for the unveiling?'

He shrugged. 'Makes no difference whether I am. They're coming, ready or not.'

I said lightly, 'We'll keep some champagne on ice.'

He met my gaze full on for the first time and I drew back at its intensity.

'Why? Is there something to celebrate?'

He left, but as he did I asked him about Mircea. I had not seen him for weeks – not since our unsettling midnight meeting.

'He left.'

'Left? Where? Why?'

But he only shook his head. His eyes were the oldest I had ever seen.

Jude paused in the hall. 'You're welcome to join me at the hotel, Lăzărescu, provided you follow the strict aim of the expedition.'

'Which is?'

'Getting utterly and irretrievably drunk. No exceptions.'

I smiled. 'Simple yet elegant. Sadly I don't think vodka will solve this headache.'

'Gin, then? It's a free country.' I raised my eyebrow and he amended, 'Sort of.'

I fended him off, and once he'd gone, I went for a walk under the leering sky, inhaling in great gasps so the cold air poured down my throat, pooling between my ribs, stretching the walls of my cells. The year was old, the trees silent. No birds sang; even the gate-bird had lost its voice, while the snowdrifts had been there so long, I could scarcely believe there was anything beneath. I pictured the white cracking open and myself falling, falling, not through ice but through nothing, as if that great sky had slithered beneath me and I might fall forever.

I tapped my foot nervously on the path, as if reassuring myself it was still there. Unconsciously I had arrived at the beehives: I surveyed the six neat white boxes. Ecaterina had said one was destroyed, and it was a sign of my immaturity as a lawyer that I still expected the crime to mark the land-scape. I well knew how misdeeds could be concealed in innocuous balance statements and company filings, yet the primitive part of me, the part that hears the things that go bump in the night – that part expected to see a black cloud hanging over those poor boxes.

Some instinct took me to the hive closest to the mansion. I looked in, and had to grasp the wall for support.

It was a graveyard. Tiny black and yellow corpses littered every surface, furred with snow, tragic in their pitifulness. Death had curled them round themselves and each other, a last frozen embrace. The hexagonal combs gaped empty, like a picture the creatures had never had time to finish. I felt the loss of something I could never now understand.

The lid lay on the ground, where it had presumably fallen. Or been dropped. I thought of Ecaterina's fevered cheeks, of her enchanting sister, of the malign buzz in the walls of the house they shared, and recalled something I had once read about insects.

There is always the possibility that the queen is not a queen, but a slave.

CHAPTER THIRTY-FOUR

The destroyed hive left me feeling grubby in a manner that had nothing to do with the slush on my boots. I had a shower, my second of the day, turning the water spitefully hot. My body displeased me, my limbs too pale, a strip of fat clinging to my belly like a changeling. Placing a hand over my navel I felt a little vacuum form beneath my palm, as if my flesh sought to suck into itself and disappear.

I dressed and reached automatically for my mother's watch, but it was not in its customary position on the bedside table. Where? Not my coat, nor my trouser pockets, nor any of the usual places. Had I even had it that morning? Another wave of dizziness: I could not think with this raw absence on my wrist. I had definitely had it when working the afternoon previously; I'd checked it several times when the pace grew really slow. Could it somehow have become detached? But it had never done that before. I always took it off last thing at night, after I got into bed. Had I done so yesterday? I thought so, but in my heady distracted state I could not remember. If I had, and I had put it on the bedside table . . . The realisation crawled across my skull. Someone must have come in during the night and taken it. Who?

Marija? Apostol? One of the staff? I was shaken by the notion of someone else in here, gazing down upon me as I slept.

But why would anyone take it? It was not expensive – quite the opposite, a cheap communist production. It was a miracle it had lasted as long as it had. They must have known it mattered to me, and that was unsettling in the extreme.

Or perhaps I was just being paranoid, and it would soon magically turn up.

In distress I went down to the Lair and flung myself into my usual chair, but some idiot had adjusted it. The arms were all wrong, the seat too low. I yanked at the lever in frustration. Nothing.

'For fuck's sake,' I muttered.

'Merry Christmas to you too.'

I spun around, or tried to, but the seat foiled me, snapping obstinately back into position. Getting up, I saw Patrick in one of the green leather armchairs.

'Oh. It's you.' The armchairs were tall, secretive pieces of furniture with wings protruding on either side, secluding the sitter. We never used them. I think Pavel considered comfort in some way as cheating. You were either at your desk, working, or you were not, it was as simple as that.

Patrick grinned, peering out from behind the frame. 'Thanks for the enthusiasm.'

'You're welcome.'

Exhausted by this lengthy conversation, I sat back into my own chair, forgetting the adjustment. I yanked at the lever again, unreasonably furious at my own ineffectiveness, at the absence of my mother's watch. How had I lost her only gift?

'Stop! You'll have your eye out.' He came over. 'Let me.'

He kneeled beside me, low enough that I could see the top of his head. He had a tiny bald patch, right on the crown. He pulled the lever and immediately, miraculously, I sank about seven inches.

'What the . . .'

'Sorry! Sorry.' There was smothered laughter in his voice and I suddenly found myself also resisting the urge to giggle. 'Stand up again. OK, that's it.'

The chair rose and I sat, regally. 'Arms,' I commanded. He obeyed without comment, that small naked patch still visible. Unexpectedly I found myself wanting to place a finger on the bare skin.

'Was it you who adjusted this thing?'

'Guilty, your Majesty.'

My brow creased. 'What were you doing? You can't be in here! This stuff is confidential.' I began hurriedly sweeping up the Iubită files. In the beginning we had locked the doors, both to the Lair and to Pavel and Mr Gabor's office, yet as time passed and our exhaustion increased, security had grown lax. A dormouse could probably have broken in. I recalled the missing inventory. Just how locked had that little study been?

'Calm down,' Patrick said. 'I just needed a place to work.'

'I am calm. In our office?'

'I didn't realise you were here. Thought you were all off doing festive activities. Puppy kicking. Seal clubbing. Whatever lawyers do on their day off.'

I was unconvinced.

'Look, I'll even show you what I've been doing.' He gestured to a ring binder on the coffee table that bore the First Loyalty logo. 'It's not easy to work from some ridiculous chaise longue. This place has actual office chairs.'

I sank back in my chair. In truth, I was tired. Tired of paranoia, tired of shadows. I wanted to lose myself in this man who had that earnest, disinfected openness common to Americans.

'All right,' I said, relenting. 'I do understand the appeal of a spinny chair.'

He smiled, and I saw he knew he had been let off the hook. Oddly, I did not mind. 'We race them in the office between deals. I didn't want to say anything, but actually you're talking to the current eighth-floor champion.'

'Gosh. Thank goodness you kept that to yourself till now, otherwise . . .'

He raised an eyebrow. 'Otherwise what?'

'Nothing.' I remembered that stupid ring on his finger. I remembered my boyfriend, if that was what I was still calling him. I had phoned Andrei several days ago to say I would not be returning for Christmas.

'Actually, I'm going to Brighton,' he had interrupted.

'Oh.' I thought, his ex lives in Brighton. But I didn't ask. I couldn't. Partly because I felt I no longer had the right, and partly, if I was being completely honest, because an image of Patrick had flashed into my mind unbidden. We'd exchanged a few meaningless pleasantries, like strangers; after he hung up, I went back to work.

'Work. I need to do some.' My voice was dull, parrot-like.

'What? Laura, no.' Patrick grabbed the chair and twirled me around to face him. 'You are *not* working on Christmas Day.'

'No rest—'

'For the wicked? Don't give me that. *I'm* done working.'

'And you're so wicked?'

That smile again. 'Diabolical. Anyway, I have something better.'

'Better than work? I don't believe you.'

'Come here.'

Beside the mantelpiece was a squat wooden cupboard, two or three feet high. It had always been there so I had never paid it any attention. Patrick knelt and took out a long box, which he offered up to me like a prayer.

'You must love Monopoly. Don't answer, I know I'm right. Well, may I present . . . the communist version.'

I stared at the package and its faded cartoons. 'That makes literally no sense.'

'I know. Wonderful, isn't it? Well, actually the name means something like "Manage Your Finances Wisely".' Again I was impressed by his Yanussian. Where had he picked it up? 'You have to compete to furnish your house. The big prize, the Mayfair of this thing, is – wait for it – a sofa.'

He smiled up at me with unadulterated optimism, the kind of gaze I had not seen in a long while.

'You know Ceaușescu banned Scrabble.'

'Sensible man. Now, Monopoly . . .'

I looked away. Could he break through my claustrophobia? Would it be wrong to use him so? But he was also clearly after a pick-me-up, like a puppy that has been shut up too long and is desperate to play.

It was not wrong if each of us sought the same thing, and above all for the same agenda. Yes, I thought. If the agenda differs, there is the crime.

'All right. But I want the boot, or the communist equivalent.'

Patrick set up and we played, seated across from one another on the floor, cross-legged like children. He chose a leg of lamb; there was no boot, so I plumped for a milk bucket. I started to wonder how long the game had been hidden there and who had last played it, but then I chased those thoughts away.

'I'll be the banker, of course,' he said with a seriousness I found amusing. I rolled a four: a sewing machine was mine for the purchase. Patrick rolled five and landed on the equivalent of Chance, which commanded him to invest in a savings account. He handed over the flimsy paper money, grumbling, 'Doesn't even *mention* the interest rate.' But he brightened when I was stuck in a grocery rations queue for two turns.

'How come you're not home for Christmas? Where even is home?'

'London these days. But I'm a New Yorker.'

'Why are you here?'

'I told you, I'm advising the government on its privatisation programme.'

'What about that . . . thing you have going with Ecaterina?'

'What thing?'

'You know what I mean.'

He moved his piece along the board. 'Can't tell you that.'

'All right. Why do you speak Yanussian?'

'My wife.'

I tried not to react. 'What about her?'

He grinned as if he knew what I was thinking, and I felt naked. It was not unlike being with Marija.

'She's Yanussian. She emigrated, oh, six years ago. Had to escape Ms Popa and her charming husband on a more . . . permanent basis. She needed a Green Card. I was twenty-six, young and dumb. A friend of a friend introduced us and I volunteered. Learned her favourite colours, the food she liked, second cousins, that kind of stuff. Went off without a hitch. Or *with* a hitch, really.' He grinned and I wanted to slap him.

'And now?'

'We're deeply in love and welcoming our seventh child.' His grin widened at my expression. 'Kidding. We're separated. Amicably. She wanted to go live in Utah. Of all the places in the world, that's where she picked. Something about the open spaces, she says. Keep meaning to divorce, but work is so busy. Anyway, that's why I speak some pretty shaky Yanussian, and that's why First Loyalty sent me here.'

'Why do you still wear your wedding ring?'

He glanced down as if he had forgotten about the golden band. 'I actually have no idea. I guess I just got used to it. Doesn't mean anything.'

I frowned. 'Can something simply stop having meaning, just like that?'

'Oh, don't be so literal. Things mean what you want them to mean. Take Yanussia. First communism, now capitalism. Just different ways of making money for those at the top. Did you know that when Yugoslavia caught Yanussians sneaking across the border, Popa would pay fifteen tonnes of salt to have them back? Then he sent them to the salt mines. They had to dig out another hundred tonnes to be let out. So, a profit of eighty-five tonnes. Good business.' He laughed at my expression. 'I'm not condoning it. I'm just saying the communists weren't against business, not by a long way. Everything has a price, including people. Especially people.'

'With that attitude, did you always want to work in finance?'

'Do I get points if I say I wanted to set up a cats' home? Nope. Maybe I didn't *specifically* write "First Loyalty vice president" in my "What I want to be when I grow up" essay, but life has a way of pushing us towards our secret channels, don't you think? Look at Marija. She was an actress before she married Popa. Makes complete sense.'

'Why?'

'Because she makes you *believe*.'

He was right. Like a church, or a cemetery, she carried belief around her, within her. She reeked of it. I had blurted out as much in our first encounter. They were just words, or so I had thought; now I recognised them as the first incantation of the hymn or spell. It wasn't just her. The undercurrent of belief in Yanussia was old, older than

327

organised religion. It was why they brought unleavened wheat and wine to the dead who lay in state, why some not only worshipped the gods but also stars and time. It was why even Popa had not quite dared bulldoze some of the older temples and churches, instead allowing his architects to mount them on purpose-built wheeled platforms and move them out the way. What dusty gods had gasped in anger among those torn foundations?

'Why don't you tell me about where you're from,' I said, changing the subject.

'Grew up on a farm in upstate New York. My parents are American as apple pie. You'd probably hate them.'

'I wouldn't.'

That smile again. 'Well, they're pretty standard. My dad is a chiropractor. My mom taught for a while then gave it up to look after me and my brother. My ill-gotten gains mean they can go on a cruise every year. God knows why they want to. Perhaps it's some weird way of punishing themselves for how their kids turned out. My brother is a corporate lawyer.'

I raised my eyebrows in mock gravity. 'Dreadful.'

'Yup. Every time they come back, my mom and I have the exact same conversation about how the pineapple at the breakfast buffet was just a *touch* on the warm side. Why did you go into law?'

The question caught me off guard. 'I like how it relies on what's really there.' I had not thought the words until I said them, but I realised they were true.

'In what way?'

'In law there always has to be evidence. Motive.' I rolled the dice, though I was no longer quite sure what game we were playing. 'People have a reason for doing what they do.'

'Sounds nice.'

'Meaning?'

'Well, it would be handy to see the world in black and white, right and wrong, rather than people doing what they do merely because they're people. Chance.'

'What?'

'The card.'

I picked it up and held it before me, looking without seeing. 'Are there questions in life that you don't ask?'

'As in, do I have blind spots?' His eyes creased thoughtfully. 'Are these questions that I don't ask myself, or other people?'

'The first. Both.'

'That's a difficult one. I suppose there are questions I don't ask because I don't need to, and those that I don't because I do. In the first category are the easy ones. Am I breathing? Does J. G. Melon do the best burgers in New York City? Do my parents love me? Easy peasy. Yes, yes, yes.'

The card in my hand told me I had been stung by a black marketeer for several thousand *piesta*, but the words slid meaninglessly off the paper. Don't look up, I told myself furiously. Don't let him see . . .

'And the second category?'

'That's a little harder, because obviously I try not to ask them. But that can still be revealing. Like, if you have to ask if you're an asshole, maybe you already have the answer, see? So the only way for most people not to ask is not to conceive them at all.' He paused. 'Still, if I were a wiser man, I would probably know that's where the real stuff is hiding. The bits that tell us who we really are.'

'But what defines us? Is it the answers themselves, or the courage to look for them?'

He shook his head. 'That I don't know.'

At this my crossed legs, unaccustomed to their youthful positioning, gave a spasm. Patrick, surprisingly agile, sprang to his feet and helped me up, one hand on either arm, his grip firm but gentle. Gradually he raised me, ignoring my moans of discomfort, until I was at eye level.

I darted a look up at him. Amusement was playing around one corner of that soft mouth – a mouth that curved rather nicely at the edges, I finally allowed myself to notice. He was still holding me close, and there was a short, hot moment in which I could not work out whether every muscle was tensed or relaxed.

'Patrick?'

'Yes, Laura?'

'Are you always this deep over Monopoly?'

He smiled. This time it was warm, uncomplicated.

'This is nothing. You should see me at Trivial Pursuit.'

A spark awoke, tracing its slow, lazy way somewhere behind my stomach. He pressed the tiniest touch closer. Behind us, someone coughed.

Apostol stood there, watching.

'She needs you.'

CHAPTER THIRTY-FIVE

I followed him into the hall, shaking my head to clear it, my vision blurring in the chandeliers' glitter. Ecaterina was passing through, a large woven rope basket on her arm.

'Did you find what you needed?' she asked Apostol, who nodded. I half peered into the basket, but she shifted so I could not see the contents.

'You're going out?' I asked.

'I am visiting today.'

'One of your prison visits?'

She glanced at me. She appeared to be deciding something. 'Yes. A friend is sick. Up here.' She tapped her head and then she was gone, the front door swinging closed with a chilly snap.

We went on up the stairs, past the mirror, and I could not help but look in. My cheeks were flushed, my eyes unnaturally bright, dark hair coiled around my shoulders. I looked like someone else. We passed along the corridor. Towards Marija's rooms.

The door handle was bright and polished, our reflections twisting back. This time I did not wait for Apostol. I opened it myself and stepped inside.

She was seated at the window, gazing out at something I could not see. She wore a long dressing gown of red silk, the collar fluttering as she breathed. I saw the exposed line of her neck, the faint ribbing of her white throat; I wanted to touch it as I had once touched her flowers to check that they were real. The plants themselves were still here, ripe, almost too ripe, drooping under their own bounty. The rest of the room was soft: soft furnishings, soft colours, soft light smoothing the edges of everything. I might have been back in the womb.

'I am running out of time, Laura.'

'Doamna, we are doing everything we can.'

'Like playing games?' Her tone was direct but not angry. I flushed and could not speak. She shrugged. 'It is a good metaphor. You lawyers are playing one game. I am playing another. In my country you go to court when you have already lost. And as I told you already, I do not intend to lose.

'Do you know why I wear red?' She did not wait for an answer. 'Partly because they expect it. How could I dress like an accountant? They say they do not care what I wear, but that is not true. They want a show. And yes, I have found the show helpful. But now the curtain is coming down. So why else? My detractors say because it is the colour of blood. This is closer to the truth. Why blood? Because it connects every part of us. Because when our mother's milk is withdrawn, it is our blood that feeds us. And of course, because we women are so familiar with it.'

'*The Woman in Red*,' I murmured.

'My Picasso. They say they have found it.'

'Haven't they?'

Her eyes glittered. 'It is a beautiful painting. They call it my portrait, although of course Pablo created it long before I came along. Have you noticed how it is composed of a single line? Like blood – a single connection. To me it shows a woman who is truly alive. A woman who chooses to be both perfectly self-contained and connected to everything.'

'You think it an accurate depiction.'

'Oh yes. But not of me.'

She was looking at me intensely. I felt a long, slow blush crawl up my neck.

'I am nothing like that.'

'Not yet, no. But I have very much enjoyed watching you . . .' she paused, '*becoming*.'

I put a hand automatically to my neck. My pulse beat there, a riddle, quick and light. Was the transformation she spoke of metamorphosis, or resurrection?

She gestured towards the silent piano. 'I need a favour.'

A piece of paper lay on the instrument's gleaming surface. I crossed to it, her eyes following me all the while. The paper had been folded neatly, the crease sharpened with a finger-nail. I opened it: written on it was an address I did not recognise.

'Go to him. He will give you what I need.' She was looking out the window again, her attention drawing away like the sea pulls the sand from beneath the feet. 'It is my last card. The only one I have left.'

The quiet loss in her voice threw me utterly. I grasped a chair at a surge of dizziness, black crosses dancing across my vision. *Did you do it?*

'Doamna, I . . .' I halted. 'If I am to do this, I need . . .' I gathered myself and dared to chase that elusive ocean. 'What you said about your husband in the Winter Garden – I need more. We have come so far. Just show me the rest of the way.'

She was looking at me again and I was washed in seawater, salt stinging my skin. I had never felt so alive.

'You need to believe,' she said.

'Yes.'

She seemed to consider. Then she stood and, in a movement too quick for me to follow, tugged at the belt of her dressing gown. It fell away, rippling like the parting of waters, and the breath froze in my throat.

Beneath it she was naked. Beneath it, the Little Mother was covered in scars. Constellations of them, galaxies. Everywhere that was usually concealed by her carefully tailored clothing there was a livid white mark: her chest, her breasts, her stomach, her upper arms. Some were little more than scratches, while others burned bright as stars, warping the surrounding flesh, pulling it into themselves as if to tear her apart.

'Now do you understand?'

The paper crumpled in my hands. I fled, those scars sparkling in my vision, those eyes boring into my back.

CHAPTER THIRTY-SIX

The taxi driver knew the address but with the traffic it still took more than half an hour to get to Poartă's eastern quarter. Afterwards, on the way home, I sat paralysed in the back, watching the light fade, thinking of Marija and of how I could not bear it. For all our technological advances there is no way to un-see, and as my body pressed into the torn leather seat I thought that if I were a scientist I would pour my resources above all into this.

In my lap was a slender yellow packet. The man who had given it to me had looked at me closely, wearing an expression that I could not decipher. He was dressed in casual clothing but had the greyed face and tempered build of an official. I had the curious idea I had seen him somewhere before.

'She has decided, then,' he said.

'I beg your pardon?'

He shook his head, glanced up at the dimming sky. 'God help us all.'

The door closed, and though I knocked repeatedly, it did not open again.

The taxi stopped and I looked out. 'This isn't it.'

The driver pointed. The street ahead was crammed with people. 'Protest.'

How could I have forgotten? The Christmas Day demonstration. These people had sprung up from nowhere, like dragons' teeth.

A thought: Marija would not have forgotten. Again I sensed a fragment fluttering just out of reach.

I got out, the cold night swooping down, grasping the car door to help myself upright. The crowd was thin at its edges, its individual components distinguishable. I had been shut up in the house so long, I had forgotten what it was to be surrounded by people, that thrill of being part of an organism larger than oneself. I felt the warmth of their bodies, heard their feet scuffling on the cobblestones, saw the white traces of their eyes. Students passing a bottle between them. A mother bouncing a whining child on her hip. A snatch of laughter. Just for a moment I allowed myself to breathe, until a middle-aged couple went by, pinched with cold and holding up a large banner with Marija's face superimposed onto the body of a large spider. Then I remembered I was not one of them.

I took a deep breath and waded into the throng, making my way towards the front entrance. The gates could not have been more than a hundred yards away, but they were utterly invisible. I pictured the guards playing goldfish in their glass hut, and prayed they would still be there to let me in. The people thickened and now I had to push my way through, my coat whispering as it rubbed against others; surrounded by the mutter of Yanussian, I had to fight the sensation that there was more than one tongue here I did not understand. Then the shallows dropped abruptly away and I found myself in the depths of the crowd proper, dark waves heaving beneath a black sky. I was nowhere, I was lost, dizzy, carried along helplessly as the waters rose higher.

336

A tide of nausea swept through me as I realised that I could no longer see the edges, that the gates seemed like figments of my own imagination, for here was nothing but the swell and surge of the throng, its secret currents drawing ever deeper. I could lose myself, and if I did, who would ever find me?

A chant rose and people began to jump, their boots thudding against the tarmac. There were none of the amateur theatrics of the previous demonstrations; instead I sensed a cold, professional determination at work. A red-haired woman gave me an odd look and obediently I started jumping too, entering the sway of an unknown puppet master. Her eyes hovered on me and I knew, then, that I must not be seen. I pressed on, away from her, towards where I thought the gates might be, still jumping so I moved with a ridiculous hop, a bunny rabbit amidst a pack of wolves. Those around me did not stop, their eyes glinting, their colouring strange under the street lights, and the air grew warm from the friction of all those leaping bodies. No longer was I in a black sea – this was more like sticks rubbing together to create flames.

Răsculat. Răsculat. The chant began hoarsely at first, then spread, louder, louder, and deeper still, voices baying the militant group's name. The rhythm grew faster, faster, and changed. The crowd made a sudden rush forwards and I was swept along towards the gates, close, closer, near enough now to hear shouts and see yellow-black flashes of a barrier of policemen. I could not be far. I would slip through and show my ID and be admitted to safety. But we were pressing in, and in, and I had the mad idea that as one we could pass through the iron gates, through the brick walls, our anger making us ghosts—

A tremendous bang and everything turned to smoke. The air became a visible, writhing thing, burning my throat, clawing my eyes. Tear gas. The pressure was released, the spell broken, and the crowd fell apart into a mere mess of coughing, gasping people. I bent over, struggling for air, hardly able to see. Someone placed a hand on my back.

'OK?' a voice said.

I managed to straighten, coughing into the face of a thin, wiry young man. 'Thank you.'

'No problem. English?'

I nodded, searching through the smoke for the gates. I had completely lost my bearings. I turned round and met the young man's eyes. He was still looking. Really looking.

I saw it coming, but it was too late.

'Hey,' he said quietly, his gaze flicking to three men gathered between us and the gates, then quickly back at me. Too late I remembered the newspaper article about the Black Widow's defence team. Too late I remembered Jude mocking my photograph.

He knew who I was.

He called to his friends again, louder this time but not yelling, as if I were a wild animal he did not want to frighten, and it was this very gentleness that told me the truth. He would kill me. I knew it immediately, absolutely, and the heat of it poured through my blood, flooding my ears, pooling in my boots. Whether he noticed the change I cannot say, but his friends were still talking, they had not heard him. Frustrated, he raised his voice, shouted—

I ran. I turned and ran, through my dizziness and my nausea, away from him and his friends, away from the beckoning gates and along the wall of the mansion, pushing through the people, my feet already clogged with the snow, which champed greedily at my heels. I heard his angry yell and it was taken up by other voices – his friends had joined the hunt – but I did not look back, pushing through the haze of people and tear gas. *Răsculat. Răsculat.* Their howls

338

pursued me, but there was a side gate at the end of an alley, I remembered now, there would be a guard who could let me in. *Too late, too late*: the words danced mockingly in my brain, but I had crashed through the crowd and was now horribly exposed, running alone along the blackened wall. I sprinted harder, the brick leaping at the edge of my vision, my lungs heaving in my chest. Oblivion beckoned, and never had I wanted it less.

All I had desired in coming to Yanussia was to discover the source of my mother's anger and contempt towards me. Then, I had believed, I would know how to overthrow the anger and contempt I held towards myself.

The protesters' noise had died away. So, hideously, had the baying of my pursuers. Now I heard only my heart and the feet of the pack behind, their silent determination worse than any howl. The gate, where was the gate? I gave a sob of terror. There! The alleyway. I wheeled right quickly, too quickly, the snow gleefully giving way to ice, which snatched my feet from under me. A single yell of excitement behind – they had seen me fall. I struggled up, boots slipping, and ran on, slamming into the gate at the exact moment I saw the large padlock clamping it shut.

CHAPTER THIRTY-SEVEN

My pursuers had turned down the alley. They would be here in seconds. There was nobody here, no guard, no one to save me. I rattled uselessly at the bars, scratched for hand-holds in the wall that were not there.

I looked up. There were no stars.

And then a sound, a clanking, and the gate was suddenly, miraculously open, hands grabbing me and pulling me inside.

'Shut it, shut it!' I was hysterical now, and thank God my rescuer was already pulling the chain through, snapping the padlock into position and dragging me into the wall's shadow at the exact moment they arrived. I could hear their breath, see its clouds drifting through the gate with ghastly ease.

A narrow hand took hold of the bars and shook them viciously. I could make out the individual hairs on the thumb.

'We know you there,' he said in English. 'Lawyer.' He spat the word. 'Come and play with the Răsculat.' Silence again, and then there was a scrabbling noise, the awful sound of fingers seeking purchase on brick. I stared up at the point where the wall met the night, expecting hands and limbs to appear and violence to drop down like rain.

Nothing. Nothing but us and the unconcerned moon. At

last there was a yell of fury and a boot slammed into the wall.

'Bitch.'

They were gone. The figure beside me stirred. I turned and looked into the last face I had expected.

Apostol. He regarded me, his eyes black.

'How . . . how did you know?'

'I told you, Lăzărescu. Because of her, we are friends. Friends watch each other always.'

She was still at the window, gazing out, though the light was long gone and the protesters must have been only another shade of black. Her neck was marble; her eyes glimmered. The scars were concealed again beneath her gown, but when I closed my eyes I saw them still.

The yellow package was still in my hand. I had held on to it through everything.

I offered it to her but she did not take it. Nor did she thank me. Instead she motioned to a bowl piled high with perfect fruits, gleaming as though they had been polished.

'You are hungry,' she said. It wasn't a question. My head spun as I watched her pluck a bunch of grapes, fat ones with an unnatural violet sheen. Her fingertips took on their hue, as if etched with bruises. I blinked. My vision was darkening at the edges; I could hardly stand. She offered them to me, and I, at the brink of it all, did not hesitate. I was starving. Why deny myself any more? I had stepped into empty air long since.

I went to her, as close as I could come. She gazed up at me. Up, for the first time. I bent towards her, my lips parting.

'Here.' She pressed the fruits into my hands, her arms forming a barrier. Her eyes had moved away. Wordlessly I took them; our fingers brushed. Her hands were dry and cool.

The first grape exploded in my mouth. As though it was the first time, the last time, as though I had never tasted before. My teeth met the thin skin, the pressure mounting until I broke through, crushing into the cold velveteen flesh, juice bursting over and under my tongue. The second was just as delicious, and the third, and the fourth. I let out a quiet moan. I ate until my mouth was stained and sticky. I ate the whole bunch.

Only then did she take the yellow package from me. The room was still, but I was falling, falling.

'Mine,' she said, with the coiled satisfaction of a cat. I looked up at her, fingers and eyes streaming, and knew it was not the package she meant.

CHAPTER THIRTY-EIGHT

Dawn awoke me, light blanching through. I had forgotten to close the curtains and the room seemed raw, devoid of shadows. Somebody once said that just because the sun has come up a million million times, it does not mean it will do so tomorrow. I felt that way, as if everything I had ever known was up for grabs. I lay for some time, empty but for a fierce, unnatural joy that coursed tiger-like through my veins. A nub of my soul had been exposed and I sensed everything.

I worked for the next few days in untainted clarity, without distraction. The little pills propelled me on as the trial date hovered closer, closer. Eight days to go, then seven, then six. Pavel smothered us in work, but the thing within me burned through it all as if it were not there. Swiss papers documenting the transactions of a certain foundation; allegations that an American bank was part owned by the Popas and had been used in various illicit affairs; charges related to the Yanussian treasury, whose funds had allegedly been funnelled into Western real estate. Even Jude stopped complaining, our minds three red arrows directed to the same target. Since the protest I'd flamed with a strange fire: it would not take long for it to consume me, but then again, I did not need long. Five days to go. Four. I could not sleep, because I risked missing what I felt certain was unfolding itself before my eyes. I had not slept since the protest, yet I took the little pills nightly and enjoyed the understanding we shared, the things they showed me, the memories they smoothed away. And if I saw the odd strange figment, who cared? It was only the house revealing its true nature. I saw Camelia's face in the most peculiar corners, watched that rim of white around Pavel's pupils and thought of the border we had both crossed. There was no going back, not now.

In the Lair (a ridiculous name – there were no monsters here), Jude set a coffee mug in front of me.

'No thanks.' I did not want to obscure the hot salt of freedom on my tongue.

'What, you don't like coffee now?'

Steam coiled up before me then dissolved. I wanted to chase it into the air, to pursue it among the billions of restless atoms.

'No. Never have.'

We worked on. Backdated documents used in the purchase of five elegant townhouses in London. Bundles of cash removed from a Yanussian bank branch in New York and delivered to a suite at the Waldorf Astoria.

New Year's Eve. Three days before the trial, and that evening I went slowly upstairs to discover my bedroom floor dotted with the corpses of ladybirds. Something had awoken them from hibernation and already they had starved to death, all but one moving slowly along the skirting board. I scooped up its dead comrades and flushed them down the toilet, then searched for the source of the infestation but found none. It disturbed me, a flicker of filth amid my new-found purity. I removed the photograph from its hiding place in the wardrobe and stared for a long, long time at those shining faces. I had taken to doing so for hours during those sleep-free nights, long enough that whether my eyes were closed or open it made no difference.

But there was something else in the wardrobe. A garment bag hung there, one I had never seen before, long and sleek. It did not belong to me.

I unzipped it down the front, slowly, voluptuously, half knowing what I would find before I did. A dress, a blood-red dress. A dress for a courtroom, for a drama. Comedy or tragedy? I took it out and held it against myself. It was a simple sheath, perfectly cut. There was no label. It must have been tailored.

I removed my black suit and put it on, smoothing it into position so it skimmed every line of my body. It fitted exactly; perfect from every angle. I looked in the mirror and a woman in red looked back.

Some people are alive; some are merely not dead. Something was coming, I could feel it. I lay on the bed and awaited my own resurrection.

It wasn't long before somebody knocked. I opened the door, rolled away the stone: Patrick. I gazed at him without surprise.

'Can I come in?'

I looked at him, at the amused expression that carried a hint of concern, at that odd, almost feminine mouth.

'Yes,' I said, and shut him in.

Things can be what you want them to be. Was that what he'd said? No matter. With him stood awkwardly in the corner, a trapped animal, I felt the hot truth of it. The air was stuffy, the walls close. Another time I might have opened a window, but now I remained precisely where I was, observing him, like my hunter-protester who had not wanted me to run.

'I enjoyed our game,' he said.

'What? Oh. The Monopoly.' I attempted to make my face convincing.

'Are you all right?' He was watching me, trying to work out what was different. 'You seem . . .'

'Yes?'

'Nothing.' He shifted from foot to foot, uneasy and unsure why. I moved closer so I could make out the faint pulse of his heart, rising and falling through the skin of his throat. 'How are those blind spots coming?'

I smiled, careful not to reveal my teeth. 'Fine. Take that off.'

'Excuse me?'

I motioned to his wedding ring. His voice died as he stared down at the band. I saw the workings of his mind, saw it all. Eventually he did as I asked, as I'd known he would, as I'd known before he knocked on the door, before his shoes trod the corridor's agreeable carpet, maybe even before he had knelt and offered me a game as if it were a prayer. Was this what it was like being her, the usual human haze cleared, the uncertainty gone? My mind was pared and prepared. A mind that saw only function; the mind of a predator.

Slowly he placed the ring on the bedside table. The *chink* was unnaturally loud. I took him in. He was uncomplicated, a blank canvas. Perfect.

I moved to him and there beneath the hangings I kissed him, hard, harder, on the mouth. It was not truly a woman's mouth, not up close, but it had the quality I sought. It *yielded*. He made a sound, perhaps of protest, but I kissed him until it stopped. I put a hand to his neck: the nape was soft enough for belief, and did I not carry belief in me, didn't

we all, like children greedy for amulets and trinkets? I wanted
to grab for him, to seize him between my fingers and create
mountains and valleys of his flesh, to look upon the landscape I'd created and see that it was good. I unbuttoned his
shirt; he reached for the zip of my red dress but I would
not let him touch it. I took it down myself and pushed him
onto the bed. His chest was smooth, hairless: it made the
pretence even easier. The need to use screamed within me;
the hunger inside rose and took over everything. I closed
my eyes and scars exploded across my vision; I grasped his
shoulders and he gave a moan, realising, kissing his way
down my breasts, my stomach. I gazed up at the hangings
and saw all the way through to the hot red sky. I thought
of the woman I had left in her bedroom, of myself opened
like a tin of fruit, of sticky sweetness and of red mouths and
dresses. I thought of flowers growing fetid with their own
voluptuousness. I thought of coming to life.

He was there when I woke up, running a hand along the
hollows at the base of my back. It was still dark. I thought
of polar stillness, of the midnight sun. I had been the hunter,
the seducer – or had I? I rolled over and felt the tug of
strings.

He sat up amid a rasp of bedclothes and said my name.

'You are lovely,' he said, and his manner was so simple
and open that I blushed. Did he know? Could he tell how
he had been used? But he was oblivious, suggesting a shower
with a wicked gleam. Before I could answer, another, quite
different voice called my name.

'Laura? It's Jude. Sorry to interrupt some much-needed
beauty sleep, but you have to come down. There's something
you need to see.'

The warmth of our little climate evaporated; the spell broke. I swore under my breath. 'Hide,' I mouthed, casting around for my clothes – not the red dress, of course. They would not understand.

'Are you in there? Dear God, don't make me come in.'

'One minute!'

I turned, half dressed, to see Patrick lying exactly where he was.

'What are you doing? Get up!'

He raised his eyebrows. 'You're not a teenager any more. So what if he finds out?'

'Don't be a prick, Patrick.' We caught one another's eye: the inadvertent rhyme saved us from disaster.

'A poet, truly.'

I hesitated. 'You don't feel . . .'

'What?' He was watching me quizzically, yet I somehow felt he already knew what I was about to say.

'Exploited.'

'Don't be crazy.' He kissed me, then, half-smiling: 'Who's to say I'm not the one exploiting you?'

'Laura!' Jude's muffled exclamation came again.

I wasn't sure what Patrick meant, but there was no time now. I kissed him back, and the need was back, a red wave surging . . .

'Ow!' I'd kissed him hard enough to draw blood. His, not mine. He wore an expression I had never seen before, on anybody, at least not with relation to me. I pushed him into the bathroom, and with clothes on my back and salt on my lips I opened the door.

'What's up?'

'Remember Gheorghe Funar?'

'Popa's financial adviser? What about him?'

'He's dead.'

'*What?*'

I followed Jude to the Lair, where Pavel was huddled around the television. To my surprise, Mr Gabor was also there, red-eyed and wearing his coat, as if he had just come in. I looked at the clock: quarter to midnight. A drum of worry beat in my chest.

'What happened?'

They parted slightly to reveal the image onscreen. With a lurch I recognised Funar's thick black brows.

'Hanged himself in his cell,' Jude said. 'The news just broke.'

'Where would he get a rope from?' We turned and looked at Mr Gabor, who spread his hands wide. 'There are no belts, no shoelaces. I should know. I have visited often enough.'

'You think he was murdered?'

'I do not think anything. I only say what I know.'

The camera cut to show the outside of the prison, eerily lit by the flashing lights of police cars and ambulances.

'They're not much use,' Jude said. 'He's dead.' When nobody replied, he said, 'But this is *good* news, isn't it? Three days before the trial. Funar was the opposition's star witness.'

Still nobody spoke. Around us the shadows grew a little deeper.

'It's good news,' Jude repeated, but even he did not sound convinced. Any benefit from Funar's missing testimony would be more than outweighed by how bad this looked. Mr Gabor had once said this case was nothing but PR, and there was no worse PR than this. The attack on Ursu paled in comparison.

The crudeness of the situation, too, shocked me. It was so one-dimensional, so . . . ugly. Everyone would think Marija was responsible, yet I knew she would never have done something this *unattractive*. So who had? From the corner of my eye I studied Pavel, staring blankly at the screen. Troubled, yes. Killer, no. He had nothing to do with this. Nor did Jude, nor did Mr Gabor. But the person who was working against us must have realised they were running out of time.

I tore off a piece of nail, barely noticing the pain. Who could it be? Who among us had the capacity to end a life?

As if coming to a decision, Pavel abruptly stood up and walked out.

'I'll go,' Jude said, and hurried after him. Only Mr Gabor and I remained, the television casting a strange, dancing light upon our faces.

'If we lose,' I began (I'd never dared voice the possibility before, and now I realised why), 'if we lose . . . how do they do it?'

He did not need to ask what I meant.

'Hanging. Always they hang. It is a peculiarly Yanussian way to die. Look at Funar. Your predecessor, Cristescu, chose it too.'

He was right. It was less an end than a suspension, a question left unanswered.

'We have run out of time,' he went on. 'I cannot conduct all the witness interviews required. I know you three are working like slaves, but you will never finish the evidence cache. We must change tack.'

'But how?'

'I will think of something.' He stood to leave, but I remained seated in the old green armchair.

'Mr Gabor, do you think – do you think it's just bad timing?' Even to me the question sounded hopeless.

I heard him stop, his voice low. 'What I say to you, Laura, is to think about a life spent in the shadows. After a time you begin to be wary of the light. Without it, after all, there would be no shadows. So when I meet darkness, I do not waste time searching for its heart. Instead, I look for the source of the light.'

I gazed at the flickering screen. Bad news for us, good news for – who? Who had the cunning and capability to sabotage Marija in this way?

I turned quickly, an idea on my tongue, but nobody was there.

Outside, the faint voices of the protesters took up a chant. It took a moment to identify it as a countdown.

Five . . .

Four . . .

Three . . .

Two . . .

One . . .

It was New Year's Day.

CHAPTER THIRTY-NINE

This time I did not knock. The door was unlocked; maybe it always had been. I opened it soundlessly and slipped inside. There, among the flowers, I watched her.

She was seated at her dressing table, brushing her hair. The window beyond was black. The motion in her stillness was akin to the beating of a heart, going nowhere yet pulsing at the centre of everything. I had tried to go through Patrick in pursuit of her, but it was not enough.

Her hair fell smoothly, a shining curtain, the performance it concealed about to begin, or end. I craved to see her face. The brush swept down slowly, slowly, over and over. It was the hair of a young woman and for the first time I wondered if it might not be a wig, the Little Mother no more than a balding crone, combing in falsehoods so the enchantment might go on just a little longer. The scent of the flowers had changed too, grown earthier, danker. Those green stems were bending, the toothy white of the nearest orchid stained with brown. I was reminded of the odour in my mother's bedroom. Never had I imagined that cancer could stink.

The brush stopped and she turned and looked directly at me.

'Funar is dead,' I said. *But you know that already.*

'They will think I killed him.'

'Did you?' Too much had gone unsaid. How much tragedy would be averted if only we could talk to one another? She regarded me, expressionless, then returned to the mirror. I watched her reflected eyes just as I had in our first meeting, those amber irises pulling me through the looking glass. And what exactly had I found here? I could think nothing, do nothing, only look. That was what I had always done, pressing my nose against the window of life and whining to be let in. After the trial I would return home to England. To what? I had achieved nothing. Of the two of us, it was I who had the death sentence. She had *lived*; the signs were there in that plumped unnatural skin, as if she had drawn her body's energies upwards, outwards, scarring her torso in return for a face as smooth and bewitching as a child's.

She put down the brush and picked up a lipstick. The tube dislocated from its socket with a soft *pop*. 'I did not kill Gheorghe.'

'Then who did?'

She sighed. She was a prima donna preparing for closing night, chest heaving in the lights as thousands of bloody roses cascaded from the stalls, scratching her arms and face, until she might die of flowers.

'Do you know the Chinese word for "enemy"? *Chou jia.* It means "hated household". The people who are closest to you will hurt you the most. Jiang Qing, Mao's wife, told me that.' She paused, the lipstick at her mouth. 'You know what they did to her? After her husband died, men locked her up and forced her to sew dolls. In defiance she embroidered her name on the chest of every one. She had been declared anathema by then, so branding them like this meant they could not be sold.' A scornful smile. 'A taste for the dramatic.'

My mouth cracked open. 'She was an actress too.'

'Not a very good one, I think.' She was painting her lips, now, smearing red across them as if in a butcher's shop. 'Let them send me to my death, Laura. I don't care. But I will leave behind nothing – *nothing* – that they can use. Let them burn with my name emblazoned across their chests. Do you understand?'

I understood. She would rather set the world aflame than have her own fires quenched. I had moved unconsciously closer as she spoke. The mirror could no longer contain her, but I could; I could hold the entirety of her in my eyes, just as with the photograph of her and my mother and all those dead women. For I knew they were dead, of course they were. Something – someone – had killed them, my mother included. I had hoped to find answers here; instead I had found only deeper confusion, the path behind me long gone and that ahead nigh impossible to see.

'Come to me the day after tomorrow,' she said. 'The morning of the trial. I have something for you.'

I nodded. She was close enough now that I could have reached out and touched her. So I did. I reached for her arm and took it. This was my final opportunity to push through, to walk through walls. I had failed with my mother. I would not fail again.

She tried to pull away but I would not allow it. I saw the register of surprise, the faint, intoxicating knowledge that she had, at the last, lost control. It gave me the final courage I needed. I moved close, closer to her and . . .

She put her hand out between us, bringing me to a soft halt, then slowly brought that hand to my mouth. Her fingers brushed against my lips, then pressed, gently, indenting them. I could have tasted her, the life that leapt within her like a flame.

Then she leaned in towards me, so near that I felt the vibrations in the narrow air between us, and whispered:

'*Let them burn.*'

I closed the door, hands shaking, and leaned my head against the varnished wood. I cannot tell you the headiness of that moment, despite my disappointment, despite my knowledge that I had gone so far and yet still it had not been enough. Inside I raved, insatiable.

Then I turned, gasped.

Pavel stood there. His expression was one of extreme shock. He gazed at me, wordless, then said finally: 'What were you doing in there?'

And I did not know what to say.

CHAPTER FORTY

Cristian Pavel sat across from me in the small study. He seemed unable to speak.

Once I might have helped him. Now I merely watched. It was that time before dawn when it is impossible to imagine the oncoming light. Jude, scratchy from lack of sleep, had been sent to make coffee.

'That's a junior associate's job,' he complained, but Pavel just stared at him until two dots of pink appeared in his cheeks and he went out.

Now it was only the two of us. My boss, my rival, seemed to be having trouble looking at me, his gaze darting across, then back again. Or maybe he was finding it hard to look away. I shifted, my chair emitting a small, undignified squeak.

I was not who he'd thought. He'd believed he had her to himself, but he'd been wrong.

Eventually he stirred, smoothing back his hair like the old Pavel would. It hadn't been dyed in some time and the white was peeping through. He looked old.

'Pavel, I—'

'Trial starts in two days.'

'Yes.'

'I'm sending you back.' *Squeak.* I stared at him. 'There's a flight. You'll go back to London the morning it begins.'

'Pavel. For Christ's sake.'

His eyes were as flat as his voice. 'It's my fault. I shouldn't have kept you here after your mother passed.'

'This has nothing to do with her.'

'Doesn't it?' he said sharply, a gut-punch, and my hands flew to my throat. Then hideous politeness again. He gave me his best five-hundred-pounds-an-hour smile. 'Don't worry, we'll get you home. It was too much.'

'I'm not going home.'

'It was too much,' he repeated robotically.

'Pavel. Please.'

'Get out.' His voice was so quiet I could barely hear him. The chair squeaked again, though I hadn't moved.

'*Get out!*' He sprang to his feet, eyes wild. I went. There was no point talking to him. He was not in his right mind.

Jealousy will do that to a person.

CHAPTER FORTY-ONE

The trial had arrived, and I was leaving. I rolled the words around and could not understand them. Leaving tomorrow? Impossible. It was like trying to picture being outside the universe, that same nausea. The sleeping pill had not worked and I was on my bed, staring up at the canopy as if it had something to tell me, my eyelids stretched wide, wide open, my skull pulsing. It was dark outside – it was always dark now. Perhaps the hours had stopped when my mother's watch disappeared.

Funny, I had almost forgotten about it. When she had given it to me, I had taken it as a sign of hope, a secret signal that some day everything would be different, that loving me was only a matter of time. At first I spent that time like a guilty beggar, lavishly, fruitlessly, lying on my bed watching the dial trace round and round, pacing its cage, thirsting for a freedom that never came. Later, as my hope dwindled, I dreamed that as I slept, the watch's hands crept out from behind the glass, traced their loving way up my back and strangled me. Later still I wore it not for hope, nor even for love, but for despair.

Patrick had been right, at least in part: an object could

signify many things. Love, or the lack of it. Hope, or the loss of it.

I had thought, in coming here, that I would find my mother. In a way I had, though she was not the person I'd thought. My skull pulsed again. I had wanted the truth of my past and my parents, but Marija Popa was so much more than that. Tomorrow we would meet for the last time. She had something for me, she'd said. The falling would slow, stop, and I would find myself on solid earth.

Or would I? Another pulse. The house was watching me, scuttling into the shadows, taking care to do so slowly enough that I might catch a glimpse. Oh, it was clever. I felt as though I had lived a thousand years in this place, yet I was leaving tomorrow and what, after all, had I seen? Snatches and shimmers, nothing more.

'Where are you?' I said into the thick silence.

Nothing. Then I saw it. A solitary ladybird, crawling out from the skirting board with its wriggling insect legs.

I fell to my knees, tearing at the skirting board with my nails, scrabbling beneath it as I searched dizzily for a crack, a hole, any way at all of ripping this house open and tearing through the evil swirling at its heart.

'*Where are you?*' It was watching me, taunting me like it always did. I attacked the board until red flowered across the wall, until I could smell iron and flesh, and I thought at last that I had dug my way through, that I could reach in and pull out its entrails, until I saw it was my nails that had torn, my blood staining the white. A red wave came over me and the world turned black.

I dreamed I was walking down a street in Poartă, a wide, traffic-less boulevard, bright under the morning sun. I was following someone, but it was easy, not something to concern a person like me. I understood the language, after all, my Yanussian was perfect but for a slight accent that piqued the intrigue of good-looking men in bars. My satisfaction was of one who belongs, and I moved effortlessly through the sparse crowds in my blood-red dress. I knew I was elegant, attractive, and I felt strangers watching in appreciation. My hips undulated under their gaze.

My quarry crossed the road, and I paused and waited to do the same, but a tram came and blocked my view. It was a perfectly ordinary tram in every respect, red and white with the company name emblazoned upon it, although I had the odd notion that in other times, perhaps even until extremely recently, it had borne another name, one just as familiar but which had vanished from my mind entirely, as if scrubbed out. There was no time to be distracted, however, for the person was gaining on me and I itched to follow.

The tram began to move off, and as it did so, a woman beside me began to cry out. She had been there all the while the people got on and off, gnawing at her nails, but nobody had paid her any attention. We were all shocked when she began to exclaim, her voice improperly loud, pointing after the departing tram. What is it? I asked her. Are you missing something? I felt pleased at my own intervention, felt other strangers watching my empathy with approval, but the woman herself took no notice, kept crying out, her voice building and her hands clawing over and over, trying to grasp something that was not there. And it came to me that she was speaking in Yanussian, which I of course spoke fluently, yet I had absolutely no idea what she was saying. A crowd gathered round, chattering excitedly, and now I could not understand them either. Her voice rose to a scream. I had never seen such a concentrated expression of grief on a person's face.

I had to get out, away from these incomprehensible people.

I pushed through the throng, aiming for the wide sky, and as I did so, their looks shifted from the front of their eyes to the sides. I pressed on, but a stranger's bag caught my red dress, ripping it wide open, and my skin came with it, my torso simply opening like curtains. I began to run, shedding cloth and hair, for the person I'd been following was retreating into the distance and was almost lost from view. I stumbled up the sunless boulevard, flesh peeling away, muscles gasping in the cold air, following the faceless figure until what was left of me arrived on the hill where Sorin's statue stood.

There was the figure. It had halted, its back to me. It began to turn, slowly, and I realised that on no account did I want to see what it was, but my shredded feet would not move, and my eyes were gripped in my skull so I could not choose but look. I could not think why I had believed I was the hunter, when all along I had been the hunted.

The figure turned, and at last I saw who it was.

Now I have you, Marija said. Then she moved closer and asked for my eyes.

But I need my eyes, I said.

She shrugged, as if this did not much matter.

Besides, I would not know how to give them to you.

Oh, but that is easy, the Black Widow said. You already have. And in two quick steps she was before me, something clenched in each fist. She opened her hands and there were my eyes nestled in her palms. And I could no longer see, but my eyes could, and they lay in her hands and gazed up at the empty sky.

The knock awoke me. Patrick. I blinked at him eyelessly. He brushed my fingertips and I felt nothing but the fact of it.

I told him I was leaving. He nodded slowly, scratching at his leg through his chinos so I heard the rasp of cloth and hair. I had always loathed that sound, and it made me hate him, a reminder of the unending exhaustion of tolerating people who are not ourselves. How many times had I blamed Andrei, faultless, motherless, adulterated Andrei, for not picking up on a reference, or for failing to perform something I had only mentally willed him to do? I had sought someone to understand me; I had been terrified I would find them. And I had. It was not that she had seen me: rather, she had seen *through* me, all the way through and out the other side. Under her gaze I had become a transparency. I had thought I wanted to find my self, when it turned out that what I really wanted was to lose it.

What disappointment, what despair, when we discover we are not the person we are in our dreams! For what is growing up but the slow disinterment of our own frailties, the gradual realisation of our limits? The hopeful fog of adolescence clears and we begin to trace the true shape of who we are, with all its desolate hollows, its lonely, gloamy cul-de-sacs. And then? No cause for congratulation, for then the single question emerges: how do we live with ourselves, knowing what we know?

He moved closer, leaned in to kiss me, and I could not help myself: I flinched. I thought of how my father had shied from my touch, and at last I understood him. I did not want Patrick any more, and is there anything so repulsive as someone you do not want?

He pulled back; his face flickered. He *almost* said something, I knew it and he knew it, and there was a moment when the barrier could have been broken almost as it was made. But he said nothing, and its weight settled irrevocably between us.

'London?' he said instead.

'Yes.'

'I'm heading out too. Pennsylvania.'

The name awoke a memory. It shuddered through me. 'What's in Pennsylvania?'

It took some time for him to answer. His shadow was a blue so deep as to be indistinguishable from black.

'A buyer.'

'What are you selling?'

I could not see his face, but the air changed. There are so many unseen currents. In the silence I heard my heart beat, once, twice; I heard once more his response when I had worried he felt exploited. *Who's to say I'm not the one exploiting you?*

'Patrick. What are you selling?'

'You already know.'

The light snapped on, though whether by my hand or his I could not say. It was directly behind his head, the shadows slanting, peculiar. I stared at him, and with a sick thrill, I knew, I knew what it was.

CHAPTER FORTY-TWO

She was not in her rooms. Pavel was nowhere to be found, nor Jude, nor Mr Gabor. Seven a.m. They must have left for the courthouse already. I ran through the corridors, searching for somebody, anybody. Sorin? But it was the morning of his statue's unveiling. Even Apostol would have sufficed. My flight was in four hours and Pavel had already told me the guards would ensure I was on it. I was Cassandra, without even an audience to disbelieve her: the house had opened its maw and swallowed them all whole. For the first time I could detect nothing about it: its slimy horns had retreated into the silence. In the Lair, Jude's posters stared emptily back; in the pink drawing room the rabbit clock was still, its creatures frozen in motion, trying their hardest not to blink. The evidence room was quiet as the grave and the mirror showed nothing but my reflection. Nothing to see, nothing to see. My footsteps were absorbed by the cunning carpet, the absence of furniture and paint- ings so many hollow screams. Perhaps the house had consumed them too, absorbed them into its walls along with my companions and Andrei's mother. I sensed long- fingered ghosts drifting after me, though when I wheeled round, they hid themselves in a light bulb's filament, a plaster crack.

I opened the door of the Winter Garden. Nothing. It was silent; no birds sang. Now I walked the lower passage of the east wing, past the dining room where Ecaterina had picked so meagrely at her food, past those innocuous doors that opened up into more innocuous rooms. It was the same path I had walked on my first night. I was Drake, returning to the place I had begun, yet in that time I had seen all these monsters.

The basement door was before me. *I know what you are.* It remained as it was, the same grey that made it oddly hard to see – yet was it my imagination that red was seeping across it, oozing down its smooth surfaces, pooling in the keyhole?

I was distracted by the end of the passage: a light suddenly glowed on. It wasn't there and then it was, blurring gold through the frosted pane.

A shadow across my oppressed brain. I moved towards it.

CHAPTER FORTY-THREE

The light was not issuing from the changing room, but from the chamber beyond. I stepped inside; the door swung shut behind. In the gloom the cold tiles squirmed with fantastic creatures, hopeless victims of comingling: a manticore, a cynocephalus, a griffin. As if it were myth, not humanity, that made monsters.

No swimsuit awaited me this time. I changed anyway, simply removing my clothing and letting it fall so it obscured those twisting tails, those cumbersome claws. Naked, I pressed my fingertips against the door. It opened without resistance.

No one there.

I walked to the edge, the very edge, where concrete liquefied to water. At first the pool seemed still, but then I looked into that artificial blue and saw how it trembled with a myriad primal movements. Babies could swim – it was only later that one had to learn how. Perhaps all of life is remembering what we have forgotten.

I dived in. Simple; complex beyond words. I watched it happen from a vantage point beyond my body, the body I had used on Patrick as a last resort, and it had not worked, it had not been enough. The hunger still clawed within. I watched my knees slowly bend, a clench of muscle shading the line of the calf. My tapering arms extended, groping for the empty air; my back rotated gently down like the hand of a clock to meet its end at my buttocks, gouged by tension. I leapt, my toes creasing then lengthening, a small mole on my left thigh, and now we were in the golden moment when I was horizontal, perfect, suspended above the yawning, glowing blue. Had I possessed the power to stop myself falling all along? If so, it was all too cruel.

I returned in time to see my fingertips connect with the surface, its film bulging, hollowing, the silver millisecond when water fought flesh.

And yielded.

She was there when I surfaced, the last true heir of the Iubită empire. Her skeletal face was a pale parody of her sister's, a photo negative developed all wrong, its hollows deepened by the pool's wavering light. I might have been on the edge of a skyscraper a hundred storeys tall. I had felt those eyes before.

'It was you. When I was here with Marija before. You watched us.'

Ecaterina's features were expressionless.

'You're selling the Iubită company. You betrayed her.'

She moved suddenly closer. *Chou jia.* Hated household. In the blue light I saw the mandibles of her jaw, the nose that seemed to twist and lengthen, the yellow shadows of her cheeks. I saw the bunch of keys she carried at her hip, keys to every door in the mansion, including the locked little office where the inventory had lain. I saw the frozen face of Gheorghe Funar and the rope basket she had carried the day she went on one of her prison visits.

Where would he get a rope from? Mr Gabor had said.

'Why?' Water, water everywhere but my throat as dry as dust. The reflections flitted and coiled, hieroglyphs across her paper skin. I thought she would not answer.

Then: 'Do you know what happens when a queen bee grows old and weak?' She spoke conversationally. The skyscraper dissolved and now we were at tea in a well-heeled part of London, clinking genteelly as the traffic howled by.

'The bees *smell* it. Strange but true. They scent her vulnerability and they cluster round. I told you how they huddle in winter to keep her warm. It is like that, but something has changed. Now they crowd in until she is unable to move, more and more of them, warming her with their wings. But it is not love on their minds any more. It is death.

'The queen's body grows hot, hotter. The swarm whirs, tighter . . . tighter. At last she dies, burned from the outside in. And another takes her place.'

I looked at Marija's sister and finally I saw not the White Queen but the other queen. The queen that stalks her rival in the hive's winding dark.

'Yes, I leaked the inventory. Not Pavel. You suspected he was collaborating with Ursu? No, my dear. That day in the Justice building he not only returned that dratted sugar bowl – he also begged for a late plea bargain. Marija had refused such a deal, and First Minister Anghelescu had already publicly ruled it out, so he had to reach out covertly. He did not do very well, you know. Lust is such a useless emotion. Ursu was halfway to agreeing when he became worried about the political sensitivity and told Anghelescu, who was so angry they'd discussed it – all that sneaking around, all those silly code names – that he ordered Judge Ardelean to bring the trial forward to focus both sides' minds. So in that sense, it *was* Pavel you sought. The accidental traitor.'

'But why sell Iubită? Why now?'

Ecaterina's eyes went black. 'I told you my sister once did me a favour. Well. I was young, and I was in love. You are surprised, but love may be found in the dustiest corners. He was our languages tutor, English and French. I was twenty, Marija fourteen. I had never met anyone with blue eyes before and ah, he was handsome. The way he pushed back his hair as he bent over my work . . .' She was gazing at something far away.

'I did not tell him I loved him. When you are young, such words are cotton in the mouth. But I was young for my age, naive. It must have been obvious, not to my parents – they were focused on another daughter by then – but certainly he knew it. He responded to my swift looks, allowed his hand to fall carelessly on mine. I let myself hope.'

Her voice twisted, became bitter. 'But I was wrong to do so. He was only using me. If he loved anything, it was my wealth. Still, when it became clear what he truly wanted, I wished it had just been the money.'

I was back atop the skyscraper now, clutching the side, blood pumping through my fingers as the wind rose around me. 'What did he want?'

'My sister.' The words were little more than a whisper. 'I found them one day. He had her pushed up against the wall of our schoolroom, his hands all over her body, muttering things in her ear, things he never dreamed of saying to me.

'After he was sacked, I asked for Marija's help and she gave it. Or so I thought.' Her expression was yellow and black. 'I wanted him dead. She had friends from her orphanage days: already she was powerful on the streets. She promised she would see to it, that she wanted vengeance too, for her violation and mine. Sure enough, I never heard from him again. Until, that is, the day of the press conference. He was there, pawing Camelia's body.'

369

I remembered the two men who had gone to her side, and how Ecaterina had gazed at the blond one as if the screen might swallow her up.

'I confronted her. She admitted freely that she had lied, that she had never intended to kill him. All this time he has been living in Ravec, not twenty kilometres from Poartă.' Her nostrils flared. 'I realised what a fool I had been. It was not Tomas who had pursued Marija. It was the other way round. She stole him from me, seduced him because she knew I wanted him. Because she felt like it. Because she could.'

I shook my head, disbelieving. 'She was fourteen.'

'She is a spider! What she is, she has always been. Everything she does is for control, and if you do not see it, Laura, you are a bigger fool than me. Why do you think she invites me to dinners? I cannot bear the sight of food and it amuses her to watch. During my hospital stays she sends me huge fruit baskets. Isn't your sister kind? the nurses say. She isn't a person, she's a puppeteer. She discovers what you are, what you can and cannot bear, and *uses* it.'

'What about the Iubită? How can you sell your family company?'

'It is the only way! After sucking the money out of my business, she and her husband have left me with no choice. When she is hanged, the government will seize the company and put it up for sale – with my permission, of course, as the last rightful heir.' I clenched my fists, my nose rank with the stench of her betrayal. 'We have Anghelescu's full support. Patrick Hanagan and Alexandru Ungur at the Ministry of Industry are managing the sale. I get a portion of the proceeds, the Treasury gets the rest, and the factory will reopen again under my management.'

'How can you do that to her?' I said. 'After what Constantin did?'

This was my trump card. I waited, holding my breath – but unexpectedly she smiled.

'Ah. Showed you her scars, did she? I thought she might. They have been so useful to her, I would not be surprised if she did some of them herself.' The skyscraper lurched under my feet. 'Do not look at me as if I am mad. She weaponises your trust, turns it against you. She learned that from childhood. I told you about the orphanage, how they lined the children up in two rows as a punishment and told them to hit the other. How Marija was put opposite her best friend. Well, many years later, after she had been drinking with one of her pet ministers, she told me what happened next.

'All around her the other children hesitated, or tried to pull their punches. You go first, Alina said to Marija. She was a large, doughy girl and there was strength in her, but she trusted her friend. So Marija stepped forward, looked into Alina's timid face. Then, with a single blow, she knocked her out, and two of her teeth along with it. It was no accident. By doing so, you see, she knew she would not be hit back.'

The water was growing cold, my flesh above the line spiked with goose bumps.

'Even her godchild, little Marija. You have heard of her too? For the first time, I did think it was different. Păstrăv was close to Constantin; he was powerful. I watched her smiling into the cradle.' A shrug. 'Perhaps she really did love the child. But then Păstrăv, the idiot, began plotting a coup. They picked it up through the hidden microphones. Dinu was all for having him shot, but Marija was cleverer. She invited the Păstrăv family for tea. They suspected nothing. We were in the banquet room: there were madeleines from Paris, melons from Tel Aviv. The works, as you English would say. She cradled little Marija, dandling her on her

371

knee, crooning a nursery rhyme she had learned Lord knew where.

'I knew what was coming. Constantin waited for the tea to be poured, then asked Păstrăv politely when exactly he planned on taking power.

'Păstrăv's face went white. So did his wife's. He began to bluster to Dinu. Everyone had forgotten about the two Marijas until the little one made a strange sound and we all looked over.

'The older Marija was sitting there quietly, still smiling at her smaller namesake. But the baby's face was growing pink, then red. Her hands were wrapped around its small chest. I can see it now, how *little* that chest looked. Her nails were not painted. They looked like talons. And that grip – that grip was no longer so loving. It was tight, growing tighter.'

I thought of the video I had seen, how I had been struck by Păstrăv's clawing hands.

Dragos will not let me see her. The skyscraper lurched again, violently, and I slipped over the edge and fell, the wind screaming around me.

'Păstrăv lunged for his child but the waiters pinned him and his wife to their chairs. They were Strajă agents. Dinu grinned and said he would ask one more time.

'The Păstrăvs didn't last five seconds. They were imprisoned, and little Marija was left to grow up with her aunt. My so-called sister will sacrifice anything, anyone, to save herself. Everything she touches, she destroys.'

'I don't believe you.' I couldn't. I was falling much too fast, and above and below was nothing but black.

Ecaterina snorted. 'Of course. You believe her. She makes belief cheap. Why else do you think Funar had to go? He was refusing to testify. He *believed* in her, like they all do.' She straightened, unbending within the chrysalis of her clothes. 'I am leaving now for the unveiling of the statue. Then the courthouse. As one world ends, another begins. My beloved factory will be restored and my family will be together again.'

She crossed to the door, then stopped, bony hand on the frosted pane, the generators humming like a thousand bees. Her smile was a three-inch sting.

'Run to Mummy if you want. It's over.'

CHAPTER FORTY-FOUR

I did. I ran. Belief was all I had – belief is stories, and now I suddenly, desperately needed to know I had been telling myself the right one. I cursed my blindness, that curiously human ability to see everything except how things really are.

I ran straight to her rooms, knowing with that strange sixth sense that this time she would be there. Her presence was all around me, flitting down the corridors and spreading along the walls, pulsing in time to my heaving breath, a thousand Marijas all at once, aged fifteen and fifty-eight, scything through the swimming pool and gliding through the halls of state, unblemished yet scarred to pieces, laughing at me with blackened hair and whitened teeth.

Three hours until my flight. The guards would come to escort me to the airport within the hour. There was no time; there was nothing but. My eyes burned. I pushed my sodden hair from my cold cheeks, straightened my hastily flung-on clothes, feeling as if, in this frozen country, it was I who was dissolving.

It took all my courage to turn the handle, and when I did I was immediately hit by the smell. Those beautiful, beautiful flowers had rotted, their loveliness corroded to black, a vegetal stench in the too-hot air as if the enchantress in her distraction had let the spell slide. Or had I simply failed to notice before? There was a fire in the grate, hot and stifling. A tendril trailed its putrefied growth along my skin and I could not suppress a shudder.

She stood there, the end of an empire. The prima donna when the run has ended, the crowds gone home and only the theatre ghosts for company.

'Doamna. Marija.' I took a deep breath, drawing in the decay. 'It's Ecaterina. She did this.'

She became very still.

'You are sure?'

'Yes.'

A long moment in which the silence scratched at us both. At last she turned away – I saw her dress was unzipped, revealing the long V of her scarred back. I could not speak.

'Help me.' Her voice was utterly calm.

I moved forward, helpless. Her eyes watched me in the mirror. I could have placed my hand on her skin, but I did not. Naturally she would wear red for the court. But even as I did up the fastening, slowly obscuring those shining scars, I no longer believed the colour symbolised her own blood alone.

With her back still to me she said, 'I told you before that survival matters above all else. It seems I was wrong.' She sighed. 'The true skill is knowing the moment to sacrifice yourself. To have the strength not to do it too early, and the wisdom to do it before it is too late. That moment has come. All I need is the assistance of someone I trust.'

She turned and faced me for the first time, the last time. I was hurtling down, fast, faster. I had thought I'd glimpsed the bottom, but the deepest place I could possibly have envisaged would have been a fingernail scratch in the abyss I now found myself in.

'You, Laura. It has to be you. It could only ever be you. I told you about Jiang Qing, about *chou jia*. She taught me another word. *Yuanfen*. It means something that was meant to happen. If there is no *yuanfen* between two people, they can stand face to face and never meet. If there is, they will always find one another, even if they are miles apart.' Cool fingers enclosed my face like petals. 'Laura, our meeting was fate. No one should go through life without being seen by another. I have seen myself in you, and I know you have seen yourself in me.'

Then she placed those fingers on my eyes. The air caught in my throat, my whole being trapped. I never forgot that moment. Nor did I ever know truly what it meant.

She came closer, so close that I felt the warmth of her breath as she whispered, 'We are twin souls. I want you to know that.'

Her fingers released me, leaving ten different absences in their place. I could not speak. I was being brought to life. So what, if I died of the pain?

Like a dumb animal I watched her put on her coat, coiling her hair over and around the collar, preparing herself for all those other eyes that would feast upon her, raking over her until they were sated. I could not bear it.

'I have left something for you. In there.' She inclined her head towards her bedroom. 'It will explain everything. I hope you will not be too quick to condemn an old woman. I hope, one day, you will understand.'

I stood unlocked and motionless as she moved towards the door. Just before she opened it, she turned.

'Goodbye, daughter.'

And she left, the door closing behind her. I heard the sound of the lock turning, as if she had taken my whole soul with her and thrown away the key.

CHAPTER FORTY-FIVE

I went automatically to the door and tried to turn the handle, but it was hopeless. I pressed my ear against the wood and listened. Nothing. She had gone. Around me, petals wept to the carpet.

I went towards the bedroom, skirting the piano, and as I did so a single note sounded, reverberating. The sound woke the house. Without her protection it returned with a vengeance, exerting all its force onto my shoulders so it was all I could do to stagger on, the hares on the wallpaper baring their teeth in a snarl. For it is human to change and therefore it was no wonder this timeless ruin, buried up to its neck in the past, wanted no part in the future. I fought on, on, until I entered the bedroom and the pressure withdrew as suddenly as it came. It had no power here.

No wonder. I took in the bare little room, its single bed with a plain coverlet, everything white, white as bone. There was nothing in here to influence or control. It was where she let the world fall away.

On the bed the yellow packet lay like a discoloured tooth, the only colour in the room. It was the same one I had collected from that mysterious official, the one I had nearly died retrieving. Of course she had known the risks. She had known everything. No wonder she had never been unduly concerned by imprisonment: she was a gamma ray, cutting through walls. When she looked at life, she saw through to its bones.

There was nothing else to do. I opened the envelope, and even as it disgorged its contents, my heart was already thrumming in recognition.

A file, stamped with the mark of the National Records Office. I opened it with trembling hands. The first page bore my mother's name.

My mother's missing file, the one I had failed to find at the NRO. Here it was, the meat of the matter. I set it carefully on the bed and backed away. I was ready; I was not ready. I wanted to know; I never wanted to know.

She had known.

I wrenched open the window, gasping into the frozen air. The sun shone wretchedly above the horizon, half obscured by the smoking spire of the iron mill. To the west rose Sorin's statue, denuded of scaffolding for its grand opening. A movement there caught my attention. Something . . .

But I could not see what it was. I could not see what it was, I told myself, even as my stomach convulsed. My hair, half frozen by the cold air, crackled as I went quickly to the living room and snatched up a set of binoculars. The strap caught on a side table and I yanked it so hard that the table fell to the floor, smashing some humanitarian award, but I was already back in the bedroom and shoving the window further open, ignoring the crack and whine of the ice. Somewhere the gate-bird screamed. I thrust the lenses to my eyes and placed a hand against the sill to steady myself as I searched through the white sky until I came to the object

(no, person)

hanging from the outstretched hand of Lady Justice.

CHAPTER FORTY-SIX

I had always pictured the hanged as suspended in space: immune (too late) to gravity, pinned to the white air as if someone had drawn them there, like the game on paper. Never had I imagined this awful swaying. Back and forth, back and forth the slender body went, the wind seizing it lasciviously; then, finding a new amusement, it began to twist, first clockwise, then anticlockwise, tracing an awful circle. Its back was to me but it was turning. I could not look; I had to look.

Sorin. His beautiful, ruined face tilted blankly down. Blue with blood and distance, the eyes were mere milky smears, the delicate cheekbones swallowed by swollen flesh. I turned and vomited onto the carpet.

I should call for help, but he was beyond helping. I was too late. I was failing, I was falling – no, I had failed, I was fallen. Black feathers at the window and the gate-bird screamed again, out there, in here, inside my own head, raking the underside of my scalp as I gasped and ducked, Baba Mierlă angling for my tongue. I had asked questions all right, but they had not been the right ones.

Slowly, with shaking knees and heart, I returned to the bed and took up the slender folder. It was time.

The first page was dated April 1963. Six years after the Popas came to power. It did not mention my mother. Instead it described the results of a clinical trial for a drug called eroxane: a high-ranking special committee had approved its use by the state after trials on a test population. Puzzled, I turned the page. The next document, in slightly stilted English, detailed its performance.

> Stage I trials (1961–63) proved successful in the boosting of fertility rates among the test population of 800 females aged 20–40. The increase was 65 per cent. Due to pressures implemented by the special committee there has been no possibility to examine any long-term effects. We have approved regular dosage of test population, as well as immediate roll-out to wider population. Beyond raising testosterone levels, there is no proving effect in men, but the rationing and unique branding of the product should ensure limitation within the female community.

I turned another, newer page, entitled 'Twelve-Year Follow-Up'. My eye snagged on a word.

> After the subjects are followed for a decade post-introduction into food supply, we are finding a significantly increased incidence (RR = 2.27; 94% CI: 1.07–4.81) of thyroid and ovarian cancer risk among the test and general population (Table IV). We note that other studies[4] show women are two to three times more likely to develop thyroid cancer than men.
>
> The increased risk was principally due to a four-fold increased incidence in multiparous women (those giving birth to multiple children). In the test environment of 800 women

alone, there emerged 348 cases of thyroid cancer during the follow-up period.[5] Most diagnoses are occurring a decade or more after the beginning of treatment, albeit they were given doses at a multiple of several times the dose elsewhere in the population. We note that there is a high probability of further incidences that will be evolving beyond the timeframe of this study.

Although the special committee has deemed this an 'acceptable risk', since thyroid cancer is generally treatable, we are concerned that out of the 348 cases, 95 had symptoms – and indeed are dying, or have died – of the far rarer anaplastic thyroid cancer (27.3% incidence rate).

We notice that anaplastic thyroid cancer typically accounts for some 1% of all thyroid cases. Prognoses for anaplastic thyroid cancer are severe, with sufferers living on average for less than a year after diagnosis . . .

Notwithstanding the relatively small sample size of the study, we find its far higher incidence here alarming. Some of these cases took as long as a decade to emerge, and in five instances were diagnosed after the subject had left the testing environment, raising the possibility of further undiagnosed cases.

Due to the impossibility of tracking the entire population affected by the roll-out, it is unclear what the incidence rates may be in the rest of the country . . .

It is not our position to question the judgement of the special committee, and its visionary approach to Yanussia's issues of demography. We have previously noted the existence of the Western drug clomiphene, which would have the same impact as eroxane but minus the undesirable side effects. However, since it would obviously be unacceptable to use a foreign pharmaceutical, we merely seek fresh approval for the continuing use of this drug and to decline all liability . . .

With trembling fingers I turned the page. The following leaves looked different and were slightly bent, as if stuffed in by a hasty hand. The Iubită accounts. Except this time the numbers included spending on the development of the ingredient eroxane. This time the numbers added up.

I could not breathe. Another page, turning it slowly as if it were made of lead. This was dated 1975 and marked continuing approval for eroxane usage by the special committee. On it were the committee's signatures. There were only three.

One for the Minister for the Treasury and Popa's special adviser, Gheorghe Funar.

One for the General Secretary of the Communist Party, Fearless Leader of the Marovia Region, First Worker, First Minister of the People's Republic, and Executive President of Yanussia, Constantin Popa.

And one for the Minister for Language and Culture, Minister for Women and Family, Beloved Little Mother and First Lady of the People's Republic of Yanussia.

Marija Popa. I closed my eyes. It made no difference: the text glowed through the lids.

Marija was Minister for Women. She had the iubită *made by an all-female workforce.*

The 'test environment' referred to in the papers. The eight hundred lucky Iubită workers, all of them women, all with a heart-shaped *iubită* sweet permanently in their mouths. Marija's laboratory at the top of the factory, used for research, and the spinning machines below, the same kind used in pharmaceuticals, with the clever tubes into which one could feed dyes, or drugs. The unstoppable Movement for a Million Children. The photograph's slow death march of black crosses across smiling faces.

My mother belongs to my heart; my heart belongs to my mother. She'd meant it literally. She'd captured these women's

382

bodies for her own use. The Minister for Women. Jobs for women. What a sick joke. Not women, but one woman, grasping at power and self-preservation no matter the cost. I had admired her for weaponising her infertility. I had not thought the metaphor so accurate.

My legs gave way and I was kneeling beside my mother's bed again, smelling that sweet, fruity, sickly smell, seeing the rotting lump on her neck, as if she had swallowed one of the sweethearts and it had stuck. As if the factory had followed us to England.

Which, of course, it had.

I remembered her words on my thirteenth birthday, the terror in her eyes. *You don't know what I sacrificed.*

What she had sacrificed, it turned out, was everything. And I – I was the awful product. I was a Iubită child, a poisonous child, a child that had murdered its mother before it took its first breath. Marija had known. She had always known. Our time together had been nothing but her leading me down this path to this precise point, a pig fed to fatness on lies. She'd poisoned her own women in order to supercharge their fertility, breeding them like animals. She'd told me herself that she was a survivor, that she had stayed alive this long by knowing exactly what to sacrifice and when. No wonder they had never found Popa's missing remote control. It was *she* who had seen it was all over for the regime, she who'd realised the protesters would not stop until they had slaked their bloodlust. She had opened those doors and sacrificed her husband for her own survival. Sorin had practically told me as much and I had refused to see it.

There was no oxygen anywhere, only dreadful space. I had been falling and now finally I could see the end, and it was not what I had sought. No relief, no solace, no one to catch me. Only the hard, blind ground.

Think. The house that had seen so much death was

watching me, hunger in its eye, but I forced my mind to coalesce around the white-hot star of my rage. We had spent months checking for anything with Marija's name on it, and now here it was, on the defining programme of the Popa regime – the icy tip, it turned out, of something far more damaging.

Why give this to me? If it got out, we would lose. Even if excluded as evidence, which of the population would believe that a woman capable of pumping fertility drugs into her people like so many lab rats was not also capable of pulling illicit financial strings? The allure of Marija consisted of her ambiguity; this would eliminate it at a stroke. She would be condemned to death and the Iubită empire would die with her. For who would buy a company whose brand had been, quite literally, poisoned?

A thought electrified me. What if this destruction was what she wanted? What if it was exactly the point? I thought through the consequences. Ecaterina's plans would be ruined, and the Yanussian Central Bank would lose a great deal of much-needed money. *I will leave behind nothing* – nothing – *that they can use.* A pyrrhic victory, and who had she appointed as her avenging angel? Not Pavel, the useful but overly devoted pup. Not Mr Gabor, who knew what she was and would shudder at her touch, nor Jude, who was too self-involved to care. She had needed someone to destroy her and her case, someone who already carried the seed of self-destruction within.

It has to be you, she'd said. I'd thought I understood her, but I understood nothing. There was no bond between us – I was simply one of her Million Children, one of her factory daughters, the convenient, corrupted fruit of my true mother's poisoning. *Yuanfen* indeed. It was just as Sorin had said. I thought she had been teaching me to love myself when in fact she had taught me to hate.

Footsteps drummed outside, voices called my name. They were coming to take me away.

At the bottom of the page was a phone number and the name of the *Popor* newspaper. Dully I picked up the phone and prepared to carry out the sentence on my betrayer. On myself.

CHAPTER FORTY-SEVEN

But my finger did not dial the newspaper offices. Instead it called the one number I should always have called, since the beginning, had it not been for my fear and my despair.

No, not fear. Give it its true, shameful name.

Cowardice.

He picked up on the fourth ring.

'Hello, Tată,' I said quietly, and I told him what I knew.

When I finished, there was a long silence. I caught sight of myself in the tall, thin mirror. I was trembling with nervous hope.

'Did you know?' I asked him as the silence stretched.

'Yes. We knew.'

'You should have told me.' My voice was shaky. 'We should have talked about it. Mamă and me. We could have—'

'What?' His voice was a splinter. 'It would have changed nothing.'

He began talking, really talking. It was the first time in my life we had discussed anything at all. A dangerous operation, removing the carapace from our hearts. I had no idea if we would survive it.

'When you were born, Laura, you were so loved. We had

a difficult time of it. Your mother was thirty when you finally arrived. For a while we thought you never would. It was our duty to create workers, but it didn't feel that way. The world opened up yet it also became focused in a way I had never experienced. Everything was centred on you. Your mother spent the first year of your life with her face buried in your hair: she loved to caress the place where your skull hadn't meshed together. It gave her access to your baby thoughts, she said. Our neighbours told us we were going soft, that the novelty would wear off once we'd had our second child. We didn't listen.

'But we knew you could not grow up there. As you got older we saw the regime's shadow edging across your face. We saw the Popas in the drawing-in of your cheekbones, in the largeness of your eyes. We could not raise you there, let alone another child. We made plans to leave and we succeeded.

'In Yanussia it had been our duty to create workers. In England we could have you for your own sake. I cannot tell you the relief. We quickly decided to have another child, but nothing happened. Your mother went for tests, prodded and poked in a strange country, hardly able to make herself understood. The results came back. They found a translator and she told us in our own tongue, her face flat, hardly looking at us.

'There was an unknown chemical in her blood. It had similar properties to a Western fertility drug, she said, but they didn't know exactly what it was for or what the long-term impact might be. Nevertheless they thought it ill-advised to have another child – it might affect her more if she was multiparous. They wanted to know how she had ingested it, who had administered it, but your mother kept silent. She was so used to silence by then. It had seeped under her skin.

'Alone, however, it did not take long to work out the

truth. Something given to her regularly, in consistent amounts, over a long period? Food was already irregular when we left. My own tests were negative. What else could it have been but the *iubită* rations? They gave them extra at the factory. She was a lab rat, but for what purpose we could not know. All we knew was that somehow the Popas had followed us.' He stopped, a crack in his voice; the little fissure broke my heart. 'We thought we were safe. We were wrong.'

'Why . . . why didn't you tell me?'

His pause contained everything. 'Because she loved you.'

'No.' My voice was helpless, sunken. 'She didn't. She couldn't even look at me.'

'You think love is a thing of light? You think it's *easy*?' His voice flamed. 'Have you learned nothing? There are shadows to make hatred pale in comparison. Your mother knew that something was coming for her, knew the Popas had hijacked her fertility. Every time she looked at you she was reminded of it. She wasn't trying to hurt you. She was trying to protect you. She refused to let you know the pain of your own origins. She carried that knowledge on her own. Can you blame her for keeping her distance, for fear that she might break?'

With a devastating blow I recalled the sharp smell of blood and vinegar, my thirteenth birthday, the ruinous reminder of my own biology and the expression on my mother's face. I'd thought it was anger, when it had in fact been terror – not for herself, but for me. My eyes were hot with tears. She must have been so afraid.

'We tried to find out what awaited her, but it was too risky to contact our friends. We hadn't even told them we were leaving because it would have put them in danger. They must have thought we'd died in some secret prison. After 1989, we searched for them and . . .'

A tiny silence, but he pushed through it.

'They were dead, or as good as. All her colleagues. Anaplastic thyroid cancer. I suppose because they had not managed to escape like we had, they were more exposed over time. The children were fine – it was the mothers who died. Your mother had always known, in a way, but here was the final proof. After that there was no avoiding what was coming. You were loved, Laura, so bloody loved. You just couldn't see it. I remember you stopped swimming because you thought she'd thrown out your trophy . . . she has that trophy still, hidden safely in our room, where no one can take it away. She kept it polished until the day she died. When you took the case of the very woman who did this to us, your mother said nothing, so you would never know what she sacrificed to have you. She kept you safe right until the end.'

I thought of the grey, exhausted face, of my rage as it turned away for the last time. The hands around my throat tightened. I could hardly breathe.

'You really can't understand why she never said anything? Sometimes, when you undergo something like that, there isn't enough of you left to do any more.' At last his voice broke. 'You got the whole of her, Laura. I just got the remnants.'

He was speaking the truth, for only truth could sear like that. I had been so wrong, so blind. I thought of my mother, of the diamond-rare moments of happiness between us. Her passing me a knife to use on a block of cheese. The unexpected tenderness in her voice when she asked me if I had a coat, it was cold outside. And then how her face would cloud, as if remembering something, and she would turn away.

A knock began at the door, persistent. The handle twisted, returned, twisted again.

'And you?' I managed. 'What about you?'

'Yes,' he said at last, heavily. 'I loved you, once.'

Once.

'But watching your mother wither . . . I couldn't help it. I blamed you.'

'Tată . . .'

'I still do, if that's what you're going to ask. I still blame you. The Popas ruined us. *You* ruined us.' His voice was black infinity. 'It's not fair, I know, but I can't help it. I'm sorry.'

And he did sound sorry. It made it worse. I had always believed he loved me, had traced it hungrily in his eyes across the no-man's-land of the dining table as my mother sat opposite, a darkness I could not penetrate. Yet all along it was Gabriela Lăzărescu who had been my light, my own watchful angel. Even as part of me took the raw fact of her love and began to repair itself, everything else was tearing itself asunder. I had been wrong about everything. My mother had loved me, my father did not. Marija Popa did not. Wrong, wrong and wrong again.

CHAPTER FORTY-EIGHT

The knocking at the door was louder now. Voices were shouting my name. The line went dead and for a moment I lost all concentration, forgot entirely who and what I was. Then I remembered, and I had never in all my life felt so much pain.

I caught sight of myself in the thin mirror, thin enough that I could almost see through it. For how long had I simply existed, a mere sliver of light on glass? Now the walls were coming apart, the pictures gliding from their frames, the mirror sidling off into its own dimension. I could no longer be a pale reflection of what I ought to be.

I took up a glass figurine, perhaps another humanitarian award – I hoped so – and swung it against my doppelgänger so that she smashed noisily to pieces, shards of flying silver, nothing more. My hand exploded into something that might have been pain. The voices outside paused then redoubled, yelling for me in a dreary chorus. There was a crash and the door shook in its frame. I did not have long. Before me the telephone squatted, expectant. I considered the documents in my hands.

I could send them out into this recovering country. I could

do it, and I could watch them tear it apart. There would be inquiries, trials, autopsies, even exhumations, blame and anguish in an endless cycle, for knowledge is the one thing for which there is no cure. The public, with all its motherless victims, would discover what I had. They would live under the same grief, always, for even if we came to acceptance, why would that bring relief? What was acceptance, after all, but giving up? I thought of my mother: poisoned, yes, but by something worse than a foreign chemical. Memory had been her true killer. She had sacrificed herself at her daughter's altar and kept the knowledge to herself, but its grief had seeped out the sides and ruined the two of us for each other. The awful deed was long done, but she had never been able to let it go, never been able to permit herself to love me. The umbilical cord had always twisted round our necks.

The voices outside had risen to fever pitch. When did the cycle end? At what point could someone say, Enough? My mother had done her best, and still it wasn't enough. Could I succeed where she had not? *Truth is dangerous*, Apostol had said. No one knew that better than a liar. Did people want truth, or did they really just want to live, in the best way they knew how?

Another crash: the lock on the door splintered.

Whatever I did, Marija would win. She was too clever, too much a survivor, not to. But this went far beyond her. It always had.

The papers whispered in my hands. I looked down at the narrowing text, then out at the blue, blue sky, and thought how a world without secrets would be terrible indeed.

The fire in the grate was almost out. I moved closer, blew until it flowered. I could not allow the past to destroy the future. Not any more.

Gently I placed the papers into the flames. They hissed

and spat, their edges already blackening. For a moment, in the broken mirror, I thought I saw a face gazing out at me, an expression of surprise in its amber eyes. But then I blinked and it was gone.

CHAPTER FORTY-NINE

1 April 1994

MARIJA POPA,
COMMUNISM'S 'BLACK WIDOW', FREED

Marija Popa, former First Lady of Yanussia, has been sensationally acquitted on all charges of money laundering, fraud, bribery and corruption.

Mrs Popa, the notorious, beautiful widow of communist dictator Constantin 'Dinu' Popa, had faced the death penalty but was found not guilty after a tense three-month trial that captured the world's attention and became a symbol of how the former Eastern Bloc is tackling its tumultuous past. The so-called Black Widow wept elegant tears as the jury read out the verdict, leaving the court in uproar. Departing the courtroom, she spoke briefly to a media scrum, calling it a 'victory for justice'.

'The law says I did nothing wrong; therefore I did nothing wrong,' she said.

Other commentators, however, branded it a scandal and an insult to the memory of the estimated 130

Yanussians who died in the 1989 uprisings, and the thousands more who languished in secret prisons.

Throughout the trial, Mrs Popa, 58, in a series of red couture dresses – symbolising, she said, the violence done against women in their husbands' names – stood firm against an onslaught by the state prosecution. That included the testimony of more than a hundred witnesses and evidence ranging from bank and legal documents to boxes of cash and jewellery.

In one tense exchange, asked repeatedly where she kept her money, Ms Popa removed a banknote worth 15 YPR (£5) from her handbag and flung it at Judge Ardelean, saying it was all she had left. At other times she wept, particularly during the descriptions of her impoverished childhood.

The ruling came as a shock to the many who had thought her trial a foregone conclusion in a country not known for its fair judicial processes. Her court lawyer, Mr Radutu Gabor, boldly declined to call witnesses and declared there was no case to answer, not only claiming that her husband's alleged thefts of art were constitutionally legal under the regime, but also that she had no idea of the source of the money she splashed on shopping sprees in expensive European capitals. He appealed to the sympathy of the jurors, claiming that she had a passion for couture because as an orphan she had possessed only rags.

Ultimately Gabor's risk-taking paid off: the jury declared the prosecution unable to build a sufficient case. The state was particularly hampered by the lack of any paper trail to connect Mrs Popa with the many foreign-held bank accounts with which she, through her husband, was allegedly connected. A key argument, concerning the 1986 purchase of a Picasso with eight million dollars of allegedly laundered money, collapsed when the painting discovered by authorities in a Swiss bank vault was sensationally revealed to be a fake. The location of the real *Woman in Red* remains unknown.

'No matter who her husband was, it was perfectly clear that the Little Mother was merely a wife and a woman,' one juror told *The Times*. 'She could not have been expected to know, and nor did she know, about her husband's extraordinarily complex financial arrangements. The prosecution tried to smear her for her shopping habits, but would a good housewife question the source of her grocery money?'

The jury took four days to deliberate. Members privately criticised the prosecution for a lack of organisation and complained they were overwhelmed by the number of witnesses – 115 in total – many of whom, they said, were not directly relevant to the case and failed to prove wrongdoing by Mrs Popa beyond reasonable doubt.

Mrs Popa's case was undoubtedly helped by the death of Mr Gheorghe Funar, the ruling couple's chief financial adviser, who was found hanged in prison on New Year's Eve. His death has been ruled a suicide.

The Black Widow is not out of her tangled legal web yet, however. She faces a number of civil suits, including one regarding her connections with the famed Iubită candy company, which reports had claimed the government was seeking to privatise in order to raise much-needed funds for infrastructure. That sale has reportedly been put on ice, for reasons currently unknown.

Read more: High (Fashion) Stakes – what the Black Widow wore in court, p.25

CHAPTER FIFTY

2018

Pavel was stirring his coffee. Round and round the spoon went. Tiny little circles. Curious, the orbits we find ourselves in.

I wondered what Marija had been like, at the end. Had those amber eyes dimmed, those white scars gradually stretched to encompass her body till she was nothing more than a wound? I could not imagine it. The Little Mother had so many skins, I had no doubt she had one for every occasion. Even dying.

'What did they say at the funeral?'

The spoon moved with an uneasy compulsiveness, but his tone was offhand.

'Oh, the usual. Shame you didn't get an invitation.'

I wasn't twenty-eight any more. I looked at him levelly until he coughed and answered.

'Her duty to her country. Her love for her husband. They were very careful not to say anything in particular. We make the dead so two-dimensional, don't you think? It's a disservice.'

Two-dimensional. But then weren't all ghosts? I felt my own phantoms now, clustered at my shoulder. My mother and father, both long dead. It was at my father's funeral that I cried the tears I should have wept at my mother's; it was then that I accepted him, and her, and myself, and everything we were and weren't. Once upon a time I had thought of acceptance as giving up. Perhaps so, but after a lifetime of struggling to stand erect, there is a deep relief to bowing one's head. Their shades were constant presences in my life, but not unwelcome. Sometimes I thought I caught glimpses, in the skeleton of an autumn leaf, in the faint scent of earth when I opened the patio door. You have to learn to live with the dead. They outnumber us, after all.

It was true I was more aware of the past than most. Perhaps Marija and her factory were not my burden to carry, but why should they be anyone else's? My mother had taken on my secret; I had taken on my country's. The long scars at Yanussia's back were healing, and if the sacrifice was that I alone bore the weight of its abortive past, so be it. Some might have said it was the easy way out, that it was simpler to leave buried than to exhume. After a quarter of a century, I knew the opposite was true. Far simpler to bring up the bodies and let the world deal with the stink than at some point to tamp down the soil and say, Enough. Truth and guilt, guilt and truth: I died a little every day, and every day, so far, I had resurrected myself. I chose to live with, to live *through*, the pain. It was not easy, but nor is anything that matters.

I did not ask myself, any more, whether burning the file was the right thing. It was *a* right thing, the very best I could do. They had broken down the doors and found me staring into the fire. As we left for the airport, I asked them to wait. They would not leave me on my own, so I brought them to the Winter Garden and left them at the door. The birds inside twittered in their cages, eyes pressed so close to the wire they could hardly see it any more.

Opening the first cage was surprisingly easy, the others no

less so. The creatures were dazed, hopping back and forth, unsure what to do with all that freedom. Finally a canary plunged forth from its prison, sinking at first with the weight of unaccustomed space. But it discovered its wings and, flapping desperately, rose up, up, up and disappeared. Seeing their sister's example, the others followed suit, a spiralling flutter of colour and movement, exactly as they were meant to be. The fire on the ground beneath them had consumed itself. With triumphant cries they found a skylight and vanished.

Upon returning to England, I resigned from HSG, not even staying until bonus season.

'But with this case on your files, you could do anything,' the managing partner said in exasperation.

Exactly. No longer would I be caught up in other people's webs. I vowed to forge my own path, and that was what I did. Set up a pro bono legal charity. Got married. Got unmarried. Had children, whom I loved fiercely, without caution or regret. Sometimes I loved them so much that, just for a moment, I could not look at them – but then the sun would emerge from behind the clouds, the lump in my throat would flee and I would find the strength to turn back.

'Has it been enough?' I asked Pavel.

'What?'

I expanded my hands. 'Everything.'

The steam from my tea obscured his face. 'I had a ninety-two per cent success rate. I retired a month after winning the biggest trial of my career. Even now that case opens doors. You know that.'

I waited.

'What do you want me to say?' He shrugged irritably, the movement chasing the vapour. 'Of course it wasn't enough. With her, it never was. I would have liked . . . I don't know. A sign. Something to say she was grateful.'

I knew exactly what he meant.

'It's a shame you missed the trial,' he went on, and that little pearl of sympathy slipped through my fingers. I did not bother to comment on his choice of words. Let the bodies lie. 'We were in each other's company so often. I really felt I came to know her.'

He paused, licked his dry lips. 'What about you? Did you . . . know her?'

I sat back in my chair, remembering the last time I saw the dictator's wife. *No one should go through life without being seen by another*, she had said. And she was right, though as ever it was for all the wrong reasons.

My secret squatted in my mouth. I felt its weight on my tongue.

You don't know what I sacrificed.

If I was ever to tell anyone, it had to be here, now, to him. A tiny opportunity had opened, a temporary aperture in the material of the universe.

I opened my mouth and . . .

A sacrifice was supposed to be to the gods, but really it was to yourself. It was the point at which you traced your very edges, where you discovered what mattered to you and what did not, which was the same as what you were and what you were not. The moment when you had to try not to lose yourself, whatever the stakes.

To speak now would add to the misery of the world. To speak would mean my freedom.

The air trembled. The leaper paused at the very edge, where something disappears into nothing. The line was blurred and hard to see.

Slowly, carefully, I stepped back.

'No,' I said slowly. 'I don't think I knew her at all.'

Pavel sat back with a sigh. Disappointment? No – relief. His suit jacket had flopped open. The scarlet lining was spanking new.

'Good. Good. Well, I shouldn't worry. I can see she played you to the last.' He gave a knowing smile. 'The space in the hearts of the great is limited. I think by the end I occupied a special place.'

I glanced involuntarily at the window. It had the faintest mirror-like sheen, though when I blinked there was only my reflection.

Pavel saw I had nothing to say. 'I must be going.' He glanced ostentatiously at his watch. 'There's a drinks function this afternoon.'

I took him in, his sharp suit and smoothed hair, and saw what he was, saw that he would never change. Our lives are the tales we tell ourselves. Did it matter, at the last, if the accounts varied? I thought of Ecaterina, a woman who had always lived the other side of the story. She died two years after her sister's acquittal, withered by her anorexia and her grief. Andrei too was gone, killed in a freak car accident on his book tour (*Mother/less: A Yanussian son's quest for meaning*), six years to the day after I told him about the grey door. Patrick, Mircea, who knew what had happened to them?

Oddly, it was Jude and I who remained friends. He would ring a couple of times a year to offer me high-paying corporate counsel jobs, and I would refuse, and he would moan at what he called the uselessness of conscience. It was a ritual we had; I was glad I knew him. We choose who we allow to hurt us, in the end. The important thing is to let the right ones in.

A breeze blew through, wrapping itself round my ankles, and I shivered. For a moment I thought I caught the scent of blood, and flowers. The door had opened; someone had come in. I realised that Pavel and I were now the only customers.

The stranger was a slender, officious-looking man, clearly

Yanussian, with those slanting almond eyes. In his arms, incongruously, was a large, flat package. It was wrapped in brown paper, perhaps three feet wide and long.

'I think I remember this chap from the funeral,' Pavel said. 'I gave out my card. He probably wants to talk.'

The man approached and set the package carefully down against the table. It sounded heavy.

'Yes, my good fellow?' Pavel said. 'May I help you?'

He received a blank stare.

'I am a former senior partner at Harris Stroud Glyn. I have just come from the Doamna's funeral. If I can be of assistance—'

The man cut him off with a jerk of his head. 'Lăzărescu?' he said, and I started, my chair emitting a metallic protest.

'Yes?'

'At last. Package for you. Tried to find you at the funeral. Someone said you went this way.'

'Oh, I wasn't invited to that,' I said hastily. 'You must be thinking of someone else.'

His eyes glittered. 'She said you would be there.'

'She?' Pavel was confused, looking back and forth between us.

'This is for you.' The man tapped the parcel. 'And this.' He removed something from his pocket and dropped it into my palm, unwrapped.

'A watch?' Pavel said. 'Who's given you a watch?'

I gazed at it, at the silver strap, at the dark, unknowable face. My mother's watch. Someone had kept it clean, polished it carefully, all these years.

I murmured something.

'What's that? Speak up.'

I raised my head. 'Not given,' I said. 'Returned.'

I gazed at it again, a warmth spreading through me as I saw how it had been looked after with care. With love, even.

I had worn it to keep its previous owner close. It looked like someone else had done the same.

I studied the package again. It was quite large. About the size of a painting.

She said you would be there.

The woman in red had indeed played me to the last. But perhaps it wasn't about winning or losing. Perhaps it was about being courageous enough to carry on, long after the game has ended. How do we live with ourselves? That is the greatest question of all.

'Is there something wrong?' Pavel interrupted my thoughts. I blinked, realising my hands were wrapped around my throat. Slowly but surely, I released myself.

'I'm fine.'

'Good.' He was staring at the package and I caught the yellow of his eyes. 'Aren't you going to open it?' he snapped at last, twisting his old hands.

I gazed down at the solid form, up at Pavel, then out of the window at life. The reflection I thought I'd caught smiling down had gone; now there was only the sunlight beaming through, drenching us in warm gold, while the cup before me issued a delicate spire of steam. In the air was tea and people and spring.

'No,' I said at last, the rushing sound in my ears quieting, my feet landing gently on the welcoming floor. A slight curve pushed at the corners of my mouth. 'No, I don't think I need to.'

ACKNOWLEDGEMENTS

Yanussia might be a made up country, but a lot of real life research went into it, chiefly three invaluable months in eastern Europe. Huge thank yous to Ciprian and Radu, who took me to the 2017 government protests on my first night in Bucharest, rescued me from tear gas and introduced me to the capital's decadent underground bar scene; to Oana, who brought me to the Timișoara demonstrations and gave me my first taste of țuică; and to Mila, who shared her wartime stories after we met on the overnight bus to Sarajevo. To Kemaludin, who showed me the wilderness of that city, and to Zsófia in Budapest, who recounted life under the Ceaușescus. To the innumerable tour guides and taxi drivers whose thoughts and stories I have layered in here: thank you. I am aware that my 'making stuff up' has leaned heavily on difficult lives really lived. It is a privilege.

In the UK, I am extremely grateful to Milan, who unflinchingly told me of his family's Balkan history. On the legal front, I owe particular thanks to the following men and women of law, none of whom charged me Pavel's five hundred pounds an hour: to Hugh Owen, for his experiences of nineties eastern Europe and his corporate war stories; to

Julian Malins QC, for not raising an eyebrow when I asked how one might launder money, and for his superb anecdotes. To Helen Malcolm QC, for rescuing me from embarrassment on several points of law. Any remaining errors are entirely mine. To James Bell, for patiently answering my basic questions on what lawyers actually do, and to James Henry Metter, for giving constructive answers to my wild ideas. Thank you to James Luckhurst – terrible jokes but excellent introductions.

Facts are one thing; fiction is quite another. I am extremely grateful to Piers Torday for his kindly tips and encouragement when the going got tough (again). To Professor Adrian Poole and Lucy Griffiths, for teaching me to think. To Hugh Dougherty, my politics editor, for telling me I could write. To my beta readers, who are alpha in every other way.

No acknowledgements would be complete without the people who turned this from Word document to actual book. To James Wills, my kickass agent who demands nothing less than perfection, and while he might not get it (at least from me), his patience, ideas and unerring eye took this novel to another level. To my brilliant editor Sherise Hobbs, for absolutely and immediately understanding what I was trying to do, and then deploying her bottomless creativity and wise words to help me get there. My deepest thanks to you both and all the team at Headline and Watson Little, for your tireless work and faith.

Lastly, my family. Thank you to my brothers, who said it needed more dragons. (Sorry, dudes.) Thank you to my aunt Melloney, for her quiet encouragement. I owe more than I can say to my husband Rory, who lifts me up more than he can know: you are everything, Dean Moriarty. And above all, to my parents, who didn't roll their eyes when I said I was going to write a book, and who only tried to persuade me back into useful employment once or twice.

Thank you for enduring a million rereadings with tireless encouragement and good cheer; but ultimately, thank you for your infinite generosity, your support and your love, always. It means the world and I owe you everything – not least several months' rent.